For my Emma
This story is just for you.
You're my sunshine.

And for all the stars who feel like they've stopped shining.
You're the brightest star in my galaxy.

FOREWORD

"But in a solitary life, there are rare moments when another soul dips near yours, as stars once a year brush the earth. Such a constellation was he to me."

MADELINE MILLER, CIRCE

PLAYLIST

Style – Taylor Swift
Teenage Dream – Olivia Rodrigo
But Daddy I Love Him — Taylor Swift
Ever Since New York — Harry Styles
Live Cinema — Ellie Williams
About You — The 1975
Supernatural — Ariana Grande
Best Part (feat. H.E.R.) — Daniel Caesar
Stargirl Interlude — The Weeknd
Beautiful — Bazzi
Passanger — Noah Kahan
Get Him Back — Olivia Rodrigo
Die For You — The Weeknd
My Kind Of Woman — Mac DeMarco
Sedated — Hozier
Sleep Well — Hozier
Saturn — SZA

PROLOGUE
NORA — SIX MONTHS AGO

"YOU'RE ADORABLE, BUT NO WAY."

Those are not exactly the words you want to hear after kissing someone for the first time.

I press my fingers to my lips, keeping one hand curled in his hair.

"No way, what?" My words are a breathy whisper into the space between us.

The party is loud but not loud enough to hide the sound of his heavy breathing. Our heartbeats are like one, and our chests press flush against each other. His hand is still wrapped in my hair from that passionate kiss, and his other hand is around my waist. I can feel his hands all over my body, and I can't get that feeling to stop—that confusing feeling of *wanting* but still needing to pull away.

"How do I say this?" he mutters, detangling his hand from my hair. He stares at his shoes before meeting my eyes. "Me and you, Nor? It's not going to happen. I know I've joked around about it, but you and Ryan are–"

Does he really think I wanted to kiss him for real?

I lean away from him, but he keeps his hands around my

waist, desperate to keep us close. "Oh my god, Wes. I don't want to date you."

"Y– You don't?"

"No."

His eyebrows furrow, his gray eyes squinting. He just stands and blinks at me. He usually has a lot of shit to say, but for once, he's silent.

I sigh and pull myself out of his grip.

I need to get out of here and fast. It's one thing being up at the asscrack of dawn to organize a birthday party for your boyfriend's twentieth, but it's another thing to witness him fucking some girl at said party. It's a whole *other* thing to kiss your best friend to make him jealous, just for your now *ex*-boyfriend to not give a shit.

I can feel and hear Wes trailing behind me like a lost puppy. As we get to a stop in the crowd, the music blaring in my ears, his huge hand rests on my waist. Leaning into me, he whispers, "Then what was that about?"

"That was me trying to gain some sort of control in my life," I groan. I turn to him, but what I'm saying clearly doesn't register on his face. I roll my eyes, hating that I have to say these words aloud. "Ryan cheated on me. He's *been* cheating on me, apparently."

His hand on my waist stills like he's lost consciousness for a second. I blink at him, willing him to say something. He just lets out an agitated breath as he maneuvers us nearer to the crowded kitchen. "Oh, shit. I'm sorry." His voice is low and thick, heavy with a kind of seriousness I never would have expected from my best friend. "I've always hated him."

"Yeah, I know," I mutter.

My brother and all of my friends have never been fond of Ryan Valla. We've been dating since high school, and I was convinced that he was the man I would marry. Since he asked me out with a bouquet of flowers and a CD with all my favorite musical songs, I knew he was the one for me.

Correction: I *thought* he was the one for me.

We spent every minute of every day together during high school, and then we both got into the performing arts program at Drayton. We knew we were destined to be together. It felt like the world had done us a favor, pushing us closer together until I had pathetic dreams of us co-starring in a lead rom-com one day.

As much as he did things to annoy me – like chewing really loud or talking during a movie – I just thought it was what boys do. I've never had a boyfriend before him, and he made having one seem like the best thing in the world.

Until he didn't.

"Wanna key his car?"

Wes is the kind of person to say the stupidest things in the most serious way. It usually takes me a whole minute of just staring at him to figure out if he's joking or not. Most times, he's not joking, and he really is just an insanely funny and stupid person.

"What?" I gawk, rubbing at my temples. I've had too much to drink, and I desperately want to go home to the comfort of my own bed. And maybe throw in some ice cream, too. Classic sad snack.

"It's the puke-coloured truck out front, isn't it?" Wes asks, pulling out the keys to his car and swinging them around his finger. He's so casual about it, I almost believe he's being serious. The motion distracts me from his idiocy for a second before I shake my head, trying to regain control of the situation.

"Wes, we're not going to key his car. Do you know how much trouble we'd get into?"

He shrugs, brushing past me. "Fine. Then I'll do it."

This time, I'm the one trailing behind him, trying to catch up with him before he does something stupid and gets us both arrested. The party has had a decent turnout – not that it's to my benefit now, and I almost lose Wes in the crowd before he gets through the front door.

The chill hits me when I finally catch up with him. I pull his arm, urging him to turn around to me. "Wesley, I'm not letting you key his car. Do you *want* to get in trouble?"

He smirks. "I thought that was *your* middle name, not mine." He leans down, his broad chest obstructing my view. "It was you who got caught having sex in the janitor's closet last month, wasn't it? Or am I mistaken?"

My whole body tenses at the thought of the shit I used to get up to with Ryan. I was a complete fool for him. Anything he'd ask me to do, I'd do it. He'd tell me to jump, and I'd leap. Every time he'd apologize on his knees with his face between my legs, I'd forgive him. He made me feel wanted, and I was broken enough to settle for what he gave me.

I push at Wes's chest, crossing my arms against my own as he looks down at me with challenge in his eyes. If this guy weren't completely attached to my hip at all times, he would have gone off the rails by now.

I say his name like it's a bad word, with pure and utter disbelief that this is the idiot I chose to be my best friend. "Wes."

"Nora," he purrs. I don't give him the satisfaction of letting him think he won this fight, and I stand my ground. He groans, throwing his head back. "Fine. I'm not going to key it, but he *will* pay for what he did to you."

I shake my head. "No. He's not worth it."

"Oh, now you realize that," he mocks. I don't even have the energy to glare at him. He shakes his head, swallowing as he shoves his keys into his pocket. "So, what are you going to do?"

"Go home, cry, and sleep," I admit. There's nothing more comforting than those three things right now. I don't even want to face my roommates tonight. I just want to put on the saddest songs from the *Les Mis* soundtrack and forget tonight ever happened.

"Can I come?" he asks.

"So you can watch me cry? No thanks," I say through a laugh. He blinks at me, his fists closing and opening at his sides like he's debating what he should do or say. I'm not going to stand here and watch his internal overprotective-dude-man struggle.

Before I can say bye and finally get on my way, I turn back to the house to see Ryan running through the door, his shirt a mess, and his jeans unbuttoned. He couldn't even have the decency to look like he hadn't just had sex with someone who wasn't his girlfriend.

"Wait! Nora, please listen to me," he shouts. "I still–"

Fuck it.

I lean up on my tiptoes, curl my hand in Wes's shirt, and press my mouth to my best friend's lips for the second time tonight.

ONE
NORA
MICRO-PENIS

YOU'D THINK that six months after being broken up with would mean you're feeling on top of the world, but it doesn't. In fact, it feels like the exact opposite. Instead of sunshine and rainbows, I feel like the dark nothingness at the bottom of a trash bag.

Uninteresting, smelly, and not something you want to spend your time around.

I've been pacing the living room of my dorm for the last.... I actually don't know how long. All I know is I've gotten to the point where my legs aren't moving because I'm telling them to, but out of the fact that I've been doing it so long, it feels like second nature.

Just back and forth.

Back and forth.

Back and fucking forth.

My two roommates are sitting on the couch, watching me pace as I go through every stage of grief for what is probably the third time this month alone. I've completely skipped having second thoughts about my life choices and gone straight to third.

"You know what? I don't even care," I mutter angrily, still pacing. I'm starting to get hungry. Maybe I should sit down and face my feelings with some food and *lots* of it. I scoff to myself at my own thoughts. *That sounds like a healthy coping mechanism.*

"You do care, Nor-Nor, and that's okay."

Do you ever wish your friends weren't so perfect and sweet all the goddamn time? Especially ones like Eleanor Harper, ballet dancer and absolute sunshine incarnate. She can be sneaky and dirty-minded when she wants to be, but in times like these, she's an absolute angel who says things to me in that lovely, innocent voice of hers, making me want to curl up into her lap and let her continue talking me out of my mind.

"I don't know what you're talking about," I say, my voice bright as I continue walking back and forth.

I'd be dizzy if I hadn't spent my entire life on a stage or trying to get on one, doing these sorts of acting drills for hours. Not getting dizzy is my superpower. Unfortunately for my friends, I'm probably making them sick by doing this.

My parents have had enough of me turning up at home unannounced as I recount the last six months of my life to them. My mom is usually the best at giving advice, but this is the one thing she can't cure with her sweet words and never-ending list of fun activities to get me out of my slump. She lucked out in the boyfriend department and got together with my dad in high school, and now she's stuck with him. Despite her surprise pregnancy with me and my twin brother, Connor, I've never seen two people more in love with each other.

"I would still be pissed if I were you," Cat says, tucking her legs beneath her on the couch. If we had to be ranked from least to most unhinged, Cat would be somewhere at the bottom. Since we were kids, she's had this wiser, calming presence around her that makes me feel like I'm floating on a cloud. Her words are frustratingly soft sometimes, but she's also one of the most stubborn people I know. She's also one of the kindest people I know.

Kind enough to have gone out of her way last year to help my brother when he was having some anxiety talking to reporters and now he's been trailing behind her for months.

"Seriously?" Elle gawks. "It's been six months, and you'd *still* be pissed? Wouldn't your anger be channeled into something else by this point? Something *healthy*."

"I can be pissed and channel it in different ways," I say to them, finally coming to a stop. I sit on the stack of romance novels on the coffee table, facing them. A deep red dances along her cheeks and stains Elle's brown skin. "This *is* healthy, Elle-Belle, trust me."

"How?" she asks, crossing her arms defensively. Cat mirrors her expression, trapping her braids under her arms. It's like having parents for best friends: a blessing and a curse.

"By imagining all the things that Daisy doesn't know about him yet. Like how he cries a lot of the time after sex, how he believed in Santa until he was fourteen, how he sings *Oklahoma* when he's sad." I list all the things on my fingers.

Really, I could keep going.

Sometimes, you're so blinded by love that you don't realize the number of things that you were so used to seeing that they became normal. Like how Ryan often forgot when we had a date planned and told me he was too tired to go. Like how I'd go to his dorm afterward and he'd be passed out drunk in his bed. And how I'd forgive him. Every. Single. Time.

You give yourself so much to someone just for them to find someone better and not need you anymore. You're so caught up in it that everyone else around you can see it before you can. You end up making excuses for people who don't deserve them.

But not anymore.

"Jesus." Cat shivers at the images I just painted of Ryan.

"Yeah. Imagine her surprise when she finds out he has a micro-penis," I mutter, shrugging innocently. Both of their eyes go wide, and Elle almost falls off her seat.

"What? Does he really?" Elle squeals, unable to stop herself from laughing as a very unladylike laugh bubbles over.

"Oh, you poor girl," Cat murmurs, shaking her head. "No wonder you never talked about your sex life with us. I understand the disappointment. Well... I don't, personally... Because my boyfriend's penis is... You know what I mean... I'm just going to stop talking."

I wave my hand in her face. "Okay, okay. I get it. I don't want to talk about what size my brother's man parts are," I shout, covering my ears. They've been dating for almost a year now, and I'm still not used to the fact that my twin brother and my best friend are madly in love. "But Ryan doesn't have a micropenis. I wish he did. It would make this whole thing a lot easier. He actually has a very normal-sized penis."

They both pout at me, a look I've come accustomed to seeing on their faces. Since the breakup, Ryan has moved on to three different women. Now, he's dating a gorgeous blonde in our acting class, Daisy. She and I were friends in freshman year, but the second her agent dropped her and I got signed to an acting agency, she's been bitter. She's always got this insanely passive look on her face like the world doesn't bother her, and she freaks me the fuck out. I didn't ask to be born this talented. Besides, I've been scouring the media with my parents to get an agent, and I was able to take the opportunity I worked for.

Whilst Ryan has been having the time of his life with multiple women, I've just been... here. My sadness took hold of me, and I managed to get fired from working at the bookstore, which became my second home. I've had little motivation to do anything other than attend class and browse LinkedIn for a job for when winter rolls around. Ryan's managed to make my life look like shit because his own is apparently so great.

It's not like I haven't had the chance to.

I've been to parties more than I have been in my bed. Yet every time I try to make a move on someone, it ends up being embarrassing for both of us.

I don't know how to get my groove back. I thought kissing my best friend would make him jealous, but he didn't even flinch. I don't know what it's going to take to get myself out of this funk and back to being the star I once was–on and off stage.

I tilt my head up to the ceiling, trying my hardest not to break down. I'm stronger than this. *Way* stronger than this. It's been too long to still be moping. I should have pulled myself together by now.

"This just sucks, you know?" I whisper, finally looking back at them. "I'll never know what I did wrong for him to stop loving me. That's what hurts the most. Because then… Maybe I could have fixed it."

Elle sighs, reaching out to rest her hand on my knee, steadying it. "You didn't do anything wrong, Nor. He's just a dick."

"Yeah, maybe," I sniffle, still not fully believing it.

I know this is one of those moments where you're supposed to listen to your friends, but what they're saying doesn't make sense to me. The truth of it is so simple. It's so clear it's practically blinding, weaving its way behind my eyelids every time I close my eyes or look in the mirror. If he had loved me enough, he would have stayed. He wouldn't have found anyone better, and I would have been enough for him. But I wasn't.

Cat stands up, suddenly full of energy. "Come on. Let's cheer you up. Shots at The Dragon. My treat. I got paid this morning, and I'm ready to sugar mama you both." She reaches out her hands and pulls me up from the table.

"Ooo, look at you, Little Miss I Have A Job Now," Elle coos, now standing beside us. She brushes her long, curly hair behind her, wrapping her slender arms around Cat's shoulders.

"I know! I'm loving it," Cat replies. She's been out of a job for years. She's never really needed the money, and I think the whole ordeal made her too anxious. But since Cat's summer internship at a local sports magazine went really well, she was able to stay on part-time writing a piece about the school. "Now I get to treat my girls."

Elle squeals, and she pulls us into a hug.

Maybe I just need one more night out. One more night of forgetting before I have to face Ryan on campus and in classes for another semester. With the smile on my best friend's faces, it's hard to say no to them, anyway.

TWO
WES
NEW ROOMATE

"NO."

There's nothing I hate more than being told no. Not because I don't like to listen – okay, I don't *love* listening, but who does — but because it sounds insanely mean no matter how nicely you try to say it. I'm constantly suggesting incredible ideas just to be shut down.

Wanna go for a drive and smoke? No.

Do you like Frank Ocean? No.

Do you also constantly battle with the fear of not being good enough? No.

Shit like that pisses me off. Not only do I feel incredibly out of place and downright insane, but it's hard to feel like anyone *gets* me the way I get other people. I spend so much time trying to make other people happy that answers, trying to understand people better than I understand myself, like that make me question my taste in friends.

As my best friend and housemate looks at me with that annoying as fuck glare in his eyes, that word is the last thing I want to hear right now.

I sigh. "Okay, at least hear me out."

"Nope. Not listening." Connor shakes his head as if he can

make me disappear. And everyone says *I'm* the dramatic one. Yeah, right. "I don't want a new roommate already, Wes. We just moved in."

"Okay, first of all, we've been living here for over two months. And second of all, nobody asked how *I* felt when Catherine started sleeping over here nearly every night."

Since Connor started dating Nora's best friend, they've been all over each other. Of course, I've known from the beginning when they were sneaking around. I've seen how my best friend looks at girls, but there's only one look he reserves just for Catherine.

It was cute as much as it was painful to watch. They finally came clean and told his sister six months ago. Since we moved out of our dorms into a new house off campus, Cat has spent more time here baking in the kitchen with Connor like an old married couple than I've spent here.

"She's my girlfriend. Not an animal," Connor says, continuing to clean up his mess on the kitchen island. It's like living with an experimental toddler. All he does is bake things that taste bad and force-feed them to me and our other housemate, Archer.

Jarvis purrs in my arms, snuggling his chubby and fuzzy face into my shirt. I pretend to cover his ears with my free hand, holding him closer to me as I rock us back and forth. "It's okay, baby. He didn't mean it."

Connor rolls his eyes at us. "You and that stupid cat can sleep outside for all I care. I don't want him here."

I wish Jarvis could growl because I would have trained him to growl every time Connor says something mean to me, which is often. "Don't call him stupid! It's not his fault he's visually impaired."

It is his kinda fault.

No matter how many times we tried to cat-proof our house growing up, this fucker managed to play with the spring next to the door a little too hard that it ended up poking him right in the eyeball. He irritated it so much that he lost sight in his right eye. Now, he walks a little lopsided. Since then, he's grown a ton and has become one very slow lump of fur that I can't get enough of.

"Wesley, you're not keeping a cat here," Connor says again. It's embarrassing for all of us that he thinks I'll listen. I've known him my entire life. You'd think he knows me better than that by now. With a chuckle, he adds, "You can barely look after yourself."

"You're not the boss of me or this house. We all pay rent," I argue. Connor acts like he's my dad half of the time and the dad of the football team the other time. He cares so much about football and all of us that it's sickening. He's constantly trying to involve me in all of his mushy feelings and tells me how much he appreciates me and all that shit.

"Fine," he sighs, pressing his hands on the island. He grimaces as Jarvis yawns in my arm, showcasing his sharp teeth. "Then ask Archer how he feels about *that* moving in."

"Fine, I will." I turn on my heels, adjusting the heavy cat in my arms. "Where is that sexy bag of bones?"

One of the many perks about moving into a house off campus is that there are way fewer rules than being in a dorm, and there's also a ton of space.

We were lucky enough to get one of the bigger houses on Fire Ridge Row. We have three bedrooms and en suites, a kitchen, dining room and living area. It's much better than living in a stuffy dorm with these two fools. Now I can live in a spacious *house* with these two fools.

And the best part? A huge backyard to do whatever the fuck we want, including – but not limited to – parties, a very easy game of hide and seek, and a perfect place to host an outdoor movie night. There are large trees on both sides of the backyard, one of them close to the bathroom window that blocks out most of the sun. It also connects to a hammock against the opposite tree. It was perfect during those last few weeks of summer sun.

And, of course, Archer Elliot puts all men to shame as he

stands outside on the cusp of winter in nothing but denim jeans and a backward cap as he chops wood.

Who does this man think he is?

I shake my head, stalking closer to him as Jarvis flinches in my arms at the harsh sounds of the axe hitting the wood. "Hey, Archie Boy."

He doesn't even turn around as he grumbles, "Don't call me that."

I let out a low whistle and get straight to the point. "How do you feel about getting a cat?"

The axe drops on the wood as he turns around, twisting around his hat as it shields him from the September sun. His eyes narrow. "What do you mean? Seems like you've already got one."

"Yes, I am very glad you have eyes, Archer," I murmur.

He ignores my comment. "Is this Jarvis?"

My eyes widen. "You remembered his name," I coo. Archer is a grump. Way grumpier than any twenty-year-old should be. There's no way he spends his free time thinking about or trying to remember my cat's name.

"Only because you don't shut up about the abuse he experiences at your mom's new place," he says, trying not to laugh as he eyes the cat suspiciously.

I wouldn't say abuse. Slightly neglected, sure.

Since my mom officially moved out a few weeks ago, the divorce with my dad has hit her like a truck. She's barely looking after herself, never mind a cat. Which means I usually have to go over there every few days and make sure she and Jarvis have eaten. The least I can do is take him off her hands for a while. Besides, I've missed my little partner in crime.

My dad couldn't care less, apparently. This is my third year at Drayton Hills with my dad coaching the football time I'm on, and he's been on my ass lately. I can't tell if he's doing that to distract me from his own guilt or because he might actually care about me. I don't know what makes him think I have to listen to him when he's been cheating on my mom for years. Fuck that.

"As long as he stays out of my room, I don't care," Archer says, turning back around to do whatever the hell he's doing.

I rub the top of Jarvis's head in the spot he likes and he meows quietly. "You hear that, buddy? You're moving in! I promise they'll warm up to you soon," I coo, walking back into the house. Connor is exactly where I left him, still cleaning up after himself. I can't help the smile that forms across my face as Connor's face falls. "It's two against one, I'm afraid."

He groans. "Fine. Whatever. Just don't let him wreck any of my stuff."

"What stuff do you even have to wreck?" I ask, genuinely confused about how empty this house is. He lobs a silicone spoon at me, but I dodge it, watching it fly past my face. I kneel down and drop Jarvis on the floor, allowing him to wander around his new home. Of course, he doesn't wander.

He just sits there.

Right at my feet.

Not moving.

Great.

"What do you think cats do, Connor? Because all he does is eat, sleep, and shit," I say, looking down at him as he curls up at my feet. "He'll just follow me around until he gets bored. He's a piece of cake, trust me."

"He better be," Connor mutters before picking up his phone when it lights up. He laughs a little when he types back a reply. "The girls are going out. Seems like they're cheering Nora up. *Again.* You in?"

For Nora Bailey, I'll do anything. But of course, I don't say that to her twin brother. Instead, I settle for, "Hell yeah."

THREE
NORA
THE DRAGON

EVERYONE SAYS they want a brother until the second they have one. Because when you have a brother, you know they're going to annoy the living crap out of you at any chance they get. You also know they're going to be breathing down your neck when you do something wrong or try to murder anyone who even looks at you. There is usually never any in-between for them.

Connor has always been the protective type — that much isn't new. He's always been a worrier for me and for his football team. Dating Cat brought him out of his shell a lot more, but he's still getting there. Since my breakup with Ryan, he's been extra cautious and protective over me wherever we go.

Part of that is my fault.

I'm known to sort of… disappear sometimes.

Most of the time, I don't realize I'm doing it. I get caught up with whatever I'm doing and could end up in the next town over. More times than not, I'm in a separate building on campus, fooling around with Ryan.

Nope. I'm not going there.

No more talk about Ryan if I can help it.

I'm supposed to be having a good time. I'm supposed to be

getting as shit-faced as possible to distract myself from the shit show my life has become and the looming results of the auditions for this year's musical.

"Are you okay? Do you want some water?" Connor asks, fidgeting with the sleeve of his Drayton football hoodie. Before I can respond, Cat wraps one of her arms around his waist, her eyes wide. "How many drinks have you had?"

"She's fine, Connie," Cat says. If there's one person that can make my brother relax, it's got to be Catherine. He looks down at her and lets out a deep breath. She turns to me. "You're good, right?"

"Yes, I'm fine. You can both stop treating me like a baby," I mutter, sulking like… Well, like a baby. Both of their eyes zero in on me, not listening to my bullshit. I try again. "I'm *fine*, seriously."

"Well, when you stop feeling *'fine,'* let us know," Connor says as he tugs Cat to his side.

"Thanks, Dad," I say, smiling wide. He rolls his eyes at my comment, and I bark out a laugh. "I'm going to the bathroom. Do either of you want to escort me?" They both shake their heads. "Thought not."

I slide past them, trying to navigate around the new bar we've been hanging out at.

Ignoring the 2000's sounds playing from the speakers that would usually get me hyped up, I make my way to the bathroom, shutting myself in a stall.

I've got this.

Flirting and talking to guys is my thing. If I can do it on stage and write about it in my screenplays, I can do it in real life.

I don't know how Ryan is still inside my head.

No matter how hard I try to move on, something goes wrong whenever I try to talk to a guy. It's been years since I've had to try to get anyone's attention, and it turns out I'm just as boring as I vowed not to be. The best way I'm going to get over this is if I can get over him emotionally and physically.

After a quick pee and a spruce-up of my makeup in the mirror, I smooth out my black dress and hope that my cowgirl look with my boots gets me in the bed of some handsome stranger tonight.

My life goes from bad to fucking unbearable when I push open the bathroom door and collide right into Ryan's chest.

Why does he have to smell so good? He has that signature *man* scent – woodsy, dark, and spicy. He recently got a buzzcut, but his dark green eyes have always been the same. They're the kind of eyes I could lose myself in.

Despite the stereotypes of what theater kids are like, he has the slight bad-boy energy about him that always drew me in. Especially now in the confines of dim lighting in the back of a bar where everything slips away for a second.

"Hey, Nor," he says, his voice gruff and low. He steps back, steadying me with one hand on my shoulder. "How are you?"

I blink up at him, words failing me. I can't remember the last time he touched me. The last time anyone has touched me. His tight grip on my shoulder sends electric jolts through my body, causing me to shiver despite the heat.

I need to get my body under control immediately.

I hold my head up. "I'm great."

That's all I can get out. No matter how attractive he is, no matter how many times we broke up and got back together, he *hurt* me more than anyone that I know. I shouldn't be getting tongue-tied over him and letting him distract me from my goal.

Right now, that means getting away from him and finally conquering the irrational fear I have about moving on.

He tilts his head. "Really? You looked a bit distracted at auditions last week."

I hate how right he is.

This year, we're doing a famous musical to perform at Drayton, as well as working on our individual end-of-year projects. The class is divided into writers, directors, actors, and editors. It gets us right in the jist of what it would be like on a Hollywood set or backstage on Broadway. This year, we're doing *Hamilton*, which just so happens to be my favorite musical. I always felt like I was born to play Angelica, but I completely butchered my audition. I've been so out of it recently, and the auditions came at the wrong fucking time. I'd be surprised if I even get to play an extra.

"Maybe I was just repulsed by seeing your face," I challenge, locking my eyes with his and keeping my voice calm.

He scoffs. "Using insults to hide the fact that you're upset. Nice one, Nor," he whispers, stepping closer to me. My back hits the wall. I try to say something, but the words fail me, and my lips part. "I think you're forgetting just how well I know you. You always do that when you're lying about how you feel."

My heartbeat increases, and my palms instantly gather sweat.

It's just the bar.

That's the only explanation as to why my body is reacting like this to *him*, of all people.

And it might have to do with the fact that he has known me longer than I can remember. He met me as an awkward teenager, and he loved me instantly.

Or, I thought he did.

I told him things I never thought I would tell anyone, and he listened to me. He understood my dreams, and he promised to help me get there. He took care of me, and when he did something wrong, he'd apologize. It was the bare minimum, but then, it was enough for me. It felt like it was *more* than enough. I would have done just about anything to feel loved.

"I'm not," I whisper finally.

"You are."

I hold my chin up higher. "Why don't you go and talk to your new girlfriend and leave me alone? Or have you forgotten about her already? Seems to be your thing, doesn't it?"

His jaw grinds together at the mention of Daisy. He leans into me again, his hand dropping on the wall beside my head. I inhale a sharp breath, my eyes dipping to his full lips for a second before meeting his gaze.

"You're jealous." I stay quiet, hoping my eyes are telling him enough. "You need to get over it, Nor."

His statement lands the blow he intended, and my stomach coils tighter with anxiety.

Again, I can't speak because he does the one thing he knows will make me weak.

He tucks a strand of hair behind my ear and brings his mouth close to my neck.

I'm letting him get under my skin again, and I shouldn't. But the gentle way he handles me makes my legs feel like jelly. When he presses the softest kiss to the tattoo just under my ear, I sigh, melting back into the wall.

"As hot as it is seeing you get jealous, baby," he whispers, his mouth still against my neck, "We both know we're not getting back together. You *really* need to get over this."

The force in his voice snaps me back to reality.

I push against his chest, feeling the embarrassment on my cheeks as I am *this* close to kissing him for real. "I *am* over it," I say with conviction, needing to believe it as I rush away from him.

What was I thinking?

I have nothing to use as an excuse. He was just there with his usual charm and sexy face, saying all the right things... Until he didn't.

When am I going to get it into my head that he doesn't need me anymore? He doesn't want me. He just wants to mess around with me and watch me fall like a star out of the sky while he takes center stage. That is his plan, and I can't let it follow through. I really–

"Hey, hey, hey. Where are you going, Sunshine?"

I stop my tantrum at the sound of my best friend's voice.

Taking a deep breath, I pause in my tracks before I turn around.

Wes Mackenzie is standing in front of me in a red shirt and black jeans, a blow-up microphone in his hand, and blue, hugely oversized glasses over his eyes. Just the sight of him causes me to calm down, which is weird, considering every time I'm around him, he's doing something stupid enough to give me a heart attack.

He steps closer to me, pulling off the glasses and tucking them in his shirt when I don't say anything. He holds up the blow-up microphone to himself, talking into it. His voice is softer this time, less urgent. "Where are you going, Sunshine?"

I roll my eyes as he holds out the microphone to me. "Home," I answer into it.

His eyes narrow, pulling the mic back to himself. "What? I can't really hear you. You're going to have to talk louder than that, Nor."

He holds out the microphone to me again. "I said I'm going home!"

"Jesus, you don't have to shout," he retorts. I lift my arms in disbelief. It's like being friends with a child. Wes shakes his head at me, pulling my hand and dragging me towards the bar, sliding into the stool. I sit in the one next to him. "Why do you wanna go already? You guys just got here."

I shrug, pulling out one of the straws from the cup and twisting it until it pops. "Yeah, well, I've got no reason to stay anymore."

"You do. You've got me." How did I know that would have been his response? Wes fully believes that he can solve every problem to ever exist with himself as the answer. Unfortunately, I don't know how much he can help right now other than distracting me from my overthinking brain for a few hours. He's pretty good at that.

"Right. How could I forget?" I pull out another straw. I hand one to him, and we twist them again until they pop.

He bumps his shoulder into mine. "Don't be such a grump, Nora."

"I can be a grump if I want to," I say, turning in my chair.

His gray eyes meet mine. "You *could*, or you could try to move on. To someone better than him, perhaps." He taps his chin, pretending to think. "Come to think of it, it shouldn't be that hard because he's an asshole."

The anger in his voice makes me want to laugh no matter how right he is. Wes is such a loveable guy that it's weird to hear him talking shit about someone. He usually saves all his bad-mouthing for characters on a TV show or on the football field. But he makes special reservations for Ryan Valla. Reservations I wish I had taken more notice of before.

"Yeah, I know," I reply, trying my hardest to ignore the ache that has been weighing on my chest for months. I change the subject. "How is training going? You know... With your dad and everything."

Talking about Wes's dad has been a sore topic since he found out his dad has been cheating on his mom with their assistant football coach. Oliva Hardon somehow had the balls to wreck someone's family when she knew his son played for the team she coaches. She has some fucking nerve. I can only imagine how hard this season will be for him, with his dad coaching the team.

"Well," he sighs, "It could be worse. Pre-season is fine for now, but I know he's going to be on my ass come October."

I groan. "This doesn't look like our year, Wessy boy."

"Says who?"

"I did. You kinda just did. The universe is clearly against us. I also saw a video saying something about how Scorpios and Geminis are going to go through it this year, so we're pretty much fucked." I list them off on my finger lazily, watching as his mouth turns into a frown.

"Me and you, Stargirl? We're going to have the best fucking year of our lives now that you've said that," he says, gripping my shoulders and shaking me. "Reverse psychology works."

"I don't think that—"

He cuts me off. "Wanna get drunk?"

When Wes Mackenzie asks me a question as stupid as that, I usually think of all the things that go wrong. I was already *this* close to crawling back into bed with my ex today, so maybe getting drunk with my friends will cure it.

Fuck it.

FOUR
NORA
AUDITION LIST

WITH THIS BEING my third year at Drayton Hills, I've learned to become very selective with my friends. Making them has always come naturally, and having my friends' back is the most important thing to me. There is nothing worse than feeling like you've got no one in your corner and no one to indulge in your delusions. I'm lucky to have friends like mine who are just as crazy as me.

Especially with this degree, I know people can stab you in the back at any given moment. It's a dog-eat-dog world, and part of me hates the fact that I love it so much.

I stayed close with Ryan and our friends Summer and Kiara until we broke up. I met Summer in high school and only met Kiara in the acting workshop we had before freshman year. I always knew Summer had a crush on him, but Ryan had chosen me, and there was little I could do about it. She's been off in Switzerland for the last two years, and we only see her around the holidays. I'm sure she'll jump at him the second she comes back.

Besides, being friends with someone first and then dating them is a disaster waiting to happen.

But Kiara Davenport is the one I know I can always trust. She might be extremely high-energy and the loudest person in our class, but she knows all the best ways to calm me down or to do the opposite.

Except for right now, as we walk to our final class of the day, she updates me on Ryan and Daisy like I actually give a fuck.

"You know, they've been dating for a lot longer than we thought," she says, bumping her shoulder into mine as she scrolls through her phone. Her dark curls fall in front of the screen, but she's somehow managing to navigate it and her way around campus.

"Do you mean a lot longer than *you* thought, Kie?" I reply, sighing. She blows a raspberry. "Why do you feel the need to tell me about what they're doing every day? I don't care. I've moved on."

She peers up at me, squaring her brown eyes. "Yeah, to who?" I just blink back at her with no response. "I saw you refreshing her feed in Jessop's class. You're not fully over it, and it's okay."

"I am, but whatever," I mutter, hitching my tote bag higher up my shoulder as we get closer to the auditorium. I've only got to put up with her and the rest of my class for an hour. I can do that. I can find out that I'm playing Angelica – my literal birthright – and get on with my day. This day has been a long time coming, and I can't wait.

"Look, all I'm saying is people will stop pitying you and treating *them* like a celeb couple once *you* start dating again," Kie explains, pocketing her phone. "People only care about Ryan and Daisy because they post constantly and weirdly... They look good together. Well, no offense to you, Nor. I think it's the whole good girl and bad boy look. I mean, she's got an insane resting bitch face, but in the rare photos where she's smiling, she's pretty cute."

I sigh, tilting my head back. There is nothing the theater kids love more than relationship drama. With people as loud and proud as Ryan and Daisy, everyone eats up whatever they feed them on their social media accounts. It's stupid, really. They're not celebrities or have famous parents. They're just theater kids from Colorado who somehow make enough things about them that people online and in-person care.

"If they both get the leads, I'm dropping out," I say, the nausea in my stomach increasing when I see how close we're to the auditorium. I can barely deal with Ryan outside of class, and having to sing and perform on stage with him would be my idea of hell.

"Oh, my parents would love that idea," Kiara laughs, linking her arm with mine as she sways us to the side a little.

I turn to her. "What do you mean, *your* parents?"

"If you drop out, I'm dropping out with you. There's no way I'm putting up with *these* animals on my own," Kiara explains, nodding down the hallway where most of our class hovers around the door, the holy grail of audition lists hanging above it.

It's normal to feel like my heart is pounding and like I'm going to throw my guts up, right? It's completely normal that I can *feel* every single vein in my body working its way through me. Like that's a normal thing to feel in my situation. I'm *definitely* not overthinking this. Right?

As if reading my thoughts, Kiara whispers, "Stop overthinking, Bails. Give your brain a rest. Your stress is going to become *my* stress, then we'll both be stressed, and it'll be one big ball of stress, and we'll never get married because everyone will know us as the two girls who are constantly stressing over nothing."

I only listen to half of that rant before my brain tunes her out as the crowd slowly disperses from the sheet. It's like the Red Sea is being split in two. Everything happens in slow motion, and it feels like I'm up on a stage and the curtains are opening. The light is shining down on me, and the crowd is cheering my name as they read it on the Playbill that I signed at the door.

Nora Bailey, it reads, *starring as…*

Eliza Schuyler.

You've got to be fucking kidding me.

I SPENT the entire class zoning in and out, listening to my favorite teacher drone on about the importance of this musical as she played clips of Lin Manuel Miranda talking about the script. Twisting the star necklace my dad gave me around my neck isn't helping like it usually would. My parents gave it to me for my tenth birthday, a silver star to remind me how much I shine. It's pathetic how dull I feel now in comparison to what my parents think of me.

Usually, I would be eating that shit up. Finding out the cast for our musicals is the thing that I look forward to every year, as well as the research trip we get to go on. They're supposed to be revolutionary, almost. It's supposed to be all I think about, in a good way. Not the way I've felt all day – like a ghost floating through this thing I'm supposed to call my life.

This isn't a big deal. I have the lead role. I have an important part, and I can't keep sulking about it. This is my *favorite* musical. It always felt like I was born to play Angelica since I watched the musical for the first time on a dodgy livestream. As much as Eliza's character is important to the story, I don't want to play the wife of Hamilton, who – we can all admit – is a huge fuckboy. Yes, he gets his redemption arc, but don't they all? I spent hours scouring the script, researching the history of the US Constitution I didn't care to think about until I watched it.

This was my chance to finally get back on the stage in the role I'd dreamed about and stop feeling like the dirt at the bottom of someone's shoe. It was supposed to be a step in the right direction with all the shit that went down with Ryan, and it feels like I've just been reduced to what I was when we first broke up. Nothing.

Adding salt to the wound, I haven't heard back from my agent in a few days over some self-tapes I submitted a few weeks ago, and the thought of not booking anything *again* is frightening. I've done a few commercials here and there when I was younger, but since I started college, it's been a lot harder to book a job. Now, without employment at BoBo's, I desperately need some sort of income. Even if it's something small from a YouTube series or something. I'll do *anything* at this point.

"If you don't stop working those gears in your brain, I'm going to personally drill a hole through your forehead and carve in a huge sign that says 'Shut the fuck up.'"

I look up at Kiara, and I roll my eyes. I've somehow been mindlessly eating fries in this greasy diner while my mind runs a million miles an hour. I honestly don't know how I managed to move from campus and drive here without having a nervous breakdown. Keeping it together has been my new normal, and I don't know how long I can keep going with it.

"You are terrifying," I mutter.

She just grins, her brown eyes flashing. "I know. It adds to the allure," she explains with a flourish, gesturing to her face and her outfit. I wholeheartedly believe Kie is one of the most stunning people I've ever met – all brown skin, long curls, beautiful doe eyes, an adorable southern cowgirl look with a slight drawl to match. No wonder she's booked so many modeling gigs. I'm just waiting for the moment she appears on my screen in a silly Netflix Original.

"And what allure is that? You're practically allergic to relationships," I say, laughing as she steals one of my fries, covering it all in ketchup.

She rolls her eyes. "I'm *not* allergic. No one has met my standards yet."

"Right," I mock. "Because it's absolutely ridiculous that not everyone can recite word for word the entire script of *Les Mis*."

"Exactly. There's got to be someone out there. I'm not settling for any less." She shrugs before picking up another one of *my* fries and pointing it at me. "And neither should you. It fucking sucked seeing you with Ryan when we both know you can do so much better than him. You're hot as shit, Bails."

"Why, thank you. Thank you very much." I give her a shy smile, tucking my hair behind my ears. I wish her words could just immediately evaporate the anxieties I have about dating again, but they don't. "If I'm being honest, I don't think that's going to happen for a while, Kie. So, you can call off any double dates you've been planning in your head."

She takes a long, dramatic sip of her milkshake. "Okay, fine, but you need to get out of this funk somehow. Seeing you sad every day, and now, with the stress of the musical, it's not your best look. I miss us going out and dancing with strangers in bars or staying in and filming videos for our imaginary YouTube channel. That was just *fun*. I miss that."

Sometimes, when Ryan and I would take 'breaks,' it finally felt like I could be free. I didn't realize how much I needed my time with my girls until he disappeared on me. I always wanted to stay faithful to him because, at the time, I thought that mattered to him. Kie and I would end up at bars across the city, line-dancing with randos and feeling like the world was at our fingertips for the night. Then, we'd spend the rest of the weekend doing self-care and making videos out of it just to laugh at later.

"I miss it too, trust me, but I just don't think I'm cut out for anything serious right now."

"Fine," she concedes, which means it's not fine. She tries to sell me on those innocent-looking eyes, but I know they're not innocent either. "Why don't you just try sleeping with someone at least? Maybe a good fuck will straighten you out a little. You're wound too tightly, and it's honestly painful to watch, Nor."

"I'm not doing that either," I say, as good as the idea sounds. My fingers and toys can only do so much for me. Ryan could piss me off, but he was never bad in bed, which sucks balls now. "In the kindest way possible, I'm not you, Kie. You've been dating casually for years. I've only been in one real relationship in my life. I've only kissed three people in my life, two of which I've had some sort of relationship with afterward. I'm just used to commitment, and I think that freaks a lot of guys out if they're looking for a casual hook-up. A friends-with-benefits situation is the very last thing I can do."

She shrugs, grinning. "Well, don't knock it until you try it."

"The first time I sleep with someone who isn't my boyfriend will be the day you finally get into a serious relationship. So…" I pretend to think. "Never."

Kiara lobs a fry at me, frowning. "I hate you."

I smile. "I love you, too."

FIVE
WES
FUCKING FOOTBALL

I TRY my hardest at all times not to use the word *hate* when talking about people.

There are some people that I strongly dislike, but I don't hate them. There are people that make me see red, and thoughts of murder are swarming around my brain, but still, I don't hate them. Mom always told me not to use that word unless I really meant it. It was like Mrs. Macallestair's threat to Kevin before he wished his family away for Christmas. She scared me so much by saying that word that I never used it unless I was talking about objects. Even then, she would remind me that I'd eventually change my mind and that I would stop hating it in a few days. She was right.

Maybe all those times that I didn't use that word when talking about people was because I was saving it for the right one. The right time to finally let how I truly feel bubble over to the surface.

I am almost one hundred percent positive that I hate my dad.

I don't need some pathetic lecture about how much you're supposed to love your parents because they love you unconditionally, because when the person you idealized for so long betrays you and your mom in the same breath, all you see is a monster. What man preaches about family and the chosen family you make on a football team just to cheat on the woman who has given him everything? A fucking coward, that's who.

We've not had a real conversation since I found out after our semi-final game last season back in January, but now, as we prepare for the start of our new season, I couldn't care less about what this man has to say. I've avoided him at all costs and spent my time checking in with my mom.

The whole team is spread out around the field to do drills together. We're doing rotations, and I'm paired up with Sam Cho, Oliver Nayman, and Connor. And every time my dad looks over at me, scolding me about something, I get closer and closer to punching that mother fucker in the–

"Wes!"

Fuck. Our team has set up cones a few yards in front of us, enough space for a quick sprint and then into a backpedal. It's an easy drill that I could do in my sleep, but I've spent so much time thinking about ripping my dad's body in half that I didn't notice it was my turn to run.

I quickly do my reps of going back and forth ten times before switching off with Oliver. I sit down on the grass, catching my breath as Connor does crunches beside me. Workout time is one of the best times of the week, but for once, I can't get my head in the game, and we really don't have any time for me to fuck this up. Especially when we're having one of those seasons where the new freshman messes up the dynamic on the team. We have a few new defensemen, and they're treating this like it's a frat party, not a serious team where some of us are actually wanting to get drafted to play in the NFL.

"What's wrong with you, dude? Your face is beet red," Connor says, not a single waver in his voice as he continues to put his body through hell. "Someone clearly hasn't been pulling their weight in the gym."

"I'm fine."

"You only say that when something is wrong. I think you're forgetting how well I know you, Wessy. You talk too much shit for you to give me two-word answers," he explains, sitting up.

We've been friends since we were in diapers, of course, he knows me better than anyone else I've ever met. And he's right, I love to talk, but when I'm in my dad's presence, I prefer to shut up and keep my thoughts to myself. I've got a big mouth, and the second I let loose around that man, no one's going to hear the end of it.

So, I lie.

"Honestly, I'm good. I'm just tired," I say, faking a yawn for some extra effect.

Connor isn't buying my bullshit. His eyebrows crunch as he turns to look at me better. "From doing what? You've been lounging around like an ass for the last two weeks."

"Oh, gee, thanks so much for checking in on my mental health. I could be really struggling, and you think I'm just lazy–"

He shakes his head. "That's not what I mean, and you know it. You always speak your mind, so quit acting like you don't. You're looking around like you've got a secret."

"I *do* have a secret," I say, keeping my voice low. He raises his eyebrows. "No one else knows about my dad and what he did. Olivia just disappeared, and no one cared enough to ask why. So excuse me if I'm still pissed."

"Oh," is all he has to say. Honestly, what am I expecting him to say? He has the best pair of parents any kid could ask for. I'm sure the thought of either one of his parents cheating has never crossed his mind. He's never had this sickening feeling of pure rage in his chest when he looks at his dad. All he sees is what I used to – admiration.

"Yeah, it's fine. It doesn't matter," I mutter, pulling at the grass. Fuck. I hate feeling like this. I'm supposed to be a happy friend. The one who doesn't have any serious problems. The one who lives their life to a set of rules that I make up on the fly. "I think I just need to get laid."

He lets out a sigh at that answer. "I can't believe I'm saying this, but I think you might be right. I've never seen you so jittery in my life, and it's making me uneasy. I'm a mess as it is. I don't need your stress to rub off on me."

"I've not even had the energy to entertain another girl, but I'm starting to think it's about time," I say, running a hand through my hair. I need a haircut, desperately, but there's nothing I love more than a girl running her hand through my hair whilst I have my face between her legs. Fuck me. I'm getting hard just thinking about it. I shoot to my feet, ready for this conversation to be over. I've decided what's wrong, and now I just need to fix it. "Wanna run laps now?"

Connor blinks at me. "T- That's it? We're not going to suggest a game plan or anything?"

"Who the fuck do you think I am? I'm a catch, Connor. I'm not like you. I don't need step-by-step instructions on how to get laid. Women practically leap at me, and all I have to do is exist," I say, speaking nothing but the truth. Being a football player certainly has its perks. I used the fuck out of said perks in my freshman and sophomore years, so I can use them again.

Connor grins, standing up as he pats me on the shoulder. "There he is."

"Who?"

"The Wes that thinks his ego is bigger than the continent, not the one who secretly thinks about murdering his dad," he says, bumping his shoulder into mine as we start off at a slow jog, Oli and Sam slowly joining us.

"I wasn't thinking about murder... Just slight psychological and physical torture."

"Right, because that's so much better."

We all settle into a routine of talking about classes and our plans for the weekend as we run around the field. Holding a conversation whilst running is an art we've all mastered from a young age, so when Oli tells us about another proposition he's gotten from Hailey Dermont, we all burst out laughing.

That poor guy has been in the shackles of a woman who isn't even his. She's had her way with all of us on the team, apart from Connor and Oli. We only hooked up once at the end of freshman year, when she gave me a BJ in the back of her car. Connor is basically married to Cat, so Oliver is the only one left that she's desperate to get a taste of. She's imprinted on him – Jacob and Renesmee style. It's fucking weird as much as it is hilarious.

"Wes! What are you doing?" My dad's voice booms across the field as he stands in the middle of the track, his eyes following me as I continue running.

"What does it look like? We're running laps. Isn't that what you told us to do, old man?" Sam and Oliver laugh at that, and Connor just groans beside me like a disappointed parent. My dad shakes his head.

"I'm supposed to check your group drills first, boys. You all know that," Coach explains.

"Sorry, Coach," Connor says. What an ass-kisser. "We'll do better next time."

"Yeah, we're just trying to tire ourselves out," I add. That only makes his face redder. What the fuck is his problem? It's like he's begging me to go over there and swing right in his adulterous face.

"You tire yourselves out when I say you do," he argues. I roll my eyes, but he just beckons a hand in my direction. "Mackenzie? A word."

Reluctantly, I drag my ass over towards him, holding my head up high, puffing my chest out. Trying to intimidate my dad is pointless. He can make me see red, but he's also a fuckton bigger than me and could probably beat the shit out of me if he wanted to. Still, I try my hardest.

"Yes, Coach?"

"What's your problem, son? You don't speak to me for

weeks, and you've managed to fuck up every training session we've had since preseason started," he says, pinning his arms against his chest, the football he was holding dropping to the floor.

"I guess fucking things up runs in the family," I mutter.

He takes a deep breath. "Look, I don't know how many times I'm going to have to apologize to you and your mom. We're still in the process of the separation, but it seems like she's handling this a lot better than you are."

I scoff. "Do you really think that living on her own in an apartment is her handling this better than me? She's hardly looking after herself, but I guess that doesn't matter to you, does it? It never really did, anyway."

He sighs again. "Wes, look–"

"Is that what you called me over her for, Coach? Just to complain about how badly I'm handling the fire *you* started?" There's a very fine line between punching him in the nose or walking out of here. I've not cared much for football over the last year or so, anyway. I doubt anyone would notice if I left.

"I just need you to know that despite all this, I'm still your coach, and I expect you to listen to me. You and Connor are key parts of the team, and if you continue acting like a brat, it's going to rub off on everyone else, too," he explains. I hate that he kinda has a point. "You have a lot riding on this season, son. A *lot*. And if you don't get your head out of your ass, I can't be the one to push scouts your way or help you get any contracts. That's all up to you. All this partying and drinking and sleeping around isn't helping your case. You need to focus more on your performance and take better care of your health if you want to be taken seriously. This whole goofball, funny guy act that you have going on isn't going to last, Wes, and the faster you get that in your head, the better."

I don't even say anything.

I swallow the bile in my throat as I look at him. Who is he to tell me to get my act together when he's spent the last few years lying to all of us and cheating on my mom? His *wife*. The mother of his only child.

Fuck this.

Fuck him.

Fuck fucking football.

I kick the ball at his feet instead of kicking him in the balls. As soon as it's off in the sky, the whole team gasps and whistles as we watch it fall to the other side of the bleachers. I immediately hang my head, knowing that I'm going to be the one who has to collect it.

My dad's growl reverberates through me. "Collect it, bring it back to the locker room, and get out of that uniform. I don't want to see you wearing that until you start acting like you're a part of the team."

I blink at him. "Are you benching me, dad?"

"Oh, so I'm back to being your dad now?" he scoffs, shaking his head. "Get the ball and change. I don't want to look at you anymore, Wes."

I sulk the whole time it takes me to find the ball, shove it into the equipment locker, and change out of my kit. I don't like feeling like this – constantly on edge, like I'm waiting for the other shoe to drop. It isn't supposed to be like this for me. I'm not supposed to get wound up about shit like this. I'm used to taking this light and breezy, and just existing is starting to feel like a chore.

I don't bother to wait for the rest of the team to join me in the locker room and I'm out of there in ten minutes. Connor drove us here from our house earlier, so I had to walk all the way back on my own. My headphones don't serve as the kind of distraction I thought they would provide. Every song doesn't sound right in my ears. I end up skipping each song that comes on my playlist before my mom's contact name fills my screen.

I stop in my tracks, swiping the answer button. "Mom?"

"You took Jarvis."

"Hello to you too, mother," I say, laughing. "I took him just over a week ago, remember? You said it was easier for me to have him for a bit until you found your feet."

She sighs, laughing a little. "Oh, right, yeah." A pause. "I'm sorry, Wes, my brain is a mess right now. A lot is going on at the moment, and I keep forgetting things, like where our cat is."

My chest pinches. "Are you getting enough sleep?"

"I'm trying to, but with the deadline and everything and the papers and–"

"Just one thing at a time, Mom," I say quietly. I hate how soft and fragile she's gotten. My mom is the toughest person I have ever known. She always has been. Growing up in Germany with a strict mother as her ballet teacher, she grew a thick skin. And I hate that my dad was the one who healed her just to break her down again. "What needs doing first?"

She pauses again, humming. I imagine her pacing around her small apartment, barefoot, her long blonde-ish-brown hair flowing down her back. "Probably grocery shopping. Then I need to get this draft to my editor by next Friday."

"Okay, okay," I say, trying to think. "How about this? I'll order the groceries to your house and they'll get to you tonight. Then, you can work on your book. How's it going?"

Mom's been working on a series of lifestyle books for as long as I can remember. She's an incredible author, and although most are about motherhood and the struggles of being a woman, they're a fun and interesting read. I'm not just saying that because she birthed me and has been doing everything for me for the last twenty years.

When she explains to me that she's not reaching her writing goal for the day, I suggest that she hang out with her friend Julia. I don't know what grown women talk about in their spare time, but I'm sure my mom's divorce would be a good conversation starter. I'd be running that story into the ground if I was her.

"Enough about me, *Sonnenchien*," she says, laughing softly. "How are you? Have you got a girlfriend yet?"

I sigh. "Same answer as always, Mom. No, I don't."

"Why not, Wes? You're always talking about how you're seeing new people."

"Doesn't mean I'm dating them seriously, Mom. It's just, uh… Just a physical thing," I say, clearing my throat. Do I really want to talk to my mom about my sex life? Not particularly. "Which we're both totally okay with and are consenting to," I add quickly.

My mom lets out an exaggerated sigh on the other end. "I don't like the sound of that, Wes."

"It's fine, honestly. I don't need to be in a relationship to be happy, or I dunno… Complete?" I say. She should be very anti-relationship after the way her last one just ended.

"Maybe not, but you need some stability. You're constantly out and drinking and… I don't know, Wes. I can't help but think you're lashing out, and I don't want to ruin your life before it's even started just because of what's going on with me and your dad."

Living life without a plan is freeing. It might not be ideal for other people, but not having to worry about expectations or something I've planned for not working out makes me feel better about myself. It feels like I'll have the opportunity to share stories with my kids about my rebellious days and that the fun parts of my personality won't die out.

"I'm going to be busy with football, but I'll think about it," I say, just to give her some peace of mind. The last thing I want is for her to worry about me above everything else that's going on. She might not believe me right now, but I'm going to have to figure out a way to prove it to her and my dad, apparently. I can't deal with either of them on my back right now.

After she ends the call, I submit a grocery order to get to her as soon as possible. When I get back to the house, finding Jarvis curled up in the blanket on my bed, I thank my lucky stars that there's at least one sane person left in our family. Jarvis will always be the best of us.

SIX
NORA / WES
STRAWBERRY ICE-CREAM

NORA

YOU KNOW you're going crazy when ideas you would have laughed at a while ago start to sound sane.

When Elle demands that we go out to a party at one of the frat houses off campus, you know it's serious. Elle is the last person I expect to want to go to a party on a random night. But she's my best friend, so it's hard to say no to her when she blinks up at me and Cat with her round doe eyes and begs us to go.

"Party, party, party!" Elle is screaming louder than anyone in this joint, and Cat and I can't stop laughing. The fact that we've been here less than an hour and this is the kind of vibe we're on pretty much sets the tone for the rest of the night. "Are you animals ready to party?!"

"Jesus, what have you taken?" I ask, pulling on her arm as she tries to drag me into the dance floor for the fifth time. Her eyes are wide and slightly red as she stares back at me with a loopy grin. "Are you high?"

"What? No!"

"I mean, it's not a problem if you are. I kinda want a hit if you have some on you," I murmur, bumping my shoulder into hers. Cat rolls her eyes, pulling on both of our arms until we stand in some weird three-way circle.

"Okay, then what's going on?" Cat asks Elle, her eyebrows furrowed with concern. "It's not like you to want to go out on a Saturday night. This must be a new world record."

Elle rolls her eyes. "Don't freak out..." Obviously, I start to freak out. I'm practically bouncing on my heels, desperately waiting for her to say something. "I'm looking for a hookup or something. Well, anything, really. A kiss, at the very least. I might even settle for a peck."

Cat and I start screeching at the same time, holding onto Elle's shoulders as we all jump around in a circle. You'd think she just told us she's about to get married, but these are the kind of small victories that we need right now. Elle's been swearing off the opposite sex for as long as I can remember, and it's about time that she gets some.

"I love this for you, Elle-Belle. We're going to do some real wing-woman shit tonight," I say, winking at her. "Trust us."

Cat sighs. "Well, Nora might have to take the lead on this one. I can *feel* Connor looking at me from here, and I know he's going to be miserable if I don't dance with him for a bit," she says. We all look over our shoulders to spot Connor with his eyes directly on Cat, Wes, Sam, and Oli standing beside him. They're like a pack of wolves. "Besides, he'll probably be leaving early, anyway. I'll catch up with you guys in a while, don't worry."

With that, she disappeared into Connor's arms, and I had to stop myself from throwing up. His arms are wrapped around her waist, dangerously close to her ass, and he's whispering something into her ear as he walks her backward into the space in the living room where people are dancing. Wes's eyes lock with mine, and he sticks his finger into his mouth, pretending to gag, and I can't help but snort. He just winks at me before grabbing Sam and Oli to walk around.

I turn back around to Elle. "So, where do you want to start? Do you have a type?"

She bites on her bottom lip. "I haven't really thought about it, but someone tall, strong, with dark features, funny, doesn't hate the fact that I have such a busy schedule."

"Okay, slow your horses, girl. You just want someone you can make out with, right?" She nods. "Right, so you don't need to plan out your whole future. Hell, maybe I should even take some of my own advice. Anyway, you're probably looking for something casual, which means you have a better chance with some of the assholes in here. You don't want to end up with someone like–"

Her eyes widen. "Ryan."

"Exactly," I say, my stomach knotting at the thought of him. "You don't want to end up with someone like him. He'll latch onto you like a snake, suck all the blood out of you, and just leave you there to dry. You do *not* want that. People like–"

"Ryan."

I laugh. "Yes, Ryan, we have established the devil's name. We don't need to keep repeating it. What I'm saying is–"

"No, Nora, I mean, he's right behind you," she whispers.

I get a weird twinge in my heart at her words, so I turn around slowly.

Yup. Ryan Valla is standing behind me, hands shoved in his pockets, his all-black outfit making the butterflies in my stomach strangely reappear. I thought they were dead and gone and buried, but apparently not. And he's fucking *smirking* at me.

"Nora," he greets, "Glad to know my name is still in your mouth."

"Unfortunately," I retort. I'm not going to let him get under my skin again.

"You always liked having your mouth full, didn't you? I could only shut you up in a way that benefited the both of us." His voice is so slow and taunting and just annoyingly sexy. He should *not* be allowed to make me feel like this. No one should be allowed to make me feel like this unless they're fictional and not able to hurt me. He's playing his signature push-and-pull game.

Elle clears her throat. "Yeah, I'm just going to… I'm just going to go… Away from whatever the fuck this is. I'll see you later, Nor."

My eyes flash to hers.

Traitor, my eyes scream.

Deal with it, hers say.

Before I can beg her to stay and not leave me alone with this monster, she runs away. I can't blame her because my feet aren't moving either. *Why the fuck aren't I moving?*

"Look, Nor, I'm glad you're here. I wanted to talk to you," Ryan says, scratching the back of his neck.

"Well, we're starting rehearsals next week, so we can talk then," I say, smiling tightly.

He shrugs. "Don't think it can wait until then."

I don't know when he started to walk closer to me. I also don't know when I started to walk further back into the wall. We have *got* to stop bumping into each other like this. The perks of dating someone in the same social circle as you, I guess. He just turns up everywhere that I am and manages to make me feel like I'm sixteen again, and he just kissed me for the first time.

"Okay," I breathe out. Maybe if he says what he needs to say now, we can pretend to like each other during rehearsals, and all will be well. He stares at me for a long moment, not saying anything, his eyes ping-ponging between mine. I get agitated under his gaze immediately. "Spit it out, then."

He takes in a deep breath. "I wasn't going to say anything, but I miss you so much, Nor. Like, so fucking much. Can't you feel this energy still between us?"

"If you mean utter hatred, then yeah, sure." I laugh despite the tears that prick at my eyes. "You're stupider than I thought."

He shakes his head. "I'm not."

"You are," I say, placing one hand on his chest so he can stop coming so close to me. "You're pretending, Ryan. It's what you do. This doesn't mean anything to you. *I don't mean anything to you, and I'm sick of being played like a fucking puppet."*

"Who said that?" he asks. *Is he fucking serious?* He blinks at me. *Oh, he's serious.*

"*You* did," I shout, "When you were fucking another girl at the party I planned for you. That I did just for you because I- I loved you, you asshole. And you were constantly doing things to hurt me, and for what? You strung me along, and I fell for it."

He shakes his head violently, breathing heavily. That's when I can smell the alcohol on his breath, and I try to step further away from him. He turns into such an asshole when he's drunk.

"What? You don't love me anymore?" he asks as if that's the main point of what I just said.

I take in a deep breath, wishing every stupid thought could leave his brain. That way, he'd have nothing else to say. "You treated me like shit, Ryan. After all the times you apologized, I went right back to you because you promised you would make it up to me, but you can't fix it now. It's over. We're over. We have been for *months.*"

I'm so sick of this back-and-forth. Feeling like he wants me one second and that he doesn't want me the other. It's two steps forward and three steps back with this guy. I don't want that anymore. I want security. I want assurance that someone is always going to have my back, no matter what. Not whatever the fuck this is.

With whatever strength I have left, I close my eyes, push at his chest, and whisper, "Just go."

His eyes flicker. "Nora, please, I–"

I've gotten to the point where my eyes are shut so tight I can only see darkness and then hear the gruffness of another male voice. "She told you to go, bud."

WES

This was not part of today's plans. Sure, I might have fantasized about ripping Ryan's head off whilst he screams hysterically before dunking it into a bucket of bleach, but that's usually for a late night when I need to blow off some steam, not for mediocre parties like these.

Nora looks fucking frightened, which scares *me* because she's one of the toughest people I know. There's no fear of him in her eyes, but it's almost like she doesn't trust herself to be alone with him. She ran back to him countless times after he broke her heart. How he tried to put it back together like a Band-Aid over a bullet hole. I know she'd do just about anything for him, but when he's all up in her face and she's telling him to leave, he needs to learn how to take the fucking hint.

Ryan turns, almost completely covering Nora with his body. "Are you fucking serious?"

"What? Got a problem with people telling you no?" I ask, inching towards him. He can act all tough now, but I know he's the same guy who exaggerated a British accent after spending a summer in London. "She told you to leave, so leave."

"We're *talking*, Wes, relax. You've always loved interrupting our conversations. Is there something I've been missing this whole time?"

He flickers his gaze between the two of us. Nora's shoulders are shaking now, the rest of her body frozen in place. I clench my jaw, waiting to see if he's got something else to say. He's always had it out for me, and honestly, I can't blame him. I care enough about Nora and the boundaries in our friendship to know I can't exactly tell her to break up with her boyfriend, but that doesn't mean I can't coincidentally turn up in places that I know they're in.

When he doesn't say anything and when I don't respond, I finally say, "Leave."

He reeks of alcohol, and I can't bear to look at this sorry excuse for a person anymore. He finally made his way across the room, and I let out a breath of relief. I do not want to be caught up in a fight right now. That alone would be enough for my dad to kick me off the team.

When my eyes focus back on Nora, she's just... Staring at a spot on my shirt. Shit. Do I have a stain or something? I look down. Nope. All good in that department.

I press two fingers under her chin, urging her to look up at me. God, she's so pretty. Even like this, seconds away from breaking down, she's still the most beautiful person I've ever seen in my life. Her brown eyes shimmer and my words come out breathy because of the weird stutter my heart does.

"You okay, Sunshine?" The second the words leave my mouth, her whole face crumbles as she covers her face with her hands. Sharp sobs rip through her, and her shoulders shake. Instantly, I wrap my arms around her, pulling her right into my chest. "Hey, you're okay. You're okay."

Fuck.

What do I do?

Am I supposed to call Connor over here to help his sister out? Or is this the sort of best friend thing you do? Where the fuck is Elle? I look over Nora's head, frantically searching for her. I spot her next to Oliver, laughing insanely loudly. If she's trying to flirt with Oli, she'd have better luck getting more action from a rock. Oli is as clueless as they come when it comes to girls.

I shake my head to get rid of the thought. Strange girl, she is. Even stranger? Nora Bailey sobbing in my arms at a *party*. This is exactly her scene. The place where she comes to life. Not the place where she falls apart.

"I've got you, Stargirl," I murmur, and she only starts to cry harder. I'm really not cut out for this. I can barely handle my own emotions, never mind someone else's.

As soothing as I thought my words were, she shakes her head. "I'm not okay. I'm really not okay, Wes. Everything keeps going wrong."

"It's okay not to be okay." I swallow back the emotion in my throat at her words. "Tell you why?"

She leans up off me, only enough to rest her chin on my chest. God, my heart might explode. Or my ribs might combust. I don't fucking know. But she's looking up at me with those wet lashes, that sweet mouth, that cute as fuck pink nose, and it's like my entire world stops. Fucking hell. I need some medical attention or some shit.

"Because nobody is one hundred percent okay all the time. If anyone says they are, they're lying. You're a good actress, Nora, but you're not *that* good. I can see right through you, you know," I explain, smiling softly as I tap her on the forehead. "And when you're not okay, you can tell me. I don't want you crying over him or how he makes you feel. He doesn't deserve it."

She nods, stepping away from me to wipe her face with both of her hands. "Thank you," she says, sniffling. "You've had some weirdly wise vibes lately, and it's freaking me out. It's like you always know the exact right thing to say."

I shrug. "I dunno. Maybe I'm just saying the right thing for you." I look around us, and when I see Cat and Connor, now with Elle and Oli, I reach out for Nora's hand. "Come on, Sunshine. Let's get out of here."

※

AFTER A QUICK RUN the grocery store, buying some serving spoons and a tub of strawberry ice cream (her choice), we're sitting on the hood of my car in the parking lot, silently enjoying each other's company. I don't even like strawberry ice cream, but I was almost ninety percent sure that she'd start crying again if she didn't get her way.

Nora bumps her shoulder into mine, stealing another huge spoonful from the tub. "Well," she whistles, sighing. "That was awkward."

My eyebrows knit together in confusion. "What was?"

"Me, crying just then," she says, swallowing the ice cream.

I resist the urge to roll my eyes. She notices my annoyance because she pulls the tub out of my lap and places it between her legs instead, guarding it with her life. I press my hands against the cold metal on either side of me, tilting my head up to the sky. For one of the first times, I can actually make out a few stars in the sky.

"Don't do that, Nor," I murmur, tilting my head down.

"Do what?"

"Don't downplay your feelings. You don't have to do that with me. We can joke around, but you know that beneath it, I'm here for you, okay? Like, always," I say. We might have known each other forever, but there are some parts of herself that I feel like she hides from me. It's fair enough. We're in college now. We're not going to share every moment with each other, but sometimes, I wish she would.

"I know," she replies, pushing around the ice cream that's starting to melt. "And I'm here for you, too."

"Great, glad that's all cleared up." She rolls her eyes. I smile. "So, what's the next step for you since you didn't get the part you wanted in the musical?"

She points the spoon in my face, ice cream dripping off it right onto my car. "How did you know about that?"

"I'm not an idiot. You wouldn't be able to shut up if you got the part you wanted, and you've not spammed my phone since the audition list came out, so just connecting the dots," I say simply, shrugging. Her eyes narrow. I lean forward and steal the melting ice cream from the spoon, keeping my eyes locked with her brown ones. Something flashes in her eyes as I do, but I pull away, and she drops the spoon into the tub.

"To be honest," she starts, tucking her hair behind her ear, displaying that fucking tattoo that I can't get enough of. "My mind is constantly spinning, so I don't know what I need to do next. I can't focus on anything, knowing that he's the lead. I just…" She closes her hands into tiny fists, and I almost choke from trying not to laugh. "I just want to hurt him like how he hurt me. He's constantly playing with my head. And I've got all this pent-up anger in me, and it's destroying me. I want to get him back, you know?"

She turns to me, a confident spark in her eyes. Fuck me if it doesn't turn me on. Maybe I'm just desperate for some action because there's no way I'm getting hot under the collar over Nora Bailey.

Sure, there's been the odd time when she's shown up to our games in my jersey, and I've thought about taking it off her, but that's completely unrelated. I've also been around when I crashed at her dorm one night after a party, and she woke up in the middle of the night, walking into the kitchen with nothing but tiny shorts and a tank top. No bra. She didn't see me because I was supposed to be asleep on the couch, but I didn't sleep a wink that night.

Fuck.

Maybe that time she kissed me to get back at Ryan really did a number on me.

I clear my throat as if that's going to shake the thoughts in my head. "Hate to break it to you, but you sound like a psychopath."

She groans, a tiny furious noise leaving her lips in a snarl. "That's what I mean. I don't know what's wrong with me. I feel like I'm going crazy." Her hands are still balled into little fists at her sides, her knuckles digging into the metal.

"No, carry on. I like it when you're angry. It's hot as fuck."

Yep. I just said that. And those words are definitely going to bite me in the ass later.

"Whatever," she says, rolling her eyes. An easy 'thank you' would also suffice. "What are your plans then? The season is going well, right?"

"Yeah, it's fine for now. It's too early to tell, but I'm not expecting us to carry a huge win this year. The team's not gelling like usual. We lost some vital players at the end of last year," I explain, somehow feeling responsible. Things like this just happen. As much as I love playing football, I can't see myself going pro. It was a dream when I was a kid, but I don't live and breathe it like Connor does. A part of me thinks I never did. "Apart from that, I've got nothing else going on. For once."

Nora hums. "No new girl you want to take for a spin?"

I bark out a laugh. "You're making me sound like an asshole. I don't sleep around that much, Nor."

"You're a commitmentphobe. That's okay," she coos, patting my thigh.

"I'm not," I say, swatting her hand away from me. Her hand doesn't need to be anywhere near my junk, or Lieutenant Benson is going to get confused. *I* might get confused. "You just love commitment *too* much."

"Oh, I'm sorry I don't love the idea of someone leaving me," she argues.

"Oh, *I'm* sorry I don't love the idea of being stuck with someone forever," I challenge.

She rocks her shoulder into mine again. "Come on, you can't possibly believe that." I scoff, giving her my answer. Nora shakes her head. "You'll find someone you'll never get sick of, and you'll want to see them *all* the time, even when you close your eyes. There will be someone you want to do all the boring stuff with, and you'll never get bored of them. When that happens, I'm going to be right here to say I told you so."

I don't know when the lump appeared in my throat, but I'm suddenly finding it hard to swallow. I've always thought that I wouldn't be enough for someone to stay with me instead of the other way around. There's no way someone would want to stick around me forever. I could easily become attached to people, and there's nothing special enough about me that would have anyone feeling the same way I do.

"We'll see," I finally say.

SEVEN
NORA
COLLEGE DROP-OUT

IF PENELOPE THOMPSON tells me to fix my face one more time, I'm walking right out of this room.

We've been in the rehearsal studio for the last two and a half hours, and I would much rather dunk my head into a bowl of ice water than be here right now. We all know this script like the back of our hands. It's been burned into our memory since it came out. But for some reason, Ryan has managed to make Hamilton that much more annoying, and every time he speaks, I want to punch him in the face. He's going back and forth between skipping over the affectionate scenes we have to do and only doing the ones where he has long expanses of speech while I have to sit in the corner with Kie and run our lines together. I mean, the play *is* called *Hamilton*, but he's taking it to a new level of arrogance.

I've never been much of a violent person, but this guy is making me question every reason I committed to treating people with kindness when really all I want to do is–

"Can you save your plotting for another day?" Kiara asks, pumping her hip into mine as we collect our stuff from the side of the rehearsal space. "You could probably channel this energy into something else. Like pottery painting or selling handmade jewelry on Etsy."

"Can't," I say simply, dropping down onto my ass to tie up my Converse. An absolute monster of a shoe. They should not be allowed to look this good and be *that* hard to put on. "Eliza's rage is important to the story. I have a right to be pissed off at Hammy."

Kie rolls her eyes. "Yeah, but not in the first act."

I shrug. "No harm in starting early. Besides, Mr. Secretary is making it pretty easy."

Kiara sighs, standing to her feet as she plants her hands on her hips. "You need to learn how to chill sometimes, Bails."

I wish I could just tell her, 'Yeah, fine, you're right,' but that just isn't me. I don't get to chill. A lot of my future in the artistic industry is riding on how I perform now. These are my golden years. These are the years I'm going to look back on with my kids and reminisce about how agile and sexy I look. I can't fuck up my chances by not taking this seriously. If Ryan doesn't fix up his fuckboy attitude and his inability to at least pretend to like me, then this is going to be a disaster. I know I bruised his ego the other day, and now he's using it against me. He knows how much I value having time to run lines with the person I need to, not my friend who is playing a different part.

"I think Kiara is right," Penny says, walking towards us. As lovely as a teacher she is, she has been on my ass all day, and I'm sick of it. She's usually my savior, my saving grace, my stage mother, but today she's been a grade-A pain in the ass. "You have to *live* like Eliza. Feel the way she feels. And from what I'm getting, you're not channeling that well into this role."

I scoff when I catch Ryan behind her, his arm slung around Daisy. So much for him begging for me back at the party. "I don't want to live like her. Her husband cheated on her, and he was in love with her sister. I don't exactly want to manifest that, Penn."

Ryan shrugs. "Well, it seems like you're halfway there."

That motherfucker just *wants* me to kill him today. "You

know what? If you don't shut your mouth, I'm going to do it for you."

He steps out from behind Penny, meeting my stride. "You're all talk and no action, Nora. I think we both know that."

I got so close to him I could easily curl my fist in his shirt and give him a nice shiner. I took a few karate lessons growing up and spent years torturing Wes and Connor. I'm sure I could take him. He looks down at me, that annoying smirk on his lips, and his dark eyes shine at me. Before I start fantasizing about which body part I want to chop off first, Penny breaks us apart. She huffs out a sigh, running her hands through her braids.

"I do not get paid to babysit you two," she says, pointing between the two of us. "I want you both in my office once you've gotten ready."

Penny's office is frustratingly cozy and calming. It always makes me want to drop right asleep, no matter how much energy I have running through my body. The small room is filled with pastel throw blankets and cushions, the chairs feeling like mattresses. She's got a pride flag hanging from one wall and the other walls filled with certificates and the Playbill from the time she filled in for another famous actress on the West End. Crystals scatter along her desk with a stack of tarot cards, and it smells like incense. No matter how angry she looks at the two of us right now, I'm convinced that she's my spirit animal. I want to be her when I grow up.

She leans forward on her desk, shaking her head. "Okay, guys, I'm going to be brutally honest with you two." The tension settles between us like an awkward fourth person in the room. The anticipation tickles my skin, making me grow uncomfortable in the seat, which I thought was impossible. "I'm regretting casting you both as the leads."

My heart sinks. Ryan's jaw drops open. "What?" We both gawk at the same time.

Penny shakes her head. "I'm regretting the fact that I thought you would be mature enough to be able to keep it together on stage. Today was a disaster, and that was hardly even a run-through."

"What are you talking about?" Ryan asks because, apparently, I have no words.

"I'm not stupid," Penny says. "I know you two broke up earlier this year, and it's severely messed up your chemistry on stage."

"Well, we can fix it. It's just another act, right?" Ryan asks hopefully. I resist the urge to kick his shin.

I take in a deep breath. "I'm not playing pretend with you," I say as calmly as I possibly can.

"She's right. I'm not asking you guys to become best buddies or start dating again. That part is none of my business. But at the very least, I need you to get along. Or, get along enough that it doesn't look like you want to tear each other apart on stage."

We both take in the idea for a minute. If this performance means as much to him as much as it does to me, he wouldn't need to jeopardize it. If he cared about me at all, like he's claimed a million times, he would put some sort of effort into making this a good act. But, no. He wants to fumble around the stage and stand on my feet like an oaf.

"Nora, it seems to me like you've got some tension that's been unresolved with Ryan," Penny says, her voice sickly sweet. I nod stiffly. "And Ryan, you seem incredibly apologetic. I think that if you just—"

I hold out a hand to stop her. "I don't want an apology, Penny. I want the last five and half years of my life back. That's not going to be fixed by a simple 'sorry.'"

"You're right, but obviously, I can't do that. You need to find some sort of peace with each other or within yourself, whichever it may be. You've clearly got all this pent-up inside you, and it's showing. Just please try to get along. For me." Penny bashes her beautiful lashes at the both of us, her brown doe eyes almost hypnotizing me.

I sigh, pushing out of my chair. "Fine."

I spend the rest of the day with an annoying ache in my chest, and the second I step through the doors to my dorm, I say, "I'm dropping out of college."

Sometimes, there's nothing better than starting a conversation with your best friends with a controversial statement that will get them immediately hooked. Elle and Cat have been lounging in the living room area of our dorm since before I left for rehearsals and they're still there by the time I come back.

I drop my bag on the floor next to the couch, where they're curled up within a large blanket. Cat's reading a romance novel that my brother bought her, and Elle is editing a video for her YouTube channel on her laptop.

Cat looks up at me, squaring her eyes as I perch myself on the edge of the coffee table. "I've heard that sentence come out of your mouth too many times for it to be true."

"Well, it is," I say seriously. I gesture at myself in the same outfit I've worn twice this week. "Get a good look at this, ladies, because you'll never lay eyes on me again."

Elle snickers, not bothering to look up as her eyes focus on her video with concentration. I never knew how intense it was to be an influencer. Cat rolls her eyes. "I'm dating your brother. I'm sure we'll bump into each other at some point."

I throw my head back, shouting in fake disbelief. "God! Don't remind me, ew!"

Cat shakes her head, laughing. "You're impossible, Nor-Nor."

"No, *you're* impossible," I argue, pointing at her.

"You know what, for all of our sakes, I *hope* you move out." Cat points her nose up, dismissing me with her hand.

Elle gasps, finally. "Wow, that was catty."

Cat shrugs, making a very posh 'hmpf' sound as she crosses her arms against her chest. The second the tiny noise leaves her mouth, we're all in a fit of hysterical laughter. There is no one on the planet I can laugh with like this over stupid arguments like the one we just had.

I'm going to value our friendship, no matter how hard life gets sometimes. I always get this looming feeling in my chest when something goes wrong, like the world is ending, but it's not. And these are the people that can bring me back to reality when I feel like that. The ones that remind me of my worth and my potential. Growing up with a twin brother was fun, but I've never wanted sisters as bad as I did when I met these two. In some way, I guess they're already my sisters.

A weird feeling washes over me, and I suddenly have the urge to call my parents. As overbearing as they can be, they're the best two people on the planet. My mom got pregnant with Connor and I when she was younger than me. I can only imagine how it must have been being eighteen and raising twins with the talkative, nerdy guy who has had a crush on you for years. Still, they managed to make it work, and they both got a degree in teaching and have been doing what they love for years. My parents have been to hell and back, and as much as I can pester my dad about going to New York or bug my mom to show me how she used to do my hair when I was a kid, they mean everything to me.

I pull my phone out of my back pocket, but I'm instead distracted by an email from Max, my agent. My heartbeat instantly starts to grow erratic, and I don't fully register the words in front of me until I've read them a few times.

MAXGREENWEEL@GREENWELLTALENT.COM

Updates on recent tapes.

Hi, Nora! I hope you're doing well. I know you've been waiting for an update, but it's been a busy month for everyone. I did manage to get some updates on the tapes you sent in August.

1 The one for the A24 project wants to send you an updated script and see if you can do another take. They're very picky, but the fact that they want you to do another tape is good news!

2 The Netflix one was a bust. Apparently, they want someone blonde, and they've changed their mind. Wigs and dyes are out of the question, apparently. Suddenly, they care about authenticity. Pathetic, right? Sorry about that one.

Also, a short film reached out to me about wanting to cast you for the lead in their film. It's created by influencers, so be careful when you have a stalk of their social media. They want someone who can work as soon as possible, but I let them know it might be unlikely due to your current class schedule. I added their message below if you want to have a look.

The A24 project is a big deal! Let me know what you're most interested in. I really want the best for you.

This is going to be your year, Nora. I know it!

Regards,

Max :)

MY HEART LEAPS in my chest as I read through the message again. When I click the link to find the short film that needs casting, it doesn't exactly check my boxes, but new things are good, right? It's a murder-mystery, suspenseful thriller with a romance side-plot. I'm open to pretty much anything that can get my name out there. Everyone wants to be an actor these days, and with the amount of talent in my generation, I don't know how I'm going to be able to make myself stand out. How I'm going to prove that I'm special.

This is probably the best news I've had in a while, so I don't take it lightly. Maybe this is finally the start of something good. I'm sick of feeling like there's another shoe about to drop and like there's a piece of my life missing.

This could be exactly what I need.

EIGHT
WES
HAPPY BIRTHDAY, I GUESS?

THERE IS nothing I hate more than traditions changing.

Ever since I've known the Baileys, they've spent their birthday together. Not only is it on the greatest night of the year – Halloween – but there's two of them, which means twice the fun. They always have a big blow-out party where I can get pissed drunk and not have to worry about anything else for the next few days. It was perfect last year. I got to spend the day at the party dressed up in a Sven costume from *Frozen*, and then I spent the night getting a manicure from Nora.

Best.

Birthday.

Ever.

I think I've always loved their birthday more than my own because who wants to celebrate someone's birthday in the middle of summer? Being born in June fucking sucks, and everyone is too hot and bothered to have a party.

This year, I was expecting them to have an even bigger party since they're turning twenty-one, but nope. Instead, Connor decided to spend the entire day with his girlfriend since she planned a scavenger hunt or some shit. I guess that's cute. Or whatever. But it sucks ass for me.

Even Nora didn't want to do anything. She spent the whole day shopping for books with Elle and then spent the night watching movies until Cat came back and hung out with them. Nora not having a party on her birthday is a crime against humanity. She might look like a good girl, but she's got sin written all over her. She causes trouble and chaos everywhere that she goes, and I love to get in on the action. But for one of the first times, I was NFI: Not Fucking Invited.

Not being able to hang out with my friends on their actual birthday was the worst, but at least we still have the morning-after ritual, which I hope will never die out. Every year, the day after their birthday, Emma and Mark Bailey prepare a brunch for us so we can get rid of our hangovers and debrief about the night before. For once, I'm not hungover, and the birthday boy is. Has Hell frozen over?

I raise my orange juice glass to my lips, shaking my head at Cat and Connor, who both have on a pair of sunglasses. Cat's head is nestled into his shoulder, and he rests his head on top of hers lazily. "Ah, how the tables have turned."

"I can hear myself breathing. I hate it," Connor grumbles.

"Awh, does the Princess finally know how it feels to be hungover?" Nora coos from beside me. I give her my hand as a secret high-five, and she clasps her hand in mine.

"Nice one," I mutter.

"Thanks," she says, grinning. Torturing Connor just happens to be one of the many things Nora and I have in common, and I'd be lying if I said we didn't use it to our own advantage sometimes. "How does it feel, Connie Wonnie? Do you finally know what it's like to live on the wild side?"

"Yes, and I hate it," he says, nuzzling his face into Catherine's hair. Elle laughs from the other side of the table. "Worst birthday present ever."

My eyes light up with the perfect segway. "Speaking of birthday presents…" I pull out the badly wrapped gift from under the table and drop it in front of Nora. She eyes the funky wrapping paper, and she can see exactly what kind of box it is.

I'm an awful gift-giver. That's just a fact. The Baileys have had an array of gifts from me over the years, and I thought that would never change. Unfortunately for Connor, I completely forgot about getting him a gift, so he gave me the whole 'I'm older and wiser, and I don't care about gifts but the people I spend time with' speech. Luckily, Nora's gift came just in time because the look on her face was priceless.

This girl has endured way too much shit these last few months to have a shitty birthday. It's the least I could do. I know who is winning the Friend of the Year award, and it's not Cat or Elle.

When she uncovers the wrapping, spotting the logo on the box but not opening it, she turns to me. "Wesley." She says my name and nothing else, treating it like a bad word that she's not allowed to say.

"Nora," I say slowly. I immediately frown, knowing that it doesn't have the same taunt the way she says my name. "It doesn't have the same effect when I do it. I wish you had a longer name."

"Don't change the subject," she warns. "What the fuck is this?"

"Shoes," I answer simply, nodding towards the Converse box in front of her.

"I can see they're shoes, Wes. Why are they in front of me?"

"Because it's your birthday, and you like shoes?" I spell it out to her. She doesn't give up scrutinizing me. "Why are you making this so hard? Just accept the damn present."

"Wes, you never get me gifts for my birthday. You write hand-written messages on the back of a cereal box or on a card you make. I mean, one year, you gave me a half-eaten pack of gum from your car and said, 'Happy Birthday, I guess.' I've never seen you spend this much money on yourself. The last thing I want to do is open this box and find a cute pair of shoes in there."

Yeah, right.

This girl loves presents. She likes feeling special and looking pretty. She likes feeling needed and cared for. I've spent so long watching her beat herself up, going back and forth between hating herself and hating Ryan and what he did to her, that I knew she needed something to cheer her up like this.

"Just shut up and open them, will you?" Slowly – so fucking slowly – she opens the lid of the box to find a pair of pink Converse All Stars with tiny, embroidered stars on them and an 'N' on the heel. It might have cost me more money than I spend on a weekly grocery shop, but the look on her face is fucking priceless.

There are only three types of smiles that Nora gives. There's the one she uses on stage or when she's thanking someone for opening the door for her. She uses it when she's not fully *there* but there enough to want to smile. Those ones are painful.

There's the regular smile that she gives when she's happy or excited about something or when she's listening to her favorite song. Those ones are cute.

Then there's the smile that she only reserves for special occasions. The smile that pulls her dimples right in. The smile that causes her eyes to light up like a fucking galaxy.

The first time she smiled at me like that, I almost died.

We were six years old, and we went to a carnival with our first-grade class. After scouring all the games, we spent all the money our parents gave us on the ring toss. We thought we had better odds that way, and as we made our way through the change, Nora won a goldfish. She had the biggest smile on her face, and I felt like I was getting dizzy just looking at her. I didn't know what to do with myself.

When we moved on to the balloon darts, and I also won a goldfish, I noticed that hers was upside down. I tried to explain to her that hers was just sleeping, but the whole day, she had this heartbreakingly sad look on her face like she didn't believe me. I mean, who would? Her parents clearly hadn't had *The Talk* with her, and I wasn't about to be the one to ruin that for her.

When we got home, I asked Emma for a favor. The next morning, she ran straight over to my house, her goldfish in a makeshift tank, and she was screaming about how it woke up. When she asked to see mine, I told her he was having a sleepover at my grandparents' house. We both sat down and stared at her goldfish and for the short time the fish lived, she never asked me where mine went.

I shrug innocently. "See, I know a thing or two about giving good gifts."

She almost knocks me out when she wraps her arms around me, melting right into me. "Thank you, thank you, thank you. This is the best present ever." She leans up off me, her whole face radiating with the joy I've missed seeing. She rolls her lips in and then back out before leaving a long kiss on my cheeks with a *smack*. "You're the best."

Connor pushes his sunglasses off his head, winking at me since I managed to distract her enough for the main event. "That's not the only surprise you've got," he whispers.

I sling my arm around her shoulder, leaning into her enough to get the sweet smell of her perfume as I whisper, "Turn around, Stargirl."

We all turn at the same time, looking into the living room through the large window where Mark and Emma walk outside with a banner that says, 'Arrivals Here,' t-shirts that read 'I 🖤 New York,' two tickets in Mark's hand as Taylor Swift's 'Welcome to New York' blasts from Elle's speaker.

I wish I could bottle the sound of Nora's hysterical scream when she understands what's going on. Well, I also don't because it's fucking terrifying. She's out of the seat and into her parent's arms before I can blink, and before I know it, we're all singing along to the song.

"Holy shit, Dad. Is this for real? You're not pranking me,

right?" she asks Mark for the third time, still jumping around in front of him. "Like, this is– This is–"

"Yes, it's for real. So, totally, for real," he responds, winking at us. Connor shakes his head, and I give him a double thumbs up. You'd think they'd be better with the Gen-Z lingo, but he's still getting a hang of it. "Me, you, and the Empire State Building. I told you I'd take you there. I've just been waiting for the right time."

"God, I love you so much!" Nora jumps into her dad's arms as if she's a baby, and Mark doesn't stumble. I'm pretty sure Emma is crying, but it's hard to tell. Nora has been dreaming about this trip since she could speak. Her parents didn't have the money when they were growing up, and she always told me that she didn't want to go when she was a kid because she knew how bad her memory was. Now, she's got the perfect opportunity. New York City won't know what hit it.

A strange pang of *something* washes through me as I watch the family in front of me. I hate the uncomfortable ache in my heart. The hole that feels too big to fill. It's fucking impossible to feel good when you're constantly reminded of something you know you'll never have.

Elle sneaks up beside me. "Feeling like the odd one out, too?"

I shrug. "A little."

"We'll be fine, Wesley. Besides, this is the first time I've seen Nora really smile in months, and I'm taking that as a win," she says, laughing at her friend, and she continues bouncing up and down, chanting about New York. "What do you say? Do you think that's a real Nora smile?"

Before I can respond, as if she could sense us talking about her, she turns around, her cheeks puffy, her hair a mess as she grins at me. She's panting now, walking towards me. I look down to see the new shoes I got her on her feet. When the fuck did she put those on?

"Hey, Wes?" She's grinning ear-to-ear, and my heart feels like it's fucking soaring. Is that a real thing? Because I don't think I can even breathe normally right now.

"Hey, Nora."

"Guess where I'm going?"

I scan around the room with all the New York decorations, deciding if I should play her little game or not. Who am I kidding? It's always going to be a yes when it comes to her.

I can't help but brush the stray strand of her that's fallen in her eye, tucking it behind her ear. My fingertips tingle, and I don't know what to do with my hands.

"Where are you going, Nor?" I whisper.

"I'm going to New York." She tells me as if it's a secret. As if it's the kind of thing that she waits all day to tell you about. Like it's just for me, even when I know it's not. Her entire face is glowing, and I have the strangest — and I mean, *strangest* – urge to kiss her. To say fuck it and take her face between my hands and finally get to taste her. I bet she tastes like strawberry ice cream, smiles, sunshine, and everything *good*. Every good thing in the world belongs to her, and I'm selfish enough to want some of that.

Instead, I shake my head and repeat her words back to her. "You're going to New York."

And when she looks up at me, her face exploding like sunlight, I know for a fact what kind of smile that is. It's a *real* Nora Bailey smile. The kind of smile I crave. And she's smiling like that.

At.

Me.

NINE
NORA
IT'S THE BEST TROPE

I DON'T THINK my heart can take any more of the love that is in it right now. I've spent so long moping and thinking about all the things that could go wrong, and the million and one things I need to do today feels like the first time I've truly *lived* in months. My whole body is tingling with love.

Deciding to have a chill birthday for one of the first times ever was the best decision I've ever made. We always have breakfast in bed together, but after Cat left to spend the day with Connor, Elle and I went around town searching for new books to fill our dorm. I always need to have some sort of massive party where it gets overwhelming and out of control, but spending the day with my girls was just what I needed.

The very last thing I was expecting was my dad to surprise me with tickets to go to New York. Since I knew about the glitz and glamor of the Broadway shows and the city life, I've dreamed of going there. As terrifying as the big city seems, there's nothing I've wanted more than to be surrounded by creatives and people who are willing to fight and work for what they want.

With all the excitement surrounding the trip and the shoes Wes got me, I make sure I get a second to talk to my brother whilst we clean up in the kitchen. Cat and Elle are watching *Modern Family* reruns with my parents in the living room, and Wes is outside, still on the porch. It baffles me that he's acting like he didn't just give me the best present ever as he sits outside alone.

"Hey, I'm sorry if I kinda overtook the birthdayness this year," I say to Connor when I hand him the sharing plate to dry. He always acts like everything is fine, but I know there are times when he feels overlooked. This is not the first time this has happened. I always feel like I take up too much space, and I have no clue how to fix that.

He shakes his head. "It's fine, Nor. I'm just glad you had a good time, and I got to celebrate yesterday. You know I don't care about parties and all that shit. Cat made yesterday really special. I don't need trips to New York or a new pair of shoes to have a good time."

I hum. "Always so humble, aren't you?"

He shrugs. "I'm just lucky." His gaze travels to where Cat is sitting, and just from the sight of the back of her head, he's smiling like a loon. "I'd trade in a million parties or gifts for a million days with her."

My heart aches at his words. There is something so special about watching my brother fall in love and that person being my best friend. Cat has had to deal with a lot in her childhood, and she and Connor just make so much sense together. I could not think of two people more perfect for each other.

"You make me sick, you know that?" I say, flicking water into his face.

"Says the one who wouldn't shut up about how much she was in love with her boyfriend," he argues.

I roll my eyes. "Yeah, and look where that got me."

His face softens. "You'll get there, sis. If anyone is going to have a great comeback after a breakup, it's you."

"Thanks, Con."

"No problem," he says, shrugging. "Just don't do anything

crazy this year, please. I don't want to see you making out with a guy in classrooms or doing God knows what in a janitor's closet."

"I'm not making any promises." I wink at him, and he rolls his eyes.

Once we've finished cleaning up, I feel like I'm walking on air. I just want to soak up this feeling and bottle it for later when I need it. But that isn't possible. So the next best thing is sitting on the porch with Wes whilst he gives me an hour-by-hour run down on how he managed to get my customized shoes. I can't help but smile up at him as he does, my cheeks hurting from smiling and laughing too hard.

When he's done with his rant, I say, "Tell you what I've just realized?" He looks up at me, still fiddling with the placemat on the table. "Every time I think something is going to go wrong, you kind of save the day. You're like a superhero or something." His eyes light up at my words. "Like when Ryan didn't turn up to my birthday last year, and you were there instead. When I found him cheating on me, you were there to, uh, distract me." I clear my throat when my cheeks heat at the way I kissed him that day. I've tried my hardest to block that day out of my memory, but that was the first and probably the last time I'll ever kiss Wes, and it feels like the taste of him is still on my lips. I hate it. "I dunno, you're just always here. I thought this year would go to shit because Ryan and I broke up, but other than the rage I have in me, I'm pretty much okay, and a lot of that is thanks to you, so..." I shrug, not sure what else to say to follow it up with.

Wes just starts laughing. Like a tears-springing-to-his-eyes kind of laugh. I roll my eyes at him, shaking my head. I swear, any time I try to compliment him or say something adjacent to a thank you, he makes it into a big thing.

His laughter finally dies down, and he lets out an exaggerated sigh. "Okay, first of all, I'm glad you've finally got it in your head that I've got your back. Second of all, can I ask you something? And you've got to promise not to get mad at me."

I narrow my eyes. "Permission granted, but I'm not making any promises."

He waves his hand as if he doesn't believe me. "Why is it so important to you to have a boyfriend? I mean, I'm not saying you shouldn't have one. You're hot, you're smart, you're kind, obviously, people are going to want you. I just don't fully understand why you put up with Ryan for so long after the way he treated you."

The fullness in my heart slowly starts to deflate at his words. "I wish I could tell you," I murmur. I bite my bottom lip, trying to really dig deep into where this desperate need to be wanted came from. Maybe I've made it all up in my head. Or maybe it's something infused in my DNA that I'll never be able to get rid of. Both thoughts are as terrifying as each other. "I think... I think I needed the security. The reassurance. And he gave that to me, most of the time. He'd tell me I was pretty, or that I was smart, or that I was going to be something, and he was the only one who did."

Wes shakes his head, a low groan escaping him. "I could have told you all those things, Nora, and you know that."

I trail a line on the glass table. "Yeah, well, there are perks to Ryan that you can't exactly offer."

His eyebrows scrunch. "What? You mean because he can recite plays from start to finish, and I–"

"Sex, Wesley," I say, cutting him off. His eyes widen. "Lots and lots of steamy hot sex. And I don't know about you, but I don't exactly want to have sex with my best friend."

His face turns red as he scratches his neck awkwardly before coughing. Jesus, he is a mess. I don't know why he's acting like he doesn't fuck girls religiously or like this is the first time he's heard about sex.

He stares at me wide-eyed for a few more seconds before he says, "Yeah." Another pause. "I get what you mean, weirdly. I think my parents want me to crave what you want, you know? They want me to be obsessed with relationships and settle down and focus on my career like you are. I guess if I had any of that, they would finally get off my back, and maybe I'll be able to turn this season around." He shrugs, sighing. "I don't know. I'm just saying words."

I laugh. "Yeah, you are."

A few moments pass, and for a second, I think the conversation is over. He lifts his head, his eyes lighting up with something I can only describe as mischief. My palms instantly grow sweaty with this look he's giving me.

"This is perfect," he breathes.

"What is?"

"We can pretend to date. You said you want to get Ryan back, and people would lose their shit if they found out we were dating. I'm a ladies' man, Nor, people are dying for a piece of me." I snort at that, trying to stop myself from laughing. "If Ryan sees you with someone else, he might finally get it in his head that he can't play mind games with you and fuck up your performance. It could help you out of your funk, too."

I digest his words. It *could* get Ryan to lay off me. It could help improve my performance, and maybe I'll be able to pull myself up enough to film some more self-tapes.

I hold my chin up. "What's in it for you?"

"My dad will finally get off my back. Not like I should listen to him anyway, but maybe settling down for a bit will help my game through the playoffs. Some stability. And my mom might actually chill out and not think I'm turning into some manwhore like my dad."

When he puts it like that, it actually seems possible. Fake dating my best friend to get back at my ex? It's the best trope. Ryan has disliked Wes since we started dating back in high school. He always thought he was trying to come between our relationship, which is so far from the truth. And Wes needs some sort of routine and stability in his life. Having his parents off his case could really help his peace of mind and the football team, too.

"It could work," I whisper.

"You're considering it?" He's practically choking on his own words, his knee bouncing under the table. He's like an overexcited puppy.

"I mean, it's not a *terrible* idea. It would really piss off Ryan too. Like, *really* piss him off," I say, sounding and feeling like an evil genius.

He leans down on the table, lowering his voice. "You want revenge?"

I lean into him, too. "More than anything."

"Then you get your revenge, Stargirl." There's a weird sense of power in his voice when he says that, and he leans back, looking down at his arms. "Holy shit. I just gave myself chills."

I look over at this idiot fawning over his goosebumps, and I realize that this will either make or break my career.

TEN
WES
THE ART OF SOFT LAUNCHING

"OKAY, DON'T BE NERVOUS."

It's been a week since Nora and I sat down with Connor, Archer, Cat, and Elle and told them our plan of action. After a lot of shouting questions we did not have the answers to, Nora and I reconvened and tried to think of a better plan.

According to Nora, fake dating isn't easy, but she's got a set of rules, which she will explain to me before our first date today. Honestly, I'm still shocked that she even agreed to this. I'm not really expecting this to work, but from the sad look in my mom's eye when I saw her last weekend and the frustration with the team after we lost the game on Tuesday, I know I have to make this work somehow.

Fake dating Nora should be a piece of cake. She might act like she's hard work, but I watch her like she's my favourite movie. I've *been* watching her for years. I might not have her for real, but I can boyfriend the shit out of her. I've already taken some initiative and posted some pictures of us that we've taken over the years with some slightly cringe captions. She's going to love it.

"I'm not nervous," I say, pushing myself off the stool at the breakfast bar as Connor and Archer coo at me like I'm a baby.

"It's like prepping a kid for their first day of school," Archer says, taking a sip of his black coffee.

I roll my eyes. "If you have a daddy kink, just say that, Elliot."

He just flips me the bird, and Connor rounds the island, standing in front of me as he inspects my outfit. Nora didn't give me any instructions as to what I should wear, so I settled on some casual black jeans and a blue shirt I thrifted a while ago.

"How does it feel, big guy?" Connor asks, clasping my shoulder. "I don't think I've ever seen you go on a date."

"Yeah, when you're not busy fucking your way through the female population at Drayton," Archer adds. I shoot him a look as I shrug off Connor's hand, straightening out my shirt.

"I'll have you both know that I've not slept with another girl in months." I hold my head high.

"That explains why you've been so uptight," Archer grumbles.

"Hey, I am *not* uptight. If anyone is uptight, it's you, Elliot, so shut your pie-hole. I'm the opposite of uptight. I'm… Down-loose," I ramble, the words rushing out of me before I can stop them. Jesus Christ. I'm a mess. This might be my breaking point.

They both burst into laughter, and Connor shakes his head at me. "Have you taken something?"

"No. Maybe I am a *little* nervous," I admit. Connor's eyes widen as if this is complete news to him. "Come on. Your sister might be my best friend, but she's terrifying. If I fuck this up for her, I can kiss my balls goodbye."

"Damn right, you will," Connor agrees. An unknown look washes over his face as he steps closer to me, all the laughter and smiles from before disappearing. "I swear on everything holy, Wes if you do anything to hurt my sister – and I do mean – *anything* you can say bye to more than just your balls. I love you, man, but I will kill for her. Even if that person happens to be you. Understood?"

I swallow at the force in his voice. "Yes, boss."

An eerie smile spreads across his face as if he didn't just threaten to kill me. He steps back, gesturing to the door. "Now go before Nora kills you for being late."

I scoff, grabbing my jacket from the chair. "Oh, please. She loves me too much," I shout over my shoulder before I run out the door, a little faster than I'd like to admit.

I DON'T EVEN GET to Nora's door before she swings it open, pulls me in, and pushes me against the door. Honestly, this view isn't too bad.

"You absolute idiot! I'm going to kill you!"

Whoa. Way too much anger in such a small person. And what is with everyone throwing the K-word today? Does no one understand how harmful these things are? I'm only human, after all.

She gives me one solid punch to the stomach. I don't flinch. "What have I done now?" I ask, politely removing her hands from me. I try to keep my voice calm to level out her hysterical screaming.

"You've already posted *fifteen* pictures of us online, you fool!"

Ohhh. That whole thing.

I slide into the stool in the kitchen. "Oh, I'm sorry. I want people to see our beautiful faces."

"You're not supposed to do that without asking me!"

"Well, maybe if you had told me some rules, I wouldn't have done it," I argue. God, it is so hard not to laugh right now. She looks so angry while looking downright adorable at the same time.

"Sorry, I've been busy trying to get my job back and not feel like I'm going nowhere with my life," she shouts back. I just blink at her. "Do you *not* know the art of soft launching?"

"Clearly not if you're screaming at me!"

"You're supposed to post subtle photos over a few months, or *weeks* at least," she explains, her voice slightly calming down.

"Right… So what I've done is a hard launch?"

Her eyes flicker. "Exactly."

"There is nothing wrong with things being hard, sunshine. If you get what I–" She punches me in the shoulder. "Right, okay. I'm sorry. I didn't mean to. I should have asked, but if you want me to remove them, I will. Are we cool?"

She takes a deep breath. "We're cool. I didn't mean to freak out on you. I'm just–"

"I get it," I say, gesturing at her to sit beside me on the stool. "Just tell me what you need me to do."

She nods. "First order of business are rules," she explains, pulling out her phone.

I groan.

"You should consider yourself lucky. I managed to boil down a thirteen-point list to three," she says. "One, I'm okay with anything up to second base in public or to post online if you are." I nod because that's the only thing I can do. Going to second base with Nora is a fucking dream come true, no matter how fake. "No telling anyone this is fake. The only people that are allowed to know are the people we live with, which means not telling your little buddies on the team."

I bump my shoulder into hers. "And you can't tell Kiara."

She swallows. "I won't. And three, under no circumstances do we try to make this more real than it is. This is a show. An act. A game. We're just friends, Wesley, and we're always going to be *just* that. Understood?"

Just friends.

I have never hated two words put together as much as those.

"Yes, ma'am," I agree reluctantly, saluting her. She rolls her eyes, and my heart does a weird flip thing. "God, I love it when you go all-teacher mode on me."

"Did you not listen to anything I just said?" Her eyes narrow, those beautiful brown eyes shining.

"Sunshine, I have been hitting on you since I knew how to. Don't try to act like that's new," I say. Flirting with Nora has been my favorite pastime for years. She might not reciprocate it, but it doesn't mean I can't have fun with her. She just blinks at me. "So, what are we telling people? Are we just fucking, or is it serious?"

She turns from me, slipping out of the chair to collect her tote bag and jacket from the couch. The summer dress she's wearing distracts me for a second. Jesus, those fucking *legs*. That fucking pink color against her slightly tanned skin. Her chestnut hair has that natural waviness in it as she pinned half of it up in a ribbon, the other half flowing loose. She's so fucking pretty. Like, insanely.

"It's serious," she answers finally.

"Right," I say, "But, like, *how* serious?"

"Serious enough," she answers.

"Okay," I say, nodding. "Oh, and back to the sex thing. How good are we saying it is on a scale of one to ten? Are you walking around with your legs wobbling, or what?"

"It's fine," she says, her back still to me as she packs and unpacks her bag.

"Whoa, Sunshine. Sex with me is not just *fine*. And I think you're forgetting what I've seen you look during a walk of shame. I doubt Ryan hardly ever pulled his weight, so you're clearly not too bad in the sack," I mutter. Even with all my teasing, I don't get so much as a sigh out of her. I slip out of the chair, making my way towards her. "Okay, what's wrong? You've let me talk for too long, and I'm starting to get sick of my own voice."

She scoffs. "That's literally impossible."

I reach her and slip my hand around her waist, swiftly turning her around and pulling her into me. Her eyes widen as she takes me in, her hands landing on my chest. My name leaves her lips in the softest pleading tone I have ever heard, and I'm *this* close to already scraping all the rules and kissing the shit out of her.

"What's going on?" I ask gently.

Her slightly panicked eyes meet mine. "Nothing," she whispers. I tilt my head to the side, and her shoulders relax. "I just… I need you to take this seriously, okay? As much as I want to get back at Ryan, this could also help my image at school, and if you keep playing these games and messing with me, it's going to ruin it before it even starts."

"We've got this figured out," I say confidently. "My parents are going to back off on me, and I might be able to help the team. You're going to give Ryan a taste of his own medicine, and you're going to crush the show." She nods, swallowing. I lean down, pressing my forehead against hers. "We're a power couple."

She laughs. "What?"

"Me and you, Nora? A power. Fucking. Couple."

She shakes her head, still laughing. "I hate that I think you're kinda right. Or, well, more like I *need* you to be right so I don't lose my mind."

"Yeah, yeah, I know," I mock, stepping away from her. "Just hold my hand and tell me how much you love me so we can get on with this already."

ELEVEN
NORA

HAMILTON WOULD BE ABSOLUTELY APPALLED

I SPEND the entire bus ride praying that this goes well while also listening to Daisy and Ryan giggling behind us. My nervous tick of twisting around the necklace on my neck doesn't do anything to soothe the weird sense of anxiety I have running through me.

There is nothing more irritating than the grating sound of both of their voices together. I wonder if they know that everyone can hear them talking to each other in baby voices and how good Ryan is going to give it to her tonight. It's revolting.

Like every year, we have a field trip to a museum to learn more about the history of the time period when our musical is set. This year, we're learning all about 18th-century America, and the non-fictional impact Hamilton's role has on our lives today. Usually, these trips would be the perfect time for Kiara and I to hang out and make fun of old garments that we spot, but I'm more on edge than ever, hoping that Wes pulls through with his side of the plan.

I'm pretty proud of myself for not spilling the truth about my and Wes's fake dating plan to Kie on the bus. She was rattling on about how we should think about going on a double date already since she saw the awful pictures that Wes posted of us on Instagram, but I kept my cool. Keeping my mouth shut is not one of my best qualities, and it's especially hard not to tell one of my best friends everything.

When we get off the bus and into the warmth of the museum, I stick with Kiara as we gawk over the random facts that we learn. She's got her arm hooked in mine as we walk around, and I can *still* hear Ryan talking as if he knows better than everyone else. He's pretending to be a tour guide, rattling facts that no one asked for. He's not the sharpest tool in the shed, and we all know that.

"Oh my god," Kiara gasps, pointing at an old sheet of paper that's enclosed in a glass box. "I didn't know Jefferson was an Aries. Everything makes so much more sense now."

"What!" I look over at what she's looking at, and she's right. Huh. "I wonder what the founding fathers would be like if they were into astrology."

Kie snickers as she tugs on my arm towards a wall of paintings. "God, I'm sure it would just be an excuse for their sassiness."

We stop in front of a painting of Alexander Hamilton, and I cross my arms against my chest. I'm convinced the only way I would ever care about the history and drama with these men is through the art of music. Otherwise, they're pretty boring old men.

"I'm sure Hammy here would somehow use his status as a Capricorn to justify his affair with Maria Reynolds," I murmur, tilting my head to the side. Kiara hums before slowly walking down the line of pictures. I stay where I am, scrutinizing the painting in front of me. He looks so fucking smug in this portrait, and so much of him reminds me of the person who is playing him in our take on the musical. It's ironic, really.

As I'm about to end the intense staring contest between me and the painting, I feel one warm hand wrap around my waist, slowly making its way to my stomach. The same hands that had pulled me into him in my dorm earlier.

"Hi, Stargirl," he whispers into my neck. *Chills.* I get fucking chills everywhere. "Fancy seeing you here."

I turn around, using the best of my acting training as I pretend to be completely smitten with my best friend. I sling my arm around Wes's neck, and he's blushing. "Hey, babe." He pulls his arm out from behind him, showcasing a bouquet of pink lilies. "Flowers? Nice touch."

He shrugs lazily. "I know a thing or two about chivalry."

"Right," I mock, slowly bringing our bodies closer. He wraps both of his hands around my waist, pressing the flowers against my back. "I'm going to look dreamily into your eyes, and you're going to tell me if Ryan and Daisy are watching. Cool?"

He leans down slightly, dropping his voice to a whisper. "Oh, they're watching alright. He had his beady little eyes on me the second I turned up in this joint." I smirk, knowing that's exactly what we both need. Still, he looks… Nervous. Like he doesn't know what he's doing. He *feels* like he knows what he's doing because his hands feel so warm and just… safe. Or that might just be him. "What is your class doing here anyway?"

He's trying to make small talk even though he knows exactly what we're doing since we both orchestrated the whole coincidental meet-up thing. "Research," I say, biting my lip as I try not to laugh.

"Oh." He swallows, and his gaze bounces around, trying not to look at me. "I haven't been on a field trip since high school. It's not fair that you–"

I curl my hands in the hair at the bottom of his neck. Twisting the soft curls around my finger, I tug his head towards mine. "Hey, Wes?"

"Yeah?"

"Shut up."

He nods once. Twice. Three times. "Right. Boyfriend shit."

"Exactly," I say, failing to my laughter. "Boyfriend shit."

His brows furrow. "And what exactly does that entail?"

I shrug. "I dunno. We just need to look affectionate."

He nods again at least ten times in a row. This nervous side of him is making me uneasy. "Right, right, right. Affection, affection, affection. I can be affectionate."

I tilt my head to the side. "Are you sure? Because right now, all I'm getting is panic, panic, panic."

Something switches when I tease him, and some of the anxieties relax on his face. Something else takes over his expression, and I can only describe it as pure hunger. The flowers drop to the ground behind me as he slowly pushes us towards a blank wall. There's a silent question in his eyes, and I'm nodding without even confirming what he means. We've both always been impulsive, and if whatever he's thinking is going to sell our fake relationship, I'm ready to jump in blind.

My entire body comes alive when Wes presses the softest lingering kiss on my jaw, creating a trail of tiny fires until he reaches my neck. I'm practically squirming under his touch, desperately grasping onto his neck as he shows me just how affectionate he can be. The searing spot feels like it's burning holes through my skin as he keeps pressing these soft, dramatic kisses that just make me *swoon*.

He tucks a strand of hair behind my ear, my pulse beating rapidly when he kisses the star tattoo. "How's this for affection?"

"Mm," is all I manage to get out. I swallow whatever is in my throat that is stopping me from speaking. "It's pretty good."

"Pretty good?" he taunts, trailing one finger down the arm that's wrapped around his neck. "These goosebumps are telling me otherwise, Nora."

"It's cold in here," I mutter, a slight edge to my voice. I hate that his warmth is so damn comforting and that he's still kissing my neck, and I want to curl into a ball at his feet. "And you're so– Why the hell are you so warm?"

He shrugs innocently. "I dunno. Maybe because I've been sitting in the parking lot for the last hour." I hum in response. He shifts his head so we're at eye level now. My mouth dries. "Do you want me to keep going?"

"Yes."

As I expect, he moves his attention to the other side of my neck, leaving achingly soft kisses there. I'm just standing there, my hands still curled in his hair as he works his magic. No wonder girls are always at his feet when he kisses like this, and it's not even on my mouth.

I start to come back to earth, and when my vision clears, I spot Ryan and Daisy walking towards us, hand in hand. Just the sight of them makes the hairs stand up at the back of my neck. I clear my throat, tugging on Wes's hair. "They're coming over here," I mutter.

He peels himself off me, clasping his hands together as if he's about to give a speech. He takes a deep breath, picking up the flowers that we almost crushed and shoving them into my hands. "Okay, are you ready for the big sell?"

He pulls me into him by the waist, and I jolt. "The big se—"

He cuts me off with a dramatic sigh, slinging his arm around my shoulder. "You know, Nora, I *still* can't believe that loser actually let you go."

"What the hell are you doing?" I ask, wide-eyed. This was not part of the plan. He just mouths, 'Trust me,' and continues pulling me along with him until we're almost in front of Daisy and Ryan.

Of course, Wes continues talking.

"You're the prettiest girl I've ever laid my eyes on. You're funny, you're smart, and that thing that you do with your tongue? Goddamn extraordinary," he says, possibly loud enough for the entire museum to hear. Jesus, he's bad at this.

"Okay, reign it in, loverboy," I mutter, jabbing him in the stomach. He just winks at me like this is the best thing to happen to him, which, in turn, means it's mortifying for me.

Ryan stops in front of us, sizing us up and down. "Hey," he says to me, giving me a douchey head nod. He turns to Wes, narrowing his eyes. "I didn't know you were allowed on these trips, fella. I thought the football team was only allowed out of their cages on weekends."

Wes gives Ryan the brightest grin I've ever seen, as if his words don't affect him. Hell, maybe they don't. Maybe I'm the one who is secretly too soft to let everything get to my head.

"Yeah, well, funny thing about places like these; they're open to the public, *fella*," Wes says, his voice extra sweet yet dangerous. His arm tightens around my shoulder. "Don't want to miss out on any quality time with my girl."

Ryan's face turns white. I swear his lips turn purple at the way I'm snuggled into Wes's side, his arm possessively wrapping around me like I might slip away from him. Daisy has the same stoic expression on her face like she always does, always pretending like nothing really matters to her.

Ryan stumbles over his words. "So– So this is actually for real? All those pictures he posted weren't just for show? You're actually a couple?"

Maybe Wes's chronic over-posting isn't such a bad thing after all. Wes puffs out his chest. "Yup," he says, smiling down at me and then back at Ryan. "Very, *very* real. Very serious, too. But hey, there's no point in me trying to tell you about serious. Clearly, that's not your thing."

Ryan lets go of Daisy's hand, and she immediately goes to check her cuticles. Honestly, I'm glad she doesn't seem to care. It makes this whole thing a lot easier. And it makes this whole broman-stand-off thing with Wes and Ryan that much hotter. They're both in each other's faces, and fists balled at their sides as if they're waiting for the other to make the first move. Part of me just wants to sit back and enjoy the show, but I don't exactly want to watch my best friend beat the shit out of my ex-boyfriend.

Who am I kidding? Of course, I want to see that.

Just maybe not today.

"You know what–"

I cut Ryan off, sticking my head between the two of them. "Whoa, hold your horses. We can all be nice to each other, can't we? Like Penny said, we need to get along. I think the first rule of that is respecting each other's significant others, right?"

Ryan scoffs. "You don't have a problem with Daisy. You just don't like that she's not you."

This time, *I* scoff. "Actually, it's the complete opposite. I'm glad I'm not dating you. I mean, after your little dating spree when we broke up, who *knows* what you might have." Now Daisy wants to tune in, her eyes widening. Ryan just blinks at me. "Oh, and congrats, Ryan. You were right. Apparently, Wes *did* have a thing for me, but he did the respectful thing and waited until we broke up. You could learn a thing or two from him."

"Damn right," Wes agrees, pressing a kiss to my cheek. It's sloppy, messy, and way over the top, but it does the job. I give Ryan and Daisy the smuggest smirk possible as Wes slips his hand around my waist, dragging it lazily across my stomach as I pretend to not be affected by it. "Let's go."

We get halfway to the lobby between the exhibitions before I'm almost screaming with excitement. Wes's back is to me as he continues walking in front of me. "Did you see his face? I have never seen him like that before. We fucking killed it."

No response.

For someone who usually has a lot to say, he's awfully quiet. He looks like he's trying to readjust his jacket in a really strange way. I jog to catch up with him as he continues walking. I don't think he's even looking where he's going.

"Hey, what's wrong?" I ask, pulling on his arm.

"Nothing," he mutters, "It's pretty hot in here, don't you think? Just trying to get this zip down."

"Oh. Do, uh, do you want help?"

"No!" His hands fly out at his sides dramatically.

"Okay, Jesus. I was just asking." I back up from him, finding a bench in the hallway as he mindlessly moves around the small space. I tilt my head to the side, trying to figure out what the hell he's doing. I'm getting restless watching him mess around, and my patience is thinning. "Will you just let me help you, you fool?"

I stand up, pulling on his arm again. "No! Just– Just keep your hands to yourself."

"Why? You're clearly struggling. Just turn around," I argue, yanking his arm. *Again.* He pulls his arm back. "Hey, stop fighting me."

"*You* stop fighting me," he grumbles, using one arm to push me back, but I'm stronger than he thinks. I reach around him with both of my hands, tickling him under the jacket he's so desperate to take off. "Nora, stop."

He's squirming now. "Why? You're not ticklish, are you?" I tease, finding out that he is indeed very ticklish. His throaty laugh escapes him, and my own giggles are contagious. I finally make my way in front of him, and as I try to reach for his zipper to put us both out of our misery, I completely mess up the proportions and accidentally brush my hand over his crotch.

We both freeze.

Whoa.

Whoa.

There's a very large warning sign blinking at me saying DO NOT TOUCH, and even though it was an accident, we're both staring at each other like the world is about to end. Wes instantly starts to panic, his face turning red, and before I can tell him to calm down, he's falling back over his own two feet, reaching out for me and pulling me right down with him.

I collapse onto his chest with a thud.

We both blink.

Breathe.

Then burst out laughing.

This guy is the most stupid person I have ever met, and I can't get enough of him. He makes me want to punch him just as much as I want to hug him. There's never a dull moment with him.

I lean up off his chest when our laughter dies down, and I'm suddenly hyper-aware that my bare legs are wrapped around him. "You stubborn idiot," I manage through my laughter, shaking my head.

Wes rolls his eyes. "Oh, shut up." He clearly doesn't know what to do with his hands in this position, so they awkwardly rest on my thighs. I try to move back so I can stand up at the same time he tries to move me forward, and we're caught again in another painfully awkward moment.

Will today just get over with itself and die already?

My eyes widen when I feel what's beneath me. "Oh my God. Are you—"

"Come on, Nora," he bites out, shaking his head. "You're straddling me right now. Of course, I'm hard."

I press my lips together in a line, desperately trying not to laugh. "But you were already *adjusting* before this. Please don't tell me a few neck kisses and waist-holding is what gets you hot under the collar." He doesn't say anything, which confirms that I'm right. I watch the color wash into his cheeks as he keeps staring up at me. I poke him in the cheek. "Wes."

He sighs. "That might have been the first time I've been close to another girl in months. It has nothing to do with you, Nora. It's just a biological thing. Don't read into it."

I am *this* close to laughing in his face again. Boys clearly have no restraint over their horniness. "We were hardly doing anything! You didn't even kiss me."

"Doesn't matter," he says, shrugging. "Lieutenant Benson doesn't know that."

"Lieutenant Be..." My voice trails off when he nods to the space between us. "Do you have a name for your dick?"

"Yes," he says seriously. "Every guy does. Now, get off me before you start feeling something you don't want to."

From the awkward repositioning, I'm now further down his

thighs than before. I pat him on the chest. "Oh, come on. You're not that big."

He tilts his head to the side. "Want to find out?"

He's looking at me like he really wants me to, and I couldn't think of anything worse. Wes always flirts with me. That much isn't new. But what I don't like is the way it feels so easy to flirt back. I'm telling myself it's because I'm single, and I actually have the option, and it doesn't feel wrong.

I open my mouth, ready to say something, but Penny and Kiara's voices fill the echoey room, laughing about something. They both stop in their tracks when they see us, and Kie's eyes bulge out of her head cartoon-style.

Penny shakes her head, clearly trying to contain her laughter. "Hamilton would be absolutely appalled."

"I don't think so," Kiara says, winking at me, "I'm sure he would heavily encourage this."

When I look down at Wes, his face red and hot all over, I wonder how well this will play out. This all feels like one big game of dress up like we're little kids again. I'm just waiting for the moment that our parents will tell us it's time to stop.

TWELVE
NORA/WES
HOME IS WHERE THE HEART IS

NORA

MAYBE I SHOULD HAVE EXPLAINED the *Wes-Situation* to Kiara before we started rehearsals because now she won't stop asking me questions. Understandably, she's very confused that I'm suddenly dating my best friend after I swore off dating for the foreseeable future.

I would tell her the truth, but I made a promise to Wes, and he would lose his shit if he found out that she knew. I trust her with my life, but I know how much she talks, and if she was left alone with Ryan, I'm not confident that she wouldn't be persuaded into telling him the truth.

Instead, I'm letting her pester me with questions as we get ready for a run-through of the first act of *Hamilton*. Really, she should be trying to save her voice since she's playing Peggy and Maria Reynolds, but apparently, that is the last thing on her mind.

"Girl, I know I said to move on, but *Wes Mackenzie?*" I can tell she's trying her hardest to be quiet as we sit on the edge of the stage, our feet dangling as we share a packet of strawberries, but Kie is the opposite of quiet. She shakes her head at me. "I mean, good for you. I'm sure he's great, but isn't that going to mess up everything between you two? You're, like, best friends."

I shrug. "Nope. It's fine. Apparently, he's had a crush on me for years, and it's the most stress-free option. Besides, Ryan *hates* him, so that's a bonus."

She gives me a slow side-eye. "Right. So, this is a whole revenge thing?"

"Well, sorta, but also not really. I actually like Wes. I wouldn't be dating him if I didn't," I admit. At least part of it is true. He *is* one of my favorite people. I shove a strawberry into my mouth, hoping my acting skills are pulling through. Although it pains me, I put on my big girl boots and add, "He's hot too."

She laughs, "I know. I've seen the way girls swarm around him on campus. He's lucky that he's funny, so he isn't half bad."

"He's really the whole package," I say before I shove more strawberries into my mouth.

I push myself up, getting ready to stand before Kie pulls my arm back down, pointing towards the entrance. "Speaking of the devil," she mutters.

I follow her line of vision to see three football players strolling into the small auditorium. Wes, Sam, and Oliver walk through the doors like it's a fucking movie, and they're the jocks who are desperate to hook up with anyone with a pulse.

Sam and Oliver are a given whenever Wes is around. I don't know what kind of power they think he holds, but they treat him like he's a God when Connor isn't around. Wes is usually Connor's second in command, but since he's decided to 'retire' from being the dad of the football team and have fun and spend time with his girlfriend, it seems like Wes is trying to fulfill that role.

Do you want to know the worst part?

He looks good doing it.

He somehow has this kind of quiet but harsh authority that can render people speechless. It should be comical that someone as chaotic as him can round people up to do his bidding, but he manages to pull it off. He ditched his football jersey and is instead sporting a Rockies shirt and black pants and has covered up his hair with a backward cap, his hair curling around his ears. I'd think he looks attractive if I didn't know any better.

But then he sees me, and his whole face splits into a grin, and I have to contain myself. Penny doesn't mind anyone coming to watch our rehearsals as long as they're quiet, but I have no clue what Wes is up to. It's only the main cast today, so we can start blocking the choreography we learned last week, and I can't wait to see the look on Ryan's face when he sees him in the crowd.

The three boys take a seat a few rows behind where Penny is sitting. Wes crosses his arms against his chest, and I know he can feel my eyes on him because when he's done looking around the space like he actually cares about all of it, he winks at me.

He fucking winks at me.

And a piece of me dies inside.

I can also feel Kie's eyes on me, so I shake my head, needing to say something before she does. "I told him I had rehearsals today, and it's like he just wants to be around me all the time. He's like an untrained puppy."

"You're telling me that like I don't already know. I've seen the way he's looked at you since I met you. Honestly, Ryan had a right to be jealous when you were together," she says, pulling me up finally to stand.

I clear my throat, a weird feeling settling in my stomach. When you're so caught up in a friendship with someone, you don't know how it looks to everyone else. Whenever I thought Wes and I were just messing around, there was a side to it that I didn't realize, and everyone tried to make it into more than it was. I didn't mind the jokes, and now it makes our arrangement much more believable.

"You know nothing has ever happened between me and Wes, right?" I say to her, quiet enough so only she can hear. "Well, not until now, at least. I would never cheat."

"I know you wouldn't," Kiara replies immediately. She looks

over her shoulder, where Wes is still looking at the two of us, and his eyes narrowed slightly as if he knows what we're talking about. "That doesn't mean Wes wouldn't have tried to convince you."

I shake my head. "You're insane."

"Whatever," she grumbles, bumping her arm into me. "So, are double dates back on the table?"

"That depends. Do you think you can find someone to put up with you?" I tease, pinching her arm.

"Very funny," she mocks. She takes another look over her shoulder, *very* obviously checking Sam out. "Is that Wes's friend?" I nod. "He's hot. Is he single?"

"From what I've gathered, yes, but he's also a player."

Kiara winks at me. "Don't worry. I can reform him."

"You can try your best."

We both burst into giggles before we turn our back to them and get on with our rehearsing.

I spent the whole time hyper-aware that Wes was watching me and listening to me sing. The script has been altered, and there's less singing and more dialogue, but it still makes me uneasy. I'm not supposed to get nervous around him, or anyone for that matter, especially when I'm on a stage. People say home is where the heart is, and this stage is my home. Having Wes here shouldn't change that fact.

We've spent the last half an hour tripping over each other's feet and getting our lines messed up. Every now and then, Wes lets out a loud cheer when we run through a song with the backing track, and the encouragement is weirdly endearing. It's nice having someone in my corner here, and I'm glad that it's him.

He's been to a lot of my shows, but him being here and I'm out of costume just doing my thing feels strangely intimate. I don't fucking know. What I do know is that Ryan is absolutely furious that he's here. He keeps biting out his lines as if I've done something personal to offend him. Hell, maybe I have.

I try my hardest to keep my cool throughout most of the rehearsals, but by the time I've sung *'Helpless'* three times and have to pretend I'm completely infatuated with Ryan, I can't wait to get out of there.

WES

I have wisely spent the last three hours watching Ryan squirm under Oli, Sam, and I's gaze, and I couldn't be happier. Deciding to ambush Nora's rehearsal was the best decision I've made because not only have I been able to listen to her sing like a fucking angel, I get to be the one to PDA all over her when rehearsals are over.

Best three hours of my life.

After their job was done, Oli and Sam got out of there and went to the field to start warming up for our game later as I waited outside the door for Nora to finish up. Honestly, I'm putting off spending time with my dad, and the more I can drag this out, the better.

She walks out with a dopey smile on her face, like she couldn't decide if she was happy to see me here or not. Even during the breaks their teacher gave them, she went off with Kiara in a corner and didn't even look my way.

"Hey," she says, walking up to me in baggy jeans and cami top. Her brown hair is down, slightly curly from the humidity as it flows past her shoulders. She has no right to look that good after practicing for three hours. And I have no right to be this attracted to her, and no part of that feels fake at all. "What a nice surprise this is."

"Yeah, how sweet of you to watch your girl practice," Kiara adds, rolling her eyes at me. Sometimes, it feels like we have unknown tension between us like I've stolen her best friend from her. I'm already sharing Nora with Cat, Elle, and her brother. I don't need another person in the mix. I'd have her all to myself if I could.

I give her a tight smile. "Be nice," Nora mumbles, bumping her in the shoulder. She bumps her back. "Didn't you want to ask for *someone's* number?"

Kiara's eyes widen as if she's been caught out on something. "Nope," she says, basically screaming. She gives Nora a kiss on the cheek before brushing past the two of us. "Bye! See you, uh, soon!"

Nora shakes her head, laughing. "Ignore her," she mutters, stepping closer to me. She hooks her thumbs into the pockets of her jeans as she rocks back on her heels. Why is she making this so fucking awkward? It's adorable as fuck, but unnecessary. She knows that she can be herself around me, and watching her perform is no different. "So...." She whistles, looking at everything but me. "What did you think of the performance? I mean, we're still a bit rusty, *obviously*. And Ryan is still acting like a—"

"Didn't pay much attention to him when you were on stage," I say simply, shrugging.

She bites her bottom lip. "Oh."

I narrow my eyes. "What? Why do you always have to do this?"

"Do what?"

"Act all shy like I've never seen you perform before. I've watched you on a stage since we were kids, and you're only getting better, so quit acting like you don't love it up there," I say, and I hook my finger in the belt loop of her jeans, tugging her closer to me as people start to walk out of the auditorium slowly.

"Ah, right." She's still not looking at me, and I don't understand why. Seeing her in her natural habitat is my favorite thing. It always has been.

"Nora," I press. "Look at me."

She closes her eyes before they land on me. "Better?"

"Much,. Now stop acting all nervous around me because you're making me antsy, and someone's going to notice. You're meant to be insanely in love with me, remember?"

She rolls her eyes. "Right. How could I forget?"

I'm about to tease her before the douchebag of the century walks through the doors, his head held high as if he wasn't shitting himself a few minutes ago. Every time that fool was talking on stage, I tried my best to burn holes through him with my eyes, and he tried his best not to notice.

Before he looks at me, he gives a very obvious perusal of the back of Nora's outfit. Even *I* don't have to stare at her from behind to know how good she looks, but the dick cheated on her, *and* he has a girlfriend, so he shouldn't be looking. He's lucky his eyes are still in his sockets.

He's still walking, his eyes on her when I pull her closer until our fronts touch. She blinks up at me, her eyes widening. "Wes," she breathes my name like it's a warning not to do something stupid.

That sound on her lips is my undoing. Ryan finally notices me, and his eyes connect with mine, a smug smirk on his lips. I lean down, my breathing suddenly erratic against Nora's ear. My words make the next move before my brain does. "Are you ready to kiss me, Stargirl?"

"Why?" Her voice doesn't sound like her own. It's distant and breathy, infused with the sound of my heartbeat. I just want to bottle the sound. Her small hands find their way onto my waist, gripping me over my jersey like she can't stand upright.

I enjoy torturing the both of us, so I press a kiss to her neck in the same spot I did at the museum. "Because he's looking at you like he wants you," I say into her skin. Her whole body is so hot beneath me. So sensitive, as if she's never been touched like this before. "I can do him one better. Tell you why?" All I get is a low hum of approval. "Because he looks at you like you're in a lineup and doesn't know who to pick. But when I walk into a room, and you're there, you're the only thing I can see. It's only *you*."

Nora swallows, and I lean off her. I catch Ryan's eye above us, and I pull Nora's face closer to mine, tilting her head up as my hands rest possessively on her delicate face. Golden brown eyes stare into mine, and she wets her bottom lip. "He– He can't hear us, can he?"

I shrug. "Dunno."

"Then why are you–"

I cut her off by pressing my lips firmly against hers.

I must be dead. This is heaven. This is what I was made for. This is everything and more.

Although it's freezing, kissing her feels like being in the heart of summer.

Her lips are soft and smooth against my rough ones. She tastes like the strawberries I saw her eating, and it takes over me. I'm surprised I didn't collapse onto the floor. The only thing keeping me upright is the hand curled into her hair as I swipe my thumb against her cheek.

Her entire body melts into mine, and I just want to hold her here forever. Everything about her just feels so fucking soft, and I can't get enough of it. When I kiss Nora, I don't remember what it feels like to be with anybody else. I can't even remember the last time I kissed someone, and Nora makes me feel like that doesn't even matter. It's like she's hit the reset button in my brain, and she's the only one I'll feel forever.

Her.

Her.

Her.

The kiss isn't as powerful as it could be, but the small tremor on her bottom lip when we pull apart tells me more than I need to know. *Whoa.* My heart stutters a little when I take her in. Her cheeks are bright pink, and her eyes are glossed over.

Ryan passes us slowly, and his eyes narrow at the both of us. There's a flash of anger in his eyes, and I fucking love it. "Hi," he grumbles to the both of us.

I force myself to look at Ryan when all I want to do is stare at her. To memorize this look on her face. "Hey, fella."

The two words are enough for him to roll his eyes and shoulder-barge me as he walks past. Good enough for me.

"Hey, are you good?" I ask Nora, shaking her shoulder slightly. She's not said a word since the kiss, and I'm afraid I might have broken her.

She finally meets my eyes again. She blinks. Then blinks again.

Then she runs past me.

Jesus Christ, this girl. If she doesn't stop freaking out and getting nervous around me, this whole fake-dating shit isn't going to work.

I hold my hands up in defeat as her fast little legs carry her away from me. "You do know I'm going to see you at the game later, right?" I shout, cupping my hands around my mouth.

She throws her hand in the air, giving me a thumbs up, still scurrying away. "I know. I-I'll see you there."

I've known her for twenty years, but I'll never understand some things about her. Like how she runs away after each time we kiss. I'm completely convinced Nora Bailey is the strangest person I've ever met.

But she's *my* strange person.

THIRTEEN
NORA/WES
OLD FASHIONED ASS-WHOOPING

NORA

RUNNING AWAY from my problems isn't new. In fact, I think I've been doing it since I was a kid. I remember getting my first report card, and my initial instinct wasn't to go home and pin it on the fridge. No, it was to run into the backyard and try to bury it. Connor caught me, and because he's a narc, he told Mom and Dad, and they never trusted me to bring my report cards home again. I thought I grew out of it, but apparently not.

Running away from Wes-related problems is… new.

After the first time I kissed him, I did the same thing. I ran straight back to my dorm, only for him to follow me and drop the bombshell that Connor was dating my best friend.

The kisses on the neck? Hot, but it's fine. I can deal with those. Hugs and a little bit of close contact? Also, fine. But full-on making out in a hallway? Nope. Can't do it.

He kisses me like a man starved. He doesn't kiss me like Ryan did, always with one foot out of the door. He gave me everything. It felt alive, electric, *timeless*. It's like he breathed life into me just for it to rush back out when we pulled apart, reminding me that this isn't real.

Truth is, I've only kissed three people in my life. Two of those being people I ended up in long-ish-term relationships with and the other being Wes. So, if my track record is anything to go by, kissing someone and being intimate is not exactly something I can do casually, even if it's fake. My feelings are bound to get mixed up in the attraction, and I'll form a semi-obsession with Wes if we keep going down this road. My brain is annoying enough to do that to me.

Every couple in Drayton Hills is constantly all over each other, making out in hallways and dry-humping in classrooms. No one would believe us if we didn't throw in a few kisses and ass grabs.

I've got to learn somehow how to turn that part of my brain off. Not every interaction has to turn into a blockbuster or a Hallmark movie. Maybe I'm just wired that way, and I'm always going to crave that sort of commitment. It's much better than dealing with the fear of being alone. My mind is a terrifying place to be stuck in, and I'd rather be distracted with sweet words and orgasms.

What scares me most about Wes is that if he spends more time with me than we already do and peels back layers of me that he's never seen, he might not want me anymore. In *any* way. He might think I'm completely insane, and he'll leave. I don't think I can handle him leaving, and the only way I might be able to control my feelings is if I don't linger around him after we make out.

The only logical thing to do was run. Now, it feels like a stupid decision because I'm in the bleachers of a very loud and chaotic football game, watching Wes move around the field like a machine.

Coming to watch football games has been one of my favorite things about starting college. The atmosphere is otherworldly. People are constantly screaming and chanting, booing the opposing team, and yelling at the top of their lungs insults to the referees. Only me and Cat are watching today as Elle had a late dance practice, and we are trying our hardest to enjoy ourselves.

There's only one problem.

The Titans are playing *terribly*.

I have never seen them play so poorly. My brother is shouting louder than I've heard him in years, and everyone is getting sick of them getting their ass beat. We usually try our hardest in the crowds to encourage them, but there's something deeper that a few chants can't help with. We're on home turf; the entire stadium is filled with support, and yet they can't seem to get it together.

Cat said something about them having a few players leave and switch to other colleges, so their spots have been filled, but not to the same standard. She said Connor hasn't been able to stop talking about it and how badly the team is merging together. This isn't something new that happens in sports teams. Players get traded all the time, but for the Titans, they're getting run into the ground with the team from Greenwich. This is the same team they usually beat every season or during friendly games they do during the summer. They're not going easy on the Titans, and I actually feel bad for them.

"This is painfully hard to watch," I mutter, shoving my face into my hands as I check the clock on the huge screen. There's only ten minutes left until the game is over, and I've had enough of screaming at them. Clearly, all I'm going to get out of this is an even raspier voice and a headache.

"Tell me about it," Cat murmurs. I bite the inside of my cheek as I take in her furious expression. It's funny seeing her turn into a football fan in the last few months. Before having to work with the team for the newspaper she was writing, she never cared much for it. I'd always suggest for her to come along to games with me, but she'd say no. Now, she's almost at my level of crazy. "I still don't know what's going on, and I'm *pissed*. How is this even legal?"

"It's not as bad as it looks," I say as sweetly as I can. I look at the scoreboard, and it's 17-30 to the other team. I grimace.

It doesn't even have to *look* bad because, from our seats, we can hear Coach Mackenzie scolding the players beneath us. Connor has said he's been on everyone's ass this season, and I don't blame him. A lot of the boys take this seriously, but due to the influx of new players who are mostly freshmen, the playing field for those who want to do well and those who don't care is very uneven.

Apparently, the only one who actually cares is Hayes Cohen. His dad is Michael Cohen, Drayton Alumni and current assistant coach for the Colorado Buffaloes. Despite the scandal he was involved in two years ago, he's a God to many of the football players, and now that his son is on the team, everyone expected an easy victory, but we're already getting our asses handed to us.

Listening to Coach Mackenzie talk to Wes in the way he is now makes my heart ache for him. I understand that his dad can't go easy on him, so he's playing fair, but he only reserves a bite in his tone for Wes. I've not been able to look at him the same since I found out what he did. Nolan and May Mackenzie have been like a second set of parents to me since I was born, but I've never felt more disconnected from them than I do now.

And there's only one person to blame for that.

WES

My head is thumping. My ears are ringing. My pulse is hammering against my neck and on my wrist. It feels like my chest is caving in on itself, and at any given moment, I'm going to stop breathing.

Since the second I got on that field, my dad has been using me like his punching bag. For one of the first times, I actually wanted to play well. I know how bad we've been in training sessions, and I want us to win this season, no matter how out of reach it feels right now. But as soon as my dad started to get pissy with my defense tactics – the ones he's instilled in me since I could walk – I was ready to throw it out of the window. He made me sub over five times just within the first half and only let me back on the field for five minutes of the second half.

I'm agitated and pissed, and the last thing I want to do is to be stuck in here with the team as everyone complains about how poorly we played. Coach hasn't been into the locker room yet, and I'm about to get showered and out of here as fast as humanly possible.

Connor sits beside me on the bench when the team rushes in after I've showered and gotten ready. He's finishing up the pep talk that he loves to give after a game. We need one of his famous speeches now more than ever. Although most of what he says is negative, I know we have to take it with a grain of salt. Connor's the best leader our team could have, and I hope to God he isn't doing that pathetic thing where he thinks that everything is his fault.

Knowing I won't be able to let it go, I knock my knee against his. "You did good out there."

He sighs, tilting his head back. "Could've done better."

I shrug. "Nah, you were fine. It's the rest of the team. They're not taking it seriously."

Connor hums. "Yeah, you're right," he says. He shakes his head before adding, "About them not taking it seriously, I mean. I wasn't fine. I was less than my best, and it shouldn't piss me off as much as it does, but it's true."

Connor worked hard on letting go of the team and being able to let us do our best without the pressure of the world on his back. He's constantly trying to make sure we're always incredible, but that's impossible. We're going to have days like today, games like today, and sometimes there's nothing we can do about it other than train harder and listen to whatever Connor or my dad has to say.

I take in a deep breath, changing the subject. "Do you want to grab some food after this?"

"Can't," he says simply, which is code for *I'm going to work out my frustration by fucking my girlfriend into oblivion where the whole house can hear.*

I'm honestly sick of those two. If I'm not getting any action, why should they? I'm also sick of Cat trying to sneak out in the morning like I didn't know she was there. I think they're still caught up in the fact that they had to hide their relationship. She's over at our place nearly every night, and I have no idea when Connor is going to pop the question and ask her to move in.

"Ah, it's cool. I'll see if anyone else is free," I say awkwardly. I sound desperate. This guy is my best friend. Of course, I'd rather him hang out with me than his girlfriend.

He pushes himself up, grabbing his duffel bag from the space next to him, but he turns back around and frowns at me. He rolls his eyes before pointing a finger in my face like I've done something wrong. "You've reminded me."

"Of what?" I ask.

"My parents invited your parents to ours for Thanksgiving if you want to come. I know things are hard, but I don't think they know yet, and I haven't told them," he explains. "Now that you and Nora are… together, they want you around more. So, if you want to swing by with just your mom, feel free. Just let me know if you want me to make up an excuse for why Coach can't go."

Thanksgiving with the Baileys is magical. Their life is like a fairy tale come true, and holidays are no different. Their lodge in Aspen is filled with the childlike adventure that I've always loved. It's tucked between huge forests, winding roads, and mountains, and it feels like somewhere you can escape. I could really use some of that right now, but I can't.

It's always the time of year when all of our families can get together without any stress. Christmas usually makes everyone freak out, and we'd rather spend it with our biological families, but Thanksgiving is always special. It *was* always special. Now it's just going to be another day trying to talk my mom out of her mind and encourage her to leave the house while my dad does fuck knows what across town. I know my mom wouldn't want to be around people and couples in love, so I plan to spend the day with her instead.

"What reminded you of that?" is what I ask. "The fact that you're blowing me off to hang out with your girl?"

His eyes narrow. "No, Wes, it was the sad look on your face. You look like a puppy who hasn't been adopted at the pound."

I don't know why his words sting, but they do. I don't want his pity. I don't want to look like a lost puppy. I want to be Wes Mackenzie, the funny friend with the jokes, smiles, and an endless line of girls. I don't want to be the one who is always on edge and stressed over things that never seemed to matter before, like my career and my future and all that bullshit.

I settle for a joke instead of my actual thoughts. "Oh, shut up. Girls love it when a guy is miserable," I say, chuckling weakly.

Connor shakes his head. "Yeah, usually when they are the ones making a guy miserable." Then he looks at me and reminds me of the answer to all of my problems. "Besides, Wesley, you've got a girlfriend now, remember?"

The second the words leave his mouth, the rest of the team swarm around me like I'm a piece of live bait. Connor blows me a kiss as he walks out, knowing the guys are going to torture me on every detail about my and Nora's relationship.

Luckily for them, I could talk about her for hours.

FOURTEEN
WES/NORA
AN EXISTENTIAL THANKSGIVING

WES

MOM'S NEW APARTMENT SUCKS, and I mean that in the nicest way possible.

I thought she'd move into a huge house with all the money she had saved and turn it into a library or some shit. I thought it would give me an out to live with her instead of Connor and Archer. As much as I love those guys, they're a pain in the ass, and the thought of living with my mom doesn't sound half bad.

Instead, her apartment is pretty much a bigger version of the office she used to have at home. *Home.* I hate calling it that. Without her there and just all my dad's shit and my childhood bedroom, it feels like the furthest thing from a home.

Here, there's wide floor-to-ceiling windows, dark wood panels, fancy transparent chairs, and a sleek kitchen that always looks clean. It's almost *too* clean like she never does anything in there. There's a huge bookshelf filled with all of the classics and an abundance of signed copies of her own books. There are only black and white stock photos in the large frames that hang on the walls in the living room area.

The only good thing about this place is the fact that my mom is here, safe, somewhere she can call a *real* home. Better at least than the place where she used to be.

As I walk up the steps to her apartment, I try my best to push away all the resentment I have towards my dad and try to focus on making my mom feel better. This is her first holiday without him, even though she never really celebrated Thanksgiving until she met my dad. I just want today to go well for her. For her to have some sort of normalcy in the midst of the current chaos.

I hold up the carrier in my hand as Jarvis coos quietly. "Are you ready to surprise your mom, bud?" Obviously, he doesn't respond, but from the soft way he nuzzles his face into his hand, I'd say he's up for the job. I didn't wrestle this fucker into wearing a bowtie for no reason. I'm making a show out of my outfit so he might as well, too.

Before I can even knock on the door, it swings open and my mom practically launches herself at me, smelling so distinctly as vanilla as her slender arms wrap around me. "Oh, Wes. I saw you get out of the cab from the window, and I couldn't help myself."

"It's good to see you too, Mom," I muffle against her blonde hair. She pulls away from me, pouting as she leans down to take the carrier out of my hand. I take a second to look at her. She looks better than one of the first times I came over. She's not wearing loungewear today and is instead sporting a plain black dress and pairing it with her fluffy slippers. I don't think she's wearing any makeup, but I could never tell the difference anyway. The main thing is she's smiling.

"And you brought my favorite boy," she coos, turning around to let Jarvis out so he can roam around the apartment. He doesn't, though. He just sniffs along the carpet before he plants himself next to the television, curling up into a little ball.

I shut the door behind me as I follow them in. "I thought *I* was your favorite boy?" I ask playfully, toeing off my shoes beside the door.

She throws me a frown over her shoulder. "You're *both* my favorite boys. How about that?"

I laugh in response as she flops herself down onto the couch, reaching down to pick up Jarvis. He couldn't care less where he's seated as long as he's not walking around, so he doesn't fuss when my mom plants him into her lap so she can stroke him.

I take a quick look around the apartment, and just as I expected, everything is spotless. I sit down at the other end of the couch, trying not to sound judgemental as I ask, "Are you not cooking today?"

She turns to me, her blue eyes shining. "Nope. I don't think there's much point, is there, Wes?" She says the words as if they're just... *right*. As if there is no questioning that this is how things will go from now on. As if this isn't the first family holiday where her family isn't together. She scratches Jarvis's head before straightening out his bowtie. "We can just order takeout and look pretty."

I don't know why the way she seems so okay with this bugs me. If she's fine, then I don't need to worry. But I can't help but think that this is all a front she's putting on so she doesn't break down in front of me. I'm never fully going to understand her position as much as I try, and maybe the sooner I come to terms with that, the better.

"Yeah, I guess so," is what I find myself saying when my mind stops spinning.

She gives me a weak smile. "Hey, no sad energy in this place, okay?" She lifts her arms up as if she's raising the invisible roof. "This is a party house. A fun-zone."

I can't stop the snort that leaves me. "Okay, mom."

Silence settles over us for a few seconds before her favorite French drama captures her attention. I try to focus on it, but I don't understand much. She tried to help me learn French as a kid, as well as German, but I was too stubborn to take it seriously. I gave up on French, but I had no choice but to learn German. Sometimes, she'd go a whole day not speaking English just so I was forced to understand her. I'd have the odd meltdown, but eventually, being bilingual has come in handy. It just means new ways to curse, if I'm honest.

After the show's finale wraps up, she switches it to a classic romcom, and I can't help but flinch. Is a romantic movie really the best thing she should be doing right now? I mean, she's settling a divorce with her husband, who *cheated* on her. If I were her, I wouldn't want to listen to a dumb movie that talks about how love is infinite and life-changing. I'd just want to smash some shit.

"How are things with you? You seem quiet, *Schatz*," my mom says, turning to me.

I shrug. "I'm okay. Everything's... okay."

Her eyes narrow. She settles against the arm of the couch, turning to face me fully. "Come on, Wes, talk to me. I'm dying over here in silence. You and I don't keep secrets from each other. Remember?"

I hate how right she is. I'm a huge softie. Everyone knows that. And that soft side is all because of my mom and how she raised me and allowed my personality to flourish. Despite my talkative and eccentric behavior, my mom has always made sure it's important that we communicate no matter what. I've told her nearly everything growing up, and I don't see how that's going to change now.

"I know, I'm just..." I take a deep breath, running my hand through my hair. "The team is doing awful this season, Mom, and I don't know if we're going to make it through."

"Oh," is all she says. Her nose wrinkles. "Do they know about–"

"No," I say, cutting her off. "Nobody on the team knows about what happened with... *her*. Only Connor knows, and it's going to stay that way, I promise."

Mom nods. "So, what's going on?" I try my best to explain to her how the team isn't gelling, and there's not much we can really do about it other than doing more team-building drills. I tell her about the last two games and how we just managed to pull through at the end of our most recent one. "Is your dad giving you a hard time?"

I sigh at the hesitation in her voice. Neither one of us has brought up what happened directly, and I don't want to unless she does. "Sort of, but I think it's also my fault. I just don't think my heart is fully in it, and I can't figure out why. I just… I don't know if I'm that serious about football anymore."

My own words shock me. They've been floating around in my head for months, but I've been too afraid to say it aloud. I've always loved playing and competing. It's been one of the constants in my life since I was a kid, but doing it professionally, doing it as a job, I don't know if I want that.

I don't want to be tied down to a contract or, worse, not make it to the NFL at all. If I'm going to strive for something, I want to be sure. And recently, football hasn't felt like that thing. I want to travel. I want to see new places and meet new people, not sticking to diets and ridiculous workout schedules. I just want to have *fun*. And playing football until I eventually break doesn't exactly sound like my idea of fun.

"What do you mean? You've always loved football. Ever since you were a boy," my mom whispers, her tone gentle, like she's afraid I'll break.

"I know, and I appreciate everything you and Dad have sacrificed to get me where I am, but I just…" I trail off again because, for once in my life, I don't know what to say. I'm confused, irritated, and downright stressed. I hate feeling like there's a rock lodged in my chest, but that has been happening more times than not recently. "I don't know, Mom. I don't feel like I used to. Maybe I need to discover more options and see what else I might be good at."

I shrug, feeling pathetic at my answer, but my mom just nods. A frightened expression takes over her face as her eyes widen. "This isn't about your dad giving you a hard time, is it? I don't want what's going on between us to drive you away from your passion, Wes. That's the very last thing I want for you."

"It's not him," I say, not really meaning it. He's obviously a factor in this somehow. "I just need to think about it. I'm probably stressing over nothing." My mom bites the inside of her cheek, clearly thinking about what to say, but I say something before she does. "No sad vibes, remember? Let's think of something to eat."

When mom looks at me like she's regretting everything that's happened in the last few months, I have the urge to tell her that it's not her fault. To tell her that no one is going to be able to fix the weird numbness I'm feeling in my chest. It's a problem I'm just going to have to deal with and figure out eventually.

After we submit an order for a pizza and chicken wings, I try to lighten the mood with some good news. "You know when you told me I should think about dating more seriously," I say as casually as I can, leaning over to pet Jarvis. Mom's eyes light up. "Well, I did. I've been seeing someone, and we're dating. Officially."

"Oh, Wes, seriously?" She exclaims like an excited teenager.

"Yup," I say, puffing out my chest. "You're going to love her. In fact, I think you already do." Her eyebrows quirk, and I let out a short laugh. "Nora Bailey," I add simply.

Her eyes soften, and she lets out the dreamiest sigh as if I've told her the best news in the world. "You finally asked her out?"

Finally.

That word hangs in the air like a firework about to explode. I've always had a thing for Nora. I think anyone with eyes can see that. I've waited around like a fool for years, waiting for her to see me the same way I see her, but I've come to terms with the fact that I'll only be her friend. I've spent nights with her in bars or at parties, trying my hardest to keep my hands to myself. I've spent weeks turning over ideas in my head, thinking of how I'd finally be able to ask her to be mine. This whole fake dating thing could work out perfectly for her, and we'll go back to the way it was. Her with a new guy and me being the idiot that has to watch.

"Yeah, I did," I answer.

"She's so sweet, Wes," Mom says, fawning over her like she's not a she-devil. I snort at that, shaking my head. She knows how much we terrorized each other as kids. She's a lot of things, but she isn't as sweet as my mom makes out. "I'm happy for you. Just don't rush into anything if you're not ready. I don't want you to have done it just because I suggested it."

I swallow.

There's nothing I wouldn't do to make my mom happy. To ease some of the tension and the pain she's feeling. If I can lessen that by making her think I'm fine and that my life isn't spinning out of control, I'm going to do it. There is nothing more important than the smile on her face, even if I have to lie to get it.

NORA

> How do you feel about Hamilton?

WESSY
The musical or the founding father of our great nation?

> Both...?

WESSY
I have no particular feelings towards Hamilton.

> Really? I swore I heard you listening to My Obedient Servant last month...

WESSY
I was deep in an LMM rabbit hole. Sue me.

> Wow, you're even using the abbreviations. I hate to break it to you, but you're a true fan, Wesley.

> **WESSY**
> What do you want from me, woman?

> There's a showing of the musical at the drive in a few towns over. We can go if you want? Would be great for photos, and maybe my own personal gain...

> **WESSY**
> If you want to make out with me again, just say it. Or, I dunno, run away again? That seems to be your thing.

> Shut up.

> It's next weekend. Pick me up at 12. We're taking your car because it's bigger.

> **WESSY**
> Guess I don't have a choice.
>
> See you there, Sunshine ;)

I've spent the better half of today trying to shield myself from Cat and Connor making out or doing *something* at the dinner table.

Thanksgiving with my parents is always my favorite time of the year. We always try to get together with Elle and Wes's family too, but with everything going on with the Mackenzies, I wasn't expecting them to show up. Elle's relationship with her moms is hard as it is, and I don't think the distance she's putting between them is helping her case. Instead, it's just me, my parents, Connor, Cat, and Cat's grandma JoJo.

I'm fully convinced that JoJo is my spirit animal. She's witty, fierce, strong, and *highly* competitive. After completely sweeping both of my parents in a game of Go, I dared to even look her in the eye. Even now, as she argues with my dad over the rules of chess, she's slightly terrifying but incredibly inspirational. After losing her daughter, she's become a huge constant in Cat's life, therefore making her a constant in our lives too. She might live half an hour away in a care home, but I know how important it is for Cat to be close to her around the holidays.

"What are you smiling at?" Cat asks when we've all finished our dessert, and she slides into the seat on the couch next to me. Connor follows her like the lovesick puppy he is and takes the seat across from me.

I didn't even realize I was still smiling at the texts between Wes and me until she started talking. I click my phone shut, shoving it between my thighs. "Nothin'," I say, shrugging. The country accent does nothing to hide the blush on my cheeks.

"Who were you texting?" Cat presses, poking her finger into my knee.

"Just Wes."

"Ah, the boyfriend," Cat muses.

"*Fake* boyfriend," Connor adds.

"How's that going?" Cat asks, ignoring Connor's comment as she takes a sip of the margarita in front of her.

"Good," I say. Her eyes narrow. "What? Everything's fine. It's just a little…. Strange."

"Strange how? What has he done?" Connor presses, pushing to the edge of his seat as if he's going to go across town to find him.

"Nothing," I shout, holding my hand up to him. "He's not done anything wrong. I'm pretty sure it's just me." I take a deep breath. "I'm just worried how easy this all is. I've only been in serious relationships, but pretending to be in one with my best friend just feels like I'm setting myself up for something that's going to go wrong."

Connor coughs and excuses himself. He doesn't really need to be present for my meltdown. Not like he's ever much help anyway. Cat inches closer to me. "What do you mean?"

"I kinda… ran away after we kissed. The same way I did the first time," I admit.

Cat furrows her eyebrows. "What? Why?"

I take a deep breath and all the words I've been holding spill out of me.

"What if I fall for him?" I blurt out. Her eyes widen. "What if he gets too good at this, and we get too into it, and all the lines start to blur? What if none of it works, and we've just made out a bunch of times and touched each other, and it just fucks up our friendship? What if it's not convincing enough, and it's all for nothing? Or…" I swallow, my throat tightening. "What if he stops liking me after this? If he realizes how genuinely unbearable I am, he won't even want to be friends with me anymore." I take in another gulp of air, unable to stop. "I know this is going to sound crazy, Cat, but… I need Wes in ways that I can't describe sometimes. He's always been there. Through every single rough patch we've hit, he's just *there*, and I don't want this to drive him away."

All the words rush out of me like I've been holding them in, and the vault has finally opened. Since we kissed after my rehearsals, I've not been able to stop thinking about this. My brain won't stop telling me the worst possible outcomes of this. I don't know when I became such a pessimist, but after everything that has happened in the last few months, it feels like second nature. I don't want to have rushed into this to make *another* mistake. To push another person away. My overthinking has never done me any good, and it sure as shit isn't going to now.

"First of all, everything you said is valid," Cat whispers. I take a deep breath. "But some of it is also bullshit, Nora."

"What?" I choke out.

"That boy loves you more than anyone, and he has done since we were kids. I don't think a few make-out sessions and some cute pictures together are going to ruin what you two have," she explains. "You've just got to prioritize your friendship. Just think of it as an extension of that. You're an actress. You can pretend to be in love with people, right?"

"With people I don't know personally, yes. This is different. I know Wes better than anyone. I know how he is, how he thinks. I don't know people like that when I'm acting with them. Everything with him just feels so... safe."

Her eyes soften. "Isn't that a good thing? Aren't you sick of fighting or of questioning your worth? If Wes doesn't make you feel like that, maybe this is a good thing for you, Nor."

"I've only been with one person. What if I don't know what I like or what I don't like? What if I–"

Cat cuts me off by placing both of her hands on the sides of my face, shaking my head. "Nora, babe. I love you, but you're driving me crazy," she mutters angrily. "Ryan must have really fucked you up if you keep thinking that you're not capable of doing something like this. Just because you love easily and fall quickly doesn't mean you can't control your emotions. Hell, maybe you don't have to at all. Just trust your instincts and yourself. You're trying to play two steps ahead, and it's stressing you out. Just focus on the now, okay?" I just nod, my eyes stinging. "You've got this. It's going to work out."

She presses a kiss to my cheek before she pulls back. I take in a deep breath. Maybe she has a point. Maybe I'm just spiraling for no real reason. Maybe this *is* good for me. Maybe a model of a healthy relationship can help me move on in the future. Focusing on now might be the only thing I can do.

"You're right," I say finally.

Cat grins. "I know I am."

I laugh, resting my head on the back of the couch. "Sorry to go all existentialist on you."

She reaches out and squeezes my hand. "You're my favorite person to have an existentialist crisis with, Nora."

When she says that, I instantly start to feel a little less crazy.

FIFTEEN
WES
PEOPLE WATCHING

THE MORE TIME I spent fake dating Nora Bailey, the more I realize how little I knew about boyfriend etiquette.

I like to think of myself as a decent guy. I might have slept around in the past, but I've never intentionally tried to lead anyone on or hurt anyone's feelings. I'm always clear with what I want and I'm usually the one that's in control. I tell my hookups that I'm not looking for anything serious, but I still treat them with respect, and I have never had any complaints.

Being a boyfriend is not something I have expertise in. Not like that matters anyway since Nora knows exactly what she wants and when she wants it. I'm just the puppet she's playing with, and I hate that I love being bossed around so much. Nora has pretty much controlled every aspect of our relationship since we were kids, so I wasn't expecting it to stop now.

SUNSHINE
Wear your jersey today.

Good morning to you, too, Sunshine.

> **Any particular reason, or do you just want me to sit and look pretty?**

SUNSHINE
It adds to your appeal. Got to let everyone know I'm dating a hot football player.

Photo ops, remember?

> **Right.**
>
> **Don't think I'm skipping over the fact that you called me hot, btw.**

SUNSHINE
Wouldn't dream of it.

> **I'll change then pick you up. Cool?**

SUNSHINE
Perfect.

See you then, boyfriend.

THE WORD 'BOYFRIEND' shouldn't make my heart stutter especially when it's coming from Nora. And *especially* when I know she's only saying it as a joke. But it does something strange to my insides like they need to be rearranged or some shit.

I ignore the weird tingles I get, change into my Titan's jersey with my last name and number twelve on the back, and get my ass into my car. Per Nora's instructions, taking my truck instead of her Nissan Leaf was better, so I shove all the snacks and blankets into the back before I drive over to campus.

I'm sitting on the hood of my car, waiting for her to walk through the back entrance to meet me, when the swarming thoughts enter my mind again.

I've hardly spoken to my dad over the Thanksgiving break,

and despite our game which we managed to win on Tuesday, he's not said a word to me. Would he even care if I dropped out of football? He's never pressured me into playing, but I've never shown any interest in anything else, which is a whole other crisis of its own. If I don't play, what's next for me? As much as my literature degree is interesting, I'm not about to become a best-selling author or have the same knack for writing like Cat and my mom do. Football might be the only thing I'm good at.

The dark thoughts swirl around my head before Nora walks through the door, and suddenly, things seem to be a little brighter. The road ahead seems a little bit clearer when Nora is beside me. Her eyes widen and I have no idea why she's surprised to see me. I'm wearing the jersey she told me to wear, but I'm just as shocked as she is as I notice she's wearing my jersey, too.

Fuck.

She's wearing skin-tight black leggings and an oversized Titan's jersey, my name and number written on the back. It's not just any jersey she picked up on the school site. It's the one I let her borrow one time after a concert we went to. She had thrown up on her dress, and the only thing I had clean was my jersey in the back of my car. It practically swallows her whole, falling down to her knees, and the sleeves puff out. Her hair is slicked back into a bun, giving her this whole *clean* look. She just looks *good,* almost like she was made to wear my clothes.

My Nora. *My* Sunshine. In *my* clothes. I could get used to this.

"You should take a picture. It'll last longer," she quips, beaming as she speeds up her walk towards me.

"Already got too many pictures of you in my phone," I say, opening the passenger side door for her. Her mouth curves up at the gesture. I don't usually go around holding doors open for people, but just being with her makes me want to do all this shit.

"Well, then, what's one more?" She winks at me before she slides into her seat.

This woman might actually kill me.

I shut the car door, rounding it until I get back behind the wheel. When I turn to her, she's got this dopey look on her face like she always has happy dreams. Like she's thinking about something that brings her complete and utter joy.

"You're in a good mood," I say when we pull out of the parking lot.

She hums happily. "Maybe I'm just excited to watch my favorite musical."

I scoff because she's seen it a million times. "Or maybe it's something else," I offer.

She turns to me, squaring her eyes, and I realize she's put a bit of makeup on. There's a slight green shimmer around her eyes that matches the jersey. Nora hardly ever wears makeup, but when she does, she looks fucking stunning. She doesn't need it, obviously. She already has the whole effortless look-down pat. Knowing how she is and how her brain races, I can't help but imagine her in the mirror, a tiny brush or something in her hand as she traces the outline of her eyes, her tongue poking out the corner of her mouth as she concentrates. I've caught her doing that so many times – when she's driving, crocheting, or trying to read something far away. It's fucking adorable.

Her sigh is soft and light, and she says, "Maybe I'm just excited for *you* to watch it all the way through. Every time I try to watch it with you, you fall asleep."

"Not on purpose. You just choose the wrong time, like right after a game or when we've been out all day," I argue. It takes a lot for me to sit through more than an hour and a half of television. If it's something that I need to pay attention to, I often do the opposite.

"Yeah, whatever," she says sarcastically.

I take one hand off the wheel and grip her hand reassuringly. I don't want her to think I don't care about the things she enjoys because I do. I can't help my overactive brain and my attention span. "Hey, I'm going to love it. I'm sure. If I fall asleep, you can hit me."

She grins at that. "Deal." She squeezes my hand back, but as I pull away, she gasps, pulling out her phone from between her thighs. I grip back onto the steering wheel, steadying myself on the clear road. "Gimme your hand."

I glance at her as she opens her camera app and then back at the road. "What?"

"You can drive with one hand. Gimme your other one," she demands, holding out her palm to me. I think better than to question her, and I give her my hand. I don't even want to look at the size difference of our hands because it'll make me spiral. I think I've had enough Nora-related spirals in the last twenty years of my life to endure any more.

She guides my hand to where she wants it to be, which happens to be the inside of her thigh. My hand instantly flexes before I force myself to relax. Her thigh is so warm, and from where she placed my hand, it feels too fucking close to parts of her I have no business being close to.

"What are you doing?" I breathe out.

"Just relax," she says, not even a waver in her voice whilst I sound like I've just run up thirteen flights of stairs. "It'll be a cute photo."

"Right," I say. Obviously, it's for a picture. That's what this whole thing has been about. It's fake. She wouldn't just invite my hand to touch her for no reason. I keep my eyes on the road, not daring to look at her. "And what exactly am I supposed to do now?"

She snorts. "Nothing. Just let me get a few pictures. I'm trying to get one with both of our shirts in it. Real coupley."

I glance at her then, noting the faint redness on her cheeks. Then I make the dumb as fuck decision to look at the position my hand is in. My veins are pronounced, my whole hand practically covering all of her thigh. The material of her leggings doesn't feel thick enough the more I look and the more I touch. It feels like I can touch her skin. And it makes me realize how fucking badly I want to.

"All done," she says, clearing her throat. "Nice work, boyfriend."

All I get out is a hum in response as I continue driving.

How have I been missing out on this for years? Having a girlfriend fucking rocks. She can wear my jersey, and I can touch her thigh for stability as I drive along the road. I might have a raging hard-on, but who cares? Everything about this – about *us* – just feels good. And I haven't had that feeling in a long time.

When my thumb absently rubs against her, she whispers, "Wes?"

"Yeah, Sunshine?"

"You can– You can move your hand now," she murmurs.

"Do you want me to?" I ask gruffly. I can only imagine how comfortable this is for her if it feels like heaven for me. I feel like she's closer to me like this, and I love that.

"I mean, I've taken all the pictures, so…." She trails off, but she doesn't go to move my hand. If she wanted my hand gone, she would have moved it by now. That's just the kind of person she is.

"That's not what I asked," I taunt. I don't know what the fuck I'm inviting. Friends can rest their hand on the other's thigh whilst they drive, right? There's nothing completely wrong with that.

As I turn to her, ready to ask her again, her eyes widen, and she grips onto the steering wheel. We swerve on the road, and my heart thrashes against my chest. The sound of a blaring horn takes over my hearing for a second, and I almost lose control. I immediately put my hand across her chest, pushing her back as I regain control of the car again.

I sigh when my brain catches up. It wasn't anything major. I was slowly swerving between the lines, and it could have gotten ugly if I hadn't indicated or completely changed lanes.

"Are you okay?" I ask Nora, my voice filled with concern. I keep my eyes on the road for everyone's sake.

"Yeah, I'm fine," she huffs out, a slight bit of panic lacing her tone. "Are *you* okay?"

"I'm good," I say, blinking a few times.

She takes a deep breath. "Just keep both eyes on the road and both hands on the wheel, okay?"

I nod, and I spend the rest of the drive wondering what would have happened if we hadn't been interrupted.

***

Pulling up to the field where the Drive-In is being held makes me think that the five-hour drive wasn't so bad. There's nothing interesting in our small town just outside Fort Collins, anyway. Nora had told me that it was so far away I wouldn't have wanted to come, but of course, she only let me know once we were on the interstate. We spent most of that time listening to different music. Whilst her music taste is upbeat and poppy, mine is a bit more mellow with some slow rock songs thrown in there. She was lucky enough to get some sleep for an hour since she had 'tired herself out from thinking.' Whatever that means. She had fallen asleep right after she said that, and I desperately wanted to know what she had meant.

We set up our blankets and snacks into the cargo bed as a short film plays on the screen in front of us. We've got a pretty decent view, and the fairy lights that are weaved around the spotlights above us make this whole place look dreamlike. When we get comfortable enough, Nora snaps some more pictures of us before going to find the closest porta potty. I salute her for good luck before she disappears. When she's gone, my attention snags onto the couple in the car next to us.

I hate to be nosey, but they're not exactly talking quietly, and this short film that is playing is not interesting. Their truck is similar to mine in style, but a different style and color. It's silver, and it has a sticker on the side that reads *Folkwhores*. What the fuck does that mean?

"Miles, we did not drive all the way here for us to have sex in your car," the girl whisper-shouts at her very unbothered boyfriend. She's got blonde hair and bundled up in a scarf and a jacket.

The guy – Miles – pulls her into him regardless of her chiding and kisses her on the forehead. "We can be a bit reckless sometimes, baby. You've just got to trust me."

She scoffs. "I do trust you. That's the scary part."

They continue to chatter quietly, and I do my best to tune them out. I don't want to be caught being the weirdo who listens to couple's conversations because he's bored.

I don't know if they can tell I'm listening, but I try my best to look innocent when the guy stands up and gets a little closer to my car. I do the normal thing and whistle and look away to not give myself away.

"Hey," the guy says, and I have no choice but to look at him. I nod in response. He looks around my age – curly brown hair and a tall enough frame, but he's got a face that looks like a model. I look over to his car, and it's now empty. "Would you mind taking a picture of my shirt for me? My girl's refusing to do it. She thinks it's stupid."

"Yeah, sure," I say, and he hands me his phone. He turns around, and I immediately start laughing. There's a picture of the dude who created *Hamilton* in a very odd position with the words '*I am not throwing away my shot*' written above it. It looks like a DIY project gone wrong. "Who wouldn't want to take a picture of this?"

After I've taken a few pictures, he turns around, looking through them with a cheesy grin on his face. "My girlfriend, apparently," he murmurs. "Thanks for that, man. Are you a fan?"

I shrug. "No, but my girlfriend is."

Just as I say that, Nora appears back from the bathroom, and she slips into the car beside me, smiling at the stranger. I look at her like I haven't seen her in years, and my heart does that weird *soaring* thing again. Jesus, I'm pathetic.

"Opposite way around for me," Miles says to me as he walks back to sit in his car. We're close enough together that he doesn't have to shout. "Wren, my girlfriend, is absolutely embarrassed of me. She couldn't even handle watching *you* take the photo so she got up to do a lap. Real pain in the ass sometimes, but I love the hell out of her."

I laugh at that. "Same with this one."

Nora swats me in the arm. "Hey, I am *not* a pain in the ass."

"See what I mean," I mock and Miles bursts out laughing. Playing pretend with her isn't just easy, it's *fun*. We make basic small talk with Miles and he tells us he's a hockey player at North University and how his girlfriend is a figure skater. We tell him a little about us too, which Nora takes the lead on.

As we're wrapping up our anecdotes, his girlfriend turns up again. Her back is to us as she walks straight up to Miles, not noticing that we are talking. When she climbs into the truck, I get a better look at her face. She's stunning. All blonde hair and bright eyes. Who the fuck made these people? They should be in a TV Show or something.

"Ohmigod," she's basically wailing, pulling on Miles's arm. "You should have seen the concessions stand. They *only* had Oreo's. I was going to send a video to Evan to see if he has a meltdown, but I'm pretty sure he still doesn't know that we–"

"Baby," Miles says, cutting her off, and his mouth clamps shut. He hikes a thumb over his shoulder, and her eyes widen, a blush spreading across her cheeks.

"Oh, shit, sorry," she says, giving us a wave. Nora snorts. Wren nudges Miles in the ribs, wiggling her eyebrows. "I didn't know you made some friends, Milesy. Found someone to take a picture of your shirt?"

"As a matter of fact, I did," he says to her before gesturing to us. "This is Wes and Nora. They go to Drayton Hills."

Wren's eyes spark with something, and I can't tell if it's just the fairy lights now that the film is about to begin or if it's something else. She glances at me for a second before her gaze lands on Nora. "Oh, isn't that where E–"

Miles cuts her off, rubbing her back as he gets completely engrossed into the opening credits of the movie. "Shhh. It's starting."

Nora and I decide to leave them alone after that and I actually manage to sit through the first half of the musical. I knew it was good from the way Nora talked about it, but I found myself on the literal edge of my seat. If all my history classes in high school were like this musical, I'd learn a lot faster.

During the interval, Nora snuggles closer to me under the blanket, our legs touching. She doesn't look at me like she notices. Or like she even cares. She nuzzles her cheek into my chest and snaps a few more pictures of us. I can't help but smile in every single one of them because having her here, happy, watching something that makes her happy, somehow makes *me* just as happy.

When she's taken the photos, she looks over into the couple's truck beside us. "They're literally like us," she whispers, looking at them with a soft smile. They're taking similar pictures to ours, too, but there's a lot more kissing and groping involved. We both turn away, deciding to give them a bit of privacy.

"Yeah, well, that seems a lot more real than what we're doing," I mutter, turning to her. Her eyes light up, humor dancing within them.

"Are you saying you want to palm my boobs, Wes?" she asks innocently, pretending to be shocked. Nora Bailey saying my name and 'boobs' in the same sentence has to be some sort of dream. I just blink at her, my throat drying at the thought alone. I cannot go down this road again. I can't start fantasizing about all the things I would do to her or all the places I want my hands on her body. When no words come, she says, "I'm kidding.

Besides, who knows, they could just be really good at faking it too."

I take another glance over at them. Wren is now on her back, and Miles is on top of her. "I'm pretty sure his tongue is lodged down her throat." I grimace, turning away. "Nothing fake about that, Sunshine. That's two people fully in love."

Her eyes dart away, and she looks back up at the screen. "Yeah, I guess you're right," she says quietly, and we don't say much for the rest of the night.

***

The second half of the movie wasn't half bad. I retained enough information to answer some of the questions Nora asks me as we drive back, and I even listen to the soundtrack with her, singing along. Apart from the very loud makeout session between Wren and Miles, it was, all in all, a good day. I know my phone is going to blow up with texts once Nora and I post the pictures online, so I try my best to hold onto the parts of the day that are kept just between us.

When the sunset has faded, and we're still driving, I work up the courage to say, "Okay, I have a confession to make."

I don't have to turn to see how quickly Nora's face whips towards mine. "Okay…"

I leave a long pause for dramatic effect, drumming my fingers against the steering wheel and staring out into the line of cars ahead of us.

"I love Hamilton."

Nora lets out a noise between a sigh and a laugh. "Fucking hell, Wes," she breathes, "You gave me a heart attack. I thought you were about to confess your crimes to me or some shit. Of course, you loved it. Who wouldn't?"

I resist the urge to roll my eyes as I think about what we just watched. "Don't you feel any pressure playing Eliza? Those are some big boots to fill from what I've seen."

She sighs. "I'm not trying to beat or compete with Phillipa

Soo. That's *literally* impossible. I'm just going to put my own spin on it. You'll see."

I look over at her, and she's got this smug look on her face like she has a million secrets and things she can't wait to show me. "I can't wait, Sunshine," I say, and her smile doubles. She turns to look outside the window to hide how big she's smiling, and I love that about her.

I'd watch Nora Bailey do just about anything. If she wanted me to watch her watch a three-hour-long movie, I'd do it. If she wants me to sit around in a waiting room just for the thought of seeing her, I'd do it. I'm quickly beginning to realize that I'd do anything she asked me. Even the things she's afraid to ask me out loud.

SIXTEEN
NORA/WES
THE FERRIS WHEEL

NORA

> DADDY-O
> Call me when you've finished classes, honey.

That one text is enough to put me on edge for the entire day. Mark Bailey is the softest, most fun-loving, go-lucky person I have ever met. He doesn't have one sad or mean bone in his body. It's like he was built on sunshine and happiness, and it makes me wonder if he was always built to be a dad. *My* dad.

Not a day goes by when I don't think about how lucky I am. How insanely grateful I am to have two parents who push me to do better without being overbearing. Who loves me unconditionally and knows how to talk me out of my mind. They've single-handedly taught me how to be brave and not to be afraid to take risks. Because of their happy nature, a text like that from my dad sends me into a spiral. I thought about calling him earlier, but if I don't start to pay more attention in classes, I can kiss my degree goodbye.

The second I finish my last lecture of the day, I walk in the opposite direction of Kie and hit the call button. My dad answers immediately. "Dad? Is everything okay?"

"I can't go to New York with you."

I stop still in the middle of the hallway.

I get concerned looks from others who are passing me, but I can't bring myself to care. My heart roars in my ears; it feels like I've been cemented to this spot. I want to move, but I just *can't*. His words ring in my brain, and I can't control the emotion lodged in my throat. Out of everything he could say, this was the last thing I expected. The trip isn't booked until the New Year, and it's the perfect time to go before my schedule gets more hectic with exams and the lead-up to the opening night of the show.

"What?" I choke out, still standing in the middle of the hallway.

My dad's soft, hushed voice vibrates through the phone. "I'm so sorry, sweetie. I wanted to tell you as soon as I heard, and I didn't want to do the whole lead-up, so I just told you straight away. I know you're shocked. I'm sorry to do this, Nor."

I swallow. Hard. "What do you mean you can't go?" I know I sound like a child on the verge of tears, but I can't help it. This trip has only been a dream because of him. Because of the stories he told and the movies we watched together. I'd want nothing to do with New York if it wasn't for him.

"Something came up at the school, and it's important that I'm there to–"

I cut him off. I've officially hit rock bottom. I'm sobbing on the phone in the hallway. "But, Dad, you *promised*. You've been saying this for years. When I go, you go, remember? I can't go to New York for the first time without you."

A sob lurches from me, my voice breaking, and I finally manage to move my feet. I'm getting too many stares, and I'm starting to get uncomfortable. I push through the main doors of the building, hit by the December chill as I stand at the side of the building.

"I'm not going if it's not with you," I sob, my chest aching just at the thought.

"I'm sorry, Nora," my dad says quietly, "If I could change it, you *know* I would. This is the perfect time for you to go. You're only going to get busier after this month, and then you've got camp, and you'll be working during the summer, and then it's your final year. I don't want to postpone this for you, and then you won't end up going until you've finished college entirely." I don't even have the energy to argue with him. My whole body feels numb, and my chest can't stop shaking. I'm surprised I'm still standing upright when his next words hit me. "Go with Wes."

"What?"

"Bring Wes. You're dating now, aren't you?" My dad's question shouldn't catch me off guard. Fake dating Wes has been the only thing keeping me sane these last few weeks, and it's slowly paying off. For me, more so than him. I just sniffle. "You would never be able to decide between picking Elle or Cat, so take Wes. I know you two would have fun together."

I sigh, leaning my head against the wall behind me. "This was supposed to be *our* trip, Dad. Just me and you."

"I know, I know," he says. "But New York isn't going anywhere, okay? When we're both able to, we'll go again. We'll go for longer, too. I promise."

I resist the urge to give him shit on his promises, but I think better of it and mumble out an 'Okay' before I end the call. The feeling I get after the call ends *sucks*. It's like someone has taken a sledgehammer to my chest and wrecked me in two.

I shouldn't be so torn up about this. The New York trip is still going ahead. No matter who I go with, I'm still going to be in the city of my dreams, and that's all that really matters. I try my hardest to collect myself as I go to text Wes, but I get a text from Ryan instead. He sent me a picture that Wes and I took at the drive-in with a message attached.

THEDEVIL

I was there too. How come I didn't see you?

> Maybe I was too busy with my tongue down my boyfriend's throat.

THEDEVIL

I bet you were.

What is so good about him, Nora? Even when we were together, I could tell something was going on. You deserve better than that.

> HAHAHAHAHAHA.

> Are YOU seriously trying to tell ME I deserve better after I was stuck with you for five years??? Next joke.

THEDEVIL

I'm being serious.

> Sure you are, bud.

> Do you want to know what's so good about him?

THEDEVIL

Yes.

> For starters, he isn't you.

I CLOSE Ryan's text thread, and I want to delete his number. I also don't want to because of the strange feeling I get in my stomach knowing that I've pissed him off. Being able to get under his skin is exactly what I need to blow off some steam. I take a deep breath, swiping onto Wes's contact.

> Thoughts on New York?

> **WESSY**
>
> Is this the same as the Hamilton situation?

> ....

> **WESSY**
>
> Never been, but it seems like your scene if your birthday is anything to go by.

> Do you want to go with me? My dad can't go anymore, and I can't pick between Elle and Cat since I only have two tickets. You're the last resort.

> **WESSY**
>
> Wow. Way to make a guy feel special.

> Do you want to go or not?

> **WESSY**
>
> I'll go anywhere with you, Stargirl. You know that.

WES

I've never really cared for Christmas.

Well, I used to love it. I used to love my parents waking me up with a smile on their faces, a hot chocolate in their hands, and a present for me to open in bed. We'd spend the whole morning under the tree in our pajamas, and my parents never failed to make me feel special. Being an only child both sucked and was the greatest thing on days like those. I had their attention on me at all times, and there was never a moment where I felt alone.

Until now.

Now, Christmas time feels like it's just going to be a

whole period where everyone is happy and with their families and in love, and I can barely look my dad in the eye. We've managed to get through some more games without any major setbacks, and if all goes well, we might even make it to the semis. Connor, Oli, Sam, and I have had a talk with the freshmen, and hopefully, they'll start to pull their weight. I haven't told anyone about how I'm feeling about football in general, and it might stay that way. The last thing I want is for them to either pressure me into staying on or pity me for not having a clue what I want to do with my life.

I have to suck it up since I'm in the middle of the Christmas markets in Fort Collins with my best friends and my fake girlfriend. Fake dating duties are supposedly off the table for today since we've had this group hang-out session planned for a while. Nora's still standing next to me, her arm hooked in mine as we slowly make our way around.

"Penny for your thoughts?" she asks, peering up at me. Her hair is a mess of waves today, covered by a beanie, and she's wrapped up tight in a scarf and puffer jacket. Her adorable nose is red with cold and her cheeks are pink.

"Got nothin' going on up here, Sunshine," I say, but she frowns at me.

"Come on, Wessy. You've been quiet all day, and you even let Connor make fun of you for losing the ring toss. That's not like you."

I hate that she knows me so well. That she understands when I'm quiet and when I have nothing to say. I honestly don't know what's wrong with me. I'm just… numb. Too many things are going on in my head that just settling on one thing to worry about is stressing me out more than anything.

I give Nora my best grin so she doesn't have to worry. "I'm just thinking about how I'm going to kick your ass on the crepe-making station."

She snorts. "You do know it's not a competition, right? It's just a fun way to make your own dessert. No need to make it into something it isn't."

"That's just what losers say," I tease. I turn back to the rest of the group. Cat and Connor are nowhere to be seen, probably making out behind one of the huts. Elle is standing in front of a jewelry stall, and Archer is beside her. She's talking to him, but he's a man of little words, so I'm guessing he's just blinking at her. "Guess it's just me and you, Stargirl."

She giggles. I almost faint. God, I just can't get enough of her. How is that even possible? I've spent nearly every day with her since we were kids, and I *still* want more. "Guess so," she gets out, pulling my arm as she leads us to the station.

Maybe I did underestimate her crepe-making skills because hers looks a lot better than mine. I'm sure they've given me some fucked up batter or something because whilst hers looks all smooth and delicious, mine just looks like lumps of batter with Nutella thrown on top.

"Gimme some of yours," I demand, leaning over her as we walk around the markets, the Christmas lights shining around us. She holds her cone higher, which only makes it easier for me.

"No! You've already eaten your own," she argues.

"I'm pretty sure mine was raw. I might *die*, Nora. You can't let me die without a good taste of your crepe," I whine, still trying to steal her cone.

"Maybe I do want that to happen," she says, stopping still and pointing to me with a look.

My mouth pops open. "Nora Bailey, you sick, sick woman."

It only takes one look at her with my gorgeous doe eyes before she sighs, holding the one up to me. "Fine. Don't eat a lot, or I'll kill you myself."

"You really need to stop with these threats, Nor," I mutter, leaning down to take a bite of her crepe. She watches me carefully so I don't take too much, and when I bite a piece off, my eyes connect with hers. Her mouth twitches slightly as she continues staring at me, and I can't tear my eyes away from her.

Of course, it tastes delicious, and all the Nutella and strawberries make so much sense together. I groan when I swallow.

"Good?" Her voice is all but a rasp.

"So fucking good," I whisper. Her mouth turns up into a smile and she turns away from me, continuing to eat her crepe whilst I'm left wondering if the blush on her cheeks was because of me or the cold.

"Wanna go on the Ferris Wheel now? We could take some pictures up there, too," Nora suggests when we get closer to the line for the wheel. I look up and gulp. Jesus Christ. How tall is that thing? I try not to make my nerves obvious, but she nudges her arm into mine. "We don't have to if you don't want to."

"No," I say quickly. Maybe even too quickly. I don't fucking know. "We can go." She throws me a skeptical look before thinking better of it and walking us toward the end of the line.

I pull out my phone whilst I wait, seeing if I have any new messages. There's a few from my dad trying to confirm what I'm doing for Christmas, and I sure as hell aren't spending it with him. There's one from Connor saying he and Cat have left early and are going back to the house, and there's a few in our team group chat.

RED

If we don't make it to the semis, what then?

SAM

Dunno. Sit and cry.

RED

I don't like the sound of that.

OLI

Neither do I.

CONNOR

There'll be no sitting and crying if you actually pay attention. Which means no pissing about over Christmas break.

RED

Yeah, and what are you doing? I can see all the pics of you at the markets, dumbass.

CONNOR

Hanging out with my girlfriend isn't a crime.

SAM

Where's Wesley? I haven't seen him around in a hot minute. I miss my bestie.

RED

Too busy playing Loverboy.

I'm right here, Assholes.

RED

Ah! Came out for a breather from between your girl's legs?

Yeah, actually, thanks for checking in.

CONNOR

That's my sister, chill.

SAM

LMFAO. You're pussy whipped.

CONNOR

Again, she's my sister, so watch it.

As a matter of fact, I am.

RED

You bringing her to the NYE party? Oli's hosting.

OLI

Since when?

> **RED**
> Since now...
>
> **OLI**
> Fuck that. There's a party at The Dragon.
>
> Yeah, I'll bring her. Might stick my tongue down her throat in front of you all to shut you up.
>
> **CONNOR**
> She's still my sister.

MY PHONE almost drops out of my hand when a shrill voice brings me back to reality.

"Nora!"

We both turn to see a tall blonde running towards us in the line. She is *not* dressed for this weather at all. Whilst we're all bundled up and cozy, she's wearing a summer dress, no tights, and flats. Her face and legs are completely red like she's been rolling around in snow.

"Summer?" Nora asks, detangling her arm from mine as the girl gets closer. I have no clue who this is, but the surprise in Nora's voice is saying something. The girl reaches us, and she gives me a once over, smirking like she knows something. "Oh my god! It's been forever. How's Switzerland?"

"Cold," the blonde– Summer– replies. She's panting like she ran all the way over here. "How are you? How's Ryan?"

Nora stiffens. "Uh, we actually broke up a few months ago."

"Seriously?" Summer's blue eyes almost bulge right out of her head. What was the best news to me sounds to her like the world is ending. "I thought you two were going to get married. Endgame, or whatever."

"Nope," Nora says, and there's an edge to her voice. I can't tell if she loves or hates this girl. I kinda need to know so I know whether or not *I* should hate her too. "This is my boyfriend, Wes. You remember him, right?"

I'm never going to get tired of her saying my name and 'boyfriend' in the same sentence. I smile at her, giving her a firm nod. "How could I forget?" she purrs, her eyes so *obviously* trying to fuck me. Yeah, I've decided on my own. I don't like her. Not at all.

Still, I find myself doing the polite thing and saying, "Hi. It's nice to see you." I don't even remember this chick. It's hard to notice anyone when I'm around Nora. So, if she had introduced her as her friend one time, I would have blocked her out. Part of me is glad that I did. She seems like bad news.

"You too," she says, and I *swear* she winks at me. She turns to Nora. "So… Ryan's single then, huh?"

Nora tuts, shaking her head. "Ah, no. He's with Daisy from our class. Oh, well, he was with Megan before that, and then there was Belle from his internship…." Fucking hell. The sass on this woman just makes her that much more fucking attractive. "Ugh," she says, rolling her eyes, "It's so hard to keep up now. But you're more than welcome to wait around to see if he gets bored."

Oh.

Oh.

She was *that* kind of friend.

That makes a lot more sense now. I just stand there quietly as Nora shoots daggers at this girl who clearly had a thing for Ryan when they were dating. I'm sure she couldn't care less about Ryan in the situation and more about how she felt being betrayed by her friend. Friends like that suck, and they shouldn't be allowed around people who are in relationships.

Summer's eyes widen. "What makes you think that–"

"Oh, come on, Sum," Nora says, sighing. "I've seen the way you looked at him when we were together. I never said anything because… well, he was mine, and he made me believe he was faithful. Turns out, he was cheating on me anyway. Seems like you could have had a chance."

Summer scoffs. "Whatever," she mutters. She points between the two of us. "Ryan is going to hate this, you know. You two together, I mean."

Nora just shrugs. "He'll get over it."

"Not so sure he will," Summer says like she knows something I don't. I'm not a fan of this girl. "See you around, Lovebirds."

And then, she's gone.

We're both quiet until we get seated on the Ferris Wheel. I try to make conversation with her, but I'm too busy trying not to have a panic attack. I breathe in through my nose and then out through my mouth. Nora snuggles close to me on the bench, and I thought her proximity would soothe the nausea, but it's not helping.

"Am I evil for enjoying every second of that?" Nora asks, trying not to laugh.

"Not at all," I breathe out, turning away from her to look out to the skyline and the markets beneath us. Big mistake. I suck in a breath, closing my eyes as I tilt my head back.

She doesn't notice my discomfort because she continues talking. "It's so pretty from up here, don't you think? Everything just seems so much quieter. Muted. It's like nothing bad could happen up here."

Her soft words calm me for a second, and I open my eyes. As terrifying as it is, she's right. We can see the tips of the trees up here, the tops of houses, and the stalls in the market. Christmas lights shine everywhere, and it feels like we're in a separate universe altogether. It reminds me of the childlike wonder the holidays used to bring.

But when I look at her, watching her watch everything else, that's a sight that can beat what's beneath us. I go quiet again, turning away to look back down to the scene below. Maybe this isn't so bad. When the car jolts slightly when we stop at the top, I gasp.

"What's wrong?" she asks tentatively, somehow moving closer to me. Her thigh brushes against mine, and I bite the inside of my cheek. "You've not got a hard-on again, have you?"

Just the word hard is enough for me to shift in my seat. "You wish," I bite out. I take in a deep breath, and when I turn to her, my heart settles slightly. She's got this worried expression on her face like I was about to jump out or something. "Let's just say I don't love heights."

"Are you being serious?" she gawks, "Why would you agree to come on here?"

"Why do you think?" I mutter.

She just blinks at me. I blink back. Unspoken words settle beneath us, and I think she realizes that I'd do anything she asked me to, no matter how fucking terrified I am right now. She closes her eyes, choosing her words carefully as if she doesn't want to upset me.

"You can say no to me sometimes, you know," she whispers softly.

"I can't."

"Wes."

Heat creeps up on my neck, making my whole body tingle. "What?"

"Come on," she says, rolling her eyes as if I'm ridiculous. "You can't be serious. Just because I like something doesn't mean you have to by proxy."

I nod. "It does. It's how we work, Nora."

"No, it's not."

"It is."

"It's not."

I sigh. "Are you really trying to argue with me right now?"

She crosses her arms against her chest, tilting her chin up. "Maybe I am."

"*Maybe* you need to shut up."

"Maybe you need to make me." Her own words catch her off guard as she slaps a hand over her mouth. I just smirk at her as she looks at me like a deer in headlights. Now, I can tell that the blush on her cheeks has nothing to do with the weather. "Oh my God. I meant like–"

"For the love of God, just shut up and kiss me."

I thought I would be the one pulling her into me, but I'm not.

Her small hands fist in my jacket, pulling me right into her, and she presses her lips to mine. My eyes widen in shock before they soften as she melts into me. She's fully in control this time as she pulls me down to her, and our bodies flush together. Even with the layers of clothes between us, it's like I can still *feel* her. She tastes sweet – forever like strawberries and the chocolate she had earlier.

I let myself get lost in her. I don't think about the fakeness of this or the part where she'll stop and push me off her. I let myself imagine for a second that this is real. That she actually wants me and not just to piss off her ex. That Nora Bailey might actually be interested in me beyond being my friend.

When my hand makes its way into her hair, her beanie falling onto the bench, she whispers my name into my mouth. *God, that sound.* If I die on the Ferris wheel right now, I'd die a happy man because Nora is beneath me, saying my name in that raspy, sexy voice of hers.

Her mouth parts, and I dare myself to slip my tongue into her mouth, but I chicken out. Suddenly, I'm not sure what we're even doing, and I can't tell myself to stop. She feels too good. Too safe. Too much like *mine*. I snap back to reality when her arm moves from beneath me, only for me to realize she is taking a picture.

She rears back from me slightly, her lips swollen, and her entire face is red. She licks her lips like she still wants to taste me. Her voice is breathless and tight. "Photo ops, remember?"

I clear my throat. "Yeah, photo ops."

SEVENTEEN
WES/NORA
SAVE A HORSE

WES

"HOW WERE THE MARKETS?" Connor asks me when I make my way into the kitchen. I haven't seen him in what feels like months. After the markets, he and Cat kinda disappeared in their little love bubble, and with the holiday's, we've not seen each other much. He got to spend it with his family and I had to painfully sit through a whole day with my mom, distracting her from her very harsh reality.

He's baking Banana bread because he's an old man and has finally managed to make an edible dessert. As much as I love teasing him about it, it actually smells good.

I take a seat on the kitchen island. "Pretty good. It seems like what we're doing is working. Ryan's pissed, and I'm... I dunno, happy for one of the first times in a while?"

Connor hums, adding some chocolate chips to his batter. "Right. And that's what you want, isn't it?"

"I guess. It's making my mom happy, which is a bonus, but my dad doesn't give a shit," I mutter. "I kinda wish he did, but this whole thing proves that he simply doesn't care about me."

Connor drops his spoon onto the counter, staring up at me. "Jesus. What?"

"Can you hear yourself right now?" Connor asks, his eyes wide. "That is so fucking sad, man. You need to talk to him."

"No, I don't," I argue.

"You do," he challenges. "What he did was stupid and selfish and fucked up, but he's your *dad*."

I sigh. "You don't get it. We don't have the kind of relationship that you have with your dad. We don't sit around drinking whilst he gives me some life-changing advice. He's just a normal, regular guy who happens to have a son. He wasn't born to be a dad like yours was, okay? And that's fine. I don't need him anyway."

My own words sting. I can't really think like that, can I? Then why does it feel so easy to say? My dad has never done anything out of the ordinary or done things that stand out to me. He's just done the regular things that dads do – minus the cheating part. We don't have the same bond that Connor has with his parents. My dad isn't built to be loving, caring, sweet or have an abundance of good advice. He's just… there.

"Jesus, Wes," Connor mutters, shaking his head at me.

"Can you stop looking at me like that? I'm not some broken person who you need to fix, Connor. I don't need you to feel sorry for me, alright?" My words are biting, and Connor leans back.

"I'm not trying to fix you, and you're not broken. You're just… sad."

"Like that's any better," I scoff. "Everything's fine, okay? Everything is always fucking fine, so stop looking at me and acting like it's not."

I don't let him respond before I storm out like a fucking child and go to my car. It's New Year's Eve, and after spending the holidays with my mom and trying not to cause an argument with my dad, I can't wait to get this season over with. Going to spend the night with my friends and my fake girlfriend is the only thing I'm looking forward to.

The team is somehow on the road to the semis, and I don't feel the way I should. I should be happy like Connor and the rest of the guys. I should be ready to take our next team and kick their asses, but I just don't care. I don't even want to win anymore. How pathetic is that?

I drive around the block a few times before I get bored of my playlist and turn it off. Silence doesn't do any better, so I pull up outside the gym and hope I can work off some of this tension. I quickly change into my clean gym clothes before I hit the treadmill. If I can't literally run away from my problems, maybe this is the next best thing. I'm listening to the shitty gym music because, for whatever reason, my own music doesn't feel the same. Everything just feels wrong, and everything keeps going wrong, and I hate it.

Just as I'm coming down from a sprint, my phone pings and I welcome the distraction. It's a text from Nora with two photos. They're both of her in front of her mirror, and the phone is held high above her head to get her full outfit in the frame. In the first one, she's wearing baggy jeans that rest comfortably low on her hips and a lace cami top, showing off her toned stomach and her boobs. The second one is her wearing a simple black dress with thin straps and silver cowboy boots. Those fucking *legs*. Those fucking *boots*.

My heart restarts when I read the message.

SUNSHINE
Which one is hotter?

Think you meant to send this to Cat and Elle.

SUNSHINE
No, I need your opinion.

It's you that's going to have your hands all over me tonight, remember?

THE IMAGE she creates makes my decision about what she should wear. Both options look so fucking good on her, and I know I won't be able to keep my hands to myself. Even in the pictures, she has this unwavering sense of confidence, and fuck me if it doesn't turn me on.

> Black dress and boots.

SUNSHINE
Perfect. Do I go full commando or not?

> That's definitely not a question you want me to answer, Sunshine.

SUNSHINE
I'm kidding.

See you later, cowboy ;)

SINCE WE GOT to the bar, my eyes have not left Nora's. Just like we agreed, she's wearing the black dress and boots. Her hair was wild, flowing down her back, and the second I picked her up, she stole my cowboy hat and plopped it on her own head. It looks way better on her, though, anyway. She's been on the dance floor for what feels like forever as she dances with her hands in the air, screaming lyrics into Kiara and Elle's faces.

I don't think I could look away if I had a person holding a gun to my head, begging me to. She's moving around the small space as if she owns it. Everyone is looking at her like she's the fucking sun, gracing us with her presence. She's shining brighter than anyone else in this joint, and it makes my heart ache. It also makes me regret not asking if she really *did* go full commando tonight.

I let her do her own thing whilst I sat with a few of my friends in a booth. Being here is a good enough distraction than being at home with Connor. I don't know why his comment got to me. It shouldn't. As easy as it is for him to suggest, I don't exactly want to talk to my dad. It's the very last thing on my mind. If he wanted to reach out and spend Christmas with me, he would have, but he didn't. So why am I going to go out of my way to try to mend something that's never going to be fixed?

Red's arm nudging me brings me back to reality. "Your girl's got a mouth on her."

"What?" I follow his line of vision, and sure enough, Nora is arguing with the DJ to play a song she wants. Elle and Kie are standing awkwardly at her sides, not sure if they should intervene or not. "Ah, she's got a very particular music taste."

"Nice ass, too," Red mutters. I hit him in the back of his head.

"Don't talk about her like that, Mikey, or I'll kill you," I say, my jaw clenching. He just looks at me with an amused smile on his face. "Sorry, that sounded like a joke. I will actually just murder you."

Red gulps, and he drops his gaze to the table in front of him. He knows when to back down when he's told. Most of the time, he just acts like a teenager who has never been in proximity with a woman before.

"Wild one she is," Sam says under his breath, shaking his head. "So is the other girl with her. She's been giving me the fuck me eyes all night."

I try not to laugh at the way Sam sounds *sad* that Kiara has been checking him out. She's forward as fuck, and Sam is clearly playing dumb. "Why don't you go for her? She seems like your type."

Sam just shrugs, looking past me and staring right at her, but when Nora's argument with the DJ gets louder, he snorts. "You might want to tighten the reins on that one."

I lean back, admiring the way she's sticking up for herself.

"Nah, I'm good. Besides, she's got my hat on right now. You know the rules."

"Save a horse, ride a cowboy," Oli murmurs quietly.

My face splits into a grin as I clasp him on the shoulder, slipping out of my seat, "Exactly."

NORA

I'm about to throw another jab at the long-haired DJ before Wes's voice pulls me back down to earth. I might be a *little* bit tipsy, and Elle and Kie are doing the very unfriendly thing and are *not* indulging in my chaos. They've disappeared, dancing together in the corner to whatever song is playing now.

"Darlin.'" I spin around at the country accent Wes has adopted for the day. He's dressed up to match the party's theme, and he's wearing black pants and a huge belt buckle, his brown button down untucked, and his hair is a mess. He just looks *good*.

He holds his hand out to me, and I don't need him to tell me anything before I slip my hand into his. "Honey," I coo, stepping away from the DJ's station. He can deal without my wrath for a few minutes.

"Care to join me for a dance?" he asks, gently squeezing my hand. I giggle as he pulls me into him. My hands instantly drop to his chest. And maybe it's the music and the bit of alcohol in my system, but for one of the first times, I find myself actually feeling Wes. Or *wanting* to feel him. His chest is hard beneath my palms but soft against the fabric of his shirt.

"I would love nothing more," I say, looking up at him.

His grey eyes hood as he clasps my hands in his, pushing me out to pull me back in. "Did you manage to bully him into letting you play a song?"

I pout, shaking my head. "Nope. Apparently, I'm not scary enough."

Wes scoffs. "You're barely five-five. Of course, you're not

scary enough." For that, I purposely stand on his foot. "Okay, okay. You're terrifying."

A loopy grin spreads across my face at his words, and the noise from the bar starts to fade. Everything about us stupidly dancing together in a bar as we wait for the countdown to start just feels right. Everything about *him* just feels right. It always has. He manages to look at me like I'm special. Like I mean something to him. He makes me feel like what I have to say and what I think matters. So when the pop song changes to something more sad and mellow, I rest my head against his chest and feel him sigh.

My arms wrap up around his neck as his hands find my waist, pulling us together and making our bodies fit perfectly. He sways us side to side as *'Wondering Why'* by The Red Clay Strays plays over the speakers, fitting tonight's theme perfectly.

I could stay like this forever, swaying on a dancefloor with my best friend. His fingers trail down my spine, and my breath hitches. The movement is so small and insignificant I'm sure he doesn't even notice he's doing it. But I do. I feel it everywhere. I feel *him* everywhere. It's the small kind of intimacy I never experienced with Ryan. It's like something I never knew I needed.

As if on instinct, my hands curl into the hair at the bottom of Wes's neck, and he lets out a sigh. There's a slight tension in his neck, but as I continue to move my fingers, he slowly relaxes.

"You having fun, Stargirl?" His voice is low and hoarse it feels like there's nothing else in the room other than the two of us.

"The most fun," I say, and then a thought pops into my head. I lean up off him, but our arms don't detangle from each other. "We should take line dancing classes."

He lets out a soft chuckle. "Whoa. One step at a time. That seems more like a fourth date kinda thing. I don't want to be offering up all my good dancing skills so quickly."

A smile stretches across my face. "Guess I've got to stick around for the good stuff, right?"

"Yup." His answer is so matter-of-fact and goofy that I can't stop the laugh that escapes me.

I tilt my head. "How about you? Are you having fun?"

"With you, Nora, I'm always having fun."

There's something hidden in his sentence that makes me want to panic, and I try my absolute hardest not to. This whole thing between us is fake, so why can I feel butterflies swarming in my stomach that I hadn't felt before? Maybe it's because of how well I know him. How well I know he can make me feel. How easy it is to be with him and have fun and not worry about him breaking my heart.

My body moves on its own accord, and I step back from him, ready to make an excuse to find my friends. I'm panicking for no reason. I *know* that. I have freaked out in too many situations to know that that's just the way I am. The way I'm wired.

"Where are you going? Why are you so far away from me?" Wes whines, shredding the small bit of space that I put between us.

"I'm not. You're just possessive," I say, slowly making my way back to him.

"Wanting you close to me doesn't make me possessive, Sunshine," he taunts. Before I can get to where we just were, he wraps his arm around my waist, making that decision for me. My hands find their way right back around his neck like they belong there.

"Where did you learn how to do that?" I mutter, looking down between us. His head quirks. "The whole grabbing my waist thing. It's hot and I hate it."

He lets out a deep laugh. "Friday nights with my mom, remember?"

I sigh wistfully. "Ah, how could I forget?"

I've walked into Wes's old house too many times as a kid, watching him watch romantic movies with his mom. I remember how she'd try to instill some good manners into him and make him the perfect man. He'd give me a full rundown the Saturday after, and we'd sit and watch the movie together. He'd then proceed to tell me every single thing that's going to happen, and I could never get him to shut up. So, I guess he's picked up on a few ways to make a girl swoon.

When I come back down from the daydream, and we're still dancing to another slow country song, it starts to fade out, and the countdown from fifteen starts around us. Without saying anything, Wes pulls me into his side, lifting up the cowboy hat that has fallen into my face. He pulls out his phone and opens the camera app, getting us both in on the screen.

Ten.

I lean up towards him, wrapping my hands around the hair at the nape of his neck. His eyes hood as his mouth parts.

Nine.

His eyes dip to my lips, and my throat instantly dries.

Eight.

I try to get closer to him, and I don't know how to. I don't know *why* I want to.

Seven.

I settle on tugging his face closer to mine.

Six.

"Are you ready to play, Stargirl?" His voice is soft and hushed. His mouth is so achingly close to mine.

Four.

"I'm always ready to play with you, Wes," I whisper.

I don't mean it to sound suggestive, but it does, and by the time the words are out of my mouth, his lips are on mine. The kiss isn't like the other ones we've shared for the sake of this plan. The only way to describe this is *desperate*.

Our mouths fight over each other, and my hands tighten in his hair. He tastes like he's constantly showering in sweet products. As if he's always just eaten something sweet. I'm getting dizzy just thinking about how his hand feels in my hair, the way the cowboy hat no longer exists, and we're just gripping at each other as if we need the release.

Then his phone falls. The video might still be recording. I don't know. But he doesn't go to pick it up. And neither do I.

We must both be aware that we're just standing in the middle of the dance floor, making out for no reason. People might be watching us. That's a good thing. But the whole point is to take pictures and videos, and neither of us are caring about that aspect of it.

Now that both of his hands are free, they curl deeper into my hair, his fingers massaging my scalp. The softness of his hands is so foreign, and I crave more of it. More of *him*. His hands move around my face like he's trying to feel every part of me, and I let him. His thumbs caress my cheeks, sliding down towards my neck, where he squeezes me softly.

Holy fuuuckk.

I did not expect to like that so much, but I did, and I'm craving more of it. He must know the way my body reacts to it because he keeps his hand on my neck, holding me there, squeezing me hard enough that the pleasure ripples through my entire body.

My tongue slips into his mouth, and that's when I know for sure that this is something else. He groans in response, tasting me back, and my knees go weak. We keep going back and forth, pushing and retreating, tasting and claiming. I don't know how long we keep doing that, but I eventually come up for air.

I'm panting. My chest is heaving, and from the friction of rubbing my chest against his, my nipples are pebbled. And Wes looks... So fucking good. His hair is even more of a mess than it was before. His pupils are dilated, and his lips are slightly swollen. We both look at each other for a second before he leans down again.

And he kisses me.

There's something significant about this second kiss, but I don't give myself a chance to overthink it before I pull apart from him and turn around. I need to get my head on straight. I'm clearly drunk and gripping onto him for dear life because he's the only person giving me attention right now. I'm being selfish and taking more of him than I'm allowed to have. That's it.

"No," Wes bites out, his hand gripping onto my forearm. He pulls me back into him, and I stumble.

"What?"

"We're not doing that," he says simply. "You don't get to run away every time we kiss, okay?"

I catch myself and swallow. I look up to him and I can't place the dissatisfied look on his face like this has really been bothering him. "Wes... That was–"

He grins. "Insane."

"Yes, but..." I shake my head, trying to find something to say. Something to blame my mood on. "Your phone fell."

"And?"

"And what's the point of us making out when no one is going to see it," I argue.

"There's around a hundred people in here, Nor, someone must have seen," he says easily as if he didn't just stick his tongue down my throat.

I don't bring up the fact that we clearly indulged in that for ourselves. If he's not saying anything, why should I? Maybe it didn't mean anything to him. Maybe it's just me and my brain that loves to over analyze every single interaction I have and turn it into a big deal. Maybe I'm just too in my head and confused about what's real and what's fake.

Wes has always been upfront, and I don't see why that would change now. So when I look up at him and I say nothing, I wait for him to ease the weird feeling I have in my chest.

He doesn't.

He just picks up his phone and his hat, plopping it right back on my head before he kisses my cheek. "This suits you, Stargirl. You should keep it."

"Don't say that, Wesley, or I might start taking more of your things," I tease, tipping my hat to him.

"You can take anything you want as far as I'm concerned," he says, winking, and I burst into a fit of laughter.

And just like that, we're back to pretending that kiss didn't just happen.

EIGHTEEN
WES / NORA
MAMA'S BOY

WES

MY MOM IS LOOKING RIGHT at me like she's a kid at Christmas. You'd think I'd just surprised her with a million-dollar painting, or a brand-new car, or literally *anything else*. But no. She's smiling like that at me because I'm in her apartment with Nora Bailey beside me. In some ways, maybe having Nora here does equate to all those things. All those things and more.

She's just been staring at us since we got here, and I'm sure Nora is getting creeped out. They've met a million times growing up, but this is different. I'm not introducing her as the girl I make mud pies with or who I sneak out to see after dinner. She's now my girlfriend, and from the look on Mom's face, she might as well be my wife.

"Mom, can you stop looking at her like that?" I grunt as we pass each other in the kitchen, trying to put together a chicken salad.

Nora's sitting at the island, her head propped into her hands as she watches me and my mom walk around each other. "Please don't stop on my account. It's doing wonderful things for my ego."

I roll my eyes, pointing my spatula at her whilst giving my mom a look. "See?"

"See what? All I see is a woman who knows her worth," Mom says, winking at Nora before taking a sip of her wine.

"You two are a nightmare already," I mutter, doing the finishing touches to the salad. "And are you both seriously drinking right now? It's two in the afternoon."

"It's five o'clock somewhere," Nora says with a shrug.

I look over at her, and she's smiling like a loon. Of course, my mom loves her. Who wouldn't? She's charming, funny and sweet. She always knows the right thing to say, and my mom needs that right now. When I look at them both in this kitchen, talking like they're best friends, I get a jolt in my chest, reminding me how heartbroken she's going to be when we stop whatever it is we're doing.

Nora is still rehearsing for the show. I'm still in a state of purgatory on the football team, doing the best I can to keep us afloat. We've got the semis in just over a week, and I can't wait to get this season over with. I've performed worse than I have ever done in my life, and the more I try to fix it, the worse I feel.

When we've managed to sit around the small dining table and eat our salad, I can't help but think about how well Nora fits in here. She talks to my mom about her classes whilst my mom talks about her book. They laugh, and they smile, and it just feels *good*. Everything about Nora being here, making my mom happy, and therefore making me happy just makes me wish it could be like this forever.

"So, Wes," my mom starts, shuffling some playing cards in her hands. We never actually play a card game. I don't think she actually knows how. I think she just likes holding them. "Got any special plans for next month? It is the month of love, after all."

Nora quirks her head to the side playfully. "Yeah, Wesley, what's your big plan?"

"Can't tell you if it's a surprise, Sunshine," I say, grinning.

Truth is, I haven't thought that far ahead. Anything past the football season being over has completely been blocked out of my mind. "What about you? This relationship works both ways, you know."

"Oh, I know it does. That's why I've been pulling most of the weight," she argues. My mom laughs at that, and I just shake my head. Nora shrugs innocently. "I could have a few tricks up my sleeve."

"Really?"

"Yup," she quips, holding her chin high, "I guess we'll have to see."

I hold her stare. "I guess we will."

We continue looking at each other for a second too long, and it painfully reminds me of the split second I took to look at her before I kissed her again at the New Year's party.

My mom sighs wistfully. "Look at you two. I've never seen you more smitten."

Nora drops her gaze then, pushing around the food she had left on her plate as if that'll somehow distract my mom from looking between us like we're her favorite movie. I embrace it, and I smile back at my mom. She needs this. She needs to know that I'm doing okay. That soon, she'll be able to get back on her feet and we'll establish a new kind of normal.

"Oh, Wes. Have you thought about what you're going to do about football?"

Her question gets Nora's attention, and her head shoots up. Those pretty brown eyes bore into mine, and I pull my gaze away from her. I haven't told her, or anyone, about what's going on in my head. Mostly because I don't know what that is. All I know is that football is not bringing me the same excitement it once was and that passion for playing is slowly fading away. The more time I spend on the field, the more I'm beginning to realize how much I don't want to be out there. Vocalizing that to my mom is enough. I don't know how or if I will tell Nora.

As I battle with coming clean or just answering my mom's

question and moving on, my phone lights up with a text. Saved by the bell.

> **NOLAN MACKENZIE**
> Call me when you get the chance. It's important.

THE LAST THING I want to do is talk to this man, but it's about time I stop trying to run away from my problems. I excuse myself from the table and walk outside my mom's bedroom, terrified about what my dad has to say to me.

NORA

I can't wait to grow up just so I can retire. Although May's life has been turned upside down recently, I still want what she has. I want to work on my own schedule and live in an apartment filled with plants and posters. I want to only have to worry about cooking my own meals and waiting for someone to come home to me at night. I want a son who comes home from college to visit me with his partner. I want someone who's going to love me unconditionally and never make me doubt my worth. I crave that. I crave the thought of being needed and appreciated. Of doing something good. *Being* good.

Just thinking about it makes my heart twinge. I can't wait for the day that happens. When I've completed everything, I've wanted to in life and I'm just *happy*. Comfortable. Safe. May must recognize the loopy look on my face because she points one of her playing cards at me that she folded into a boat.

"Can I tell you something?" she whispers, dramatic as always.

"Of course." I lean into her from across the table.

"I've known you since you were a baby, Nora, and I don't think I've seen you look at anyone the way you look at Wes." My eyes instantly prickle. "I'm just glad you've finally given him a chance."

My eyebrows furrow. "What do you mean, *finally*?"

She sighs, leaning over me slightly to check if Wes is listening. He's talking quietly on the phone down the other end of the apartment. "Don't act like you don't know, sweetheart. The poor boy has been at your feet for *years*. He begged me to let him play with you every day when you were kids. He asked me to help him create gifts for your birthday with the crafts we had lying around. He was always trying so hard to impress you."

"I thought that was just the kind of person he is. He's kind to everyone. I'm no one special," I say, forcing out a laugh so I don't cry.

"He wasn't like that with anyone else. It was just you," she whispers, tapping a spot on the table in front of me. My chest rises and falls, a feeling twirling around inside my chest that I can't fully explain. May continues talking. "He's such a good person, Nora. You know that. There's something so inherently *good* within, and I just hope what's happened doesn't fuck that up."

My eyes widen at her cursing. I've only ever heard May curse a handful of times in my life, and she only does it when she's being serious. "I know. I hope so, too." I reach for my glass of wine, taking a generous sip, somehow feeling like I need it.

"Good. Now that's out of the way," May murmurs, unfolding her paper boat. "Can we talk about the wedding details?"

I almost choke. "*Wedding*?"

She shrugs as if this is the most casual thing she's ever encountered. "I know that boy has not been obsessed with you for years to let you go so easily."

A piece of my heart breaks for her because of how real she thinks this is. I don't know how I'm going to stomach telling her when we 'break up.' She's got this almost child-like wonder in her eyes as if this is the toy she's been waiting to open. As if all of Wes's happiness can become hers. And I hate myself for playing along with this trick just so she's happy for a moment.

"Respectfully, that's insane," I say, dismissing the idea as I reach for my glass again.

"No, sweetie. *You're* insane," she argues. God, I love this woman almost too much. I see so much of her in Wes, both physically and in their personalities. It's like he's taken all the good parts of both of his parents and made them even better.

Speaking of the devil…

Wes's footsteps pad along the wooden floor as he makes his way back over into the small dining area. There's a passive look on his face. If he was on the phone with his dad for the last five minutes, I'm not surprised. When he doesn't take a seat and just stands by the table, I ask, "Is everything okay?"

He comes back to life for a second, then gives me a reassuring smile before turning to his mom. He slides his hand around my shoulder from where he's stood, squeezing me gently. "Everything is fine. Dad just wants to see me. Is it okay if we go?"

I watch the way May's eyes dim at the mention of Wes's dad. Her smile is wobbly, but it's a smile nonetheless. "Yeah, that's okay." She lets out a short laugh, adding, "I was thinking of excuses on how to get you out of here anyway."

Wes frowns. "I'm sorry, Mom. If it didn't sound serious, I wouldn't go, I promise."

May just nods, and Wes helps me slip on my jacket like the gentleman he is. I can't help but notice how distracted he is as we make our way out of the apartment complex. I try to keep up with his long strides, but he's making it frustratingly difficult.

"I'll just drop you off at your dorm first," Wes says as we make our way across the parking lot.

"Actually, can you bring me to your place? I'll hang out with Cat and Connor until they're sick of me. Elle's got practice this afternoon, and I don't want to be there on my own," I say, falling in step beside him.

"Whatever you want, Sunshine." He doesn't say it like he usually does. The nickname somehow sounds bitter, and I can't figure out why. He turns to me as he unlocks the car from the driver's side. "I don't know how long I'll be, so don't wait up for me."

I nod, and when the car unlocks, I slip into the seat. We drive in silence, and it's deafening. One of us usually has something to say. I'm too anxious to say something and have to deal with the embarrassment of getting a one-word response out of him. Clearly, something is going on in his head, and he's not letting me in. He's not letting me see past the funny, flirty side of him, and it sucks.

When we pull up outside of his house, and I get out of the car, I stop myself, turning back to him. I lean on the open window, searching for his eyes as he looks out at the dashboard. "Hey, are you okay?"

He nods, slowly turning to me. "I'm always okay, Sunshine."

My chest tightens. "That's not what I asked."

"You don't have to worry about me, I swear. I'm fine."

"I do worry about you, Wes," I say shakily. My voice wobbles, and my mouth etches into a frown. "All the time. I *care* about you, you know. And I feel like you don't know that."

He just swallows, turning away from me. "I know."

Trying to talk to him when he's like this doesn't get us anywhere. There's only been a few times where he gets these moods and I never know how to fully pull him out of them. He would just turn up at our house one day and sleep over, disappearing back to his house the next morning. Or he won't speak to me for a few days and then come back like nothing was wrong. It's like he wants to be close to me without fully letting me in, and I can't find my way around it.

So, I let him go.

NINETEEN
WES
DADDY ISSUES

I SWALLOW the bile in my throat as I drive away from Nora.

I hate leaving her like that, knowing she has questions, but just the thought of saying what I'm thinking aloud – *whatever that is* – is terrifying. Especially to someone who wouldn't fully understand. So I keep it hidden, push it down deep inside of me until I'm forced to deal with it. Like right now.

Meeting up with my dad was the very last thing I wanted to do today, but I need to suck it up. I've come to the point where I actually *want* to hear him out. There's no point in dancing around it now since it's not getting us anywhere. I'm sick of feeling angry all the time. Sick of feeling useless and like I've not been doing enough for both the team and my mom. So, I push down the resentment I have towards my dad and drive to my old house.

Everything about being here doesn't sit right with me. The porch that we'd vandalize with chalk is plain, and it's losing its color. The front yard is empty. There's not a football in sight, and the tree I spent so many years trying to climb looks sad and abandoned.

Worst of all? When I walk into the house to find my dad in the living room, a part of me feels bad for not being here. For shutting him out. For being the stubborn idiot that I am because he looks sad. I thought he had always looked like a young parent despite his age, but when I look at him, I no longer see the guy who pushed me on the swings or taught me how to kick a football. He looks like the world has torn him down, pulled him apart, and turned into someone I don't recognize.

We've been sitting in silence for almost five minutes before he blurts out, "We need to talk about your performance."

I don't get to control the laugh that escapes me. He shakes his head before reaching for the glass of bourbon in front of him, taking a long swig. "Are you fucking serious? Did you really call me over here so we can talk about *football?*"

My dad doesn't meet my gaze. He stares straight ahead, thinking as if he needs to choose his next words carefully. "Yes."

"Why?"

"Because I can tell when you're not doing well, son, and I want the best for you," he says slowly. He's talking to me like he's a saint. Like I'm a child, and he knows so much better than I do. That's all bullshit.

"You don't want that, Dad. You wouldn't have cheated on your wife with the assistant coach if you did. Unless that was somehow in my best interest," I argue. My hands are balled into fists on my knees, itching for them to do something. To grab something. Break something. To do literally *anything* to get this anger out of my body.

He turns to me. His eyes are bloodshot. His hair is graying a lot more than it was a few months ago, and there are hard lines etched across his face as if he's had his mouth in a permanent frown. "You want to do this right now?"

My eyes flash. "Yes, I want to do this right now because we're never going to have this fucking conversation if we keep dancing around it."

He takes in a deep breath, his eyes still on mine. His gaze feels scrutinizing. Like he can see right through me and pick out everything that I'm thinking. I fucking hate it. "What do you want to know?"

"Why?"

He reels back. "What?"

"Why did you cheat?" I ask, clarifying my question. My jaw ticks, and I try my hardest to reign myself in. "What was so wrong with mom, huh? She gave everything to you. She gave up her *life* for you. For *us*. And you threw it all down the drain for what? For a few moments reliving your glory days?"

Again, he takes his time to answer. He swishes around the drink in his glass, looking down at it before drinking some. "Your mom and I were growing apart," he says matter-of-factly. His tone is so even and sure.

"That's bullshit," I mutter.

"It's true. Ask her."

"I don't believe you."

He sighs. "We were having problems, Wes. You knew that. Which is why Thanksgiving and Christmas were hard last year. You *knew* that."

I try to keep track of my memories from last year. I know they were arguing more often than before. I just thought it was because my dad was so busy with work, and my mom had a million deadlines to meet. I shake my head, not wanting to think about the times I was away from my dorm and had to sit through painful dinners with my parents. "T-That wasn't to do with you. That was because of–"

"It *was* to do with us. We didn't tell you because you didn't need to know. You were busy with school and football, and we weren't going to load all of our problems onto you," he explains.

"So you cheated on her? That doesn't make any fucking sense. From…" I stop, remembering the night I found the messages on my dad's phone. The day I drank myself stupid to try to forget it. "Those messages were going on for years."

He takes another generous sip, shrugging lazily as if this

doesn't mean anything to him. Maybe it doesn't. Maybe he's just as heartless as they come, and his excuse for cheating is that he was having problems with his wife instead of communicating like a normal fucking person.

"Maybe we were just good at hiding our problems from you. God knows we've been doing it for years," he says, his voice low and gruff. "Do you want to know why?" I just stare at him. "Because you wouldn't be able to handle it. You walk around with this idea that everything is going to be perfect and things will always work out, but the truth is, Wes, they just don't. And every time we try to prove that to you, you have a meltdown. Look how well that's been going since you found out about this."

I swallow. Hard. "What are you talking about?"

His head drops to the space between us. "Football, Wes."

"My performance has nothing to do with you and Mom," I say, which is only half true. Maybe what has happened has slightly contributed to this weird *something* that is in my chest. This annoying ache that won't leave me alone. I shrug one shoulder, ready to rip off the bandaid. "I don't think football is for me anymore."

I was half expecting my dad to stand up, push me against the wall, and banish me from the house. I grew up on football. It's always been the main hobby in my life, and I've never stepped in any other direction. Maybe I'm missing out on something good because I'm so used to following what is expected of me. But he doesn't do that. His gaze lifts to mine, and his eyes narrow. And for once, it doesn't feel like he's ready to lecture me or tell me to get my act together.

"What makes you think that?" he asks. His voice is gentle and soft. Reminding me of what he used to be like. Of what I used to look up to.

"I don't feel like I used to when I play," I admit.

Again, with his annoying as fuck soft voice, he asks, "And why's that?"

I roll my eyes. "Come on, this isn't some fucking up family therapy session. I just don't enjoy it, okay? I haven't for a while, *way* before any of this shit was going on. And maybe I've been too afraid to tell you that I want to quit because of how hard we've trained and how much…" My voice trails off when something catches in my throat. "How much you believe in me."

My dad blinks at me for a second. "I wouldn't want you to do something you don't enjoy."

His words are supposed to cure everything. They're supposed to heal the wound I've let get infected for months, but nothing happens. I still feel numb. Empty. Like I've got this big gaping hole in my chest, and nothing is ever going to be able to fill it again.

"Okay," is all I manage to get out.

"Okay?"

"Yes, okay. Now, what am I supposed to do? I told you how I feel, now what? How do I get back? How do I feel something that isn't fucking sadness or anger? I'm sick of it," I bite out, feeling truly and utterly lost. No road makes sense to me. No vision of my life looks clear. And I need it too. Badly. Desperately.

"I can't just hand that over to you. It doesn't work like that. If I could, I would, Wes," he says. "You navigating how you feel about football and your career, whatever that may be, is something you need to find. I can't push you because, clearly, that didn't work the first time. And I know you're angry with me and at the situation, and I am in no position to tell you what you can and can't do. You're… You're on your own, kid."

His words feel like a brick being thrown through my chest. It feels like my body is caving in on itself. I did not expect to have an existential crisis today. I reserve those for weekends or a long shower.

Suddenly, everything I had once envisioned for my life didn't exist. Everything that I do is constantly going to get messed up, and I'm never going to get anywhere with my life. Maybe I was born to just fuck everything up and have no real purpose than be the friend people lean on, the person people come to when they need some comedic relief because, beyond that, I'm nothing.

The words don't leave my mind on the entire ride back to my house. Music doesn't help, like usual. There's just a constant buzzing sound in my head. A constant reminder that I'm going to become a failure. A reminder that this feeling is going to last forever. The only thing that calms me is the sound of heavy rainfall on the hood of the car.

I step out of the car, my hands and legs shaking as if I've just run a marathon as the harsh raindrops beat down on me. I need a hot shower and to faceplant into my bed. Human interaction is the last thing on my mind, so when I hear the soft sound of Jarvis meowing in the yard, I welcome the distraction. I bet Connor left a window open, and this fucker has managed to get outside again. It's only when I listen closer that his meows sound more distressed and... higher up.

The automatic lights in the yard turn on, and when I look up at the massive tree, there Jarvis is, casually sitting in the tree in all his glory. Of course, today is going to get worse. The poor cat grips onto the tree branch for dear life, his fur completely drenched in the rain.

"Jarvis," I call up to him, thinking he'd respond. Of course, he doesn't. He's a stubborn idiot, and he's dumb enough to get himself killed. He's only got one eye, for God's sake. He's clearly not the sharpest tool in the shed. "Get down, boy. I'll even let you play with the laser if you do."

He doesn't budge.

I consider the option of climbing the tree myself. It's tall enough to reach the second-story window where the bathroom is, but too tall for me to climb. I don't have the traits of a cat to be able to grip onto the tree the way Jarvis has. The last time I checked, we didn't have a ladder long enough to reach him.

I try to encourage him to get down again. I'm practically

choking on the amount of rain that is pouring down on me. "Come on, Jar-Jar. You can't stay up there all night."

He doesn't move or even meow in response. He just grips the tree tighter when the wind shakes it, and he lets out a distressed cry. The noise almost breaks me. I'm having a shit day as it is, and the last thing I need is for something to happen to him. If *anything* happened, I'd never forgive myself.

As I'm about to say fuck it and climb the tree, the door swings open.

"Wes? What are you doing?" Nora's soft voice forces me to take a deep breath. I face to look at her and she's still wearing the same outfit she was earlier. Skin-tight jeans and a sweatshirt. The only difference is that her cute hairstyle from before is now a mess as if she's been rolling around or something.

"What are you still doing here?" I ask, shouting over the relentless wind.

"I fell asleep when I was watching a movie with Cat and Connor. They let me sleep on the couch." That explains the messy hair. "What are you doing?"

I sigh. "Jarvis is stuck, and I... I can't get him down."

"Just call a firefighter or something. Come inside. You're going to get sick." She's shivering just by being in the doorway and I fight the urge to just shove her back inside to where I know she'll be warm.

"Thanks for the concern, Sunshine, but he's my cat, and I'm going to get him down. I can't– I can't just leave him."

She steps out of the door, and I hold my hand up to her, making sure she stays put. "Wes."

"Just go back inside, Nora." I don't mean to sound harsh or rude, but it comes off that way, and the words are out of my mouth before I can stop them. She flinches, but she listens, taking a step back. I feel like the biggest asshole, but the last thing I want is to drag her into my shit with me. "Please."

"Okay," she says quietly. She glances up to the tree and then back down to me. "Okay."

After she shuts the door, I spend the next ten minutes freezing my ass off, trying to get this dumbass down from the tree. Maybe this is my calling. Maybe this is what I was made to do. I was made to try to convince my cat to jump into my arms by bribing him with all of his favorite things. Even that isn't going well. I need to do this one thing right. Just *one* thing.

When I've had enough of standing in the rain, moving around the tree, I run up into the house and to the bathroom window. He's still closer to the spine of the tree than the window, but it's worth a shot. I crack open the window as best I can, trying to move the smaller branches out of the way. I call his name a few times, urging him to get closer to me. Why the fuck is this so hard? He's supposed to trust me. He's supposed to want to come to me for safety. I'm supposed to be his beacon, and he's holding on to the branch, frightened as fuck as if I told him we're out of treats.

"Come on, buddy, you're killing me here," I shout, my voice wobbling from the cold. I'm pretty sure I have hypothermia by now. Jarvis just meows in response, but it's louder than before. "Come on. You can do it, Jar. I believe in you, okay?"

As if he can understand my words of encouragement, he slowly starts to shuffle a bit closer. He's still gripping onto the branch with all his legs, but he's making sure progress towards me.

"That's it," I coo. "You're almost there, Jar."

He continues moving. Just a *tiny bit further*, and I'll be able to reach out and pull him in. For both of our sakes, I hope he doesn't look down because even from the safety of the house, this height is terrifying. He keeps scooting and I finally reach out and pull him inside. I shut the window, blocking out the cold as I pull him to me.

"Jesus Christ, bud. You gave me a fucking heart attack," I sigh, pulling his cold body into mine. He nuzzles his chubby cheek into my chest, and I think that's his version of a thank you.

I place him down into the bathtub and do my very best to clean him up. Bath time is the *worst* with this one, but he seems to have learned his lesson and doesn't put up much of a fight. Once he's all washed and dried, I crack open the bathroom door and let him wander out. I follow behind him to go to my room to pick out some clean clothes until I bump into Nora.

"Jesus, woman," I mutter, pulling apart from her.

She just blinks up at me. Her eyes are dark and serious. I don't know why she didn't just go back to sleep when she went into the house. I didn't even bother to look in the living room when I came up to the bathroom. I just want today to be over with.

"What's going on, Wes?" Her voice is quiet within the silence of the house.

"Nothing."

I try to turn away from her, ready to go to my room and sleep, but she stops me. Her small hand rests on my damp cheek, and she lifts her head up to mine. I'm a few inches taller than her, so I have to crane my neck to look at her as she whispers. "Don't lie to me. You don't have to hide from me."

That's what does it.

Those words.

Those eyes.

That *mouth*.

I shake my head, but she only holds on to me tighter. "I'm just so fucking tired, Nor. Like, my brain is just *exhausted*."

Nora's mouth lifts. "I know. Being a cat dad is hard."

I narrow my eyes. "No, I mean–"

"I know what you mean," she says, laughing slightly. "You don't have to be perfect all the time, Wes, or feel like you have things together. That's impossible. Life is messy. Sometimes, things don't work out, or you lose your head a little and get into a dark place. I saw the look on your face when you left earlier, and I didn't say anything, but I've been beating myself up about it since you left." She shakes her head this time as if she needs to clear her thoughts. "When you get into a dark place, you've got to let the light in."

The tightness in my chest slowly starts to deflate. "That's what you are, Nora. The light."

I can't tell if she laughs or cries, but her arms are around my middle in an instant. She presses her head to my chest, and I can't help but hug her back. I hold her so close to me that it fucking hurts. My arms tighten around her as if she's the anchor weighing me down. As if she holds the answer to every problem I'll ever have. As if she just *gets* it. Gets *me*.

"You're going to get sick," I murmur, swallowing the lump in my throat as she snuggles her head deeper into my chest.

She sighs deeply. "Don't care."

I don't know how long we stay like that, just tangled up in each other, but it feels glorious. For a minute, I forget about everything that happened today. I forget about my dad and the team and football and my future. I forget about the noise in my head, and I'm only left with *her*. She clears my thoughts just by existing in my orbit.

I don't know which one of us pulls apart, but one of us does, and I clear my throat. "I was going to take a shower, but you can, uh, you can use it if you want? I didn't mean to get you wet." Her eyes sparkle. "Not like that. I mean–"

"Sure you didn't, big guy," she jokes. I let out a laugh, and she shakes her head. "I don't have any clothes here."

"You can wear something of mine."

Her head quirks as if she's thinking about questioning me on what I just suggested, but she thinks better of it. "Yeah, okay."

"I'll grab you a towel and some fresh clothes from my room," I say, and she nods, just standing there in the hallway. I turn to walk back before turning back around. "Oh, and bring your stuff from downstairs. You're sleeping in my room tonight."

She blinks at me. "What?"

I shrug. "I can't have my girlfriend sleeping on the couch."

I SWEAR girls take their sweet time when they're in the shower. She must be having a fucking pamper party in there because, by the time I'm in and out of the ensuite, she's still in the bathroom down the hall, humming softly.

Part of me thinks she's stalling so she doesn't have to sleep in the same room as me. We've slept in the same bed before. A lot of the time, we're drunk, and it's never a big deal. But me inviting her to sleep in my bed *is* a big deal. I don't like the thought of her sleeping on the couch when I'm dozing off on my king-sized mattress. It's just not fair. It's the gentlemanly thing to do. The *friendly* thing to do.

"Okay, don't laugh at me." I hear Nora's voice from the other side of my door.

"Why would I laugh?"

"Because you have ugly pyjamas," she grumbles.

"I'll have you know they were a great Secret Santa present from Sam," I say proudly. She huffs out a disbelieving laugh before she slowly pushes the door open. My jaw hangs open. "Holy shit."

The set she's wearing was indeed a gift from one of my teammates from a few years back. The white pants she's wearing have cut-out pictures of my gorgeous face on them, and the top is the same. They're a few sizes too big for her, and she's tried to roll up the pants, but she just looks ridiculous. Her hair is tied up into a messy bun, and it looks damp which could explain what was taking her so long. I don't think I've ever seen her look hotter. Which says a lot more about me than it does her.

"I told you not to laugh." She sulks, stalking towards me. I flip open the left side of the bed so she can get in.

"Oh, I'm not laughing, Sunshine. Trust me," I say, biting the inside of my cheek. She just rolls her eyes at me before she reluctantly slips in the bed. The big light is already off, so when she slips in beside me, the orange glow from my lamp gives her this whole dreamy look like she isn't real. Sometimes I don't think she is. As she makes herself comfortable, I get a whiff of her shampoo. Or... "Did you use my shampoo?"

She presses her lips together, her cheeks heating. "I had to take my chance to figure out why your hair is so soft."

I wish I could tease her about it, but all I can think about is Nora Bailey in my shower, using *my* shampoo on her hair. I adjust to lay on my back, letting out a noncommittal "Huh."

She turns to me. "You do know you could have let me sleep on the couch, right?"

"I know," I say, still looking at the ceiling.

"Then why didn't you?" I open my mouth to respond, but she cuts me off. "And *don't* say it's because of the whole fake dating thing."

"Fine," I bite out. "I just want you close to me. Is that a crime?"

"No," she giggles. I can feel her wiggling under the covers. She still manages to be chaotic even when she's sleeping. "It's like we're having a sleepover."

"An *adult* sleepover," I say, and I turn to wink at her. She scoffs, turning her back to me. Lucky for her, I just get another smell of the shampoo and my body wash that makes her feel like mine.

"You're disgusting," she mutters, and I can just tell she's smiling.

I turn my back to her, too, staring at the blank wall. Just knowing that she's in my bed with me relaxes the nerves in my stomach. I settle in the moment for a second, and when a thought pops into my mind, I hope she hasn't fallen asleep.

"Hey, Nora?"

She shifts under the sheets. She lets out a soft snort as she mocks, "Hey, Wes."

"Ryan's an idiot."

"What?"

"Ryan's an idiot, Nora," I manage to say, my voice low and quiet. "If I had you, I'd never let you go."

She's quiet for a beat. The silence stretches over us, and I feel like I've said the wrong thing. I know her brain is over analyzing everything I just said, and all she says is, "Oh."

"Yeah, oh," I tease, shaking my head to get rid of whatever stupid thing I was about to say next. Instead, I settle on the only sane response. The *friendly* thing to say.

"Goodnight, Sunshine."

"Goodnight, Wes."

TWENTY
WES
QUARTER LIFE CRISIS

THERE IS nothing like the atmosphere before a football game —a semi-final one at that. I don't think I've seen so many pissed-off faces in my life. We've been breaking our backs all week training and trying our hardest to work together, but nothing is fucking working.

My dad has laid off me slightly since our talk, but there's still this look in his eye like he's waiting for me to snap. Honestly, I'm waiting for it too. I have no idea what will happen after this game, and I have no clue what I'm going to do with my life. Maybe I don't have to have a backup plan even when everybody else does.

The expression on Connor's face right now could give my dad a run for his money.

I've hardly spent a day away from Connor since we were born. Even though I can torment him for my own personal gain, I love him like a brother. He's always treated me like that, but he's also got this overprotective energy that makes me feel like he's talking down to me and like I can't figure my shit out on my own. I know he means well, but I feel like such a fuck-up compared to him.

"Hey, look," he starts. *Finally.* He's ready to head out onto the field, but he's been circling me for the past few minutes, and I just need him to spit out whatever it is he has to say to me. "I want to apologise for the other day. I've got no right to tell you how to fix your relationship with your dad. I don't want to be fighting with you, Wes."

I look up at him from my position on the bench. "We're not fighting."

"We're not?"

"No, because surprisingly, Connor, what's going on isn't about you or what you said," I explain, leaning down to do up my laces.

"Then what's going on? You've been shutting yourself off from me, from *everyone*, for weeks. I know you're going to hate me saying this, but I'm worried about you." My head snaps up to him, and I try my hardest to keep my cool.

"Don't be." He just continues staring at me and I take a deep breath. Might as well rip off the Band-Aid now, I guess. "I've been thinking about it, and I don't think football is for me anymore."

Connor scoffs. "What are you talking about?"

"I don't want what you want, Con," I explain, leaning back. "I don't want to go into the NFL and work myself until there's nothing left of me. This isn't… This isn't fun for me anymore."

He laughs incredulously, shaking his head as if this is a joke to him. "Are you being serious?"

My jaw clenches. "Yes, I'm being serious."

"Then what are you going to do? Quit? Because I don't think that Lit degree is going to get you very far," he says, still shaking his head. Is *he* being serious?

I stand to my full height. "What does that mean?"

"Nothing. I just–"

"Look, if you don't believe that I can make something of myself outside of football, I'd rather you just say that." Connor just blinks at me. "Exactly." My dad's voice booms through the walls as he beckons Connor to get out of the changing room. I tilt my head at him. "Seems like you've got some *very* serious captain business to take care of, pretty boy."

He grabs his helmet from the bench, muttering, "Don't be like this, Wes."

I barge past him, shoving him in the shoulder. "Let's just get on with the fucking game already."

I've never been more agitated and on edge in my life. I've spent the last few days since talking with my dad, trying to find something else I can do for my last year of Drayton in the fall. The more days that pass, the closer I feel like I'm going to get to graduation with no direction after that. I hardly know where I'm going after this game, never mind when graduation comes.

I swear I try my hardest to focus. I correct every mistake Coach throws at me, and even with the triumphant cheers from the crowd, nothing is clicking. It's a fucking mystery how we've managed to pull through for this long. It seems like other teams across the country are dealing with the same decline we have, but we've still managed to come on top.

Until we don't.

I hang my head low when we're back in the locker rooms. I can't look at my dad right now. He might be okay with me not wanting to do this anymore, but that doesn't stop him from looking at me and the rest of the team with a disappointed look on his face.

"To say I'm disappointed is an understatement." My dad's voice echoes off the walls. We're all eerily silent as we peel off our clothes, and the only sound is the steady thrum of the showers and my dad's voice. "I've been coaching some of you since you came to the campus whilst you were still in high school. I thought we were better than this, but apparently not. That is the worst performance I have witnessed in my life."

I flinch at his words.

Sam sighs beside me. "What did you want us to do, coach? We tried."

"You didn't try hard enough, Cho. If you did, you wouldn't

be sitting in here with your heads down looking like abandoned puppies," Coach booms. "You have the next rest of the month to recover from whatever the fuck that was, but I want to see you back in the weight room and on the field by February. If I don't see any improvements by March, I'll be reconsidering some of your positions on the team. Have I made myself clear?"

"Yes, Coach," we all respond in unison.

I thought the silence would break once my dad left the room, but it didn't. We continue silently working around each other, getting ready to return home. I couldn't even bear to look at Nora and the girls in the crowd. I don't want them to see me like this. If I thought I was at rock bottom before, I've got another thing coming.

"Still on it to sit and cry, Red?" Sam asks Mike as he walks around the benches in his boxers. He sits opposite us, shaking out his ginger hair before pulling on some sweats from beside him.

"Honestly? It doesn't sound like such a bad idea," Red mumbles.

"Come on, don't act like that, Mikey," Connor says. He's been awfully quiet, considering he usually has a lot to say when it comes to the team. He looks around at us, and the pretentious look on his face is enough to make me reel. "We've just got to train better. I was thinking of holding some sessions with the Freshman to see if they'll listen to me over coach. It's a long shot, but it might work."

Sam, Oli and Red hum in agreement. "Are you sure you're cut out for it?" Sam asks, pointing his water bottle at Connor. "I mean, they're like fucking children, dude. It'll take a lot of work."

"I'm up for it," Connor says confidently. "With a bit more work, we'll be perfect."

I scoff. "Not everything is going to be perfect, Connor. You know that, right?"

He narrows his eyes at me. "Just because you're ready to

throw yourself and your own career under the bus doesn't mean you have to drag everyone else down with you."

"I'm not doing that," I argue. Connor stands then, coming right in front of me. I lean back, crossing my arms against my chest. "Got something to say, bud?"

"Yeah, actually," he challenges. "If what you said before the game was true, did you mess up on purpose, huh? It seems fitting that you suddenly want to tell me about how little you care right before our semi-final just so you can fuck it up for the rest of us."

"Are you being serious right now?" I stand, too, squaring up to him. The whole team is watching us, ready for something to happen. He's been getting on my last nerve recently, and if he carries on like this, it's not going to be pretty.

Connor tilts his head to the side. "If you don't care, why are you here at all?"

I jab my finger into his chest, signaling him to back the fuck up. "No, Connor, I do care. I just don't *only* care about football."

"Yeah? What else do you care about?"

I throw my hands out in exasperation. "I don't know! Anything that isn't this. Traveling, swimming, helping people, making other people happy. Just something that is fun, and this…" I gesture to the room around us. "This isn't fun. The way I feel like I'm suffocating out there isn't what I want. And I know it won't last forever, but life is way too fucking short for me to stick around with this."

"You can't go around expecting life to be fun and games, Wes," Connor says in that condescending voice of his. "You just need to work harder and put more effort in."

"I'm not doing that. You're not listening to anything I'm saying because you're so fucking used to everyone agreeing with you, but guess what, Connor? Not everyone wants what you want. I don't want to run around on a field with a ball in my hands forever. And you can't expect me to just go along with you like I have done since we were kids. I'm not doing that anymore."

The words rush out of me, and I can't tell if I'm going to punch him in the face or break down in tears. I grab the rest of my shit from the bench and shove them into my bag. I need to get out of here and fast.

Connor's in front of me when I turn around. "Hey, come on. I didn't mean it like that, Wes. I'm just worried about you."

I brush past him, and he follows me out of the locker rooms. "Well, stop worrying."

"Hey," he says, grabbing onto my arm and pulling me back into him. "I just want what's best for you."

"I want what's best for me, too, believe it or not. I'm grabbing my shit, and I'm staying at my mom's house until I go to New York," I say, pushing his hand off me.

Connor takes a deep breath, tilting his head to the ceiling before he faces me again. "Be safe, okay? Don't give Nora shit for whatever happened just then."

"I'd never do that to her, Connor," I say, finally getting away from them.

IT FEELS like I haven't slept in weeks by the time I pull up to my mom's apartment. Being away from the house is exactly what I need right now. I need to start getting my head on right before I lose myself in a spiral.

These things just happen, and the sooner I realize that, the better. Everyone goes through moments like these in life where the world feels like it's ending and nothing is going to plan. But somehow, you make it through. You *have* to make it through.

"What am I going to do with you, *Leinster*?" My mom whispers as she sets another cup of hot cocoa in front of me. We're both sitting on the couch, and it's well into the next morning. Since I got here with Jarvis, she's given me a new haircut – *finally* – we've ordered pizza, and we've been watching another French soap opera.

"I don't even know what I'm doing with myself," I sigh, leaning my head back on the couch.

"Is football completely out of the question?" she asks tentatively.

"For now, definitely. I can't see myself on that field again."

She hums. "What makes you happy? What makes your heart... I don't know. *Flutter?*" I snort, and she swats my knee. "I'm being serious. There's got to be something that makes you feel like that. It's how I fell in love with reading."

"I don't know. I just like making people happy. That's the only way I can describe it, and I don't exactly think I'm funny enough to be a full-time comedian. I need something I can get a degree in so I feel more stable," I explain.

"Have you ever thought about teaching, maybe? You were really good with those kids at the football camp with your dad last spring," she says, her blue eyes hopeful.

I shrug. "No one's going to listen to me. It was fine when Dad was there, but apart from that, I'm just a big joke."

"You don't have to be, Wes, and I think that's what you're forgetting," she says softly. "You can be something other than the funny guy, you know? I've seen every side of you, and you're the most natural when you're helping."

"I guess."

"We don't have to figure this out now, but you'll find it, *Schatz*," my mom says, and it's like she can just magic all my worries away. "I think you need a little break from your mind and the worries here, including me."

"I'm not worried about you, Mom," I say.

She tilts her head to the side. "Really? Then why have you been checking up on me nearly every day since I moved in here?"

"Because I love you?"

"I know you do, and I love you too. But you should never have to worry about me. That's my job, okay?" There's a soft smile on her mouth, and I don't know why it breaks my heart. I want her to smile at me for real. Smile the same way she used to. Not this facade that she's doing to make me feel better. "Just because you think I'm going a bit crazy on my own doesn't mean you need to be worried."

I swallow back the emotion lodged in my throat. "I'm always going to worry about you, mom."

Her eyes widen as a grin splits across her face. "Ha! See, you admitted it."

I don't even bother to argue with her. I just let her think she's caught me out on something because the future feels a little less daunting when she pulls me into her side. I know that there are always going to be people pushing me forward, even when I don't know where I'm going.

TWENTY-ONE
NORA
OUTER SPACE

I'VE SPENT the last week and a half trying to pack my suitcase for the New York trip. I don't have long I've got until Wes comes to pick me up, but I've had a million meltdowns over what to bring. We're only going for a couple of days, but I need to look my best. Who knows? A casting agent could casually be walking around and want me to star in an upcoming blockbuster. I change my outfit too many times on a daily basis, and I can only imagine how much worse it's going to be in my dream city.

Elle and Cat have been trying to help me pack, but they keep pushing the minimalist agenda onto me, and I completely disagree with their suggestions. If I'm going to spend a few days in my idea of heaven, I've got to look phenomenal. Even if that means packing over half of my wardrobe.

"Do you really think you need to bring your ukulele?" Elle asks, shuffling through my overflowing suitcase.

"You never know when musical inspiration could strike," I say, shrugging.

"Right," she whistles, and I catch her rolling her eyes at Cat, and they both snicker. She picks up a pink lingerie set I'm bringing and hangs the bra off one finger. "And what excuse do you have for this?"

"I want to feel pretty, Elle. Don't judge me." I snatch it off her and shove it back into my suitcase.

Cat snorts. "For Wes?"

"No, actually, for *me*," I argue. "Anything could happen in New York. I might even give him a show if he's good."

Cat's eyebrows lift in surprise. "I'm pretty sure he would pass out, Nor. I'd save that for someone else."

I shrug, folding up the last of the t-shirts before shoving them into a storage cube. I'm fully aware that I've gone overboard with the packing, but it'll make me less stressed when I'm there. The only issue is going to be repacking this after we've spent a few days there.

"So, any updates on your sexploits?" I ask Elle as she fiddles with a plushie she found in my room. My room is filled with them. It's like a tiny army of assorted fruits and animals taking over.

"Nope," she says, her smile still bright. "Something needs to happen this summer, though. I don't think I can stomach going into my last year here as a virgin."

"You don't have to rush, you know," Cat says, poking her in the knee. "Everyone goes at their own speed. And when you find someone, it'll be worth it."

"I know, but everyone says that before they've already done it. I mean, you can't really complain because Connor is fucking your brains out every other day," she says, sighing. She shoots me a look when I gag. "Sorry, Nor."

"It's cool," I say. "And you're both right in a way. I think you need to find out what works for you, Elle-Belle."

"I don't know what I want," she huffs, running her hands through the ends of her curly hair. "I don't want a relationship because I've never had that. I don't just want a physical thing because I've never had that either. I don't know how much time I'm going to have if I'm going back to dance camp this summer. I just want to try things out without things getting complicated, but that seems impossible. Don't get me wrong, vibrators are lifesavers, but I want to experience it for real. At least *once* before senior year."

"We get you," I say, squeezing Elle's hand. "And we're here to help you with whatever you need. We're your wing women, remember?"

"When I figure that out, you'll be the first to know," she says, laughing. Cat throws her a toothy smile, and I smile back.

"Okay," I whistle, looking at my case. "Let's get this sorted so I don't miss the plane."

We get to work and manage to shut the suitcase. Well, Elle and I had to sit on it first whilst Cat zipped it up. When I roll it into the living room, waiting for Wes, I feel lighter already. We might not be thousands of feet up in the air yet, but just the thought of traveling excites me. All of the stress with the show and with Ryan is what I'm leaving here. For a few days at least.

Wes turns up on time, and I jump to my feet when he opens the door. "Ready to go, Sunshine?" he asks, leaning his hip against the counter as he crosses his arms against his chest.

He looks different somehow. I haven't seen him much over the week, but Connor told me that he's been staying at his mom's house. Neither of them has told me why, but it must be doing him some good. His face is fresh and clean. His gray sweatpants sit comfortably on his hips, and my mouth almost – and I mean *almost* – waters. He looks so comfortable. And his hair looks different.

I walk closer to him, circling my finger in a spinning motion. "Turn around."

"Why? You wanna see my ass?" he smirks, looking down at me.

I roll my eyes. "No. Just turn around." He does as I ask, and he turns. Holy fuck. I thought I was wrong, but I'm not. Wes has naturally wavy brown hair, but he never really styles it. Sometimes, he gets it trimmed, but never like this. *This* is something else. "You got a mullet."

It's not long, but it's shaven in all the right places, and it looks insanely good on him. He turns back around and shoves his hands in his pockets. "I told you I'd do anything for you, Sunshine."

Confusion fogs my brain. "I didn't tell you to do that."

"Yes, you did. In your sleep," he explains. I just blink at him, and he laughs. "Remember? A few weeks ago, when you stayed over."

I cross my arms against my chest. "I don't sleep talk."

"Well, you do when you're sleeping with me. Must be because of all of my hair products that you used. Got you dreaming about me and shit," he says lazily. I roll my eyes. "Do you like it?"

"Yeah. You look good," is all I manage to get out. Who am I kidding? This man looks hot. Like, hotter than I've ever seen him. "It suits you."

He steps closer to me, his mouth lifting up. "Yeah?"

"Mm-hm." I press my lips together, smiling brightly. "Now help me with this suitcase so we can get on our way, big guy."

GETTING on the plane was a lot less stressful than I thought it would be. Surprisingly, Wes is a good travel buddy, and he didn't make me want to pull his hair out when we went through security. He *is* making me antsy now as we're buckled into our seats for the four-hour plane ride.

He wanted to sit by the window, but I'm not so sure that was a good idea, considering his fear of heights. He's looked anxious since he sat down, and I don't know how to pull him back to reality. I haven't flown much, but it doesn't bother me when I do. If I close my eyes enough, I can make it feel like a train ride in my mind. Wes hasn't got that memo, apparently.

"Do you want to hold my hand?" I suggest once I've had enough of his fidgeting.

"Huh?" He's still looking out the window, his hand gripping the armrest between us.

"Do you want to hold my hand?" I repeat, and he turns to me. "You said you didn't like heights, so I can imagine how hard this is going to be for you."

His eyes narrow. "Should I be concerned that you're being nice to me? Are you and the pilot in cahoots, and you're going to crash the plane?"

I bark out a laugh. "Oh, shut up. I'm always nice to you."

"You're not really putting up a good fight, Sunshine," he mutters, tutting at me. I hold out my hand to him. He looks at it and then back to me. After he's finished debating what he should do, his huge hand slips into mine, and I link our fingers together. He sighs and rests against the headrest.

"Better?" I ask.

"Much better," he replies, a loopy grin on his face.

AN HOUR into the flight Wes's hand is still clasped onto mine. I'm sure he can tell that both of our hands are sweaty now, but he isn't moving. Trying to read a book with one hand is not for the weak, so I've had to listen to music for most of the journey. Before I doze off into another nap, I spot a tiny hand peeking through the seats in front of us. I can't help but smile at the tiny human on the other side. I've always loved kids. They're like little comedians without even realizing it. Wes and I give each other a look before the hand turns into half of a little boy's face as he squishes his cheeks between the seats.

I don't know how long he switches between waving at us and pushing his face between the seats, but Wes and I can't stop laughing. I can't tell if the kid knows he's making us laugh so hard or if that's just how he is.

"Hi," he says when he chooses what he wants to do.

"Hiya, buddy," Wes says, his voice extra sweet and gentle as he leans forward a little. "Are you spying on us?"

The little boy nods. Then he shakes his head. Then he nods again. His eyes widen before he decides what he's doing. "No. My mommy said it's bad to spy on people, so I'm not spying. Promise."

"Okay," I say slowly. "Then what *are* you doing?"

He sighs heavily like he really needs us to hear his frustration. I try not to snort. "I'm scared," he whispers. "And my mommy's sleeping. And she sleeps through *everything*. Even a plane crash."

Wes scoffs. "Well, that's not going to happen."

The kid frowns. "Says who?"

"Says me." Wes's smile is bright as he leans in further to the kid, and my chest does a weird flip thing. "Can I tell you a secret?" The little boy nods, his eyes fresh with tears that haven't fallen yet. "I'm scared, too."

Wes leans back as the kid gasps. "Of what? You're a grown-up. You can't be scared."

"Of course grown-ups can be scared," Wes says before lifting our interlocked hands up and giving them a shake. "See? I'm having to hold my girlfriend's hand so I don't start crying." The boy's mouth pops open in an 'O' shape as he marvels at the two of us. Wes shakes his head. "But I'm scared of something *worse* than crashing. What if we turn into a spaceship and end up flying into outer space, and there's aliens that live there!"

The kid's eyes widen, and his face turns a deep red. "That would be so cool!"

Wes gasps, holding our hands to his chest in fake shock. I can't help but continue watching them interact. He's a complete natural. "What? No, it wouldn't. The aliens would attack us."

"No, they won't," the kid argues. "I'll protect us."

"You will?" Wes asks, hopeful.

"Yeah! My dad and I play astronauts and aliens *all* the time. I know what to do!"

Wes sighs, wiping his free hand across his forehead. "Oh, thank goodness. That makes me feel a lot better."

"Me too," the kid replies before turning back around. And when I look back over at Wes, it seems like the interaction has actually calmed him down, too, because he doesn't grip my hand as tight. Instead, he just rubs small circles of his thumb against my hand right until we land.

BY THE TIME we're in the elevator to our room at the hotel, my messages start to come through, and my heart drops at my dad's text. My head is already spinning from being in the air for a few hours and the rush of the airport has finally caught up with me.

> **DADDY-O**
>
> I hope you got there safe. Sorry for not being able to be with you, but I upgraded your and Wes's room for you. My treat. Have fun, honey.

AS EXPECTED, my dad upgraded us to the couple's suite. So, instead of two single beds, there's one large king-size mattress in the middle of the room with rose petals in the shape of a heart. When Wes walks over to the bedside table, fawning over the bottle of champagne, I have to resist the urge to roll my eyes.

"Don't get any ideas, Wesley," I say, dropping my carry-on at the end of the bed.

"And what kind of ideas would those be?" he asks, reading the label on the bottle like he actually knows what it means.

"Alcoholic ideas," I say, pointing to the bottle in his hands and then to the bed. "Cuddling and spooning ideas."

"What?! No spooning?! My day has been ruined," he exclaims, placing the bottle back down before sitting on the bed. "If there's no spooning, then what's the point? At least that way, you won't hog the covers."

I scoff. "I am *not* a cover hogger."

"I hate to break it to you, but you are," he says as I walk over towards him. "You sleep talk, you hog the covers, *and* you always end up sprawled all over me whenever we share a bed. If anything, *I'm* the victim in this situation."

My cheeks heat at the thought of sharing a bed with him, especially if that's really how I sleep. Knowing Wes, he'd never really complain about me sleeping on top of him. I bet there's some weird part of him that enjoys it, which is mortifying for me.

"Whatever," is what I settle on saying instead.

This trip was never meant to be a romantic escape, despite my dad's last-minute attempts to spin it that way. But can't complain because the window of our twenty-first-floor hotel room, the New York City skyline stretches out like a vast, twinkling canvas. *That's* the real reason I'm here.

As I gaze out at the city, my eyes light up with excitement. It's a quiet moment, yet the energy of a thousand possibilities buzzes in the air like electricity. The city feels like it's pulsing at my fingertips, and I'm eager to dive into the heartbeat of it all.

We spend the rest of the evening unpacking our stuff before we order room service. It's like we've been floating around all day, but when the food arrives and we're sitting on the floor watching a random game show, everything finally feels settled. We're quiet as we eat, and I couldn't think of anything better. Still, there's a thought nagging at me that I can't tell to go away.

"Hey, Wes?"

The side of his mouth tips up. "Hey, Nora," he mocks before giving me a suspicious glance as he takes a sip from his drink.

We're sitting across from each other, our carefully selected platter covering the space between us.

I rip the Band-Aid right off. "What's going on with you? And I know you're going to say it's fine and that I don't need to worry about you, but you're my best friend, and I *do* worry about you. Since that day we were at your mom's house, you've been off. And you've not brought up the semis once since the game." I sigh as I lean over and clasp both of my hands at the sides of his head, shaking him. "Just let me into your brain, dude."

"Okay," he whispers as I continue shaking him. I slowly drop my hands and shuffle away as he closes his eyes for a second before opening them. "I haven't brought up football because I'm glad that we lost."

I take a second to process his words. "What?"

He meets my gaze. "I don't want to play football anymore, Nora."

"Oh," I whisper. I catch the hurt in his eyes, and I try for a softer approach. "That's okay. You don't have to keep playing if you don't want to."

He sighs. "I know, but if I'm not playing, then what am I?"

"You're... Just Wes."

"*Just Wes?*" he repeats, grimacing.

"Not in a bad way. I mean, you're still *you* without football. You're not your sport or your passion. No one is." I explain, putting it a bit gentler.

"I guess." He shrugs, reaching over for a chip. "I don't have a plan for my life like you do. I think I never did, and now I'm realizing that I've never been good at anything else, and maybe it's too late."

"It's not too late."

He shrugs, running a hand through his hair. "Let's just forget about it for the next few days, okay? When we get back, you can do all your manic overthinking thing then."

"I don't do that," I argue.

"Sure, you don't," he teases, throwing me a sarcastic wink.

"I just want you to be happy, Wes."

"I am happy, Nora. Being here, with you, I'm happy. You've just got to trust me." He holds my gaze, and I try my hardest to believe him. I want so desperately to believe him. "Okay?"

"Okay," I say.

I don't press him anymore on it as we clean up all of our shit, and I go in the shower. I let the clean water wash away all of my feelings and anxieties for the day. I don't want to spend the entire trip thinking about what's going to go wrong or what's going on in Wes's head. Well, that's what I keep telling myself anyway because my mind is still spinning once I'm settled in bed and the door to the bathroom opens.

Wes walks out in nothing but his boxers, and I don't know how I don't burst into flames. I've seen him topless before, but this somehow feels different. I'm blaming it on the sleep deprivation because there is no way I'm absolutely eye-fucking Wes Mackenzie right now. It's like I've just noticed how tall he is. How thick his thighs are. How broad his shoulders are. How toned his stomach is and how many fucking abs he has.

When I think he's going to put me out of my misery and put on a shirt, he doesn't. He just walks around like he fucking owns this place. I sit up properly, placing my book on the bedside table. "What are you doing?"

He turns to me, stretching as he scratches his stomach. "Going to bed. What are *you* doing?"

"Since when do you sleep without a shirt on?" I gawk, trying my absolute hardest to keep eye contact with him as he walks to my side of the bed.

"Since always," he says, smirking. He catches the way my cheeks flush, and he tilts his head to the side. "What? Is it a problem?"

"No. *No*. I just forgot you have all… that." My own words make me cringe, and I clear my throat. When I was with Ryan, it felt wrong to even look at another man besides him. Clearly, that was never a problem for him to be looking at other girls. Looking at Wes now, I want to punch myself for not looking before.

"All what? A chest?" he teases, gesturing to himself.

I roll my eyes. "You know what I mean."

My breath hitches when he slides onto the bed beside me. The heat of his body sends electric jolts down my spine, and I try my best to ignore it as I slide down until I'm on my back. Wes does nothing to put any distance between us and instead cages me in with one arm on the side of my head, the entirety of him obstructing my view.

"I don't think I know what you mean," he teases, brushing the hair that's fallen in front of my face. My mouth instantly dries. "You're going to have to spell it out for me, Stargirl."

If he wants to play, I'm more than happy to put on a show.

I bring my index finger to the top of his chest, feeling the warmth right on my fingertip. "I mean," I drawl, slowly dragging my finger down the middle of his chest. He's flexing beneath my touch, and it makes me feel like a fucking God. "I guess I'm just so incredibly turned on by you. All this muscle is really getting me going."

His eyes flash to mine. "Yeah?"

"Yeah," I echo. I continue trailing my finger down his stomach, and he doesn't move. I tip my mouth right to his, and he's so close I can practically taste him. He leans into me, but I keep the game going right until I punch him in the stomach. He groans, clutching his abdomen as he keels over onto his side of the bed. "Sweet dreams, Wes."

TWENTY-TWO
WES/NORA
TOURIST SHIT

WES

I DIDN'T SLEEP a fucking wink last night.

Not only is my brain still on overdrive from losing the game, but I haven't been able to stop thinking about Nora touching my chest the way she did last night. Having her body so close to mine, her skin on me, was maddening. I don't know how I managed to get up this morning, managing to convince myself that I only wanted a friendship from her. We've got a lot to do in the next few days, so there's no point in wasting time thinking about things I definitely should *not* be thinking about.

"Are you ready to be a small-town boy in a big city?" Nora teases, tying up the Converse that I got her in the chair across from the bed.

"As I'll ever be," I reply. Her face splits into an uncontrollable grin. "Are you?"

"I was *born* ready, Wesley. We're going to be the most touristy tourists to ever tourist," she says, jumping to her feet to collect her tote bag that she dropped near the door.

I laugh as I swing open the door, holding out my hand to her. "The Empire State Building awaits, Miss Bailey."

She giggles, clasping her hand in mine as we walk out of the door. "Ooh, I like the sound of that."

"Yeah?"

"Hell yeah," she giggles, hooking her arm into mine. "I feel like royalty."

"I'll keep that in mind," I say. When I look down at her, I see that *real* Nora Bailey smile. Just the look on her face makes my chest tighten, and my clothes suddenly feel two sizes too small for me. It makes me want to pull her right into my chest, feel her close to me, and see if she could transfer some of that energy into me.

A huge part of me is glad that Mark backed out on the trip. Something about being with her in her dream city makes me one lucky motherfucker. I love watching her come to life. I love watching the way her whole face transforms when she sees something she likes or when she's simply in my presence. She's able to calm the storm in my brain by existing.

Well, that was until she tried to give me a heart attack at the top of the Empire State Building. For someone who doesn't like heights, New York is not the place I should be.

"You okay, Wessy?" she asks, beaming up at me with her back to the glass, meaning I can see the top of every single building from our view. Something churns in my stomach, and I cough to swallow the feeling.

"Never been better," I bite out.

"You sure? You look like you're about to puke," she teases, poking me in the stomach. I swat her hands away from me, pinning them together with one hand.

"Stop," I warn.

"It's okay," she coos, "I'm not deathly afraid of vomit like Elle. I can handle it."

I roll my eyes. "Just shut up and look out the damn window."

She snorts before she turns around and does as I asked. Her chestnut curls distract me for a second as I watch her watch the skyline. It's still pretty early in the afternoon, but from the way she's looking out at the scene, I take a second to see the city from her eyes. This is the place where she wants to spend the rest of her life. The place where she can see herself getting the career she's always dreamed of. The place where she'll call me from when I'm doing whatever the fuck I'm doing back in Colorado.

She glances back at me as if she felt my gaze on her. "Look at this view."

"I'm looking," I whisper, keeping my eyes locked with hers.

"You're not," she argues, letting out a breathy laugh. "Look at the *actual* view, Wes. I know you're a bit scared, but you'll regret it if you don't look."

She's got this serious look on her face like she really believes that this is the first and only time we'll be here together. I'm sure I'll have a better look next time, but right now, I just want to bathe in her glory. So, I say, "I think my view is much better."

She scoffs, hitting me in the arm "Shut up."

I finally take a better look at what she's making a big fuss over. It's pretty, but it's not as pretty as her. I don't think there's anything that can compare to her. That can compare to her inner and outer beauty. There's nothing in my life that is more special and worthy of my time than Nora Bailey. And when she realizes that, I don't think I'm strong enough to take the heartbreak. So, I shove all my feelings for her down into the depths of my stomach and grab her hand. When her hand melts into mine and she squeezes it, I take a deep breath.

"Thank you," I whisper.

She turns to me. "For what?"

"For letting me come with you and for holding my hand," I say roughly. I don't think I thank her enough for all the shit she's put up with for me. She always makes sure I know how much she cares about me, even when I shut her out.

"You don't have to thank me. Besides, I can't let my boyfriend freak out because he's afraid of heights," she says before she steps into me a little more. "I'll always hold your hand, Wes."

"Always?"

"Yeah, always," she says and my heart stops. "Plus, your hand was basically stuck to mine the entire flight. Sweaty palms and all. I've gotten used to it."

"You were doing so well up until that last part," I mutter.

She rolls her eyes before she turns back to the view, and I still have my eyes on her.

IF I HAD KNOWN how busy New York *really* was, I don't think I would have come. I'm not bad with crowds, but not only is it crowded and smelly, it's *loud* too. Everything about the city back home feels like nothing compared to this. Every sense feels like it's at full volume, and just existing in this atmosphere feels like I'm in some sort of simulation.

After getting the subway to Times Square and grabbing hotdogs when we got here, I've been trailing behind Nora as she walks around this city like she fucking owns it. I would be lying if I said that being here doesn't suit her personality. She was made for a big city like this, and I feel like a selfish motherfucker for getting to be in her spotlight like this.

We've spent the entire day looking around at the giant screens, taking in the awful smell and the lights that are giving us both headaches. After shopping around and collecting anything that Nora believed her parents would like, we perched ourselves on a sidewalk as we waited for our Uber to arrive. I told her we could grab a cab and save ourselves the embarrassment, but apparently, she 'needed to experience this at least once.' I can't complain much, though. My feet are aching, and

I'm more than ready to hit the shower and go straight to sleep when we get back to the hotel.

"When's it going to get here?" she asks me, stretching her legs out in front of her. We chose the least busy street possible, so there's a slim chance her feet will get run over, but it still scares the fuck out of me.

I lean forward, scooping her legs up until she wraps her arms around her knees. Nora turns to me, unimpressed. "Soon," I say, quickly checking my phone.

"I'm getting impatient," she grumbles.

"Yeah, no shit. Is the city life tiring you out already?" I bump my shoulder into hers, and she bumps me back before jumping to her feet.

"It could never," she screams.

She spins in a full circle, the bags of souvenirs we've collected over the day falling off one of her arms. I just watch her in her element, crossing my arms against my chest before she slowly sinks back down next to me.

She links her arm into mine, resting her head against my shoulder as she sighs heavily. "God, I can't wait to live here." She glances up at me with a dreamy look in her eyes.

"I can't wait to visit you when you're here."

She lets out another happy sigh. "Imagine it, Wes," she starts, looking out into the town in front of us. "I can show you around like I'm a real local. We'll go for dinner at my favorite restaurant. You'll be a gentleman and open all the doors for me. Your wife will call you, and you'll leave early so you can get back in time to tuck your kids in bed. And—"

"What will you do?"

My interruption shrugs. "I dunno. Go back to my apartment, maybe? Get high with my show friends?"

I let out a chuckle as she beams up at me. "No husband?"

Her features grow softer, and I feel like I've said the wrong thing. I don't like the thought of her being on her own here, even if it's just her hypothetical future. There's no future I can imagine myself in where we're apart. And just the idea of that fucking scares me more than being on top of the Empire State Building.

She shakes her head. "No one's going to marry me, Wes," she whispers. Those words coming out of her mouth feel like a punch straight to the stomach. How does she not know how insanely special she is? How incredibly fascinated I am by her. She takes a deep breath. "I'll swear off men by the time I'm thirty, trust me. I don't want to be with someone who holds me back."

I swallow. "What if you find someone who doesn't hold you back?"

Her mouth twitches into a smile. "Then I might just keep them."

The air between us thickens, and I think for the hundredth time if I should just say fuck it and kiss her. If it takes me doing that for her to finally get it into her head that I've wanted to date her for real for years, then I'd do it. But I value our friendship too much, and the thought of being rejected by Nora Bailey is enough to keep my hands to myself.

NORA

Is it possible to feel like you're floating? It's like I've taken a dip into an alternate reality because this doesn't feel like real life. I've spent so many days lying awake, thinking of what it would be like if I got to step foot in my dream place. I might have imagined being with my dad instead of Wes, but his company is just as good, if not better.

As touristy as today has been, I can't wait to spend days in my future doing exactly this. Shopping until my feet hurt. Picking up burgers or hotdogs from my favorite food stands. Spontaneously going to see a show *just because*. Sitting on sidewalks whilst I wait for our Uber to come. I want all the small things about this place and all the big things. I want it all.

We've been waiting for the Uber for almost ten minutes

before my phone starts to ring. Wes nods at me to answer it since he was in the middle of telling me why they should make a musical out of the Spiderman franchise.

I look down at the caller ID, and my heart stutters in my chest when I see my agent's contact name.

"Hey, Nora! How are you?" Max's shrill voice shocks me back to the reality of being at home. Unemployed. Seemingly untalented. Having to do a show with someone I can't stand.

I shake my head to get rid of the thoughts. "Hi, I'm great. How about you?"

Max lets out a dreamy sigh on the other end. "I'm great. I just wanted to check in on how that tape for the A24 project is going. It's really important you get it in by the end of next month. I don't want them to think you've lost interest... Unless you *have* lost interest. In that case, you need to let me know."

"No, no, no," I say quickly. Wes shoots me a look, and I wave my hand dismissively. "I haven't lost interest. I'm working on the tape, and I just haven't had time to rehearse outside of classes and... uh, stuff."

Wes winks at me then, and I press my lips in a thin line to hide my laugh. "So I've heard," Max says. "Your online presence is growing a lot since you got this new boyfriend of yours."

My chest blooms with hope. I've never really taken my social media that seriously, but since Wes and I started dating, I've gotten a lot more confident in posting pictures and sharing my life online. Couple content is easy to reach people, and it gets everyone engaged quickly. Still, it's a slippery slope when things get too much. "Is that– Is that a good thing?"

"It's amazing, Nora. You've just got to be careful with this kind of attention," he warns. "And get me that tape when you can. This project could be great for you."

"Thank you, Max. I'll get it done as soon as possible," I say. He agrees, and we exchange goodbyes. When the call ends, I let out a long sigh, and Wes's knee bumps into mine.

"What's all that about?" he asks.

I bump my knee back into his. "Movie star stuff. You wouldn't get it."

He scoffs. "Oh, God. How *ever* are we going to communicate when you become a big star?"

"I dunno, Wesley. You'll be talking through my assistant, not me."

I turn to him as his face glows from the streetlights above us. His face just looks so... soft. Like if I reached out right now he'd melt like butter in my hands. It's strange and endearing all at once. "That's how it's going to be, huh?"

"Yup," I say, leaning closer to him. He smells like the city, but only the good parts of it. Mostly like the florist we quickly passed through, all fresh and earthy. As I lean in, our shoulders brush lightly, sending a ripple of anticipation through me. The city around us feels alive, vibrant, and suddenly, so does everything between us. "Five years from now, you'll be on your knees for me, Wes."

"We don't have to wait five years for that, Sunshine." Our faces are now so close to each other that I could lean a little further into him if I wanted. I let my eyes drop to the fullness of his lips for a second and my breath catches in my throat.

"No?"

"I'll do anything you want me to. I'll *be* anything you want me to be. Give me the word, and I'll get on my knees right now."

His voice comes out gruffer than I was expecting and it lights a fire in my stomach. A fire I need to put out *immediately*. But all I find myself doing is leaning closer to him. Or he's leaning closer to me. I can't tell. My hands hit the hot sidewalk behind me as he towers over me, and I'm pathetically doing everything I can to get closer to him.

"I mean," I start, my voice strangled. My eyes dip into the small space between our bodies, our hips aligning. "You're already halfway there."

Wes's eyes flash and my heart drops. What the hell am I

inviting? Do I *want* something to happen, or am I just someone who is turned on by a hot guy who she didn't realize was *this* hot until a few days ago? I'm going with the latter.

That must be the only reason why my mouth tilts up to his. We're both hesitating, silently waiting for the other to make the first move. The air between us thickens, every second stretching longer as we hover on the edge of a decision.

Just as our lips are a whisper apart, a horn silences through the tension.

"Uber's here," he says with ease, moving back and extending a hand to me like the gentleman he is. He pulls me up, opens the car door for me, and ushers me inside as if we hadn't just come inches away from breaking the one rule I've tried so desperately to uphold.

TWENTY-THREE
NORA/WES
NEW YORK, NEW YORK

NORA

I HAVEN'T BEEN able to stop fidgeting since we sat down. I've seen a few shows at local theaters in Colorado, but never anything on a scale like this. Being in the audience on Broadway has been a dream of mine since I was a kid, and sitting here while waiting for the curtains to open for *Mamma Mia!* I feel on top of the world.

Despite everything that has happened in the last few weeks with Ryan and the show, this somehow makes my dreams feel that much more achievable. It's like I can reach out and grab them. As if I'll be able to get through this next year and a bit at Drayton and get my name out there.

Only minor problem is actually following through with all these tapes and auditions. As fun as the process is, there's always that doubt seeping in, telling me I'm not good enough. I spend too much time scrolling through social media, seeing girls my age who are prettier and more talented than me, and wonder if I'm in way over my head.

It's been years since I've booked something real. There's been a few modeling roles for upcoming swim lines and short adverts for popular brands. Apart from that, getting a TV or Film gig has been hard as fuck.

There's so much more to consider when taking a role in a show. If they want recurring characters, my schedule won't allow it. If it's a popular show and I'm thrown in for a few minutes, people will have a field day with random actors being dropped into a pool of nepo babies. Quitting school is not an option. I pride myself on getting a degree and even having the opportunity to go to college. I don't want to launch that out of the window just for a few minutes of screen time. I want to be serious about a role if I'm willing to commit more time to it.

There's also the very real fear of losing my spark before I get my big break. I've spent so much time holed up in my room and in my mind that being creative or leaving the time for it has been a chore. I've had no time to get my acting groove back that isn't channeled into my work for college, and that's what is going to fuck over my next audition for this new project.

Wes appears back in our seat with a bucket of popcorn, startling me from my daydream which took a left turn. As he shuffles back into the row, he gives me a big, dopey grin. "God, it's like the Hunger Games out there."

I chuckle. "Is it busy?"

"Very," he concedes, flopping down into the seat beside me. He hands over a bottle of water and then the popcorn. "It's sweet. We can share."

My eyebrows crunch. "I thought you didn't like sweet popcorn."

He just shrugs. "I don't." He ignores the skeptical look I give him and he shucks off his jacket and pulls out his phone. "Wanna take a few pics to post?"

"Yeah," I say, swallowing the popcorn I immediately shoved in my mouth. "Your Instagram is getting a lot of attention, loverboy."

"What can I say? They all think I'm obsessed with you," he mutters, nudging his arm into mine.

"Well, that's *kinda* true," I tease, turning to him.

"I guess it's pretty accurate," he whispers. He brings his fingers to my chin, his thumb brushing the side of my mouth. My whole body erupts into flames at the smallest contact. "Got a bit of popcorn there, Sunshine."

I just nod because I can't tell if he's staring right at my lips or at the spot that supposedly got popcorn stuck there. Our eyes lock. Hold. Burn. For a second, I let myself imagine that this is real. That I'm sitting in the rows of the Broadway theater with someone who is actually my boyfriend. Someone who wants to see me succeed and doesn't compete with me. Someone who just gets me for me.

I clear my throat, wiggling out of his grip. "All good?"

He nods, slinging his arm around my shoulder naturally and trying to get us as close as possible. I let myself get lost in his scent for a second as he held me closer. The picture turns out cute, and for once, I see how good of a couple we are.

Somehow, our slightly red faces and outfits complement each other really well. As sweet as Wes is, he has this slight rough-around-the-edges vibe. His hair is a little messy, and whilst mine is half tied back in a pink ribbon, it's a bit messy, too. Where my blue and white dress is slightly creased, Wes's blue polo isn't perfect either. We just look comfortable together, and I don't think I've seen anything better.

Wes flicks through the program before handing it to me. "Right here," he says, pointing at the cover.

"What?"

"Your name is going to be right here, Stargirl." The serious tone in his voice mixed with my favorite nickname makes my stomach crowd with butterflies. I swallow, looking down at the piece of paper and imagining my name on there instead of the current cast. "You're going to do so many great things, and I can't wait to watch you grow into the person you want to become. I believe wholeheartedly that we will come back here twenty years from now, and you will have your name right here." He points at the program again. "And your name is going to be carved into stone all the way down in Hollywood. I can see it, Nora Bailey. You were born to be a star."

My eyes prickle with tears at the praise. "Do you think so?"

"Of course. I've seen you perform my whole life, and you've only gotten better. I want to see you on a stage here one day."

I look out onto the stage, and I picture it. A dreamlike sensation washes over me at the thought. If I look for long enough, I start to see it. I can see myself *right* there. Manifestation can only get me part of the way. I'm going to have to work a lot harder to get there from here.

"You will," I whisper.

Wes's eyes sparkle. "Yeah?"

"Yeah. You'll be sitting in the front row with a t-shirt with my name on it," I tease.

He leans over and presses a kiss to my cheek before settling back in his seat. "I can't wait."

LEAVING THE THEATER, I'm practically buzzing with energy. It's racing through my entire body, one sharp whizz at a time. The atmosphere inside was electric, like all those clips I've endlessly watched online, but a thousand times more exhilarating. Every moment felt alive, each note, each movement—so vivid, so incredibly real. Stepping out onto the bustling streets of New York City, I'm still floating, caught up in the magic of it all.

"Did you see that, Wes!" I'm basically screaming in the middle of the street as we get lost in the crowd, trying to find our way back to the hotel.

"I was right there, Sunshine," he says, turning back to me. He's leading the way as I grip his hand for dear life so I don't lose him.

"Yeah, but it was insane. I feel like I'm dreaming but also insanely awake at the same time," I laugh, unable to stop myself.

"It was that good, huh?"

"Yeah," I sigh dreamily. "You had to have been there." He turns back to me and narrows his eyes before shaking his head. "You know what? You should definitely try out for community theatre when we get back."

"Nora."

"I'm being serious. You have a great face for acting. You're nailing this fake boyfriend shit. You'd be amazing," I admit, shoving the last bit of popcorn into my mouth before throwing it in the trash. Wes latches onto my jacket, making me gasp as he pulls me back into him.

"I have a great face because I was born naturally beautiful. I'm nailing the fake boyfriend shit because you're an incredible fake girlfriend, and I don't exactly take your word when you say I'm amazing."

"Okay, we'll circle back to the amazing girlfriend bit later... Why wouldn't you believe me?" I collide right with his back when the crowd stops at the crossing. Wes turns to me, resting his hands on my shoulders.

"You said it was amazing to skip class in senior year of high school so we could get high in your parent's backyard. You also said it was amazing to crowd surf at a small band concert last year, and that didn't end well for anyone involved. And let's not forget when you said it was amazing to try out that new sushi place downtown, only for us both to end up with food poisoning. So, yeah, your track record for 'amazing' experiences isn't exactly perfect."

I stifle a laugh. "We had fun, didn't we?"

"That's beside the point."

"That is the *literal* point I'm making."

"It's still irrelevant."

"You're infuriating," I mutter, holding my hands up to his

face and closing my hands into fists. I want to shake his head the same way I did the first night here. I swear, he's driving me more and more crazy every day. "How long until we get back to the hotel? I'm getting hungry again."

"Not long."

WES

I'm starting to think my answer was wrong because Nora sulks beside me for the next ten minutes as we try to get out of this area of the city. I'm assuming everyone who's staying in our hotel also went to the show because we've been following the crowd, and it's going the same way where we're headed.

Nora was right. The show was incredible. I've only really gotten into theater because of her, and it's been the best decision I've ever made. I've always loved music, but listening to theater soundtracks is different. There's more of a story to be told. There are hidden meanings that you have to figure out. Everything just feels like one big puzzle that you're dying to put together.

When the crowd starts to thin out, and we're still walking, Nora tugs on my arm, her fingers squeezing my hand impatiently. "How long now?"

"Like, five minutes."

"See, if this were five minutes in a film or a musical, it would fly by. This is absolute torture." She tugs onto my arm like an impatient child, her mouth etched into a frown.

"Great idea," I say, pulling out my phone. She eyes me curiously when *Lay All Your Love on Me* starts to play from my speaker. Her eyes sparkle when she realizes what I'm doing. "Are you ready, Sophie?"

"As I'll ever be, Sky," she replies, beaming.

I start singing first — horribly — playing my part the best I can. Most of the crowd's voices are quiet when they hear how loudly I'm singing. I thought Nora would get embarrassed, but this seems to be the perfect thing for her. She's laughing uncontrollably before her eyes widen when most of the male voices in the crowd join in with me. The pre-chorus comes around, and it feels like we're all singing, completely lost in the music and the atmosphere of the city. Everyone is joining in by the time the chorus arrives, and I feel like I'm on top of the world. Everyone knows the lyrics perfectly, but when Nora's verse as Sophie comes around, I tune everyone out.

There's something so special about Nora's voice. I've listened to her sing a million times, but she manages to add her own take on every song. Even now, as she playfully sings, her singing almost brings tears to my eyes. It's so soft, slightly raspy, like it's been dipped in honey or smoothed over like butter. It's fucking perfect. *She's* fucking perfect.

By the time the song ends, we're all outside the hotel, we're clapping, all the kids are screaming and others curtsying at the applause.

Nora's beaming up at me, her whole face red, and her hair is a mess. "Thank you," she shouts. "That was incredible."

"Don't thank me," I laugh. I lean down into her, brushing her hair behind her ear. I press the softest kiss to the tattoo on her neck, and she shivers. "You're going to change lives with that voice of yours, Stargirl."

She doesn't say anything, but I watch the way her face softens before she wraps her arms around my neck. I hold her close to me, picking her up off the ground and nuzzling my face into the crease of her neck.

As I'm about to put her down, she doesn't let go of me and instead wraps her legs around my waist. If I weren't enjoying it this much, I'd ask her what she's doing. But I don't. I just hold her tighter and I carry her through the lobby.

When her feet hit the ground, and she flashes me that adorable as fuck smile, I swear my heart drops right out of my chest into the palm of her hands. I don't want anything to do with this stupid heart of mine anymore. It's all hers as far as I'm concerned.

TWENTY-FOUR
NORA/WES
ROLEPLAY

NORA

AFTER THE SHOW LAST NIGHT, Wes and I got ourselves stupidly drunk with the drinks in the mini-fridge in our hotel room and spent the entire night tripping out over conspiracy theories. We failed to hook up our phones to the TV screen, so we lay in bed, sharing the tiny screen with our bodies pressed extremely close to each other. So, I have no idea how I end up at the opposite end of the bed when I wake up.

My head throbs when I turn over to see the bright lights of the sun peeking through the blinds. I try to sit up, but my proportions are way off, and I almost fall off the edge of the bed. I settle for sneaking under the covers and burying my head into my hands with a groan. I should not be allowed to drink again. Ever. I must choose the sober route from now on.

The sheets rustle before they open, and Wes's head pops through. He's grinning like a loon. "Morning, Sunshine. Sleep well?"

"No," I grumble.

"Neither did I. You were hogging the sheets all night."

"No, I wasn't."

He tilts his head to the side, judging me with his eyes. "I don't think you even know what city we're in, Nora, so you're not necessarily at liberty to say what you did last night."

"Can you stop shouting? You're making my head hurt," I groan, opening the covers completely and sitting up. "You need to stop letting me drink."

"Like always, it was your idea." He reaches over to ruffle my hair, and I slap his hand away. When I look up at him, he looks so put together that it makes my head spin. Or that could just be the alcohol that needs to get out of my system as soon as possible. His face looks fresh and clean, his hair still damp like he's just come out of the shower, and he's wearing baggy jeans and a sweater.

I rub the sleep out of my eyes. "What are the plans for today?"

"It's our last night here, so something fun?"

"Like?"

"I dunno. That's kinda where all my ideas end." I snort. He moves to sit down beside me, crossing his arms against his chest. I notice the hot mug of coffee on the bedside table. He catches me eyeing it, and he nods to it. "This is for you."

"Thanks," I mutter, and he hands it over to me. I take a long sip, letting the warmth soothe me. "Maybe we can go for lunch and then go to a bar later?"

"Didn't you just say not to let you drink?" Wes asks, squinting his eyes at me.

"We don't have to drink, you idiot," I retort, "I just want to experience a bar in New York. It's on my bucket list."

"Sounds good to me," he replies. I search around the bed for my phone, but it's so fucking big I must have lost it. I've always been a chaotic sleeper, so I'm not surprised that I find my eye mask on the opposite end of the bed. Wes catches me frantically searching, and he rummages around behind him before he throws me over my phone. "If I didn't know any better, I'd think you were a workaholic."

I fake gasp as I immediately swipe open my phone, checking through my emails. "Why do you think that?"

"Because your screen time for your email app and Google is insane," he replies.

"Who knows, I could be streaming lots and lots of porn and using the emails to manage my subscriptions," I say, still scrolling through my messages. Nothing extremely crucial – like usual.

"Now that sounds more like it," Wes says, laughing to himself. I blow him a raspberry, but my face falls when I look back at the reminder email Max sent following up his phone call the other day. Something weird churns in my stomach, and it's hard to tell if it was the alcohol or the thought of filming another audition. "What's wrong?"

"I've got to do another audition tape, but I'm feeling pretty weird about it," I admit, sighing. Wes pats the seat down next to him, and I flip onto my back, staring up at the ceiling. "I feel like I'm still rusty. Acting in musicals is so different from acting for the screen. I have my singing to back me up and choreography to hide my awkwardness. I don't know... I just want it to go well, and I'm on a deadline."

"First of all, you need to take a deep breath," he instructs, and I do. The motion distracts me for a second, but not completely. "Good. What kind of role is it?"

"It's just a side character, but they have their own separate story arc. She's a college student, but her side gig is picking up guys at bars. She's supposed to be doing it to gain some sort of control because of her shitty childhood," I explain, hoping what I said was right. It's been a while since I looked at the script, but the new scene is a monologue that Layla gives to her friends about why she does what she does.

Wes chews the inside of his cheek before he turns to me. "That's perfect."

"What's perfect?"

"We can practice your scene at the bar tonight," he suggests, his eyes filled with wonder.

"It could work," I mumble. I've not done any sort of immersive acting in a while, and it usually helps me out of these funks. But with people like Wes, we always mess around too much, and I never get any real work done. With that thought, I turn to him, pointing. "You've got to take it seriously, Wesley. This could make or break my career."

"We've been playing pretend for the last two and a half months. I'm sure I can handle some more acting," Wes says. He swats my finger out of his face as he sits up. He turns back to me. "Now come on. Let's get a late lunch."

"It's lunchtime already?" I gawk, my eyes widening.

"It's way past lunchtime, Sunshine," Wes laughs, slipping off the bed. "You sleep like the dead."

WES

Sometimes, I wonder how in the world the universe managed to put me and Nora Bailey in the same place. As much as everyone jokes about me being attached to her hip at all times, she just feels like an extension of me. She's the only person who has truly cared to get to know me and understand me in ways I don't understand myself. The times when I want to stay inside my brain and feel sorry for myself, and she lets me do that, or she helps me get out of it. She doesn't make me feel like what I think or what I say is invalid. She lets me exist, and that's more than enough for me.

Which is probably why my jaw hangs to the floor when she walks out of the bathroom after a day of lounging around for our last day in New York. We both agreed that we'd put some effort into our outfits tonight, and the hotel bar below us looked fancier than we could comprehend. But I wasn't expecting *this*.

This is breathtaking. *She* is breathtaking. Painstakingly perfect and beautiful in all the best ways. She's a fucking dream.

Nora walks towards me in a midnight blue, floor-length dress with a long slit in the side. Her legs look so fucking long and tanned, and I can't help but imagine what they'd look like wrapped around my waist. Or my face. Her brown hair is flowing down her shoulders in that natural wavy style that I like. Her face is slightly done up with a glittery glow on her eyelids and that simple star necklace that makes my stomach flip right over. Her tits are pressing against the silky fabric, and just the thought of them makes my breath catch.

Her eyes lock with mine, and I swear I almost pass out. I'm also dressed up in black pants and a white button-down, but I'm nothing compared to her.

She's fucking magnificent. Every curve of her body. Every inch that I selfishly get to see. Every single thing about her has been sculptured to perfection, and I want to punch anyone who has ever been able to look at her like this.

"Can you help zip me up? I've been fighting with it for the last twenty minutes," she says, her voice tight. I nod because words aren't able to escape me right now. I'm not so sure if my brain is even functioning properly. I scan her body again, trying my hardest to commit this sight to memory. "Wes."

"Hm?"

"You're not moving," she whispers, and it's only then that I realize that she's turned her back to me as she looks over her shoulder.

"Right. Yeah. Me. Move. Now," I say, stepping towards her because I'm only capable of speaking in mono-syllables now. She's standing in front of the full-length mirror, and I get to see what we both look like together. The words are out of my mouth before I even register it myself. "You are stunning, Nora."

Her mouth parts, but nothing comes out. I keep my eyes on hers in the mirror before she finally whispers a soft, "Thank you."

I've complimented her a million times. I've flirted with her so many times that I've not only lost track, but it's second nature.

But saying it like this: outside of our town and in a place where we're almost untouchable, everything feels different. Everything feels real.

She brushes the hair that's fallen down her back to one side of her shoulder, holding it in place. I catch a few loose strands and push it over, too, so my view of the zip is clearer. "Thank you," she mutters, and I have the urge to tell her to stop thanking me, but instead, I get to doing what she called me over for.

I move my hands, and my thumb and forefinger clasp on the tiny zip that's just above her ass. Her whole back is on display to me, and I find myself wanting to run my fingers all over her. I want to know what her skin would feel like against mine. To finally *have* her.

I grip onto her hip for stability as I pull the zip up, and she lets out the softest sound. It rushes straight to my dick, and I freeze before zipping up the dress the rest of the way.

I clear my throat, stepping back from her. "All done."

"Thank you," she whispers again.

"Is that all you're going to say, Sunshine? *Thank you?*" I tease, pulling her hair to fall down her back. She tilts her head back, shaking her head slightly to fan out her hair. I run my hands from her shoulders down to her arms, watching the goosebumps that arise in the wake of my touch. She doesn't answer me, but her fingers slowly clasp over my right hand. The movement is so simple, but it fucks me up inside. "Nora."

She sighs, closing her eyes before opening them and keeping them locked with mine. "You're making me nervous," she admits.

"*I'm* making *you* nervous?" She nods. "How?"

"Because..." I watch her search for the words, biting on the inside of her cheek as she scans my face in the mirror. I watch her eyes travel over the two of us. Her fingers drop from my hand, and she smoothes out her dress. "Forget it. Let's just go."

With that, she brushes past me and leaves me wondering what she was going to say.

NORA

For as long as I can remember, I've imagined what my life would be like. Some parts of that would change, like the way I'd style my hair, the way I dress, or even the way I talk. One thing I never imagined was to be wearing a new dress while I waited in a bar for a guy to turn up. I don't think I've looked that deeply into my future yet, and this is the last thing that I saw coming.

I swish around the ice in my glass, tapping my nails against the bar. The fancy stool beneath me isn't uncomfortable like the ones I'm used to. This one feels like it was made for me. Made for the silky fabric of my dress to slip comfortably on it.

I watch him finally take a seat next to me. He doesn't say anything at first, and I let myself inhale his manly scent, reminding me of wood and the outdoors. He's wearing a crisp white button-down shirt with his sleeves rolled up. He leans forward on the bar, and I'm convinced the muscles beneath his shirt are going to pop right out. The veins on his arms distract me for a second before his piercing blue eyes clash with mine.

I take the opportunity by the horns and pull my glass to my lips after asking, "What brings you to the city?"

The bartender returns with his drink before disappearing again. The guy turns to me, a small smile on his lips that makes my stomach trip over itself. "Business."

I hum in response. "Business, huh?"

"Yeah. It's been a busy week closing up deals," he replies, his eyes flashing mischievously. The air suddenly feels thick when I bring myself closer to him. I trail my finger on the skin showing on his arm, feeling the warmth right on the pads of my fingers.

"Can you make *me* your business? That way, you can take care of *this* business," I reply, gesturing to the very obvious cleavage I'm showing and even lower. Our eyes lock then.

And we burst out laughing.

I push myself away from Wes, feeling stupid and ridiculous. I knew this wouldn't be able to work with him. I can't seem to take myself or this whole situation seriously. I'm trying to go off-script to put myself into the character's head, but that isn't going well. I can't seem to make myself feel like I'm in her shoes, and it's going to fuck me up for this audition.

"God, you're so bad at this," Wes snorts, crossing his arms against his chest. I roll my eyes, taking another swig of my drink. Maybe some liquid courage could help me out for once instead of making me make stupid decisions. "Let me lead."

"Are you being serious?" I spit out.

"Yeah. You need to get in the mood," he whispers, his voice dropping. The sound rushes right through me, and I feel like I'm back in the hotel room for a second when he has his hands on me. I've never felt that out of control in my life, and I don't know why I enjoyed it so much. I felt both beautiful and scared under his gaze at the same time, and I couldn't figure out if I wanted him to stop looking at me or not. "You're too in your head. We should try it another way."

I scoff. "Fine. Let's see what you've got, big guy."

He slips out of the chair, ready to re-enter the room. I move from my seat, too, bringing my glass to one of the secluded booths in the bar. The seats close people off from the other end of the bar, and it makes me feel a lot better. Maybe the privacy will help with my confidence. I wait patiently, crossing my legs as I grow more anxious until Wes remerges.

I have no idea what he did in the two minutes he left the room, but my skin prickles when he comes back into view. From the lower position, he looks a fuck ton taller and just all *man*. His chest looks broader, his arms still veiny and thick and incredibly delicious. It's a crime that he's able to look this good, and I'm basically keeping girls from climbing all over him. If I had no idea who he was, I would certainly be pouncing on him right now. But I do. So, I contain myself and swallow when he slides into the seat beside me.

He puts a small space between us, and it only makes me want him closer. "I saw you sitting here, and I thought I'd join you," he whispers, his voice low and frustratingly sexy.

I swallow *again*. "Do you like what you see?"

Wes gives a very suggestive perusal of my outfit, rubbing his thumb against his bottom lip as his eyes rake down my body, landing on the bareness of my legs that my dress fails to cover up. "Fuck yeah." His voice is a rough caress against my skin. My stomach dips. "What are you doing here by yourself?" He goes to pick up my drink, bringing it to his lips.

"I'm just seeing where—" my voice trails off when he plucks the ice from his mouth, holding it between his fingers. The movement of his lips confuses the butterflies in my stomach with my best friend and the person he's pretending to be. He shuffles closer to me. "What are you doing?"

He answers by pressing the ice onto my exposed collarbone. My body betrays me as the sensation makes me shiver before I sigh. The coolness on my skin makes my head spin until I come back down to earth. "Do you trust me, Stargirl?"

"Yes," I breathe out almost too quickly, dropping my head to the leather behind me.

"Perfect," Wes whispers, moving the ice to the other side of my collarbone as it melts against my skin. "Hot?"

I swallow as he moves the ice to the top of my shoulder. "Very."

He tilts his head to the side, clearly having way too much fun with this. "How come?"

"I met this guy earlier," I manage to get out. He continues moving the ice down my arms as I try to find the right words. "He, uh, he said he was here on business."

"Yeah?" I close my eyes at the roughness of his voice, trying to breathe normally.

"Mm hm," is all that leaves my lips before another shiver

racks through my body. "I made a complete fool of myself and I asked him to take care of *my* business. If you know what I mean."

Of course, Wes absolutely enjoys torturing me, so he trails the ice along my knee, watching it melt completely before picking up another cube. This time he pushes the ice into my mouth, letting me suck the alcohol off it before pushing it back out. He keeps our gazes locked together, his eyes hooded and hungry. "I don't think I know what you're talking about. You're going to have to spell that one out to me."

With the fresh ice cube, he brings it to the slit in my dress, running it on my thigh. I gasp, gripping on to his hand. "Wes."

"Do you want me to stop?"

I take in a deep breath, shaking my head. "No. Don't stop."

Wes nods, continuing to tease the ice against my thigh, leaning right into me so that I can just taste him. "Tell me what you meant, Nora."

I clear my throat. "I was suggesting that I let him go down on me and take care of business down there instead."

"Down here?" he teases, bringing the ice higher up my thigh. My vision blurs and everything that once felt fake feels so incredibly real.

"Yes," is all I manage to get out. He's managed to make me feel weak and completely out of control. For one of the first times, it's like my brain has finally switched off, and I'm completely immersed in the moment. It's terrifying and liberating all at once.

He continues raising his hand, and I don't know what I want him to find. The ice is getting smaller because of the heat of my body, and Wes's breath against my neck almost makes me drop into a puddle at his feet.

"Do you like it when a guy goes down on you, hm?"

I instantly feel lightheaded at his words. And all I get out is another breathy "Yes."

"Why?"

"Because it…" My breath catches when he presses a soft kiss on my neck. "It feels good."

"How good?" The ice no longer exists, and it's just Wes's hands on my body. I don't know what he's talking about anymore. If he means what he's doing to my body right now or what I prepositioned the guy he's pretending to be with. His hand moves up higher until he almost reaches the cleft of my thighs, and he rubs his thumb there.

"Wes," I whimper. His movements are soft and gentle, but they make my heart race. He just continues leaving soft kisses on my neck as his hand works wonders on the most sensitive part of my body. "*Fuck.* That feels so good."

He inhales, dragging his lips down my neck. "Do you like this game, Nora?"

"Yes," I answer immediately before I run out of air.

I look down at him as he kisses across my chest where the ice was, sucking it into his mouth. My hands finally have something to do, and I curl them in his hair, pulling his head up to face me. My eyes zero in on his lips, and they're slightly red from the ice. He doesn't say or do anything. He just lets me hold his face close to mine. I bring myself as close to him as possible, getting lost in his blue eyes. My breathing is erratic. Almost desperate. My control is *this* close to snapping, and my fingers tighten in his hair.

"Are you going to kiss me?" I whisper.

My question hangs in the air. "Do you want me to?"

"I don't know. It might seal the deal, you know. I'll have to kiss people on the show, and you're–" I swallow when his eyes dip to my lips, and he licks them. *God.* "You're right here."

"I am," he agrees. He leans into me. *Finally.* But he completely dodges my lips and brings his mouth to my ear. "But I'm not going to."

I resist the urge to roll my eyes. "Why not?"

"Because it's not supposed to go like this."

TWENTY-FIVE
NORA
GLAMPING

"YOU ALL NEED to get your asses in the car!"

I love my best friend with all of my heart, but when she says things like that in her loud voice, I instantly debate whether or not I should be friends with her.

We're at the boys' house, and I can't tell how early it is. All I know is that I should definitely be sleeping right now, *not* packing the last of our stuff into the car as we get ready for a hike and camping trip.

I walk through the doors into the entryway and grip onto Cat's shoulders as she attempts to usher Connor and Wes out of the house. "Cat, sweetie, I love you, but we just got back from New York. Can we have a break for at least two to five business days?"

Cat mentioned this camping trip almost six months ago, and I was fully convinced that she was joking. That was until she presented us with full itineraries three days ago and told us to buckle up. We've been camping together as kids, but never on our own. Trying to make plans with all of us always ends in disaster, so we stick to spontaneous outings whenever we're free. This trip feels like it's going to be hell already.

I'm stressed enough with the opening of the show and Ryan's

constant nagging, so this is supposed to be something fun, but it doesn't feel like it at all. The pressure for the show is suffocating, and instead of enjoying the moment, I'm stuck in this twisted dance of stress and disappointment. This is supposed to be our escape, a break from the chaos, but it's only adding to the chaos in my head.

"You've been back for a *week*. So, no, not really," Cat retorts, zipping up her duffle bag on the floor.

She really means it's been a week of me not allowing myself to be alone with Wes for longer than five minutes, so I've been hanging out with her and Connor. I don't know how to act around him. It's not like anything really happened. But I wanted it to. God, I wanted it to, so badly.

Figuring out that I'm attracted to Wes should not be a big deal. I think there's always been a part of me that's been too scared to admit it, but being alone with him has really fucked me up, so the more distance I put between us, the better.

He appears behind me, casually slinging his arm over my shoulder as if everything between us is perfectly fine. "Yeah, Sunshine. We've had more than enough time to recover," he says, pulling me closer to his side.

I immediately shrug him off, frustrated by how nonchalant he seems about everything. I haven't been able to stop thinking about that night in the bar, and it apparently hasn't crossed his mind.

I haven't told the girls what happened because what is there even to say? He played his part better than I ever could, and I got too caught up in it. I might have also indirectly asked him to kiss me, but that's beside the point. I'm still detangling my feelings and it seems like he's already moved on past it.

"Alright," Cat says, clapping her hands together. "Final head count. Who is coming?"

"Just us and Sam, sweetheart," Connor says, packing the rest of his lunch in the kitchen. We're only going for one night, but Connor thinks we're going to get lost or stranded. He's been in real survivor mode all morning, and it's actually pretty funny.

"Yeah, Elle backed out this morning," I add. "She's not feeling like socializing because, apparently, you were all on her ass when Wes and I were gone."

Connor rolls his eyes. "She was the one who forced us to go out nearly every night. She kept going on about how she was going to reclaim her sexuality, or whatever the fuck that means."

"Don't you think we should stay here with her, then?" Cat asks, nibbling on her bottom lip.

"Archer said he'll check on her tonight since he's not going either," Wes says.

Cat and I both sigh at the same time. As independent and strong as Elle is, I know she'll appreciate someone checking on her whilst we go. Even if that person is Archer. From what I've gathered, they have an... odd relationship. They pretty much grew up together, with his mom being Elle's dance teacher since she was three. Yet they don't say more than five words to each other when they're in the same room. Fucking weird if you ask me.

"Okay, that makes me feel better," Cat murmurs. Connor finally finishes packing up the food and kisses her on the cheek before he passes us with Wes in tow behind him. "Ready to go, Nor?"

"This is going to be awful, isn't it?" I ask, linking my arms with hers.

"It doesn't have to be," she says, swaying us to the side. "I have a good feeling about this little trip."

THE ENTIRE CAR ride is pure torture. Squished in the backseat between Wes and Sam is like being trapped in a teenage boy's locker room. The overwhelming male presence and their eye-watering stench nearly send me over the edge. They shout over each other at volumes totally unnecessary for people less than two meters apart. I can't even chat with Cat because she's too busy making googly eyes at my brother in the front seat.

By the time we park in a grassy field, I'm certain we've bitten off more than we can chew. We all stumble out of the car, disheveled and cranky, clueless about our next move.

"So, what's the plan, Catherine?" I ask, trying to muster a smile for my best friend, hoping she's got something up her sleeve to salvage this chaos.

She sighs, pulling out her phone. "Well, the map says that we continue on North, and we'll be able to find the camp spot there."

Sam shakes his head. "Nah, we've got to go East. Some guys from my high school went the other weekend, and they said the same thing, but they got lost."

"Well, Cat's saying we need to go North, so we're going North," Connor says, coming to her defense immediately. Cat looks at me like she wants to roll her eyes at their bro-off, but she just snorts.

"Why don't we go East, and you guys go North," Wes suggests, "Whoever gets their first wins."

"Sounds good to me," Connor says, straightening. There's something unspoken between his and Wes's interaction, and I don't think I want to know what the hell is going on with them. Connor looks down at me. "Whose team are you on?"

It's between spending God knows how long with my best friend and my brother, who are probably going to be making out the entire time, or with two boys who can entertain the shit out of me with their stupid conversations.

"Not your team. Sorry, bro," I say, shrugging. Connor shakes his head with disbelief as if I've completely betrayed him. I hold out my hand to him. "May the best team win."

He clasps his hand in mine. "May the best team win."

Without another word, Cat and Connor pick up their bags and head on their way. I honestly have little faith in our team, but what's the worst that could happen?

If we weren't about to spend the night in the middle of nowhere, I'd think that it's a pretty decent spot for a date or something equally as romantic. The hills and turns are sculpted perfectly, scattered with moss and the fresh smell of the outdoors. There's the gentle sound of water running in nearby streams and birds chirping as the sun is slowly setting behind the mountains and rocks. It's honestly perfect.

We're quiet for a few minutes as we follow Sam's directions, and he slings his arm around both of our shoulders.

"So, Lovebirds," he starts, swinging us to the side. "How are things in paradise?"

I've avoided eye contact or any sort of conversation with Wes for so long that my heart stutters a little when I look over at him to find him already looking at me. I clear my throat. "Everything's pretty good."

"Pretty good?" Sam repeats. I just nod. "I'm great at relationship advice. You can hit me with anything."

"There's nothing to tell," Wes says. "Everything is great."

"Sure doesn't sound that way. Cat and Connor can't deal with being apart for two minutes and I don't think I've seen you two speak more than two words to each other the whole drive here," Sam says. Jesus. Where the hell did he learn how to read people like that? As if reading my mind, he adds, "My parents are doctors, remember? I can figure things out without you having to say exactly what's wrong."

"You have no idea what you're talking about," I laugh, shrugging him off. I wrap my arms around my stomach when I have nothing to do with my hands.

"Sure I don't. Just kiss and make up so this trip isn't awkward as fuck. I'm already hating third-wheeling," Sam says.

"You didn't have to come, you know," Wes says.

"Then how would you have any fun?" Sam throws us both a

wink before he scans our surroundings. There's not much to look at now that we're on a path through the woodland area. "I'm going to go for a piss. Stay on the path, and I'll meet up with you."

The moment Wes and I are left alone, I start to feel jittery. He edges closer slowly, and I fix my gaze ahead, trying to act unaffected even though his nearness sends my heart racing. He nudges his shoulder against mine. I nudge him back silently. He bumps me again, and this time, a snort escapes me as I bump him back, the tension breaking just a little with that unexpected sound.

"Hey, what's going on with you?" he asks, his voice quiet.

"Nothing's going on."

I make the brave decision to look over at him, but he's staring at his shoes, his hands shoved into his pockets. "You've been avoiding me since we came back from New York."

I play dumb. "I haven't."

"You have. And you don't have to, you know," he says. He stops then, turning to me. I get lost in his eyes for a second. Everything else falls away when he looks at me and it's like it's just us in this world. "I haven't been able to stop thinking about it either."

We both know what *it* is, but my brain won't keep up with me. "Y- You haven't?"

"It's all I've thought about since that night, Nor, but you don't see me freaking out over it. You've got your own stuff going on, and I'm still working on what I'm going to do with football. We don't need to complicate this, okay?"

His words soothe me a little. He's right. Whatever is going on between us should be the last thing on my mind right now. After Ryan, I've become wired to label and organize my feelings, always needing to define where things stand instead of just letting them unfold. I'm always desperate to know what I am to him, what I mean to him. But maybe that approach isn't necessary anymore. Maybe I just need to let go, live in the moment, and enjoy what we have without worrying about defining it.

"Okay," I breathe.

Wes smiles softly as he holds his hand out to me. It's so damn inviting that I slip my hand right into his. He squeezes it gently before tugging me closer to him. We walk for a few more minutes, listening to the soft rock playlist that Wes has been playing from his speaker until Sam catches up with us.

"You two make up yet?" Sam calls. I hold up our linked hands as an answer. "Good. Now, Wessy, I've got a serious question for you?"

"Oh, great," Wes mumbles. "If you're going to give me shit for–"

"Why don't you want to be on the team anymore?" Sam asks, cutting Wes off.

Wes sighs. I squeeze his hand reassuringly. "I just don't want to play anymore. I've been looking at other courses at different colleges, so after my senior year, I'll probably change over."

"You're going to be in college for *years*, dude," Sam says, shaking his head.

"I've got a million options. I'll be fine," Wes explains. I can't imagine Wes staying at college for that long, but I also know he needs to do what makes him happy. If it means staying on to find more options, so be it. No matter how long it takes, it's all about gaining experience and finding his passion. If anyone is going to work hard for something, it's got to be Wes.

"How's the search going?" I ask.

He just shrugs. "Not everyone has got back to me, but hopefully, I'll have an interview or something soon. I don't know what I want, so it's harder to commit to anything."

We all hum in agreement and Sam gives some very unhinged advice as to what to do with getting an interview. For someone who bases most of their life choices on his parent's guidance, his advice is slightly misplaced. Wes and I communicate just with our eyes without saying anything, and I can tell we're not going to be able to stop laughing about this later.

By the time the sun has fully set, we're all tired and hungry again, and we're getting low on snacks. I don't know why I agreed to this in the first place because if I could, I'd turn right back around now. We've been working for so long that my legs are sore, my forehead is sweaty, and the shorts I'm wearing are riding up my thighs.

"How long until we get there?" I ask Sam. He's been powering ahead of Wes and I and I've lost count of the amount of times I've asked him how close we are to the campsite.

"We're…" Sam begins, grunting as he steps over a large rock. "Here!"

I find the strength to catch up with him, and when I get to him, I roll my eyes. "Fuck. They beat us to it."

In the large patch of grass, RV's and campers have set up their fort for the night, and it's easy to spot our large two tents in one corner. Mostly because Connor is shouting at the top of his lungs that he's won when he spots the three of us. I knew we'd lose, but it still hurts to actually have lost.

We reluctantly drag our asses over to the tent, and I'm mildly impressed with their setup. Fairy lights are strung between the two tents. There's a small fire crackling whilst five cushions surround it, and our hot dogs are on the disposable barbecue that we bought with us. I don't know how they're going to turn out, but I'll eat just about anything at this point.

"You guys took your time," Cat muses when I sit down next to her.

"You can blame Sam for that," I say, reaching over to grab a can of beer.

"Hey, I was just following the directions my friend gave me. It seemed a lot shorter in my head," he retorts, gesturing to me to throw him a beer, and I do, chucking one at Wes, too.

"It just matters that we're all here now," Connor says, turning over the sausages.

"God, you're such a dad," I murmur, rolling my eyes before taking a swig of my drink. The liquid cools me down for a second, and I feel it fizzle in my stomach. He just throws me a sarcastic smile and continues tending to the food.

Connor's words still ring in my head even when the moment has passed. There are times like these where I feel extremely settled. I'm constantly running on fumes, rushing around, trying to get shit done, but there are moments like these where I can let my brain switch off for a while and just live in the moment. Who knows where we're all going to end up in a few years from now? The future is so uncertain that it makes me want to embrace moments like this that much more. Or that could just be the alcohol talking.

"Let's play ever have I never," Sam slurs, turning down the music on the speaker.

"Do you mean never have I ever, bud?" Wes laughs, patting him on the shoulder. He might sound fine, but he's also been spewing nonsense for the past ten minutes. Drunk Wes just means a talkative Wes.

"Whatever," Sam replies. He points his cup in Connor's direction. "You go first, Cap."

"Okay," Connor laughs. I snuggle closer to Cat, resting my head on her shoulder as my eyes droop a little. Since we haven't been doing anything active, the alcohol is just making me exhausted and a little sentimental. "Never have I broken up with someone over text?"

I look around the group and only Wes and Sam drink. "You animals," I joke.

"To be fair, it was in seventh grade, so I didn't know any better," Wes argues.

"Oh. I did that last weekend," Sam says, his eyes wide, and we all burst out laughing.

Wes is up next to ask a question. "Never have I ever had sex in a public place."

I shake my head at him because I know exactly who that

question was aimed at. I take a sip of my drink and so does Sam. When I look over at Connor, he and Cat are both drinking. "Oh my god," I mutter.

Cat shrugs. "It wasn't my idea."

"Sure it wasn't, sweetheart," Connor says. I shudder at the thought. As cute as they are together, I don't think I'm ever going to get used to them being a couple. Especially as the kind of couple that has sex in public.

I turn to Wes, who is the only one who hasn't drunk. "I don't believe you," I challenge.

He just shrugs innocently. "I'm as pure as they come. Who do you think I am?"

I scoff. "I still don't believe you."

He holds my gaze for a beat, and the tension crackles between us, thick and palpable. My palms grow clammy under the intensity of his stare. I silently will myself to look away, but I'm rooted to the spot, unable to tear my eyes from his. It's as if an invisible force is drawing us closer, something unspoken hanging in the air, a question begging to be asked but feared to be answered.

I shake my head when I see it's my turn. "Never have I ever been arrested?" At that one, no one drinks. "Seriously? No one has been arrested?"

"I almost did. One time," Sam says. "I was overage drinking, but the officer let me go after I bashed my blue, pretty eyes."

Sam has brown eyes.

And he definitely meant *underage* drinking.

"Of course you did," Wes laughs. "It's your turn, Cat."

"Ummm," Cat hums, biting on her bottom lip. She thinks for a second before her eyes light up. "Never have I ever kissed my best friend."

Obviously, Wes and I are the only ones who take a drink. He winks at me over his cup, and I hate the fact that it makes my stomach flip. He's getting too good at flirting with me. He's getting too good at making this feel real and feel like something I actually want. He's getting too good at all of it. All the simple boyfriend things that he's done are making me crave the real parts of a relationship so badly.

"How cute are you two?" Cat coos, looking between the two of us.

"Cute-*ish*," I tease. Wes just snorts, and when we all burst out laughing, Sam carries on his hysterical screams for a little too long. We all turn to him, alarmed. He's like an untrained puppy, completely unaware of how ridiculous he's being. "Do we need to cut you off, Samuel?"

"Don't cut my arms off!" Sam shrieks. He stands to his feet, wobbling as he almost trips over the hotdog buns that are behind him. "I'm going to bed now. Don't cut my arms off in my sleep, please, Nora."

"I won't make any promises," I joke. His eyes are still wide, and I have to bite the inside of my cheek to stop myself from laughing. "Sweet dreams!"

It takes him a whole five minutes to walk into the tent we're sharing. It's right behind us, but his perception is embarrassingly off. Within seconds, he passed out, snoring behind us.

"We should probably clean up. I'm ready for bed, too," Connor says, yawning as he stands. We all agree and silently pack up the rest of our stuff. Despite the long trek and tipsy evening we've had, it's been a good day.

After Cat and Connor say goodnight and head to their tent, Wes and I pack up the rest of our stuff and get ready into our pajamas. The air is a lot cooler now, so I slip on my sleep shorts and a comfortable hoodie before collapsing onto the air mattress in the large tent. Wes wiggles in beside me a few minutes later onto his mattress.

I turn to him on my side, resting my head on my hand to find he's already looking at me. There's only the dim lighting of the fairy lights in the tent that illuminate his features. After avoiding him for the last week, looking at him with fresh eyes makes me regret the time I spent away from him. Sam's snoring in the background is the only noise in the tent, and the comfortable silence stretches between us as we just… stare at each other.

I can't take the quiet any longer, so I say, "I don't give you enough credit, but you're actually not too bad at this whole fake boyfriend thing."

Wes chuckles softly. "You're just realising that?"

"Yeah, I mean, I was always too focused on my own relationship, and the only time I'd see you with other women was when you were sleeping with them."

He sighs. "You know I'm not this huge manwhore that everyone makes me out to be, right? Everyone jokes about it, which is fine, but I think I've secretly always wanted a relationship. That's probably why I helped Connor so much with Cat."

His admission catches me a little off guard. I would never have pegged him for a relationship-type of guy. "Yeah?"

"Yeah," he agrees, shifting a little. "I had a list of these ideas and things that I knew I was saving for someone, but I never thought I'd actually do it."

"And you're doing them now?"

"Yeah, with you."

"With me," I repeat. My chest aches at the thought. "I'm sorry. I'm probably not what you imagined your first girlfriend to be like, and you're wasting it all on me."

"Nothing's ever a waste when it comes to you. You're *exactly* who I need." His words rattle in my chest, and he shuffles closer to me. I keep my eyes strained on his as he reaches out, his fingers brushing against the side of my face as he tucks a few strands of my hair behind my ear. I try to catch my breath that I didn't know I lost, but his next words throw me right back to square one. "You are so perfect, Nora, and I wish you heard that enough."

I blink. "Do you mean that, or are you just–"

"I mean it," he says roughly. "I *always* mean it."

The way he speaks to me feels like there's a small fire in my chest that he's constantly adding wood to. It's like he knows exactly what to say to make me feel like I'm glowing. That's just the thing about Wes. He doesn't realize how much he means to me. He doesn't realize that he's got all the qualities that I didn't know I needed.

I inch my face closer to his, our bodies becoming so close that I'm sure our heartbeats could be disguised as one. He trails his thumb across my cheek, and I nuzzle my face into his palm, desperate for his warmth. My heart has never wanted something as badly as Wes Mackenzie in this moment, and the warm fuzzy feeling in my chest to stay there forever.

I tilt my mouth to his, and I can tell there's a battle in his eyes. "Wes," I whisper.

"Hm?"

"Just– Just kiss me. Please." I'm practically begging, but if he could stop being such a fucking gentleman for two minutes, he'd give me what I've been aching for since we left that bar in New York. My heart is thrashing against his chest, debating just going for it or waiting to see what he wants.

He drops his forehead to mine, exhaling as if he's been holding his breath. "Nora, I can't."

"Why? Because we've been drinking? I'm completely sober now, I promise," I say into the space between us.

"It's not because of that, and you know it's not."

"Then what is it, Wes? Because you keep looking at me like you want this, keep saying things to me that confuse the fuck out of me, and then you shut me down. If it's about the rules—"

"If we do this, there's not enough reasons to convince ourselves to stop," is his response. I open my mouth to say something, but nothing comes out other than the rush of air that leaves my lungs. He peels himself off me and turns away. "Goodnight, Sunshine."

Once again, I'm left staring into the night, wondering what would have happened if I had just let myself fall and said fuck it to the consequences.

TWENTY-SIX
NORA/WES
DICKHEAD OF THE CENTURY

NORA

I'M STARTING to think that my safe space is no longer safe.

Stages have always been my second home. They've become the place where I can become somebody else. The place where I get to turn off my brain and be in someone else's shoes for a few hours. It's where I feel the most alive. It's where I was born to be. But today, it's the very last place I want to be.

It's our dress rehearsal today and t-minus two weeks until the opening night of the show. Not only have I been busting my ass in my classes, trying my hardest to perfect my assignment for this year, but I'm also trying to psych myself up to send my final audition tape for the project Max has been on my back about.

For most of the class, the dress rehearsals are where we feel the most pressure. Blocking choreography and running lines is one thing, but putting it all together is another. Penny stops becoming the fun-loving teacher we all adore and becomes a much stricter version of herself, which we desperately need. All of us but Ryan.

He's been leaving sly comments throughout today's session,

and I'm waiting for him to break. I know Wes and I's relationship has gotten to him, but he's yet to say something directly to me. Kiara, however, has no problem with saying what's on her mind. Part of that is my fault for finally spilling to her the truth about Wes and I's relationship, mostly because I needed to vent that he rejected me twice.

"So, did you guys fuck?" She slides onto the vanity in front of me as I take my makeup off in the mirror backstage. She gets unready insanely fast for such a chaotic person and has been pestering me with these kinds of questions all day.

"No, Kie, we didn't," I say.

"Are you sure?" I nod. "What did you do for four days? There's no way you didn't pounce on him. I saw the pictures you posted when you were all cozy in that bar. It was very... intimate."

"We have rules," is all I can come up with. I'm still hurt by the way he shut me down that night and on the camping trip. I'm not going to ask him to kiss me for the third time. I'd like to believe I have more self-respect than that.

"Rules?" she repeats. I nod again. "Since when do you follow rules?"

"Since always," I say, laughing. Kiara's about to say something else, but the dickhead of the century waltzes into the space, his bag slung around his shoulder. He looks pissed, as usual. I rear back at the dark energy he just created in the room. "You good?"

Ryan just blinks at me as if I was talking to someone behind him. "Yeah, I'm great."

"You sure? You looked a little tense over there," Kiara says.

"I'm fine, Kiara. Thanks for asking," he bites out.

"Relax, Jesus. You're the one coming in here with that sour fucking attitude," I say, closing my makeup bag. Kiara snorts beside me, and I try to hold in my laughter over how weird this encounter is.

"I wonder why that is."

"You know what? I'm wondering the same thing. Why don't you enlighten me," I challenge, swiveling in my seat so we're no longer having a conversation through the mirror.

"You and that football guy," is all he says.

I let out an exasperated sigh. "You mean Wes. My boyfriend."

"Whatever the fuck he is. You don't have to keep shoving your relationship down everyone's throats."

And off goes the canon.

I can't help feeling a little smug that this asshole has finally gotten what he deserves. I sit up straighter. "What's the problem? Is it bothering you?"

"Yes, it's fucking bothering me. I don't exactly want to see my ex-girlfriend making out with some guy all over my feed. And *New York*? That was going to be our place, Nor."

"Funny. I don't exactly want to play alongside you in the show whilst you shove your tongue down Daisy's throat during the breaks, but here we are."

He stutters. "That's different."

"Is it?"

"Yes."

"There's two easy solutions to your problem. One, unfollow me. Two, grow the fuck up. *You* cheated on *me*, remember?" I'm slowly running out of ways of getting this into his head. I'm sick of being strung along by him, feeling like I owe him something when I sure as fuck don't.

"That doesn't mean I don't still want you."

Kiara lets out a low whistle before silently leaving the room. It's empty in the space now, and his words hang in the air. Once upon a time, that would have been enough. Him telling me that he wanted me despite everything he did would have been enough for me to crawl straight back into bed with him. But I don't want that anymore. I don't want to constantly be questioning my worth or fighting with someone who would never fight for me. To be with someone who only wants to compete and see themselves as the most important thing in their lives.

I shake my head, running my palm across my forehead. "Can you hear yourself right now? You only want me because you can't have me anymore. You don't have someone to push around and do whatever the fuck you want. And the fact that you're only just realizing that says a lot about you."

"What does it say?"

"That you're going to be alone forever if you don't sort out your priorities." His lip twitches as if the words actually registered in his brain for the first time. "You're never going to be happy if you're constantly trying to one-up every person you date."

He scrubs his hand across his face, sighing. "I'm sorry."

I laugh incredulously. "You're sorry?"

"Yes, I'm sorry. For the way I treated you. For the way I've been acting. I just have a lot going on right now," he explains, his voice tight.

"Everybody does, but that doesn't give you an excuse to be fucking horrible to everyone around you. It doesn't excuse your selfishness and your need to try to put people down to succeed. I really do hope you can find some inner peace or some shit, but I'm not going to be the one to help you with that. I'm going to play my part and stay the fuck away from you. We're done for good. Got it?" Even my own words sting, but he needs to hear them.

He nods once. Twice. "I got it."

As I pack up my things and leave Ryan standing in the dressing room, an unexpected feeling washes over me. I thought I'd feel relieved after confronting him, but instead, I'm unsettled. This was what I wanted—to hit him where it hurts, and I succeeded. Yet, surprisingly, I find myself feeling sorry for him.

WES

After spending the entire day on and off phone calls and scrolling through LinkedIn, I'm grateful for some peace and quiet. My mind has been at full volume for the past couple of weeks, and finding time for myself has been fucking difficult. If I knew how hard job searching and finding a new course would be, I would have just stuck with football. Then again, I'd much rather be miserable and trying to find something else than be stuck on a team playing a sport I hate.

I've spent my spare time in the gym trying to work out my energy and get my brain to settle down. I've been avoiding Connor like the plague, not wanting to run into him and get another lecture. I just want this whole fake dating thing to be over so I can go back to being friends with Nora and stop worrying about crossing that line that we've firmly put up.

That gets thrown out the window the second I step into the backyard.

The girls have been treating our house as a new hang-out spot, and I don't usually mind it. They use the kitchen to bake and the living room to crochet and watch movies. They sometimes use the backyard to do group yoga or sing at the top of their lungs for no reason. 'It's girlhood,' they told me.

It's nothing new to see Nora playing guitar in the backyard, but it still makes my head spin. She's sitting on the grass with the guitar in her lap and with Elle beside her on her stomach, reading a book. Nora's long brown hair fans around the guitar as she strums it softly, playing a song I've never heard before.

I know she's pissed at me for what happened the other night, but I have more self-control than she thinks. I know that if we kissed, then, I'd throw her off for her performance, and that's the last thing that she needs. That either of us needs.

There's nothing quite like the serene peace on Nora's face when she's playing an instrument. I can't help but let myself think for a second what it would be like to wake up to this sight.

To have her constantly playing beautiful melodies whilst I get to bathe in her presence and listen to her sing.

"You can come out here, you know? This is *your* house." Nora calls. I realize that I've been standing in the doorway for the last five minutes, just staring at her. Elle's head pops up, and she laughs a little before directing her attention back to her book.

"I didn't want to disturb you. You were in your element," I say, walking over to them and taking a seat on the grass. She narrows her eyes at me like she doesn't believe me. I gesture to her guitar. "Don't stop now, Sunshine."

She rolls her eyes, but she continues. She's not singing anymore, but the chords are beautiful on their own.

"How are you holding up without football?" Elle asks, not tearing her eyes away from her book.

"Pretty good. I've got an interview in Denver next week for a spot on a course at Carlton University."

"That's cool. What course?"

"Um, something to do with Marine Biology?"

Nora snorts. "Do you even *like* marine biology?"

"I dunno. I might," I answer. Honestly, I have no fucking clue what I'm doing. My mom has been on my ass about expanding my interests, so I just went for it. I doubt it'll go anywhere, but it's worth a shot. "How about you, Elle-Belle? You still filming your little videos?"

Her whole face lights up. "It's actually going pretty well. No major brand deals or anything, but my name is getting out there more. I got recognized at Target last week, so I'm taking that as a win."

I hold out my hand for a high five, and she clasps her hand in mine. "Hell yeah, Harper. You're going to be famous in no time."

"Oh, for sure," Nora adds, grinning. "You'll probably make it on a billboard before me at this rate."

"Why's that?"

"Ryan sort of… apologized today. It's a whole mindfuck."

"He's sorry?"

"Kinda? His words and his actions very rarely match up. It's hard to tell with him," she says, slowing down the song she's playing.

"But that's what you wanted, right? To make him pay for what he did. For him to realize that he can't treat you like that."

"Yeah, I guess. I just didn't expect to feel bad for him, you know? He's just got a really sad life, and that sucks."

"You don't have to feel bad for him, Nor. He treated you horribly, and karma is a bitch. It's about time he got what he deserves," Elle says, and I hum in agreement.

"Yeah, you're right."

We settle into a comfortable silence, and I fall onto my back next to Nora as she continues playing. She starts the song again, and it almost puts me to sleep. There's something special about just being in Nora's orbit. It's like she's constantly pulling me into her but still keeping me at a safe distance away. I could listen to her sing this song and play for hours if she let me.

"What are you playing?" I ask.

She stops singing but continues strumming. "*Nothing / Sad Stuff* by Lizzy McAlpine."

I hum. "Never heard it."

Elle and Nora both laugh. "Of course, you haven't," Elle says as if there's a joke I'm missing.

"Well, it sounds beautiful," I concede, closing my eyes.

"Thank you," she whispers.

"Hey, can you record this and send it me?"

Nora scoffs. "You can listen to Lizzy's version on Spotify, you freak."

"I want to hear you sing it," I whisper. She studies me for a minute like she might not believe me, but she doesn't say anything. She looks away and drops her gaze back down to her guitar.

She starts singing again and I take a deep breath, desperate to not make the moment into something bigger than it is. We're getting closer and closer to the semester being over, and after summer, we'll all be in our final year at Drayton. Whilst Elle and Nora know exactly where they're going after college, I couldn't be more lost. The thoughts swarm around my brain, but I don't say anything. Instead, I settle into a comfortable silence with them and listen to Nora's soft voice.

TWENTY-SEVEN
WES
YOU'VE GOT THIS

I'VE ALWAYS BEEN confident in all the ways that matter. Ever since I was a kid, I've had this unwavering sense of confidence, and I have no fucking clue where I got it from. I think I just woke up one day and decided that I had nothing to be afraid of and that I was just a genuinely likable person. That quality came in handy when I became popular in high school and got girls to go out with me, but now, I can't seem to find who that person was.

I've been on edge for this interview for the last few days, and I'm running out of ideas as to how to calm down. I ended up going to my last resort.

Nora agreed to go to the interview with me for moral support, but her tips haven't been that useful. She's used to working a room and getting people to like her, but not in an academic sense. I didn't have to go through much of an interview process to get into DHU with my dad already working there, so this is all new to me. Luckily, my dad actually has some decent advice.

Over the last few weeks, we've had odd conversations here and there. Nothing is ever substantial or important, but he's slowly becoming more tolerable to be around. I no longer feel like punching him in the face, and everything he says doesn't feel like an insult anymore. We're still in this weird middle-ground phase, but it's better than nothing.

We've been on the phone for almost an hour as I look over my interview cards in my room when he finally changes the topic. "Hey, uh, how's your mom holding up?" he asks. The question makes me stiffen instantly.

"She's been okay. We've both been busy, so I haven't seen her much, but she's doing better," I admit, leaning back in my chair.

"That's good." A pause. "Does she... Does she talk about me?"

"Not really. Not in the way you think," I say. I know it's going to sting to hear, but I don't want my dad to think he has any chance of getting her back. I might be in the process of forgiving him, but he hurt her. She doesn't need to go through that again. "Why?"

"I was just wondering. Everything has been finalized now, and I guess it just feels weird to not have a wife anymore." His words settle between us, and it seems like one of the first times he's actually acknowledged what has happened.

"Huh," I mumble.

"What?"

"For a second there, you actually sounded sorry," I muse.

"I *am* sorry, Wes. I know you're never going to fully understand it, but there are parts of your mother and I's relationship that we kept to ourselves. And in hiding that, it damaged our relationship even more until the point it broke. I'm never going to have an excuse for cheating, but that's just the path I took. And I'm sorry that you found out in the way you did."

"It's fine. Not what you did. Obviously, that still sucks, and it hurts, but the truth is, I don't want to fight with you. I just had all this anger bottled up inside me, and I didn't express myself in the best way. Now with trying to find a new degree, it's making me look back at all the time I wasted my breath on this situation."

"I'm glad we're getting somewhere, son, I am," he says. "When's the next time you're going to see your mom?"

"I'm not sure. She's got this book signing event in..." I check the calendar app on my phone. What a coincidence. "It's in Denver, too. I'll see if I can swing by. I might have to stay the night in a hotel, though."

"Are you and Nora going?"

"Yeah."

"I can book you a room if you want. I know a few people down there, and I could get you a decent deal."

"You'd do that?" I gawk. These acts of kindness are sweet, but they're also a little frightening. But progress is progress, and I should probably treat it like it is.

"Yeah, it's no problem."

"Thanks, Dad."

"Don't mention it. I'll send you the details later. Let me know how the interview goes."

I'M BEGINNING to think that deciding to bring Nora to my interview was a bad idea. Not only will she not shut up about going to my mom's book signing after, but she's convinced that I'm a doll that she can play dress up with. We've been walking around stores in downtown Denver, and she's tried to find me an outfit to wear even though I already brought one with me.

"You can't wear jeans to an interview, Wes," she says again, scrolling through a rack of clothes. I stand behind her, trying not to fall asleep with how long this is taking.

"Why not? It shows I'm laid back," I argue.

She turns to me, narrowing her eyes. She pulls out a blue button-down and holds it against my chest, tilting her head to the side. "This goes nicely with your eyes."

"Do I have to?"

"Do you want to make a good impression?"

"Yeah?"

"Then yes, you do have to," she concedes. I follow her around this fancy shop like I'm tethered to her as she picks out clothes for me. Honestly, I could get used to this. I'd let her dress me up in anything she wants me to if it brings her this much joy. I might be bored out of my mind, but I can't bring myself to care.

I walk out of the fitting room for the third time in black pants and a white shirt when Nora holds out a black tie to me. "I think you should wear this," she says. I drop the smooth material between my hands, examining it.

"A tie? Seriously? I'm going to look like I'm trying too hard," I grumble.

"That's kinda the whole point, Wesley," she teases. She grabs the tie from out of my hands, standing on her tiptoes to slip it around my neck. "Besides, you look good in a suit."

"Yeah?"

She stands back to admire her handwork. She nods as if she likes what she sees. Her teeth sink into her bottom lip in that adorable as fuck way when her eyes meet mine. "Definitely."

If it gets her to smile like that, then I don't have much of a choice. "Tie it is."

THE SECOND I walk into the interview room, the tie feels way too tight around my neck. I think at least a million times if I should just tear it right off and walk out of the room, but I don't. I sit through the entire thing, feeling insanely on edge whilst a representative of the Marine Biology course asks me basic questions about myself, why I want to study the course, and what I want to get out of it.

Talking about myself is pretty easy, but lying about why I want to take this course is the hard part. Everyone usually comes to these things with a five-year plan ahead of them, and I don't have that. I have a million ideas thrown together, and just the sheer thought of *hoping* is what I'm rolling with.

I bullshit my way through most of the answers, and each tight smile the woman gives me feels like a punch to the gut. I have no way of knowing if what I'm saying is right or if I'm completely fucking this up. So when she thanks me for coming all this way, I get out of there as fast as I can.

The whole thing only lasted thirty minutes, but it felt like it went on for hours. When I get out of the building, I loosen my tie and take a deep breath. This is only the first of what's going to be a long, torturous process. Finding out what I'm good at and what I have a talent for isn't going to come overnight, and I'm just going to have to trust that process.

I push open the door to the hotel and find Nora lying on her stomach, watching TV from the bed. Her head snaps up when she sees me and I drop the tie over the back of a chair.

"How'd it go?"

I sigh, dropping down beside her on the bed. "Pretty good, I think."

"You'll have a million more interviews after this one. You've got nothing to worry about," she says reassuringly. I rub at my temples, but I already feel more settled.

"I know."

She scoots to sit up. "Oh, you do now?"

"Yeah, you've proved that to me a million times. I don't have to worry that much anymore. not over stuff like this," I say.

She nudges me in the shoulder. "Now you're getting it, Wesley."

"Maybe you should take a page out of your own book."

She rears back a little, squaring her eyes at me. "What do you mean?"

"I know for a fact you've been sitting in her stressing over your show." She immediately bites on her bottom lip, proving my point. "*You've* got nothing to worry about, Stargirl. You sent in your tape, haven't you?"

She nods, gesturing to her laptop on the desk under the television. "It just went through now."

"Look at us. Adulting and shit," I say, and she just laughs. "Come on. We better get going before my mom starts to freak out."

She jumps from the bed, slipping her hand into mine, and my heart does that thing again. That fucking soaring thing that only seems to happen when she's here.

TWENTY-EIGHT
NORA / WES
GRAPEJUICE

NORA

IF I KNEW book signings were this fun, I would have been to a lot more of them. Maybe that's just the magic of May Mackenzie because she has really gone all out.

Her book that was published last year is all about her life growing up as a teenage girl and all the things she wished she knew. It's funny and light-hearted whilst also dealing with serious stuff, and seeing so many women here empowered by her words, it was like taking a breath of fresh air. If Elle and Cat were here, they'd love it just as much as I do.

Even better? Watching the way Wes looks at his mom. He watches her like she's the best film he's seen in his life. Like he's so utterly captivated by every word she says, even when he'll never understand the complexities of womanhood. He just looks happy to be here, and so am I. Especially when we got to the after-party that's being held in a separate building a few blocks away from the bookstore.

There's an array of things going on here that make it hard to focus on one thing. Wes and I immediately went to the bar before going to the makeshift dance floor. I have no idea what's in the funky purple drink I ordered, but it tastes amazing.

"You having fun, Stargirl?" Wes asks, stepping with me to the beat of whatever pop song is playing.

"Of course I am. Remind me to publish a book so I can host a party as good as this one."

"You wouldn't need to publish a book to throw a party," he replies.

"You're so right," I say. He just laughs, shaking his head. "How about you? You're not stressing about the interview, are you?"

"I wasn't until you reminded me."

I wince. "Sorry. No more interview talk. Let's just have fun."

"Trust me, I'm having fun," he says. He pulls me into him by the waist, pressing our bodies together. His heat makes my head spin. Or maybe that's the alcohol. I don't know. Either way, I love it.

"Yeah?"

"If I'm on a dancefloor with you, I can guarantee that I'm going to have a good time," he whispers, his breath hot on my neck. "You have that effect on me, Nora."

"And what effect is that?" My voice is a strained whisper, not wanting to break the moment we've caged ourselves in.

"The kind that I can't get out of my mind even when we're apart," he murmurs, pressing a kiss on my neck. My mouth parts, desperate to say something, but the words don't come. "All I have to do is close my eyes, and you're right there."

"Is this some sort of fantasy of yours, Wesley?" I ask, trying to add humor to the conversation.

"No, it's my reality, and every day it's getting harder to pretend you're not all I think about."

This time I *really* try to say something. Think of something that isn't the millions of thoughts surrounding my brain. Again, nothing comes. Even when we pull apart, and I'm just blinking up at him, no words can describe the weird feeling I've got in my chest. Mostly because I'm still annoyed that he's shut me down twice and he still says things like that to me without a care in the world.

The moment passes, and we continue swaying together to the music until the *Cha-Cha Slide* comes on, and everyone moves onto the dance floor. Even May joins in next to us and we're all dancing to the classic whilst I try to keep most of my drink inside my glass. I let myself get lost in the moment, feeling ridiculous and euphoric all at the same time. I used to think partying with older people would be boring, but they're surprisingly fun. This song always gets people up and dancing, and I'm so glad to be a part of it.

When the song ends and fades into another upbeat song, Wes reaches over to grab my glass. "Hey, what are you doing?"

"Let me have some. It looks good," he says, licking his lips like he's actually thirsty. He does this all the time. He doesn't want something until I have it, and then he's all over me like a dog.

"Then go get your own. The bar is *right* there," I say, stupidly gesturing with my glass because it only gives him the leverage to take a quick sip. I find myself laughing despite his stupidity. "Wes, stop."

"Hey, just give me some," Wes argues, trying his hardest not to shout. I lift the glass higher above my head, only for him to tug my arm down.

"Go get your own, you thief," I mumble, pulling my glass closer to me.

"You're not being fair, Stargirl. I just want a taste."

His words are not purposefully sexual at all, but my body doesn't know that, so I continue playing this game with him. He pushes, and I pull back. We keep going back and forth until we're just staring into each other's eyes, not giving a damn about the full glass between us until it tips right over me and stains my white dress purple.

"Fuck," Wes breathes.

"Yeah, fuck." We both stare at my dress when the crowd starts to disperse, leaving us right in the middle of the dance floor, stupidly staring at each other. I feel the embarrassment wash right over my body. I close my eyes, hoping that what feels incredibly see-through isn't actually visible. "Can you see my–"

"Yep," Wes says, snapping his eyes up to mine. He turns his back to me, finding my hands behind him. I keep my chest close to his back as he starts walking. "Come on. Let's sort this out."

WES

Part of me wants to burst out laughing at the fact that we just completely embarrassed ourselves in the middle of this event, and another part of me wants to kill any person who got a fresh glimpse of Nora's boobs through the material of the dress.

I managed to maneuver us out of the hall as quickly as possible, fast enough to shove her into the nearest bathroom with my shirt along with her. I'm lucky I didn't get anything on me, and I'm fine with walking around topless if she's dry and covered up enough until we get back to our hotel.

I'm standing outside the bathroom door, my head tilted back into the opposite wall as I stand guard. Honestly, I should have known the night would end up like this. Every time I think it's going to be a normal night, something Nora-related is bound to mess it up. And I fucking love it. There's this constant excitement whenever she's around. You never know what's going to happen and the anticipation is more than enough for me to get drunk on.

"I'm sorry," she calls again through the bathroom door. I don't know how long she's been in there or what the hell she's doing, but she's clearly having some internal freakout.

"It's okay," I say softly.

"This is the worst thing that could have happened," she grumbles.

I laugh. "It's okay, Nora, seriously."

The door clicks open as she continues apologizing. "But it's not, and I–"

I can't tell if her voice trails off or if my brain short circuits because when she steps out of that bathroom with my shirt on, I swear I almost pass out. The button-down is more than long enough that it cuts off around mid-thigh, exposing to me her long, tanned legs that dip into the flats she's wearing. The shirt is unbuttoned at the top, and it's insanely oversized on her, but it doesn't stop me from imagining what I saw when the drink went through her dress. The sleeves are rolled up, her hair is no longer in the bun it was in before as it falls in waves on her shoulder.

I press my fist to my mouth, and my eyes shoot all over her body. Nora Bailey in *my* shirt, with almost nothing underneath. My cock stiffens at the sight, and I let out a quiet, tortured groan. She looks like trouble, and she looks like she's all mine.

When my eyes find hers again, she blinks. "What?"

"I– Nothing." I shake my head because I thought she'd disappeared the first time. But she doesn't. She's still standing in front of me, practically half-naked. "Let's go."

I start walking ahead of her until she catches up with me. "Are you annoyed at me?" I don't say anything because if any words leave my mouth, I'm going to fuck everything up. We get outside and walk along the sidewalk until we get to my car. I open the passenger door for her, but she doesn't go in right away. Instead, she turns to me and continues this conversation. "It's completely fine if you are. I made an absolute fool of myself in there, and you had to save me like–"

"Can you just get in the car?" I snap. She nods and slides into the seat.

I keep my eyes on the road the entire time it takes us to drive back to our hotel, and I don't give myself the chance to look at her until we shut ourselves in the elevator up to the twenty-third floor. The silence is eating away at me, too, but I'm not going to be the one to break it.

"Wes." Her voice shakes, and I finally turn to her. "Look, I'm sorry—"

"Don't apologize," I bite out. I take a step towards her.

"No, I'm being serious. I'm so—"

"Did you hear what I said?" I take another step closer to her now until her back hits the back wall in the elevator. I grip her chin with my fingers, forcing her to look up at me. Her lips part. "You can stop apologizing, Nor."

She shakes her head. "I know, but I just feel like the worst person ever. I can't go anywhere without something insane happening, and I embarrassed myself, and you, and probably your mom. This was a big event for her, and with everything going on with your dad, this was supposed to be something good, and I ruined that. Like always."

She takes a deep breath, blinking at me rapidly. "You didn't ruin anything, Nora," I say gently. She bites on her bottom lip, and the sight distracts me when my hands slip from her chin around her neck, curling my hands in her hair. "You need to stop telling yourself that because I hate hearing you talk about yourself like that."

"But it's true, Wes, and—"

I shut her up the only way I know how.

My mouth collides with hers, and for a second, I think I've made the wrong decision, the *selfish* decision, but her body softens against mine, and everything rushes to me in the most delicious ways. She tastes just like she always does, like sunshine and sweet fruits. My hands tighten in her hair, and she lets me, opening herself up willingly as I push my tongue into her mouth.

This is nothing like the other kisses we've had. This one is just for us. This one is passionate and adventurous, and it's *ours*. I tilt her head back, needing to deepen the kiss, and again, she lets me. My vision starts to blur, and my head thrums against my skull as I break apart from her for a second. Her lips are red, her cheeks inflamed as she looks up at me. She looks at me like the times I could have kissed her and didn't.

"God, Nora," I mutter, leaning down to kiss her again. "You just don't know when to shut up, do you?"

She blinks up at me, her eyes filled with worry. "But the rules—"

"Fuck the rules."

She takes a deep breath, searching my face for the confirmation she needs. "Fuck the rules," she repeats before kissing me again.

Both of her arms wrap around my neck as mine slide down the length of her. She touches my bare skin like she just knows exactly what to do with me. Her hands run across my shoulders; my skin becomes hyper-sensitive to her touch.

God, she feels too fucking good. Too fucking much. Her hands twine in my hair, and she lets out a soft noise when I pin her to the wall with my hips. My cock is aching, and I know for a fact she can feel it. She kisses me back harder and I'm wondering if the elevator is even moving at all. The thought doesn't last for long because when my hands move down to the exposed skin beneath the shirt, her legs lock around my waist, and I can't help but think if she's wearing any panties.

I push her against the railing, and she gasps, her head tilting up. I kiss across the redness on her neck rapidly, tasting every inch of her as if I've been starved. My hands travel across her thighs, and we're panting, trying to get the air we both need.

"Is this good?" I ask into her skin. "Is this okay?"

"Mmhm," she murmurs. I rock my erection into her, and she moans. I'm dying to swallow the sound, but I continue worshipping the sensitive skin on her neck. "Keep going."

Her voice is so desperate that it almost undoes me. "Fucking look at you, Stargirl," I mutter, looking at the space between us. "You look so good when you're wearing my clothes."

She tightens her fingers in my hair, tilting her head to the side. "That's a little narcissistic, don't you think?"

I hum, kissing along her jaw. "No. It just confirms that you've always been mine." She gets impatient and tilts my head so she can kiss me back deeply, pulling back just so she can bite on my bottom lip. Fucking hell. That motion alone drives me crazy. "You need to tell me to stop, Nora. Please tell me to stop."

"No," she whispers breathlessly. "Don't stop."

I agree and continue kissing her senseless. We're both desperately gripping each other, and when my hands find their way under the curve of her tits, I look up at her. "Is this okay?"

"More. I need more," she murmurs, frantically undoing the button of her shirt until she guides my hand where she wants it. I feel the fullness of her tit beneath my hand, and when I swipe my thumb over her nipple, her head drops backward, and a soft moan leaves her mouth. "Jesus Christ, Wes."

I lock my mouth with hers again, dying to get another taste of her. "You're going to kill me, you know that? You don't understand how long I've wanted this."

She comes up for air, smirking at me. "You've wanted me to spill a drink all over myself, have to wear your shirt, and embarrass myself at a book signing!?"

I shake my head, unable to stop laughing. "Jesus, woman. Just shut up and kiss me."

She lets out a raspy laugh. "As you wish."

I don't know how long we stay there in the elevator, feeling each other up like a bunch of horny teenagers, but when the doors ping open, we break apart and shoot to opposite ends of the cart.

We walk out silently to our room, and I have to embarrassingly rearrange the bulge in my pants as I walk past an elderly couple. Nora's shirt is buttoned incorrectly and it's only then that I really realise that I'm still topless. We both look ridiculous, and I can't help but laugh silently to myself when we walk down the lobby to our room.

The room door clicks behind us and Nora spins on her heels,

holding her fingers up to her lips. "We shouldn't have done that."

The words don't sting the way I thought they would because I know her better than that. She tries to take off to go into the ensuite but I grip her hand, bringing her to the bed. "Hey, don't run off on me now, Sunshine. We're going to talk about it."

She sighs dramatically. When I go to sit down, she just stands at the edge of the bed, starting to pace back and forth.

She glances up at me, and she rolls her eyes. "Can you put on a shirt, please?"

"You're wearing it, remember?" I wink at her, but she doesn't crack.

"Then find another one," she demands, walking the opposite way.

"Why?" I tease, leaning back on my hands. I'm having way too much fun with this. "Is all of this distracting you?"

She stops still, staring at me. "Well, considering the fact that I just stuck my tongue down your throat just then, yes, Wes, I'm distracted by your body. Sue me."

I tut as she continues pacing. "Nah, Sunshine. I think I know what this is."

"And what's that?"

"You're attracted to me, and you hate yourself for it." She just scoffs. "Oh, come on. You've wanted to do that for weeks, and now you're annoyed at yourself because your self-control snapped."

She stops then, turning to me. "You're the one that kissed *me*."

"And you begged for more."

Her cheeks beat when she remembers the way she told me to keep going and let me touch her in ways I've only dreamed about. "Oh my god. I did, didn't I? What's wrong with me?"

Her hands fly to her face, and I stand from the bed. I walk towards her, gripping her hands and pulling them down to run my thumbs over them. "Nothing. I'm just irresistible," I say sweetly. She narrows her eyes at me. "Look. What do you want to do? Do you want to pretend this never happened or let it happen some more? It's completely up to you. You can tell me to forget it, but I won't, and I think you know I won't."

She nibbles on her bottom lip, thinking intensely. "Can we— Can we put a pin in it?"

I bark out a laugh. "You want us to put a pin in it?"

"Yes. Don't laugh at me like it's not a real thing," she argues.

"It's a real thing, alright. But more in a business kind of way."

"Well, that's the best I can do for now. I've got a lot going on with the show when we go back. I can't mess this up now." She holds out her pinky to me, tilting her head to the side. "The big sell, remember?"

"The big sell," I repeat, locking my pinky with hers. I lean into her, loving this new game we've created, as I drop my forehead to hers. "You're probably right. It would be a bad idea to fuck your brains out before the show. Don't want you to damage your vocal cords."

"How do you know you won't be the one screaming?" she murmurs. I know what she's like when she's out of control, but I also know what she's like when she's bossing me around. Both of those versions of her in a sexual context could severely alter my brain chemistry.

"Fuck," I breathe into the space between us. "You're right. Let's put a pin in it."

TWENTY-NINE
WES/NORA
"I FOUND LOVE"

WES

AFTER QUITTING THE FOOTBALL TEAM, I wasn't expecting to see much of them again. I thought they'd ignore me when we passed each other in the halls, but I severely underestimated how much they actually care about me. It doesn't matter to them if I'm on the team or not, because either way, they'll still treat me like family. I've been planning something for a while now, and they're the only group of people I know who will be able to pull this off.

Or, I thought they were.

I slam my fist into the table.

I'm not usually a violent person, but there is something about this football team that makes me see red. They can play fine. They can do drills and listen to whatever the fuck my dad tells them, but whenever I try to get their attention, all their brainpower disappears.

I round the table once more, standing in front of them in the empty diner.

"The lyrics are less words than you need in an essay, guys. It's really not hard," I say for the millionth time.

Oliver looks up from his lyric sheet of the song I'm trying to get them to memorize. It's important that they sing the words right, but they're acting like I just told them to remember all the digits of pi.

"I don't get why we're doing this now. This place doesn't open until four, and it's two," Oli complains. Most of the guys hum in agreement.

I know exactly what day it is for the theater students at Drayton and where they go after their final rehearsal. The opening night of the show is tomorrow, but every year they go to this crappy diner on the outside of town where they celebrate and hype themselves up for the show. I'm never invited to these things, but I pulled a few strings for the owner to let us in so we can practice our routine before Nora, her friends, and hopefully Ryan turn up.

"Wes is right," Connor says. I never thought I would hear those words coming out of his mouth. I smile wide, and he rolls his eyes. We've come to some sort of agreement over the last few days. He might not be able to boss me around anymore, but he's finally letting go of the idea that I'll come running back to the team. "It's not that hard to remember, and we've got enough time to practice it."

"Exactly," I say, wafting my sheet in his direction in agreement. "Now, let's take it from the top, ladies."

NORA

The second rehearsals are over, and I'm practically falling over. I'm exhausted and hungry, and my brain hasn't felt right since the day of Wes's interview. I kept replaying those moments in the elevator, and all it was doing was distracting me. I want to get this show over with so I can finally have time to figure out what it is I really want.

I instantly regret our post-final rehearsal ritual because the only thing I want right now is to go to sleep. After Penny dismisses us, I run back to my dorm to shower and find something else to wear. The last thing I want is to feel disgusting the entire time while I can have some fun with my friends.

Once I've showered and gotten dressed, I walk back into my room to find Elle and Cat already sitting in there. "Uh, hi?"

"We're coming to Ruby's with you," Cat says.

"No, you're not," I say, laughing.

"We are. Traditions are changing, Nor-Nor," Elle agrees. "The last time we all went out, I tried to pry you and Wes off the dance floor several times, but neither of you would budge. This could do you some *sober* good."

"No, you don't get it. Theater kids are... A little unhinged," I say, not exactly wanting my two friend groups to merge. It's a disaster waiting to happen.

"You're unhinged," they both say at the same time. I gasp at their comment, but neither one of them seems to care.

"We can handle it," Cat says, beaming. "Besides, Connor really wants us all to hang out. He's worried about you."

"Still?" I groan. "Can't you just tell him that I'm fine? He's more likely to listen to you than he is to me. His priorities have been *so* out of whack recently."

Cat laughs, throwing her head back. "What are you talking about?"

"Before, they used to go: football, gym, mom and dad, me, Wes and then the rest of the football team. But now, it's you, football, Mom and Dad, Wes, gym, the rest of the football team, and *then* me."

Cat nibbles on her bottom lip, a sickeningly dreamy look in her eyes. "That's kinda sweet."

"No, not sweet! Very, very *not* sweet, Cat. Do you understand what this means!" I'm pretty sure I'm screaming like a crazy person right now as my best friend looks at me, wide-eyed and slightly terrified of me.

"No...."

"It means our system is breaking down," I whisper, shaking

my head at her. As overbearing as Connor is, I'm pretty sure that Cat has a special reserved spot inside of that weird brain of his, leaving little room for me.

"Hey, don't look at me like this is my fault. Your brother was the one who fell for me first," she argues, crossing her arms against her chest.

"You didn't have to love him back," I shout. She's trying so hard not to laugh, and honestly, I'm almost reaching breaking point, too.

"That's… kinda the whole point of a relationship, Nora," Elle adds, shaking her head.

Cat just laughs. "Anyway, you're insane, and I love you, but he says it's important, and I've already tried bailing, trust me."

"Fine," I grumble.

CATHERINE LATCHES onto my arm when we get to the door of the Ruby's. It's a classic old-school diner that my class claimed freshman year, and we've come here every night before the opening night of our shows. It's the only place that can fit all of us and where we can relax with some shitty food and old music.

"Don't kill me for what they're about to do, okay?"

My heart stops when she pushes open the door. "Why would I–"

Before I can finish my sentence, music starts to blare from the speakers as the lights dim. My ears and my eyes hardly get to process anything before the intro to 'Love' by Keyshia Cole starts to play. I immediately recognise it before I can comprehend that most of the football team are wearing red t-shirts slowly making their way towards me, singing as loud and as badly as possible.

When I go to reach for Elle and Cat, I find that they're out of sight and instead in one corner with her phone in front of their faces, laughing at my nightmare.

The ringleader, of course, is Wes, singing the loudest out of them, brushing his dark curls out of his face when he reaches me. He's got my name written on his cheek in red face paint, his cheeks flaming almost as much as mine are. I don't know how I can even look at him after whatever the fuck happened in that elevator.

"What are you doing?" I ask breathlessly as he pulls me into him.

He spins me out and then back in, letting the rest of the team sing the song. "Serenading you," he answers easily. He clasps his hand over mine, pressing it to his lips. I shake my head in disbelief. "Is it working?"

I can't even hide my laugh as I try to seriously say, "No."

"You're laughing. That's a good sign."

"You're stupid," I reply. The chorus ends, and before I can back away, all the boys from the team come up to me and pass me a pink rose. This feels like some really cheesy promposal, although it's not prom or anything soon. When Connor hands me a rose, I shake my head at him. "Why are you doing this, too?"

He nods towards Wes, who somehow manages to sling his arm around my shoulder. "Why do you think?" Connor murmurs, sauntering away as the rest of the team all circle me, continuing to sing the song.

Wes pulls me into him again, placing us in a waltzing position. "Tell me, Stargirl. Is this boyfriend enough of me?" he whispers.

"This is ridiculous is what it is," I say, squinting my eyes at him. He pushes a strand of hair behind my ear and my body tenses. "Why in the world would you think I'd enjoy this?"

"Because I've got a gorgeous voice, and you like romance?" I tilt my head to the side, waiting for him to sigh. "You deserve to be celebrated like this, Nora."

I nod, swallowing the emotion in my throat. "By this, do you mean very loudly?"

"Yes," he says, "You deserve to be loved loudly and no other way."

His words take me back to the first time Ryan and I ever broke up, and I thought we'd never get back together. They remind me of the times when I felt so unworthy of love that I hardly had any love left for myself. They also remind me of the amount of times Wes has shown that he's going to be there for me and embarrass me even when I don't exactly want him to.

I let go of his hand and wrap my arms around him instead. "Thank you, Wes," I whisper, instantly feeling weird for thanking him for one of the most embarrassing moments of my life. "I think I needed that."

"I know, Stargirl. I've got your back, okay?" he says, pulling apart from the hug and holding my shoulders at arm's length. "Don't forget that."

"Okay," I repeat. "Was this the big sell?"

"Almost," he mutters before pressing his lips to mine.

I let myself get lost in him, and when he holds me tighter to him, I gasp. My eyes flutter open for a second to catch Ryan and the rest of my class staring at us. I continue kissing Wes, not for the sake of pissing off Ryan – though that's a bonus – but because I *want* to. I *want* to have him like this. I *want* to constantly be questioning what he's going to do next and how he's going to one-up his last gesture. I *want* to travel places with him and hold his hand.

I think I just want *him*.

THIRTY
NORA
STARGIRL

AFTER MONTHS of torture and spending days with some of my closest friends on this stage, the day has finally come.

I'm usually an anxious mess the few days leading up to the show, but most of my anxieties disappear when the day arrives. I tell myself that I just have to give my all. Even when I'm tired, exhausted, and ready to give up, I just need to keep on pushing, and it'll be over soon. It also helps that Wes left a bouquet of pink lilies in my dorm when I woke up this morning.

> *To my Stargirl,*
> *I'd wish you luck, but I know you don't need it.*
> *You're going to be amazing.*
> *If you hear anyone screaming at the top of their lungs, that's me.*
> *Yours always, Wes.*

I MAY HAVE SHED a few tears reading that message. There's no one in the world that makes me feel the way Wes makes me feel. It's like he has this never-ending amount of hope in me. This constant belief that I'm going to make something of myself. I just wish he'd put some of that hope in himself because I have no doubt that he'll find what he's passionate about and will become the best version of himself.

Since Ryan's little outburst the other day, he's managed to make me want to punch him less. My plan finally broke through to him, and he's no longer trying to get under my skin. He might have this sad look in his eye, but I don't need to keep making myself sick over how *he* feels after the way he treated me. I want to put myself first, and that's exactly what I'm doing. He pulled through at rehearsals yesterday, and I've not stepped on his feet once today.

The first act goes perfectly. The audience was full, and when I stepped out onto the stage to find all my friends in the front row, it felt like my heart was on fire. I'm pretty sure Cat and Elle were crying. Connor just looked happy to be there. Archer looks like music has personally offended him in some way, and he'd much rather be anywhere else. I'm sure he's got a secret musical theater playlist hidden somewhere. There are a few guys from the football team, too, who are here to support as well as my parents, who are looking up at me with a dreamy look in their eyes. When my eyes connected with Wes's, it wasn't like the time he came to intimidate Ryan. I didn't feel this tiny, anxious fire in my stomach. I felt settled. Happy. Just looking at him doesn't make me worry about the next time he's going to do something to hurt me like it did when I was with Ryan.

He proves that when he startles me in the dressing room backstage.

I usually spend the intermission in my own little cave, listening to music so I'm not dragged out of my zone. Wes clearly doesn't know that because when I'm ready to leave my little station, Wes bursts into the small area, panting. It's only then that I notice the very tight-fitted shirt he's wearing... with my face on it. He chose one of the worst pictures of me from a few years ago, where I'm sticking my tongue out. Around the photo are the words, 'I 🩷 Nora Bailey.'

"Holy shit," Wes exclaims, his eyes wide as he makes his way towards me. "You were so fucking good, Nora. I'm just– Ah! You were so good."

"Thank you," I laugh, my cheeks feeling hot and red. "But you can't be in here, you know?"

He just shrugs, kneeling down in front of me. He looks up at me, resting his hands on my thighs, and my breath catches. "Don't care. I just need to tell my girl how fucking amazing she is."

I'm about to protest, but he leans up off his knees to my height on the chair and presses his lips to mine. He tastes like he was made just for me — all fresh and summery and sweet. His hands travel up my waist, where my corset is keeping me locked in, until his hands wrap around the nape of my neck. I kiss him back deeply. I could get used to this kind of intermission tradition.

"Wes," I murmur into his mouth when he tips my head back. "You're going to mess up my makeup."

"It's okay," he whispers. "We can just do it again after."

I don't bother arguing with him because having him here like this, supporting me, holding me, kissing me, is more than enough. No matter how many times my life feels like it's spinning out of control, Wes pulls me back. He brings me back down to earth, and he's going to continue doing that for as long as I let him.

I know I don't have long left before I have to get back to joining the rest of the cast, so I push him off me slightly. "Okay, loverboy. I need to do my makeup all again because of you." He sighs before pressing another kiss to my lips. I scrunch my nose at him as he looks over at my vanity and starts reorganizing my makeup for me. "What are you doing?"

He holds up a beauty blender to me. "I just have to use this, right?"

"Yes, but–"

"Okay, perfect," Wes says, tilting my face back to him.

I blink as he picks up my concealer, applying it under my eyes and above my lip. He's got his tongue sticking out, his face painted in pure concentration as he continues working his magic. He starts dabbing the beauty blender on my face and I let out a laugh.

"What are you doing?"

"What does it look like? I said *we'd* sort it out, didn't I?" His eyes have a mischievous glint when his gaze meets mine again. I shake my head, unable to stop smiling. He picks up my blush and applies it in all the right places and I have no energy to fight him on this. After he's done and I've inspected his handiwork, he just leans back down on his knees and looks up at me.

"What?" I breathe out. I feel exactly as I did as he watched me in the mirror in New York. I *never* get nervous around Wes. Only when he looks at me like this. I'll never be able to explain it, but there are times where he looks at me like he's looking right through me. It's like he just *knows* he's got me wrapped around his little finger.

"God, you're so pretty," he whispers. My heart somersaults at his soft words. He drops his head to my knees, and it feels like he's worshiping me. His back rises and falls and the position is doing weird things to my insides.

"Thank you," I say shakily. He looks back up, his mouth twitching into a small smile. "You like making me nervous, don't you?"

He nods, grinning. "I like making you blush. I like watching you squirm when I compliment you. I like you knowing how insanely gorgeous you are," he says simply. "Most of all, I just like hearing you thank me."

I can't conjure up many words, so I lean down and kiss him again. "Thank you," I murmur into his mouth, knowing I'm thanking him for a multitude of things.

THE REST of the show goes smoothly. Even when I think we're going to mess up some choreography or stumble over the harder parts of the script, we pull through. The glow on Kiara's face, as she performs her duet with Ryan, makes me feel warm and fuzzy inside like I'm somehow refracting light from the inside. It reminds me of every good reason I had to perform and why I love being on a stage so much.

That feeling expands when I run into my friend's arms, and they're screaming at me about how well I did. Cat is still gushing over my outfit, Elle is screaming about her favorite song, *Burn*, and Connor and Archer grumble about how the lighting gave them a headache. And Wes stands back, watching all my friends shower me with praise, and he just winks at me. That simple gesture tops it all off.

I try to catch my breath as we walk back to the car, and Wes's arm tugs on mine. "I hope you're not too tired, Nor."

"I just performed a three-hour musical, Wes. Yes, I'm tired," I say, turning to him.

"Come on. You must have some singing in you left," he argues.

I hum. "Don't think so. I kinda left it all on the stage."

"Too bad," he says, shrugging. "I already booked us in for a slot at a karaoke bar."

"Seems like I don't have much of a choice."

"You always have a choice, Sunshine," he chuckles, holding out his hand to me. "So, what's it gonna be?"

Fuck it.

I slip my hand into his, knowing I've made the right decision.

THIRTY-ONE
NORA
PARTY FOR A KING

"LET'S GO, let's go, let's go!"

You'd think that making plans with someone four days ago would give them more than enough time to get ready to go out. But if your friends are anything like mine, then they need another hour on top of their designated time to get ready.

The boys have invited us over for dinner, and it'll be good for all of us to hang out again. Cat is constantly moving between their house and our dorm and working. Elle lives in the studio and at the gym. Wes is still working hard on finding more interviews or a course that interests him. Now that I've stopped rehearsals and I'm preparing for my end-of-year exams, this might be the last time we get to hang out as a group.

I'm standing next to the door, my hands on my hips, when Elle and Cat finally materialize from their rooms.

"Someone's excited," Elle murmurs, opening the fridge to grab a bottle of water.

I roll my eyes. "Sorry, I'm desperate to see my boyfriend."

Cat narrows her eyes at me. "Fake boyfriend," she corrects. I just shrug. "Oh, wait. Isn't the contract over since the shows are done?"

I bite my bottom lip. "Well, uh, sort of. We're just—" I clear my throat. I told them about what happened at Wes's interview, but I'm honestly not completely sure what is going on with us. So, I add, "We're friends. That I know for sure."

"Friends who fuck," Elle says, laughing as she meets us at the door.

"Not exactly."

"Do you want that?" Cat asks gently.

"I dunno," I mumble, thinking about every single moment we've shared up until now. The way he makes me feel like I'm glowing. The way he's *always* made me feel that way, and I've been too in my head to notice it. I shrug. "I think I just want Wes."

Cat and Elle's eyes light up at my words, and they surround me in seconds, pulling me into a tight hug. I'd tell them to get off me, but I like it a little too much. Their warmth can't be compared to anything else. It's inherently *theirs*, and I wish I could feel it around me forever.

"Finally," Elle sighs.

"Jesus, you're so in love with him it makes me sick," Cat says. I push them both off me, smoothing out my sweater.

I ignore the way my heart starts to race and open the door. "Whatever. Let's just go."

***

When we walk up to the house, we all look at each other because something feels insanely wrong. The whole front yard is covered in confetti, balloons, and a huge birthday banner is slung across the front of the house.

"Whose birthday is it?" Cat asks, stepping over the decorations as we make our way through the house. It's eerily quiet for a birthday party.

"I've got no idea. Wes's birthday isn't until June, and I doubt he's arrogant enough to host it months in advance," I mumble, laughing at the thought.

More decorations scatter the living room, and a ton of jackets are thrown around haphazardly. How many people have been invited to this thing? I thought Connor was just going to cook us some food like he usually does, not host an entire party. There's no music playing. There's no loud voices like there would be at a party. Connor appears down the hallway, shaking his head like he doesn't know that we're here.

"Are we missing someone's birthday?" Elle asks, looking visibly anxious at the thought.

"It's the cat's birthday," Connor grumbles when he sees us. He helps Cat out of her jacket, kissing her on the forehead as he ushers us toward the back door.

"You mean Jarvis?" I laugh.

"Yup." He slides open the door to the backyard, and my mouth drops open. "Wes rallied the team to come to help out since, apparently, everyone has pets these days."

I try to get my brain to catch up with what I'm witnessing, but it's insanely difficult. Most of the football team at Drayton sits in a circle on the grass with an array of pets in their laps as they dress them up, clean off their paws, and comb their fur. This feels like a fever dream.

Of course, Wes is sitting there with Jarvis in his lap, petting him as he watches the rest of the boys get to work. Cat and Elle are in a fit of hysterical laughter beside me and I'm still trying to believe what I'm seeing.

"Connie?" Cat calls as he tries to walk back into the house. He turns back around. "Are you ready to be a dad?"

"What?" He gawks, his eyes bulging. Elle and I snicker.

"I'm not pregnant or anything, but I, like, really want you to put a baby in me now," she mumbles. "Whatever the hell this is, is fucking up my hormones."

"Sweetheart, you know I'd give you anything you want, but this is the one thing you have to ask me again in a couple of years," Connor says, laughing as he leans down to kiss her on the forehead.

"Whatever," she says, pushing him away from her. "Go and be a grump somewhere else. You clearly don't get what it's like to see a man with a pet or with babies. What do you have against pets, anyway?"

"They're messy and loud, and they remind me too much of Wes and his chaos."

"*I'm* messy and loud," she challenges.

"That's different. You're mine, Cat. I don't care if you're messy and loud."

Elle lets out a sitcom-worthy sigh, and I gag. "That was sweet," Cat murmurs, leaning up to kiss my brother. Gross.

"I'm going to kill Wes for putting these images in your mind," Connor grumbles, tugging her closer to him.

"Do you guys want to keep telling me how perfectly okay it is to still be a virgin? Because there's about twenty men here sitting with their pets, and I want to fuck all of them," Elle says. I just blink at her, my mouth popping open. "See? I thought not."

"You've got twenty options now, Elle-Belle," I say, gesturing towards the array of men in front of us. "I'm confident they'll all be on their knees for you if you give them one look."

"You know what?" Elle starts, shimming her shoulders. "I'm going to give it a try."

***

Connor eventually comes around and sits with one of his teammates husky, and Cat watches him with hearts in her eyes. I've made my way around nearly all of the pets, marveling over someone's pet snake and lizard as they've got little bow ties on them. It's fucking adorable.

Not so adorable? One of the boys is sitting with a very angry-looking pug in his lap with an equally angry look on his face. I scooch closer to him, scratching the dog on the head.

"What's this fella's name?" I ask his owner. The boy just sighs.

"Bruce. He bites. I'd stay away from him if I were you," he explains, but I'm not frightened that easily. I look up at the boy, and I realize that he doesn't look angry. Just bored. Like he'd much rather be spending his Thursday night literally anywhere else. What in the world does Wes say to these people to get them to do what he wants? His features look insanely familiar, and I can't put my finger on it.

"Wait," I mumble, putting his features together. I can't remember his first name, but I know where "You're Michael Cohen's son."

"Yeah...." He tears back, looking at me up and down. "You're not, like, a crazy football fan, are you?"

I snort. "God, no. I'm just friends with these idiots."

He hums. "I thought you were Wes's girlfriend."

I look up to find Wes lying on his back, sunglasses covering his eyes, and Jarvis curled up on his chest. They look so perfect together. Watching them makes my heart twinge with a feeling I've never felt before, like a tiny fire that I need to put out.

"Yeah," I murmur, "That too."

After engaging in some talk with Hayes, I make my way around the circle again. Elle has been trying to convince Archer to play with one of the animals, but he's not budging. I'm convinced she's doing it for her own fantasies to replay in her head because trying to argue with Archer is like talking to a wall.

I sit down next to Wes, and he's still lying on his back. I poke him in the cheek, and he lifts the sunglasses onto his forehead. "Hi," I say.

He grins. "Hi, Sunshine."

"What is all this?" I laugh, gesturing to the space we're in.

"It's his birthday," is his answer, stroking Jarvis as he purrs quietly. I continue staring at the two of them, still confused as to why most of the football team are here. "So, he's getting treated like a king. He might be getting old, but he needs some friends, too."

My chest expands at the sentiment. "You really care about him, huh?"

"Yup." He crosses his arms behind his head. His biceps distract me for a second before my eyes connect with his. "He's one of the four groups of people I care about. There are my friends, my family, and him."

"You said four," I correct. "What about the fourth one?"

The smile on his face falters a little as he whispers, "You."

I cover the sweetness of his words with humor, "I get my own group? How kind."

He shakes his head, laughing. "You're always going to be different from everybody else, Nora."

"Different isn't always a good thing."

"It is to me."

It's those words that seem to start slowly patching up the hole in my heart. The one that has been tearing more and more every day. Wes manages to make all the parts of myself that I hate seem beautiful. He makes *me* feel beautiful, and he doesn't even have to do anything. It's just him.

THIRTY-TWO
WES
STARRY EYES

I THOUGHT that discussing girl troubles — if you can even call it that — with my friends would mean that I'd get something out of it. Maybe they'd bless me with some life-changing advice and help me figure out the girl I can't stop thinking about. But they don't.

I don't think Archer has ever been in a real relationship in his life, so maybe he was the wrong person to go to for help, but he's my only option.

"Does she like you?" Archer asks, shoving a nacho into his mouth. Connor isn't the only person who can work his way around the kitchen. Archer and I have managed to make a few decent snacks over the last few months, and our skills come in handy when we want to chill and watch the game, like tonight. Connor's out on a date with Cat, and we'll probably hear them stumbling in later tonight, giggling like teenagers.

"Well, considering the fact that she asked me to kiss her twice, and I shut her down, then yeah," I say.

"Why'd you shut her down?"

I sigh, tilting my head back on the couch. "I didn't want her to make a mistake. I didn't want her to jump right into this just because I've been obsessed with her for years. It was hard to tell if she wanted me or if she was just turned on and I was there."

Archer hums. "That's fair. So, what's changed?"

I explained to him the whole situation we had in Denver and the elevator fiasco, leaving out the part about me palming her boobs and how I almost came just from touching her. We've been in this weird purgatory state since we came back, and I have no clue how to move on from it. I want her for real. I've wanted her for real since the day I met her, and now I finally have the chance. This is my opening.

"Sounds like you've got a lot on your hands," Archer says.

"Gee, that's helpful. Thank you," I grumble.

"What do you want me to say? You guys clearly have a thing for each other. I say fuck and get it over with."

"That's not going to solve anything, you idiot. I need to *talk* to her," I say, getting agitated.

"Then talk to her and quit fucking around." I'm about to throw another snarky comment his way, but my phone starts to ring beside me.

My dad's laid off me recently, and my mom has been busy editing her upcoming book, so I'm not expecting either of them to call me. My chest warms when I see Nora's contact fill the screen. I answer, pressing the phone to my ear, ready for her voice to soothe me.

"Wes?"

"Hey, Sunshine. What's up?"

A sharp inhale on the other side of the phone has the hairs on my neck standing up. "I need you."

"What?" I choke out. This doesn't sound like the same girl who was playing with puppies in my backyard a few days ago.

"I need you to come over," she says, her voice watery and strained. "No one's home, and I— I need you, Wes. Please, can you come over?"

I stand to my feet, not bothering to explain anything to

Archer, as I grab my jacket from the rack near the door. "Are you okay? Are you hurt?"

"No. I just–" A sharp sob rips through her, and I unlock the front door. "I just really need you here."

"It's okay, baby. I'm coming."

MY HEART THRASHES against my ribs as I pass multiple speed limits as I try to get to her. I instantly regret moving out of the dorms and into a house off campus because if she needs me like this, I need to get to her immediately. I can't be fucking around worrying about speed limits when I need to be with her.

I take the stairs three at a time when I get to her building and push through the door when I get there. Thank god for spare keys. I frantically search around the living room area and I don't find her. My pulse hammers under my skin when I get to her bedroom door, swinging it open.

Nora's sitting on the floor surrounded by the mess that was her room. Her clothes and books are lying around her, jewelry scattered everywhere. Worst of all, she's still crying.

I rush down to her, holding her damp face up to me.

"Hey, hey, hey. What's going on?" She's still crying, her eyes shut tight as if she's trying to make me disappear. "It's okay. Just breathe for me." She takes in a deep breath, her shoulders shaking on the exhale. "Yeah. That's it. Take your time."

I wait for her to calm down, rubbing my hand against her cheek as she nestles her face into my palm. Her eyes droop. "It's gone, Wes."

"What's gone?"

"The necklace. The one my dad gave me. The— The one with the star. I'm such a fucking idiot, and it's probably in the middle of New York somewhere, and I'm never going to get it back. I wear it so much that I never check that I still have it. It's just always there, and now... It's not. I'm never going to find it."

"Hey, don't say that," I say softly, swiping the tears from under her eyes. "We'll look for it."

"I've already looked!"

"Did you call me over here to shout at me or for me to help you?" She just blinks at me and I drop my forehead to hers. "Here's what we're going to do. You're going to go in the shower and relax. Don't stress or worry about it and I'll look for it. If I can't find it, we'll both look again in the morning with a fresh set of eyes and a clearer mind. You're panicked, and you're scared. You're not going to be able to find anything if you're running on fumes." I watch her take a deep breath. "Have you eaten?"

"I- I had an early dinner, but since then, I've been looking, so I haven't had anything."

"Okay, I'm going to order us some food. Is pizza good?"

"Yeah." She nods. Once. Twice. "Yeah, pizza's good."

"Look at me, pretty girl." I tilt her chin up so I can see her eyes. They're still filled with tears, red and worn out. "We're going to find it. Okay? And you're going to get your pizza, and then we're going to go to sleep, and it's all going to be okay."

"Okay."

In the time it takes her to shower, I manage to get the food delivered and have looked around her room twice. I know she's taking the time to calm down, but I'm left here freaking out. I feel like such an idiot for not paying more attention. I should have known that it was gone. I spend so much time thinking about her and trying to commit her to memory, and I don't remember the last time I saw her with it on.

When I've concluded my search for the second time, I start reorganizing her room again. I've been in here enough times to know where things go, but I still feel helpless. I feel like I should be doing more. Because I can't deal with the painfully sad look on her face when she comes out of the bathroom in pink biker shorts and an oversized white shirt. We eat mostly in silence on the floor of her room, and I don't know what to say to break the awkwardness. I'm still running on fumes, but I don't want to say the wrong thing.

After we've eaten and I've thrown away the trash, I walk back into Nora's room to find her in her bed, her knees pulled up to her chest. She seems so fragile like this. Like if I try to reach out to her, she'll break.

"Hey," I murmur, kneeling onto the bed to sit beside her. "You're okay."

She shakes her head, burying it into her knees before she turns to me, fresh tears lining her eyes. "I'm going to fuck everything up."

"Fuck what up?" I ask gently, bringing my hand to rub small circles on her back.

"Everything," she sobs. "I keep making stupid mistakes. I keep messing things up and I'm constantly knocking myself back down. I can't get any sort of acting gig. I can't even hold on to the one thing that I thought I'd never lose. Whenever I think I'm at a high, something else happens, and I'm pushed right back to where I started. And I know everyone says that it gets better, but what if it doesn't? What if I'm destined to have short-lived moments of happiness just for it to vanish? What if none of it is permanent?" She takes a deep breath. "And it's *me*, Wes. No one else is doing this. It's quite literally all my fault, and I'm just going to keep doing shit like this until there's nothing left of me."

My heart breaks for her. I don't know how many times I have to tell her that she's special. That she's got something good. That she has an abundance of talents and I'm just lucky enough to be in her orbit. I've never been good with words, and I don't know how to help her. To get her to see herself the way I see her. The way I've *always* seen her.

"Stars still shine after they die, Nora," I whisper.

She sniffles. "But what if I don't?"

"But what if you *do*?"

I don't know what it is about my words that makes her break

down, but she's sobbing harder again. I pull her into me. She wraps her arms around me, and I fall onto my back. Nora's body feels so natural against mine that I just let her mold into me. Become one with me. I run my hands through her hair, waiting for the storm to pass. She lets me hold her like this, soothing her as much as I can. When her cries soften and her breathing steadies, I trail my finger up and down her spine.

"Hey, Wes?" she whispers into the comfortable silence.

"Hey, Nora."

"You're a star too." My chest tightens at her words, making it extremely fucking difficult to breathe. I force myself to exhale when she peers up at me, her body still wrapped around mine. I don't get any words out and continue running my finger down her spine. "You might just be *my* star, but you're the brightest one. You're more like the sun. I orbit around you, Wes. Just you."

I wait for the words to come, but they don't. Just looking at her has all my words scrambled and my heart beating so fast that it might as well fall right out of my chest. I just press my lips to her forehead, sealing the moment because being the sun in Nora Bailey's eyes isn't something I can put into words.

THIRTY-THREE
NORA

"YOU'RE DOING WES."

HAVE you ever cried so hard that you forget what you're crying for? Where your chest feels like it's collapsing in on itself, and you can't get yourself to stop. Or you're crying so hard to the point where you feel ridiculous, and you just want to laugh at yourself. I'm stuck between both of them right now.

Last night was the first time in a while that I've cried that hard. Being overwhelmed with the show, still not hearing back from Max, and then losing my necklace all came crashing down on me like an avalanche. Everything felt too hard to carry. The weight of thinking I'd never be good enough sent me into a spiral. I've felt like a burden these last few months, and the last thing I wanted to do was pull Elle away from her dance rehearsal or, worse, ask Cat to call off her date just so she could deal with my meltdown.

Wes's presence has a habit of calming me down. He might be chaotic and loud and say things that don't make sense, but he's always had my back. He never judges me. He's seen all the worst parts of me, the parts that I find ugly, and he still cares about me.

Just like now as we lay in my bed, feeling like the calm after the storm. I didn't sleep much last night, but after I kept tossing and turning, Wes eventually pulled me into him and held on to me so I could get a few hours in. He didn't let go of me the entire night.

I shift in the bed, sitting up against the headboard. My head is spinning, and I desperately need some aspirin and at least a pint of water. We've been awake for a while, just silently enjoying each other's presence, and I couldn't think of anything more perfect.

Wes pushes himself up next to me, running a hand through his messy hair. "How are you feeling?"

"Tired," I say, the word instantly making me yawn. Wes chuckles quietly, shaking his head at me. He looks tired, too. There are bags under his eyes, and he's got lines on his face from the places where his face was pressed into the sheets. "Thank you for coming over yesterday. I'm sorry that I called you like that."

He shrugs, rubbing his eye, which only makes me feel worse. "You don't have to apologize," he says.

"But I do, Wes." His mouth opens as he rests his head against the headboard, turning to me. I point at him. "Don't cut me off, okay?" He nods, a sleepy grin spreading across his face. "I feel like I'm pulling you into my shit. You're already trying to figure your own life out, and I'm just making it so much worse. I know I said we'd put a pin in it, but maybe we should just take the pin out."

"And do what?" he asks softly.

"I don't know," I admit. "I just don't want you to feel like you have to continue doing *this* because we're both horny and you feel sorry for me."

"Can I say something now?" I nod. "I want this, Nora. I want *you*. And I only want to take the pin out if it means that we get to do this."

My chest tingles at his words. "And what is this?"

"This," he murmurs right before he kisses me. My entire body comes alive when Wes's lips are on mine. It's like his touch is constantly bringing me back to life, making me crave him that much more. I want the roughness of his lips against my smooth ones. I want to feel the way his hands slide into my hair. The way he tugs the strands at the nape of my neck, desperately trying to get more of me. I crave the way I open up to him, letting him take me.

His thumbs smooth across my cheeks as he rears back slightly. "God, Nora," he mutters. "I'm never going to get tired of this."

"You're not?"

"Never," he whispers. "I would look at you all day if I could. I'd spend every moment kissing you, cherishing you, doing *anything* you asked me if you gave me a chance."

His saccharine words make my heart feel like it's going to fall out of my chest. When his lips connect with mine again, I give him everything. My mouth works seamlessly with his, our tongues dancing together like we just know the exact way to make each other feel good. My hands can't stop touching and exploring his body. I twine my fingers in his curly hair, needing him closer to me, needing to feel him everywhere.

I hook one leg over his waist, pushing myself into his lap. We both gasp when his hard dick presses into me, but we don't stop. I'm frantically trying to kiss him as I pull my shirt over my head, throwing it away. I swear Wes's pupils dilate when he sees that I'm only wearing a bra. My entire chest flushes with heat before he dives right in, kissing across my chest like he was made to do it. His hands travel down my sides, squeezing my waist as he pushes me closer to him, still feasting on me.

"You feel too good," he mutters. He leaves long lingering kisses across my neck, making my head roll back. "I've missed having you like this. Since I had one taste, I've been dying for another."

"Me too," I pant, gripping his hair for stability as he trails his kisses down the valley of my breasts. "I wanted... I wanted to do this on Jarvis's birthday. I don't think I've wanted anything this badly."

He shakes his head, kissing back up my chest. "No, I mean before that. I've wanted you for years. Ever since we were kids and you confirmed to me what beauty meant. I've wanted you since then."

I disguise the tightening in my chest with humor as I pull his head up to face me. "Jesus, you're such a romantic," I mutter before I kiss him again.

My whole body feels achy from the position we're in, but it feels way to fucking good to stop. Wes rolls me over him, clearly satisfied with the moan that leaves my mouth when he does.

He pulls back from me, his eyes narrow. "Wait? Watching me pamper my cat is what did it for you?"

I bark out a laugh. "Well, that amongst other things."

He tilts his head to the side, that sexy as fuck smile on his lips. "Yeah? Like what?"

"Your haircut," I say instantly. I love a decent haircut and length on a man. Sue me. "The way you talk about me. The way you make me feel. Your humor. Your smile. Your—"

He cuts me off with a kiss. "Okay, stop, or I'm going to pass out."

I do as he says, unable to hide the huge grin that's on my face. Every touch from him feels like there's a fire inside me. Every time he says my name quietly like he's trying to remind himself that he's got me now. We're always giving ourselves to one another. Always trying to make the other feel good. He proves that to me as he keeps rolling me over him, and I can feel my arousal seeping through my shorts. My hips are doing most of the work, grinding down on him until I'm left a whimpering mess. Each time I feel like he's going to increase the speed, he just edges me and slows down again, holding tighter onto my hips.

"Wes," I whimper, my body feeling out of control from this push and pull. "That feels too good. Stop teasing me."

He hums. "Is that what I'm doing?"

"Yes," I hiss.

He just smiles, gripping onto my hips to move me over his length so fucking slowly. "Is this torturing you, baby?"

God.

Wes has a million and one nicknames for me, but this one fucks me up the most inside. Especially when he's beneath me like this, his hands branding all over my body as I desperately try to get myself off. And he's not letting me.

"Yes." The back of my neck is gathering sweat, and I'm painfully writhing in his lap.

His grin turns evil. "Great. Now you know how I've felt for the last five years watching you kiss someone that isn't me."

"You're one jealous mother—"

The loud sound of a knock at my door interrupts me. I freeze in place.

"Nora? Are you home?" Cat calls from the other side of the door. "I need a debrief after last night's date. You'll never—"

"Can we talk later?" I ask. My voice turns into a strained whimper when Wes pulls down the material of my bra, sucking my nipple into his mouth. He keeps his eyes locked with mine, and my vision blurs. The small bud hardens at the attention, a sensation I haven't felt in months. "I'm, uh, kinda busy."

"Doing what?" Cat laughs on the other side of the door, which I hope disguises the moan that leaves my mouth when Wes swirls his tongue around my nipple. He doesn't get the hint to stop, and part of me doesn't want him to because he's making me feel like a goddess right now.

He grinds my core into him.

"Wes," I cry out.

"You're *doing* Wes?" Cat asks.

He grins up at me, watching the way the heat rushes to my cheeks. I'm panting now, about to fall off the edge of the cliff with the stimulation. "Can we just talk later?"

"Sure," she replies, "Just use a condom, you freaks. I don't want any little Wes' running around when we graduate."

When I hear her footsteps pad away, I let Wes continue worshiping my body as I grind down into his lap. I've never finished with so many clothes covering me, but with the way Wes holds me, the way his hard length is pressing into me, and the way his tongue works over my nipple is bringing me closer and closer to the edge.

I do the stupid thing and look down at him, and his eyes lock with mine. I'm completely drenched, my wetness seeping onto his sweatpants. I'd be embarrassed if it didn't feel this good. His hands roam over my back, clutching me closer to him as he drags his lips up my chest. He brings his lips to my ear, whispering, "Are you going to come for me, baby?"

"Yes," I moan. I've never heard such dirty words come out of his mouth, and I fucking love it.

"That's my good girl." That's what does it. It's like a switch is flicked when he whispers those simple words in my ear. Praise from the right people has always done it for me, and hearing them come out of Wes's mouth tips me right over.

I try to catch my breath, feeling like a hot, sweaty mess, and I drop my head to Wes's shoulder. He holds me there, chuckling as he runs his hand down my spine as the sensation rattles through me. "Jesus Christ, Wes. That was—"

"Hot," he replies, bringing his hand from my back to around my neck, turning my head towards him.

"Yeah," I murmur, still panting. He holds me close to him, and the realization dawns on me. I don't want to constantly question what we are to each other like I did with Ryan. I want to know where we stand and how he feels. "What does this mean?"

He doesn't hesitate. "Whatever you want it to mean." I hum, liking that answer, but it still doesn't completely settle me. It still feels like my head is empty and full all at the same time. As if reading my mind, he asks, "What are you scared of, Sunshine? Tell me what you're thinking, and let me help you."

I sigh. "I'm scared of messing this up. Ruining the system. And you can't pretend there isn't a system. You know what it is."

I sit up better in his lap to face him, and he just shrugs. "Cat and Connor broke the system. Why can't we?"

"Because I'm a mess," I laugh, thinking about how put-together Catherine is—how perfect she is for a person like Connor. Wes and I are constantly in stupid situations, and that isn't going to change overnight.

"I want you," he says roughly, holding onto my cheeks. "I want *us*, Nora. Me and you together. That's the way it's supposed to be."

"According to who?"

"Me."

I tilt my head to the side, but he rubs his thumb softly under my eye. "And I don't get a say in it?"

"Of course you do," he whispers, pressing his forehead to mine. "What's your heart telling you, Stargirl?"

I take a deep breath. "I want you, too."

Wes closes his eyes, letting out a breath of relief. "Thank fuck, because the rest of the day would have gone to shit if you didn't."

I pull apart from him. "What are you talking about?"

I had given up trying to guess what Wes would do next when we were five years old. That way, I'm always in a constant state of surprise when I'm around him. I always feel I'm floating because, though he might keep me on Earth, he also lifts me so high that it's like I'm flying.

All I can do when someone knocks on our door is eye Wes up and down. He stands in the hallway with his arms against his chest like he just *knows* that he's got me now. Even when the huge bouquet of pink lilies is shoved in my face, he just continues smiling at me like I hung the fucking moon.

"Did you get these because of my mega dramatic meltdown yesterday?" I ask, moving the bouquet on the counter.

"No, I got them a week ago. I don't know why they took so long," he grumbles.

I snort. "Why?"

"Why did they take so long? I don't fucking know. I tried to ask—"

"No, Wes. Why did you buy me the flowers?" I ask, unable to contain my laughter. He pulls me into him by my waist, a classic move I'll never get tired of.

He shrugs. "I just wanted to."

THIRTY-FOUR
WES/NORA
ARE YOU A PRINCE?

WES

WHEN I WAS YOUNGER, my mom would sit me down every Friday, and we'd watch a romantic comedy together. After spending the week watching football with my dad or whatever stupid cartoon that rotted my brain, my mom made sure it was important that she instilled some sort of chivalry in me. Most of the films were unrealistic depictions of real life, with mermaids turning into humans and humans turning into frogs, but one thing always stayed the same.

She made me realize how important love is — platonic and romantic. It made me appreciate her and everyone in my life, and I showed it in different ways. Whilst my dad would get a very badly made cup of coffee some mornings, I'd slip my mom's slippers right next to her side of the bed so she could slide right into them when she woke up. I'd make them both Valentine's Day cards at school, and I'd not shut up about how much I cared about them. I was always sensitive like that. I'd get made fun of sometimes, but I mostly pushed it off. I'd much rather love someone loudly than in the quiet where they don't know.

It's different with Nora.

I'm pretty sure I fell in love with Nora Bailey before I could even read properly. Way before I even knew what the word meant, only the soft glowing feeling in my heart that I'd get whenever she was around. She had chubby cheeks, faint freckles dotted across the bridge of her nose, and long brown hair that I wanted to touch so badly. She was always talking, laughing, trying to make sure everybody stayed friends. She'd hold meetings during recess to discuss why people weren't friends and how to fix their problems. She always made time for me and made me feel like I could tell her anything. She made me feel like I could *be* anything, and she'd be right there with me.

Until she got a boyfriend, and I stopped seeing her as much. We'd still try to hang out, and I'd put myself in situations where I thought she'd come running and help me out. I'd flirt with her, tell her how gorgeous she was, make jokes about kissing her, and she'd laugh and ignore me. I'd do anything to get her to notice me.

Now, as we walk through a record store, Nora's holding my hand, and she finally sees me.

I'm still trying to wrap my head around the fact that I watched her fall apart in my lap this morning, and now she's walking around, humming to whatever song is playing on the speakers, in a cute as fuck pink skirt. I might get kicked out of here for public indecency or some shit with the raging hard-on she's given me by just breathing.

She stops at the Pop section and holds up a record for me. "What about this one? Have you heard any songs from this?"

"Yeah, when we were in high school," I say, laughing from the other side of the rows of vinyls. She frowns. It's Starboy by The Weeknd. "I'll get it for you if you want it."

She snorts. "Vinyls are expensive and I already have it downloaded, anyway. Save your money, Wessy. You don't have a job, remember?"

"And neither do you," I argue.

She smirks. "Touché."

"So you just want to come here and browse? You don't buy anything?" I ask, walking around to meet her on her side.

She shakes her head. "I don't have a record player."

"What? I thought you wanted to come here so you could buy something."

She just laughs, the sound harmonic and light. "Not really. I just really like music."

"Yeah?" I step in closer to her, and she nods. I wrap my arm around her waist, watching as she slowly peers up at me. "Well, I just really like you."

I press my lips to hers, and everything fades away. It's just the two of us and our desperate need to always be with each other. Our moment of peace is interrupted by a very loud "EWWWW!"

Our eyes shoot open to find two little girls standing with a basket full of storybooks. They both hold one handle each as if the basket is too heavy or they just like doing everything together. They're fucking adorable. The girl with brown hair has her hand across her eyes, and the ginger one is staring up at me with wide eyes as if she's never seen a human before. Nora laughs at the horrified look on their faces, but I crouch down to them.

"What's got you in a bind, little one?" I ask, looking back up at Nora and then back to the girls.

The one with brown hair uncovers her eyes. "You two were kissing," she whispers.

"Yup," I answer. She pulls a face. The redhead smiles. "Are you going to arrest me?"

She crosses her arms against her chest. "I might!"

"I'd like to see you try," I argue. She just holds her chin up as if she's too good of an officer to arrest me.

The redhead taps my shoulder. "Um, Sir?" I nod, trying my hardest not to laugh. "Are you a prince?"

"Definitely not," Nora says. I look up at her, and she just

shrugs as if it's not a big deal. I don't know who these kids are, but I want them to think highly of me. I want to impress them in some strange way.

"Then why are you two kissing? I thought only a prince and princesses could kiss," she says quietly, twisting her tiny foot into the carpet.

"Well, maybe she's a princess, and she's the one saving me. She could have a secret identity for all I know," I whisper to them. They both gasp.

"For real?" the redhead asks, her blue eyes lighting up. I nod my head a little too hard, and she giggles.

"I don't buy it," the brunette says, still holding her chin up to me.

"I guess we'll have to kiss again and see if I turn into a real prince," I joke. Both of their hands fly out, shaking them at us.

"No! No. Please don't!"

I laugh, throwing my head back. "Okay, okay. I won't."

"Lizzy? Gracie?" A tall brunette woman comes into my view, and she sighs when she sees the two girls laughing at me. "Oh my god. I'm so sorry. They are little terrors. I take my eyes off them for a minute, and they go harassing strangers."

"We don't mind," Nora says when I stand to my feet.

"Yeah, looks like you've got yourself two princesses," I say, winking at them. They both start giggling again, sounding slightly evil.

"More like little witches, but thank you," the woman says, gesturing for them to follow her. God, I love kids. They're so funny and innocent and weirdly easy to talk to. Maybe that's because a part of me still feels like a kid myself.

Nora tugs on my arm. "I'm a princess now, huh?"

"Of course you are. I was convinced you were one when we were kids. Now that you're my girlfriend, it's pretty fitting."

"*And* I'm your girlfriend? How did I get so lucky?"

"Wait. Shit. I was supposed to ask you properly. I had this whole speech planned, and I was supposed to tell you how–"

She leans up and kisses me, cutting off every single sane thought in my brain. When she slips her tongue into my mouth, I groan and pull apart. "Just let me ask you, woman."

"Okay," she says, her dimples pulled right in. I lift her hand, slowly sinking down to my knees. Her eyes widen. "Wesley Mackenzie, you better stand up right now."

"Okay, okay," I laugh. I bring her hand to my lips, pressing a kiss on her knuckles. "Will you, Nora Emma Bailey, make me the happiest man in the world and be my girlfriend?"

Her eyes light up. "Since you asked so nicely," she murmurs, wrapping her arms around my neck. "Hell yeah, I'll be your girlfriend, Wes."

NORA

I think I might pass out.

I one hundred percent understand where Cat is coming from when she said that seeing men with kids turns her on. Because holy fuck. If I didn't think it would get me arrested, I would have pounced on Wes. He just looks so comfortable. So natural. Which is weird because he has no younger siblings or any cousins that live close by. It's like he was born to do that. Then, he had the audacity to ask me to be his girlfriend.

I'm convinced he wants me to die.

I don't think I get any more words out until we've ordered two strawberry ice creams at the parlor across the street. The sun is hot on my skin. My bare legs are finally starting to get the tan they've been desperate for.

Wes is trying to tell me about how I should invest in a record player, but I keep getting distracted by his lips. He keeps licking the ice cream very… suggestively. Even when he's finished, I'm still thinking about the way he was licking it. Was it suggestive, or am I just a horny woman who is most definitely obsessed with her boyfriend?

Boyfriend. That word only belongs to Wes, and I feel like such an idiot for calling anyone but him that. Everything about him makes him the perfect boyfriend, and I can't believe I didn't realize earlier that it's always been him.

"Why are you looking at me like that?" He asks, slowing our walk down as he looks over at me.

I shrug. "No reason."

He bumps his shoulder into mine. "Nora."

"Wes," I mock, bumping him back as I laugh.

"What's going on in that head of yours?"

"Nothing," I say quietly, trying not to laugh at the serious look on his face. "You just... lick ice cream in a very sexual way, and it's distracting."

He chuckles. "That's what is making you hot under the collar? Because I'm eating ice cream."

The mischievous smirk on his lips makes me roll my eyes. I turn away from him. "See. *This* is why I need to keep my thoughts to myself."

His breath hovers over my neck, goosebumps spreading everywhere. "I can lick *you* in a very sexual way."

I gasp, holding my hand to my chest and spinning on my heels to face him. "Are you flirting with me right now, Wesley?" I ask, humor lacing my tone.

He wraps his arm around my waist, pulling me into him as he drops his forehead to mine. "Finally," he groans. "It's about time you noticed. When am I not flirting with you, Nora?" I giggle, pushing apart from him, but he pulls me into him anyway, keeping his arms tight around my waist. "I've got you now, and I'm not letting you go."

I swallow back the emotion in my throat. "Never?"

"Never ever. Even if the world split in two and we were on different planets."

"Even then?"

"Even then," he confirms, kissing me deeply. The promise makes me feel a million times lighter because he's right. There's nothing in this world that could break what we have. Our relationship has been built on friendship and trust for years, and now it's flourishing in an entirely different way.

A slow round of applause interrupts the moment. We're both startled for a second, our bubble bursting as we turn to the sound. Ryan is standing in front of us, swaying slightly as he slurs, "Fantastic. Amazing. Show-stopping, really."

"Ryan. What a nice surprise," I say, not an iota of interest in my tone. I thought we had buried the hatchet a long time ago. We've not spoken since the show, and I'd like to keep it that way. I don't have any space in my life for him anymore. I'm not sure why I ever made space for him in the first place. He's like a rock in my shoe – every time I think I've gotten him out, he pops right back up again.

"Not really a surprise. We live in the same part of town," he replies.

"You're right, we do," I say calmly. I don't want his weird energy to ruin the good day I'm having, and the fact that he's even in my presence is making me uneasy. I hook my arm around Wes's waist, ready to vacate whatever this is. "We're just going to—"

"Hey, I'm just saying congratulations. You know, now that you're happy and everything." I smile tightly, nodding as I try to side-step us out of his way. The sidewalk is only so big, and we're on one of the busiest streets in town. It's not exactly the place for small talk with my ex. "Daisy dumped me."

His voice doesn't sound anything like he usually does, and he smells like beer. His outfit is disheveled, and I notice the bags under his eyes. "Are you drunk?" I ask. He just waves me off, giving me his answer. "It's one in the afternoon."

Wes's arm tightens on my shoulder when Ryan steps into me. "Did you hear me? She *dumped* me."

I hold my head up. "I heard you. I just don't care." Hurt flashes in his eyes as I take another step forward. "Now, if you'll excuse us. We're trying to leave."

Ryan shakes his head so fast it's giving me a headache just looking at him. "No, no, no. This is *your* fault, Bailey. You're the one that broke up with me and now look at all the shit I'm in. She was only with me for the sake of the show. Can you believe that?"

His words aren't coming out very clearly, and there are tears lining his eyes. The part of me that still wants to treat him as a human aches a little, so I say, "Sorry to hear that, but for the third time, we're trying to go."

Ryan's face turns red as he lunges towards me. "You snarky little bi—"

Wes steps in front of me, holding his hand up to Ryan's chest. "You better watch your tone when you're talking to my girl," he snarls.

Ryan's cliché comeback is, "We're just talking."

Wes shakes his head. "I'm standing right here, bud. She's done talking to you." As much as I usually like fighting my own battles, I kind of like the way Wes is standing up for me right now. He steps in closer to Ryan, their faces achingly close together as I peer around them. "Leave."

"You're not going to tell me what to do," Ryan argues, pushing Wes out of the way. My eyes widen, and my heartbeat hammers against my chest when his huge hand wraps around my bicep. I blink up at him as he tugs onto me. Hard. "Nora, get your dog under control before—"

I don't even blink before Wes pulls Ryan off me and pins him against the brick wall of the florist we're outside. Wes has his arm up against Ryan's neck, almost choking him as his face turns pale. "You don't get to fucking touch her. You don't get to speak to her like that, and, really, you shouldn't even be *looking* at her if you still want your eyeballs in their sockets."

There's a beat of silence, and when I look at the crowd that's started to emerge from their argument, I press my palm onto Wes's lower back. "Wes, leave it," I whisper, and just at the sound of my voice, he eases off. He's still against the wall, but he doesn't look like he's about to beat the shit out of him. "Ryan, just go."

He shakes his head again. "No. You need to understand that I still want you."

His words make me wince, reminding me of all the times he's said that and never meant it. Of all the times I believed he'd change. Wes leans into his face again, keeping his voice low as he says, "Do you not know how to listen? She said leave, so leave."

Ryan's oddly calm as he swerves out of Wes's grip, brushing off his shirt. He turns to walk away, and Wes turns back to me, letting out a deep breath. I force myself to calm my racing pulse, but it's only a second late when Ryan turns back around, pushes Wes up against the wall, and punches him right in the face.

I don't even recognize my own scream when it leaves my mouth. I lurch towards them, but Wes shouts at me to stay back. He's just *letting* Ryan hit him like he's done something wrong when he hasn't. My ears are ringing, feeling like the entire world has gone silent as I painfully watch Wes get beaten like a punching bag. People are staring now, debating whether or not they should interfere.

He gets a few more blows in, and I see Ryan's mouth move as he spits something in Wes's face. And then Wes punches back. And he doesn't stop.

I'm standing there, emotionless, watching strangers interfere as they try to break up the fight. For what it's worth, Wes looks like he's winning. Each time I think they're going to stop, Ryan proves that he's always going to want the last word. He has a knack for those things but not enough balls to stay around when police sirens sound in the distance.

THIRTY-FIVE
WES
JAILBIRD

I HAD ALWAYS THOUGHT I was smart enough not to go to jail. I've made a million bad decisions and done enough stupid things to land me in hospital a few times, but this one takes first place.

I've never been a violent person. Even when I played football, any of the fights I got in were to back up one of my teammates, and even then, I was still pretty tame. But when it comes to Ryan Valla, that tame side of me does not exist. He makes me see red. Just from how he looked at Nora, my blood ran cold. I should have thrown those punches a long time ago, and it felt good to release some steam. If those strangers hadn't called the police, who just so happened to be around the corner, I don't think I would have gotten off him.

Ryan, being the rich asshole he is, managed to get out of holding within ten minutes of glaring at me from the other end. He's as stupid as he looks. He thought running would mean he wouldn't get caught, but he severely underestimated how far he could run whilst being out of his mind drunk. I, however, have to spend four hours next to three guys who smell like they've wet themselves.

It already feels like I've lived a million lives today, so the last thing I want to do is see seven people all standing outside the station when I get let out. They're all shouting and screaming, running toward me like I was placed in an actual jail cell for years, not a couple of hours. I'm too exhausted to even say anything when they're all fawning over me.

"He got a real hit on you, huh?" Connor says, clasping my shoulder as we stand in the parking lot. I haven't seen a mirror since it happened, and I'm honestly not sure how bad my face looks. All I know is that my ribs hurt, my knuckles are red, and my thighs are aching. What kind of dude aims for your thighs when fighting?

"Apparently," I grumble. Archer comes into my view now, and when I can't see much out of my peripheral, I take it upon myself to realize that my eye must be swollen. For one of the first times in my life, Archer's got a smug smirk on his face as he watches me. "Take a picture. It'll last longer."

He scoffs. "Damn, prison changed you."

"It gets to you in there," I say hauntingly, tapping my skull.

He lets out a low chuckle. "Glad to know you're okay, man."

"Thanks," I reply. Then Elle and Cat come into my view, again staring at me with a pained grimace like I look like I have no eyeballs. The medic said I'd be fine, but they're looking at me like I've been run over or something. "Thanks, girls. I really appreciate the concern."

Elle lets out a choked laugh. "We're sorry, Wessy. You just... You look horrible." Cat elbows Elle in the rib. "What? It's true." I just shake my head at them, no matter how bad it hurts, as they end up arguing about what not to say to a person who had just been in a fight and spent the last three hours in a prison cell.

My vision finally clears when I spot Nora sitting on the hood of Connor's truck. It's like she's stuck in her own world, biting her nails. I've never seen her do that before, and it worries the fuck out of me. I make my way over to her. "You okay, Sunshine?"

Her head snaps up, and she slides off the car, running

towards me. I don't get a second to breathe before she jumps at me and wraps her arms around my neck, squeezing me tight. "Oh my god, I'm so sorry. I should have gotten involved or done something or told him to fuck off, and I didn't. And now this is going to be on your record, and it's all my fault, and I feel selfish for getting worked up over it, but you scared the shit out of me, Wes."

"Hey, it's okay. I'm okay, you know?" She just nods against my neck. I hold her closer to me, thankful to have her in my arms again. I try to pry her off me when my ribs start to ache, but she doesn't budge. "Hey, Nora?"

"Hey, Wes," she sniffles.

"I don't know if you saw what happened, you know, back when I was in a fight with your ex-boyfriend and everything, but my ribs are kind of sore, and you're hurting me," I grumble.

"Fuck. I'm so sorry," she says. She jumps apart from me. "What do you want me to do? How can I help?"

"How about you kiss my bruises better?" I murmur, leaning down to her. She presses her lips together. "Come on, Nor. You're not going to make a wounded man beg, are you?"

"Trust me, I'd love to see you beg, but your parents are right over there."

I turn to follow her line of vision, and she's right. How weird is today going to get? Both of my parents are standing next to each other beside my dad's car like they've been waiting for me.

"I'll wait in the car," she says to me as I'm still staring at them like they might disappear. "Go talk to them."

I walk over to them, and my palms instantly grow sweaty. Maybe it's just the last of my energy wearing off and I'm now put on high alert again. I haven't seen them in the same place for almost a year, and now they're both casually standing there as if this is completely normal. I lift my head up when I get to them. I was expecting a lecture. Or at least one of them to tell me that what I did was stupid. But I get a hug instead.

I melt into both of their embrace, and I can feel the tears

prickling the back of my eyelids. You never know how much you need something until you don't have it. If I knew how good it would feel to have both of my parent's arms wrapped around me, I would have fought harder for this months ago. I don't know how long we all stay like this, just holding each other, but I'm almost too afraid to let go. I feel like a kid again, needing to hug both of my parents twice before going to school.

My mom pulls away first, and I see that she's crying. "Are you okay, darling? You're not hurt, are you? Well, of course, you're hurt. I mean—"

"I'm okay, Mom," I say, and she just breaks down into another fit of tears. "Hey, *weine nicht. Mir geht es gut, versprochen.*" She sniffles. "I might have got it bad, but the good part of my brain is still working."

"Are you sure you're okay?" my dad asks. He's got tears in his eyes too. God. What is with the emotion today? I don't think I can handle this right now.

I shrug. "Yes, I'm good."

"Right, I'm not happy about what happened, but when Nora told me why, I understood. Doesn't mean I'm not a little disappointed in you, Wes," he says. I just nod. "I know communication between us has been strained, but waiting for you to come out of here has made us realize that we need to try to be better for you."

"I know, Dad, and I'm sorry. If you had heard what he said about my Nora then–" The rest of his words hit me, and my sentence came to a screeching halt. "Wait. What?"

"We're still separating, but we're going to work on being friends at least, so holidays and birthdays aren't hard. The way things happened wasn't fair to anyone. Everything was up in the air and we all had a million things going on, but we want to try to make this work," my dad explains. The balloon that was lodged in my throat starts to deflate. "I know it might not be what you want, but—"

"No, it is what I want," I admit, swallowing. I look between the two of them, seeing them differently already. "As long as it's what you both want, too."

"It is, my love," my mom says, smiling softly.

When they update me about how they've started seeing a therapist and clearing the air between them, the future doesn't look too bad. It doesn't look filled with strained relationships and awkward family dinners. My path might still be a little unclear, but I've got more than enough people in my corner to help me through the fog.

"SHOULD I GET A NEW CLOTH?"

If Nora could dress up in a nurse costume instead of this annoyingly cute outfit she's had on all day, I'd be enjoying this a lot more. Surprisingly, I haven't sustained a lot of injuries in my life. Nothing that a damp paper towel couldn't fix. So, having Nora in my lap, tending to my bruises, is out of the ordinary for so many reasons.

"I think I'm okay now, Stargirl," I laugh, watching the look of concentration on her face, her tongue poking out between her lips.

"Are you sure?"

"Yes, I'm sure. Now can you get the hell out of this outfit so you can stop torturing me with that fucking skirt," I say, giving her ass a firm smack. She laughs as she slips out of my lap, and I lean back against the headboard, watching her.

I could get used to Nora walking around my room like this. I could get used to her wearing my clothes and using my shampoo whenever she wants to. I could also get used to her walking out of my bathroom in my shorts and one of my jerseys, giving Adam Sandler a run for his money. I don't care how baggy my clothes look on her; she still looks gorgeous, and she looks like she's all mine.

When she gets back in bed, she just pulls out a paperback that she was reading earlier, and I watch her get lost in her own world. My TV is playing quietly in the background, but there's no use in it being on when she's all I can focus on.

I feel like one lucky motherfucker to have her in my life. Everything that has happened to us was meant to happen so we could get here. I think she knows what I'm thinking when we both settle to go to sleep. It's fucking uncomfortable with the way my ribs are aching, but she's lying on her side, looking at me, and I have to look back.

"Can you do me a favor?" I ask into the silence.

"Anything," she murmurs.

"Don't break my heart, Nora," I say shakily, running my fingers through her hair.

She frowns. "What? Why would I do that?"

I sigh. "You know that what I feel for you goes deeper than we'd both like to admit. I just don't want you to wake up one day and realize that you need more... or less. I don't know. I just don't want you to miss out on something that could be better than me, more talented than me, or someone that fits your lifestyle better. I don't want to be a mistake that you've made." I swallow. "One that you'll regret."

Her eyes dim, and she shakes her head softly. "You know, you're the only thing that I feel like I've done right. Every decision I've made regarding you has just been *right*. I don't need anything more from you or anything better. You try harder than anyone to make me smile, to make me laugh and you're there for me in the moments where I don't feel like I want to do any of that for myself."

I take a deep breath, letting her words wash over me. She guides my hand from in her hair and presses our hands right against my heart, where it feels like it's going to fall out of my chest. "*You're* the thing I've been missing, Wes, and there's nothing in this world that is better than having you. I would never do anything to break your heart. Ever."

I nod, swallowing so I don't bawl like a fucking baby. "Good, because I don't think I even know what to do with myself sometimes when I think about you. It's like I've been spun around on a rollercoaster, and I'm in a constant state of dizziness. Just pure disbelief that you're real."

She lets out a soft laugh. "You sure that's not the pain meds talking?"

I shake my head firmly. "Do you ever think about how we were just destined to meet each other? Like, how life worked out so well in our favor."

"Like the invisible string theory?"

"Yeah, but think about it," I start and she shuffles closer to me, caging us in our own bubble. "Out of every place in the universe, it was the house across mine that your parents moved into. Sometimes, I think that you were always destined to be *this* for me. Like it was written in the stars or on the back of a rock at the bottom of the ocean. Or someone a thousand years ago predicted this would happen."

She lets out a chuckle. She probably thinks I'm crazy. It might just be the medication that's making me more sentimental than usual. But after standing up for her and fighting Ryan back about what he said about her, I'd do anything for her, and I want her to know that. "I'll never be able to understand your mind, Wes. Like ever."

"I'm being serious," I whisper. She shivers, her eyes softening. "You might be my best friend, but you're also everything else for me. You're my favorite person, Nora. Sometimes, I think you're the only person in my universe. You're the only person I see. Some people might close their eyes and see a galaxy or a whole load of nothingness, but I don't see that."

She swallows. "What do you see?"

"You," I say shakily.

"Me?"

"Just you," I confirm. "It's always been you."

THIRTY-SIX
NORA
"WHAT HAVE I DONE NOW?"

PREPARING for our end-of-year exams is a huge kick in the ass. I much prefer doing practical things like acting or directing but finishing up my screenplay and the commentary has been a nightmare.

My film is a satirical take on Homer's *The Odyssey*, mostly based around Penelope and the women in the text with a twenty-first-century lens on it. Women in classic Epics always have some sort of troubled past or are witches like Circe, which is why I wanted to make it as unhinged as possible as if these Greek legends were real people in today's society. It was fun working on it and blocking out monologues with Kiara, but actually having to edit it and reread it a million times has been a pain in the ass.

My friends and I booked a slot at the pottery painting place in town as a stress reliever. One of Connor's teammates' moms owns the shop, and she was kind enough to fit us in despite the busy schedule. There's nothing I enjoy more than watching the concentration on my friends' faces as they try to paint little designs on their chosen pieces.

I'm sitting in between Wes and Elle whilst Cat and Connor sit on the other side. Archer was here twenty minutes ago, but he didn't paint. He came and watched like the grump he is, went into the back for something, and then just disappeared. I've never got a good read on him, and I've given up on figuring him out. He might be grumpy and sometimes a little rude, but I weirdly have a lot of love and respect for him. With the way Elle watches him and the way her face drops when he disappears, I'm sure I'm not the only one.

"What are you painting, Elle-Belle?" I ask, leaning over to the heart-shaped box she's been filling in with her watercolors. I'm desperately trying to ignore the fact that Wes has been painting beside me with one hand while his other hand grips my thigh.

She sighs. "I was going to paint daisies on them, but I'm a shit painter. I'm trying something else; you'll see."

"I'm sure it will be gorgeous," I say, looking down at my monstrosity. One of the last times we were all here, Wes tackled me to the ground, and we were in a very competitive paint fight. It was one of the first times I ever felt *something* for him. He was working his charming magic on me, and the way he was pinning me to the ground did very unholy things to my insides. "It'll look better than mine."

I tilt my head to the side, hoping the new angle will make the frog look a little better. It doesn't. I swore I followed Mrs. Redford's directions properly, but my mixing of primary and secondary colors has gone horribly wrong.

Connor snorts at that. "I'm sure anything will be better than yours."

"Oh, shut up," I grumble. Wes's hand squeezes my thigh like he's telling me to back down, but I ignore it, just embracing the warmth of his hand.

"You shut up," he barks back. I narrow my eyes at him, sticking my tongue out. "You're so childish."

"I know you are, but what am I?" He doesn't say anything; he just looks down at whatever he's painting. He chose a flat circle, and it's all covered in different shades of purple. "What's that supposed to be Michaelangelo?"

"Purple roses," Cat says for him, smiling down at the *thing* he's made. They don't look like roses at all, but I don't want to burst their bubble. Connor is not the best in the creative department. "Like the ones he got me for my twentieth, remember?"

"Ah, how could I forget where he left you a note that confirmed to me that you two were sleeping together," I say sweetly. I've not been able to stop teasing them about how insanely romantic – and cheesy – the note was.

In unison, all of us but Connor say, "To my Catherine. Twenty roses for your twentieth. You're my favorite person ever. Love from, Connie."

Connor cringes at his own words, shaking his head when we all burst into a fit of uncontrollable laughter. "I'm never going to live that down, am I?"

"Unfortunately, not," Wes mumbles.

"I still think it was *very* sweet, Connie," Cat whispers, kissing my brother on the cheek. They share a look that I guess only two people in love give each other. It makes my stomach dip with how happy I am for them both and to have finally realized what *true* happiness is with Wes.

When the moment breaks, Connor turns back to the table, a serious look on his face. "So, speaking of houses…"

"No one said anything about a house," Wes says, still trailing his hand up my thigh. I squeeze my thighs together, trapping his hand. I turn to him to catch his reaction, but he's just got a satisfied grin on his face like this is the best thing that happened to him.

Connor's next words knocked the wind right out of me: "Cat's moving out, and she's moving in with me."

"Connor," Cat chides, hitting him in the arm. "I was supposed to say it."

"What?!" Elle and I gawk at the same time. The thought of any of us moving out within our years at college has never crossed my mind. We committed to sticking together in our dorm for the whole four years. *This* was not in the plan.

"The system's breaking down," Elle says, placing her palms on the table as if she's having a nervous breakdown. Honestly, she might be. And I might join her. "I can't fucking deal with this."

I stare at Cat, my eyes wide. "You're moving out? We only have a year left, Cat. It was always supposed to be just us three."

She sighs, biting her bottom lip. "I know, but I just want a change of scenery, you know? I'm at their house all the time anyway, and he doesn't mind me moving into his space. It'll be nice to live together. We were probably going to move in together after we finished college, anyway, so why not now?"

When I don't get the words out, Wes speaks for me. "Makes sense to me," Wes says, shrugging. Not the words I would have chosen. And a little too accepting for someone who constantly complains that they're always fucking.

I turn to him, my eyes narrowed. "You knew about this, and you didn't tell me?"

He grins. "Seems like they wanted to tell you themselves, Sunshine."

I take in a deep breath. This isn't the end of the world, but it kind of feels like it. It has always been us three. *Always.* Through everything, we've always been together. We've had our little traditions over the years, and seeing how much they've faded out in the last year reminds me of how much I need to keep the connection with them. When you spend so much time with someone, it's hard to let them go. It's hard to watch them go. Even if it's just a few blocks away. None of us share any classes, so we'll hardly see each other on campus. Cat moving in with Connor just means they'll spend more time together, and there'll be less room for our girl time. Before we know it, they'll be married and living across the world.

"Are you guys okay with this?" Cat asks. Elle and I both nod, but she knows just as much as me that it might take me a minute to process this. We'd never want to hold her back from something that she loves.

"I'm okay with it," I say. "It's just a shock. I've gotten so used to living with you. It's going to be weird with just us two."

"Yeah," Elle agrees. "How are we going to fill the Catherine-sized hole in our hearts?"

Cat's lip quivers as if she's about to cry. If she starts crying, we're all done for. "I'll be less than half an hour away, and I'll still see you all the time, anyway. Besides, there's a waitlist for some girls who want to transfer dorms. We can do some interviews in a few days to get to know them. That way, it won't be too bad."

That doesn't sound like an awful idea. "Ooh, like auditions!" Elle says.

"I guess?" Cat shrugs one shoulder.

"Can we make them sing '*Since U Been Gone*' like in Pitch Perfect?" I ask hopefully. The boys groan. We've had a connection with that movie since it came out, and I don't want to miss the opportunity to recreate one of the best movie sequences in cinematic history.

"If you insist," Cat says, smiling wide. "Are we good?"

I turn to Elle, and she beams at the two of us. An absolute ray of sunshine, that one. "We're always good, Cat," I reply. "We want you to be happy, and if moving in with my boring-ass brother is what makes you happy, then fine by me." We all laugh, but Connor just throws me a scowl. I know he loves me, really.

"Okay, this is great and all that, but I want to get back to painting now," Wes says, impatient as ever.

JUST LIKE WES knew about Cat and Connor dating before I found out, he knew she was going to be moving out. As much as he tells me I'm his best friend, he's a traitor. He doesn't seem to care that I'm annoyed at him because the second we get back to the dorm, he's kissing across my neck like he's not seen me in years. He's got his hands on me in every way that I can, and I'd appreciate it if I could get through my dorm without falling over.

"Can you relax?" I ask, pushing at him, but he only pushes back. He pushes my hair in front of my shoulder, kissing me from behind as I squirm under his touch. The bareness of my neck just reminds me of the necklace I'm missing, and goosebumps spread across my skin. "Wes."

"Hm?" he hums into my skin as I fumble with the key to my door.

"Can you at least let me get into my room?" I laugh. He listens then, finally stepping away from me. I unlock the door, and within seconds, my back is against it, and Wes is pressing himself into me. I gasp at the hardness in his jeans. "What are you doing?"

He kisses across my jaw, making a slow journey down my neck. "This dress has been driving me insane all fucking day." My eyes flutter closed and he murmurs, "So fucking hot."

"I know. That's why I wore it," I pant.

He just hums, kissing and sucking on my neck like a man starved.

"I'm still annoyed at you, by the way," I manage to get out when his hands travel further up my thighs, his rough hands massaging me there.

"What have I done now?"

"You kept me out of the loop. *Again*," I say. He groans in response. I have way too much fun messing with him. "You're supposed to be on my side."

"I'm always on your side." He buries his face into my neck, making shivers erupt across my entire body as he kisses and sucks me there. "I've been such a good boy, Nora," he whines.

"Not good enough."

"No?" I shake my head, trying to catch the breath I didn't

know I lost. "What can I do to prove it? Tell me what I need to do, and I'll do it. I'm desperate, Sunshine."

"I can see that you're desperate, Wes," I say, panting.

"Then do something about it," he says, peeling down the straps of my dress enough to kiss along my shoulder. The way his lips work over my skin almost makes me want to surrender myself to him. To give him all of me. He can have all of me as far as I'm concerned.

"What do you want me to do?" I ask breathlessly.

"You can start by taking off that dress of yours," he whispers. He steps back, turns me around, and walks me towards the bed. I stand with my back to it, peering up at him, suddenly not sure where I should look. "Take your time, baby. I can wait all day if my reward is seeing what's under that dress."

His words knock the wind out of me. I slowly bring my hands to the straps of my dress, keeping my eyes locked with him as I drop one down, pulling my arm out. His heated gaze makes my skin erupt in goosebumps.

I peel down the other side until both of my arms are free, and my boobs bounce out on top of the fabric. My entire body tingles when I watch his eyes travel down to my chest, and I continue pushing the dress off me until I'm wearing nothing but my panties. The look on Wes's face is almost enough to make me drop to my knees in front of him. He's worshiping me without even saying anything.

"Fucking hell," he groans, pressing his fist to his mouth. I feel awkward. I've got no clue what to do with my hands. I've never been asked to undress in front of someone, not like this, at least. And he's looking at me like he wants to eat me.

"Okay. Now what?" I ask, my voice strangled. He steps closer to me, and I step backward, the back of my knees hitting my bed.

"Get on the bed and spread those pretty legs for me. I want to see you," he says, his voice low and rough. I pathetically whimper just at his words, and he's not even doing anything. I drop onto the mattress, and he's over me in seconds, kissing me deeply. He makes his way down my chest and to my stomach. "*Fuck.* When did you get this?"

"A few years ago." I look down at him, my chest heaving as he kisses across my belly button where a golden star stud has been pierced. "I don't put it in all the time. I took it out when Ryan and I were dating. He said it wasn't flattering. I just put it in when I want to feel pretty."

He hums against my skin, kissing across the area. "You doll yourself up just for me, Sunshine?" he murmurs as he swirls the gold in his mouth.

I let out a soft "Fuck," as I watch him.

"Answer me," he demands. He kisses across my thighs, making my head spin as his teeth tug on the fabric of my panties. I don't know what's switched in him, but he's managing to turn my inside out with all these soft, lingering touches.

"No," I get out. "I do it for myself."

"Right answer." Wes bites at my panties as he keeps his gaze locked on mine. His eyes are hooded. Hungry. Almost like he's been starving himself for this. For *me*. As if reading my thoughts, he groans, "Do you know how long I've waited for this?"

My back arches at his rough voice. "How long?"

"Fucking *years*. It's been absolute torture," he whispers into my skin, running his hands up the length of me, cupping my breasts. "I won't be able to keep my hands off you after just one taste, Nora."

The desperation in his voice undoes me. So does the way he says my name. It feels like he always calls me everything *but* my actual name. It's always Nor, Sunshine, or my personal favorite, *Stargirl*. But when Wes calls me by my name, I feel like I've reached the peak of my existence.

He continues kissing along the fabric that I've drenched, pressing his lips to my clit. I moan embarrassingly loud. He doesn't seem to care, though; he just nudges his nose against me, and I let out a soft cry. The way he's just there, hovering, *smelling*, feels so fucking dirty, and I love all of it.

"How wet are you, Sunshine?"

"I think you can figure that one out on your own, Wes. Don't you think?" I would sound snarky if I weren't already out of breath. He hums, the sound vibrating against my clit, rushing right through me.

"Do you still want to play, pretty girl?"

"Always," I whisper. He doesn't seem to get the hint, and he continues peering up at me with his face between my legs. "Yes, yes, yes," I chant like I'm in some sort of cult. "I want this, Wes. I want *you*. Please."

My chest is heaving now, and he laughs at me, all deep and throaty. "I didn't say you had to beg, baby."

I'd give him some sass if it didn't feel like my entire body was on fire. I'd do anything if I didn't feel like putty in his hands. He keeps his eyes locked with mine as he slowly – so fucking slowly – works down my panties until I'm bare in front of him.

I thought that being naked in front of my best friend for the first time would make me anxious. I thought I'd get up and run. But with the way Wes is burning holes into my skin with his eyes, full of complete wonder, I don't feel scared. I feel like I'm being worshiped properly for the first time.

He never does as I expect, and he surprises me by kissing a trail across my inner thighs, licking the wetness that has gathered there just for him. He groans as he continues making a meal of me, his hands locked around my outer thighs. The sight of his face between my legs makes my head spin.

"So good," he murmurs. The sound vibrates against my pussy, and my back arches, gripping onto his hair. Wes Mackenzie's gorgeous face is between my legs, and I feel like I'm in heaven. "I've been starving for this, Nora. Fucking *starving*."

"Wes." I let out a whimper when his mouth finally met my clit in a soft pinch. He's hardly doing anything, and I'm sure I could fall apart in his hands right now. He gives me one long lick down my pussy before he starts feasting on me.

I don't think the sounds leaving my mouth are even intelligible anymore. I'm squirming beneath him as he continues licking and sucking on me like he was fucking made to do it. The muscles on his back make my vision go blurry.

He has no business being this fucking attractive. He didn't even need me to tell him that I wanted to feel him here. He just did it. In fact, he *initiated* it, which is a lot more than any guy has ever done for me before. It shows me that he wants this. That he wants *me*.

"How's this?" he murmurs into my skin, sucking my clit into his mouth.

"Wes."

He chuckles, the sound deep and throaty. "You've got to tell me if this is good, or I'll stop." My hips buck up in response, my mouth drying as words fail me. "You don't want me to stop, do you, Stargirl?"

"No," I gasp. "Please don't stop."

"I thought that would be the case," he mutters. He continues feasting on me, my body writhing beneath his touch. "Be a good girl for me and keep still."

"I– I can't."

"You can, Nora. I've got you."

His encouragement helps me relax slightly, but everything still feels like it's spinning out of control. I always get too in my head during sex, and part of me wants to let him do what he wants, and the other wants to boss him around.

I can't tell if he's purposefully edging me, but his pace has increased, and every time I feel myself about to go right over the edge, he stops. I need him to draw this out. It always feels better when I can take my time, feel myself building, and then get thrown right over.

"Wes," I beg, my hands tightening in his hair. "Go slower."

He listens immediately, changing his pace so the strokes of

his tongue are soft and taunting. He circles his tongue around my clit, slipping through the wetness, and I moan. I look down at him as he peers up at me, his mouth glistening with me. "Like this?"

"Yes, like that." The confirmation makes him get back to work, doing exactly what I need. I feel light-headed like I could pass out right now.

"If I put two fingers in your pussy, will that be good for you?" If my brain could form coherent thoughts, I'd tell him that it would. I hope the desperate gasps that are leaving my lips and desperate swivel of my hips are enough of an answer.

He teases one of his fingers at my entrance, and I cry out in response, which turns into a satisfied moan when he slips two fingers inside me. It's tight, and I feel him everywhere. He moves his tongue on my clit in tandem with his fingers, the pace painfully blissful. "*Fuck.* Yes. Just like that."

"Yeah?"

The sound rushes through me, and I sigh. "Oh, God," I whimper, my entire body sweating. I've never felt like this before. No one has ever made me feel *this* good with just their fingers and tongue. As if he reads my body just right, he increases the speed as my orgasm builds. "*Wes.*"

"Say my name like that again," he whispers into my skin. I shiver. "Please."

I don't do as he says because I end up screaming his name instead when the orgasm slams right through me. I don't know what it says about me, but the desperation in his tone, the whine, the pleading is what threw me over the cliff. He holds my body on the comedown, still licking me and tasting me like he can't get enough.

He looks up at me, sucking his fingers into his mouth with a devilish smirk. *Oh, God.* He starts to kiss his way back up my body, paying attention to my belly button piercing again before he kisses up my stomach. He swirls one of my nipples into his mouth before he gets to my neck. This is all too much. Way too much.

"I fucking adore you, Nora. I'm in awe of you," he whispers before he collapses on his back beside me. I'm still trying to catch my breath, and I slap my hand against my forehead, feeling how hot I've gotten. *I'm in awe of you.* No one has ever said that to me before. "Not got anything to say?"

"Thank you," I mutter, turning to him.

He leans over to kiss me, and I don't have time to register where his mouth has just been before I can taste me on his lips. He pushes his tongue into my mouth, and I moan. Everything about it is so dirty, and I wonder why I've never done this before.

"You like how good you taste, Stargirl?" I hum against his mouth in agreement. "Good. Now you know how addicting it's going to be for me from now on."

I chuckle. "That's a little possessive, don't you think?"

"No. It's just true." I thought he'd laugh at that, but he doesn't. He looks at me seriously and passionately, and all I want to do is be this version of myself with him forever.

THIRTY-SEVEN
NORA
SINCE YOU BEEN GONE

TRYING to find someone who will move into our dorm is *nothing* like the *Pitch Perfect* auditions. I knew Cat was joking about making these poor girls sing Kelly Clarkson's hit song, but I thought she'd actually make it fun.

All we've done this afternoon is sit in one of the common areas on campus after contacting some people off the waitlist. Cat and Elle organized the whole thing whilst I was helping Wes prep for another interview that he's got this afternoon.

Since being with Wes, I've had more orgasms than I had in the five years with Ryan, and I've returned Wes the favor more than once. Those that said sex can improve your mood were right. I've felt a million times lighter over the past few days, and it's all thanks to Wes. I can't wait to pester him with questions later since he said that he'll wait for me at my dorm when his interview has finished. Just the thought of him waiting for me in my room is enough to make my heart race.

That was until reality sank in, and I was left exhausted after talking to over a dozen girls who Elle and I have nothing in common with. We're just trying to suss out the vibes and no one is really hitting the mark.

I drop my head to Cat's shoulder. "How many more people are left? I want to go home."

"Only a few more left, little one," she coos, patting my head.

"I'm getting tired too. I had a whole day of practice just to deal with this shit," Elle mumbles on the other end of the couch.

"You know how we could easily solve this problem?" I chirp.

Cat raises her eyebrow. "How?"

"You can just stay with us," I say sweetly. "Don't move in with him, *please*?"

"*Pleasseeee*," Elle joins in.

"You're both ridiculous," Cat says, pushing both of our faces away from her. Something catches her gaze on the other end of the room before she glances down at her laptop and then back to a dark-haired girl that's walking towards us. "I think this is one of the next girls."

"Hey, you're the girls interviewing for a spare room in the dorms, right?" The girl asks when she gets to us. She's got dark brown hair and headphones slung around her neck. It's hard to tell if she's smiling or frowning. It might just be the heat, but her entire face is covered in freckles, and her outfit gives the opposite vibes for summer. She's dressed head to toe in black, with a red ribbon tied around her headphones. Odd.

"Hi. It's June, right?" Cat asks, beaming up at her.

"Yeah," she replies, sitting down at the edge of the opposite couch.

"That's a really pretty name," Elle says, clearly fangirling over her. June smiles then, and it makes my chest deflate. Resting bitch faces scare the shit out of me.

She shrugs. "Thanks. It's kinda stupid. I don't get what joy my parents got out of naming their only child after a month. The worst part is I was born in October. On Halloween, actually."

"No way. I was born on Halloween, too," I gasp.

Her eyes widen. "It's the worst, right? I mean, everyone wants to go to a party or go out, but I just want to sit at home and do nothing, you know?"

Elle and Cat laugh at my misery. I love a good party. Sometimes a little too much. "No, actually, I don't," I say. "I love partying."

June snorts. "Why?"

"Good question," I laugh, shrugging. "I think I just like getting drunk and regretting it the next morning."

"Okay, *that* I can get behind," she agrees. The girls hum in agreement, and I feel more settled. She's the only girl in the lineup so far that hasn't made me want to rip my hair out with frustration. She's the biggest oxymoron I've ever seen. She has this whole badass look, all dark features, and then these bright brown eyes. Her name sounds like summer and the warmth, but she looks like she'd murder me. I like her already.

"So, tell us more about yourself," Elle prompts. "Why do you want to move in with us?"

June sighs, rolling her eyes as she crosses her legs. "To be honest? The girls I'm currently living with are all horrible."

My heart sinks a little. "Oh god. I'm so sorry," Cat whispers, and we nod in agreement. I can't imagine living with people who don't like me or would jeopardize the space we're in. These girls have been my lifeline and support for years, and living with them has only strengthened that bond.

"Do you know why?" I ask.

"No clue," she murmurs before biting on her bottom lip. She doesn't say anything for a few seconds, and we let her have her time to collect herself. "I may have got a big, uh, investment, and maybe they were jealous. Well, it's not like I could share any of the money with them anyway since it's technically my parents. I thought they'd lay me off after a few weeks, but they're doing everything in their power to torture me. We all share a bathroom, so when it's my time to shower, they make sure that the bathroom is a mess. I tried to clean it, but if there's not a mess in there, they make sure it'll be a mess in the shared living space or literally anywhere else."

We all grimace at that. "Sounds like a biohazard," Cat murmurs.

"It *feels* like a biohazard," June agrees, shaking her head. "I just don't think I can live there again next year, and I was stupid enough to wait too long and now all the other rooms are booked up. Except for yours."

Elle smiles tightly, turning to me before facing June. "We've got a few more people to see today, but we'll let you know." When June looks back up at us before she leaves, I hope for her sake that everybody else are horrible candidates, so we have no choice but to pick her.

JUST AS I EXPECTED, Wes is in my room when I get back to the dorm. He's sprawled out on my bed, deep in a sleep where it looks like he's having a happy dream. My millions of blankets and my bedsheets are covering him, wrapping him up in my scent and a part of me wonders if he's sleeping in there to be closer to me somehow. Or is that just crazy?

I toe off my shoes at the door, gently kicking them towards the wall before I kneel down on the bed, pressing my hand to his back. His breathing is soft, and his face is pressed into the pillows like it's the first time he's slept in years. It almost hurts to look at him like this. "Wes?"

He stirs slightly at the sound of my voice, one eye-opening. "Hm?"

"You were sleeping," I whisper, laughing quietly.

His voice is all thick and gravelly when he speaks. "Oh, shit, Nor. I'm sorry."

"It's okay," I laugh, pushing his hair out of his face as he turns to look up at me. I wonder if he knows just how pretty he is. How perfect. "You can go back to sleep if you're tired. I was just going to work at my desk."

He shakes his head. "Come here," he murmurs. The instructions are so low and deep in his throat that I do just as he says. I pull off my sweatshirt so I don't overheat and slip into bed next to him in my tank top. He pulls me right into his chest, and I straddle his waist, getting as close to him as possible. "I was so tired. All that—" He yawns. "All that walking."

"It's okay," I murmur, snuggling deeper into his chest as if I could bury myself in his warmth. "How was the interview?"

He runs his hand down my spine as if it calms him down more than me. I love it when he does that. It's almost like he doesn't actually know he's doing it and has some subconscious desire just to be close to me. "It might be the best one yet," he admits. "I actually felt like I fit in there."

"Yeah?" I ask hopefully. There is nothing I want more than these interviews working out in his favor. After seeing the way he's interacted with kids over the last few weeks, I pushed him to see if there's any teacher training courses at Drayton or in the surrounding colleges. He managed to secure an interview, and this is good news.

"Yeah, they didn't speak down to me or anything like that. It was like they actually wanted to know me, and I knew what I was doing. Even when they knew all my previous history had to do with football and sports sciences." He lets out a self-deprecating chuckle. "They might really want me."

I lean up on his chest, resting my chin on him. "Of course, they'll want you, Wes. You're amazing." He presses a kiss to my forehead as a silent thank you. I melt back into his chest, hearing his heart thrum softly against my ear. Our bodies fit so perfectly together like we were both made to be here for each other. I let out a soft sigh as his hand continues trailing down my spine. "I could stay here with you like this forever. It feels like you have me better like this. It's like you're mine."

I hear him swallow. "I'm always yours, Nora. I always have been, and I always will be."

"That just reminded me," I mumble, sliding off my bed and walking over to my desk. I bought Wes something a few days ago and keep forgetting to give it to him. Now might be the perfect time to. I pull the box from my drawer, holding it behind my back as I walk back to the bed. He pulls himself up against the headboard, his eyes narrowed.

"What are you doing?" he asks slowly, eyeing me up and down as I climb back into the bed. I settle my legs on either side of him, still hiding the box as I get comfortable on his lap. His hands find my waist, pulling me into him. "Never mind. I like this view."

I pull back as he tries to kiss me. "Do you remember when we were kids, and you had that whole collection of Lego figurines?" He nods. "And when we got older, you were annoyed that they made more Marvel films, and you felt stupid collecting them in case people made fun of you." He nods again, a slow smile creeping up on his face. I pull the box out from behind me, showcasing the Spiderman Lego that sits in a transparent case. "Well, I thought maybe you could start collecting them again. I know it might be stupid, but I thought it could be something we do together. I saw this the other day, and I had to get it to start it off."

I take a deep breath once my rambling stops. Wes blinks at me like he doesn't know what to say. He looks down at the box for a second, tracing his finger down the middle. "Why are you giving me this?"

I sigh. "I just explained that to you, Wes."

"Yeah, but *why*?"

"Because I saw it, and it made me think of you," I admit, sucking in a breath as he pushes the box aside, pulling me closer until our chests touch.

"Are you sure?" He tilts his head to the side like I'm lying. What I'm saying is true. After knowing Wes my entire life, there are some things I can't see without thinking about him. It's like he's attached himself to the most basic things – like the sprinklers in the front yard of my parent's house, the Christmas markets, video game stores, football fields, the supermarket where we got strawberry ice cream and sat on the hood of his car eating it. I nod in response. "Tell me the truth, Sunshine."

"Because I'm in love with you, you idiot. Is that what you want me to say?" I bite out. I roll my head back, groaning before I connect with his gray eyes. His flirty expression softens, and the lines on his face smooth out.

He stutters, blinking at me. "You— You're—"

"I'm in love with you, Wes," I whisper, softer this time. He continues staring at me like this is the most bizarre thing in the world, but everything about it feels so natural. The words roll off my tongue easily, and I drop my forehead to his. "I'm annoyingly in love with every single thing about you. With the way you look at me, the way you take care of me, the way you talk highly of me to others. The way you're just *there*."

He swallows. "Like a superhero?"

"Like a superhero," I confirm.

He tilts his head up, and I cover his lips with mine. I'll never get tired of the way it feels to kiss Wes. The way his mouth opens up to me. The way his hands know exactly how to make me feel good, trailing up my waist as I hold onto his face like my life depends on it. He feels like an anchor, pulling me right back down, holding me there.

There's no one on earth that can make me feel the way he does – loved, safe, happy, free. He doesn't think I'm too much for him. He doesn't think I take up too much space or his time. He just wants to spend time with me and be with me, and I want to do all those things for him, too.

Even when he pulls apart from me, clearly searching for words, I still feel him tingle on my lips. He's been staring at me for a minute straight, not saying anything.

"Wes," I laugh quietly. "Can you say something?"

He blinks at me, shaking his head. "I don't know how. What do I— What are you— Are you being serious? How do I–"

"Just say what your heart is telling you," I whisper, wrapping my hand around his, bringing it to his heart. It's beating hard against our hands, and I watch him take a deep breath.

"You are the love of my life, Nora Bailey. My heart belongs to you, okay? Whatever it wants, whatever it says, it's for you. It's all yours. I've been silently loving you for years. I'm so fucking lucky that I've got the chance to finally love you the way you deserve to be loved."

Tears brimming my eyes, a sharp laugh escapes me at his sweet words. "Do you mean very loudly?"

"Yes. There's no other way," he murmurs before kissing me again.

I used to think that was a bad thing. I'm used to people hiding me, wanting me to stay out of the spotlight so they can shine, but Wes would rather push me in it. He'd much rather encourage my dreams and sit front row at one of my shows than act like he doesn't care. That's the kind of love I've been craving. The kind of love I've been missing. The kind of love I finally feel like I'm worthy of having.

I want nothing more than to be loved loudly by Wes Mackenzie.

THIRTY-EIGHT
NORA / WES
SEXTING

NORA

I'M in my second class of the day when I get my first text from Wes. I always try to avoid looking at my phone whilst I'm in classes, especially now that we only have this week before my assignments are due. Summer break is just around the corner, and I can't wait to go into my final year at Drayton. No matter how bittersweet the feeling, I'm so grateful to have stayed here this long. The amount of times I've threatened to drop out is highly concerning.

I turn my phone over.

WESSY

Can't stop thinking about you.

MY ENTIRE BODY tingles just from his words. He's always made me feel like this. Like I can do things to him without actually having to do or say anything.

I click my phone shut, planning on ignoring it. I can't afford any distractions now. Kiara has been helping me a ton with my script and my commentary, and I have been helping her out with hers, too. Since the theme was rewriting, she's done a feminist retelling of Little Red Riding Hood and it's fantastic.

I'm frantically scribbling down the last of my notes when Kie's shoulder bumps into mine. "Is that loverboy texting you?"

I shrug. "Maybe."

She snorts. "You two are adorable." I let out a happy sigh, feeling like a lovesick schoolgirl. "I'm really proud of you, Bailey."

I turn to her, catching the serious expression etched into her face. "What?"

"Yeah," she says, "You majorly turned this year around. I might not have got the double date I begged for, *but* I've been texting Sam a bit more."

I wiggle my eyebrows. "How's that going?"

"It's.... going," she mumbles, her brown skin turning a deep red. It's been a while since I've seen Kiara have a crush. She usually likes someone, sleeps with them a few times, and is out of there faster than you can say asparagus.

"Kie."

"I'm pretty sure he just wants to be my friend. Which is fine and all, but kinda sucks for me since I had the hots for him," she concedes, pointing her pen at me. "Now, don't ask any more questions, alright?"

"I promise," I laugh, holding my hands up in surrender. As our tutor continues talking, I let my eyes drift to my phone again to find another message.

WESSY
Update: still thinking about you

> More specifically, about how you looked the other night.
>
> How you felt.
>
> How you sounded.
>
> How you tasted.

I ignore the flutter I get in my chest and pick up my phone.

> Are you trying to sext me right now?

WESSY
> Is it working?

> Kind of???

WESSY
> I guess I should continue...

> I don't exactly want to think about you eating me out in the middle of class, Wes.

WESSY
> Are you getting hot and bothered, Stargirl?

> No.

WESSY
> Well, I'm thinking about you and I'm hard.

> Of course you are. You're constantly horny.

WESSY
> Of course I am. Have you seen my girlfriend???!!!
>
> I bet you're thinking about me between your legs right now, aren't you?

I've lost all hope and type out *Maybe*. My thoughts don't stop running during the next hour of the class. We have a small break before another hour, which Kiara and I fill with talk about our summers. She's going to be working on a short film in a small town on the outskirts of Colorado, and I'm going to work on some more self-tapes. I'm waiting to hear back from Max by the end of the week about whether I got the A24 role or not. That's basically going to determine my entire summer and start to senior year.

The knock at the class door snaps me out of my daydream. Our tutor, Colin, rolls his eyes as he goes to open it, and I almost choke when I see Wes on the other side of the door. Colin asks him what he's doing here, and he grins. It's so fucking bright I can see it from the other side of the room.

"Hi, good afternoon. I'm here for Nora Bailey," he says a little louder so we can all hear him. Everyone's heads spin in my direction — including Ryan, who hasn't spoken a word to me since the arrest. "I've got something important to talk to her about."

My hands, my cheeks, my neck, everything starts to burn, mostly out of sheer embarrassment but also out of curiosity. The way Wes winks at me over Colin's shoulder sends my stomach rolling.

"Is it urgent?" Colin presses.

"Yes, it really can't wait," Wes says, nodding curtly before stepping into the classroom. His eyes land on mine, and I can't help the smile that breaks out across my face. "Nora? Are you coming?"

There's a clear emphasis on the word *coming* that has me bolting out of my seat. All my sheets are haphazardly thrown back into my binder and then into my bag. I run to him at the door, shooting out an apology to Colin, who is clearly not paid enough for this shit. The second the door shuts behind us, Wes presses me against the opposing wall, covering my mouth.

"Hi," he whispers.

I grin. "Hi."

"I missed you, baby," he murmurs, kissing my cheek, across my jaw, and then down my neck.

"It's not been that long since I last saw you," I say, trying to catch my breath. "Five hours, to be exact."

"It's been torture," he mutters back to me. When his lips travel across my collarbone, my back arches off the wall, trying to get closer to him.

"Let's go back to my place," I pant. "It's the closest."

He continues kissing me, savoring whatever I have to offer. "Are Cat and Elle home?"

I shrug. "I dunno. I guess we'll find out."

WES

Seeing Nora Bailey naked in front of me is a sight I want to be burned behind my eyelids. I want to see this all the time. Every day for the rest of my fucking life. She's a masterpiece — every part of her, every dip in her stomach, the fullness of her breasts, the way her hair fans out along her shoulders and her arms.

God, she's going to ruin me.

I kneel over her on the bed, and she's just lying there, her knees slightly pulled in, propped up on her elbows as her body is on display for me. She tilts her head to the side like she's ready to make me work for her. I'd do that willingly in any other way, but in this, I need to be the one in control.

I gently push down her legs until they lie flat on the bed, and she watches me with mischief in her eyes. I grip onto her right ankle, pressing a soft kiss to the inside of her heel. She gasps at how tender I'm being.

"Hey, Wes?" Her voice isn't as strong as it usually is, the stupid game we always play not having its usual connotations. "What are you doing?"

"Playing my favorite game," I murmur.

"If this game is called 'edging' I don't want any part of it," she argues, "Either make me come or stop."

I kiss the inside of her thigh, and she shivers. I peer up at her, watching her watch me. I continue my journey up, finding my favorite part of her. She's already dripping for me, her thighs slick with need. I lick her there, tasting her, and she moans.

"Let's get one thing straight, Nora," I start, hovering my mouth over her pussy. The air on her clit sends a shiver down her entire body. "You control every other aspect of our relationship. You boss me around and tell me what to do, and I listen. But this? This is going to be different. You're not going to be in control this time, okay? And I'm going to spend every minute enjoying it."

She whimpers. "Do you mean torturing me?"

"Hm, if you say so." I finally press my mouth to where she wants me to. I suck the swollen bud into my mouth, and she moans my name. "Is that okay with you?"

"Yes," she breathes.

"Thought so," I say. I stop and drag my mouth up the length of her body instead, paying attention to my favorite gold stud on her belly button. She's fucking stunning. Flawless. I trail my tongue up her stomach, reaching her tits and swirling one nipple into my mouth.

She grips my hair, writhing beneath me. "Wes. Don't stop."

"Do you think you could come if I just played with these perfect tits?"

"Fuck. *Yes*," she whimpers, her back arching like she wants to prove it.

I ignore her plea, taking her out of my mouth. Her head rolls back between her shoulder blades, and she rolls her eyes. I lean closer to her, whispering, "Get on your knees, Sunshine."

She blinks up at me like the request is out of the ordinary. She's proven to me more than once that she is more than capable on her knees.

"But, you just—" Her face heats, annoyed at the way I worked her up. Still, she gets on her knees at the edge of the bed. I stand on the other end, waiting for her. She's blinking up at me with those fuck-me brown eyes, her tits glistening with my saliva and red from where I sucked her. She looks like she's all mine.

Finally.

She hooks her thumbs into both sides of my boxers, keeping her eyes locked with mine as she slowly tugs them down. My cock bobs in her face, and she licks her lips.

Just as I'm about to rush her, she presses a kiss to my tip, circling her tongue around me to lick off the precum. My eyes roll back in my head at the simple movement before one hand wraps around my shaft, the other on my thigh.

I'm a mess when she starts to work her magic. I push my cock deeper into her mouth with every look she gives me. Every time she looks up at me with those eyes filled with water, I push harder. Each time her nails scratch against my thigh, I go faster. Every time she moans around my cock, I push deeper.

"You're doing such a good job, Nora," I praise, trying to hide the torturous groan that's making its way through my throat. "Just keep doing that."

She keeps letting out these satisfied noises like she actually enjoys doing it. It's completely different when a girl actually enjoys getting a guy off. Most people don't like it, but from the enthusiastic pump of her hand and the occasional time her hands drift to her own body, it seems like she's having a good time.

My hands curl into her hair. "Do you like this, hm? Do you like being on your knees for me, your pretty little mouth stuffed with my cock?" She just nods around me, a strangled moan at the back of her throat. "I knew you'd be able to take me so well."

My spine tingles when she changes her pace, the slow strokes making my body ache for her. She starts off slow, kneading my balls as her hands work together with her mouth. Then, the pace picks up before it slows back down.

"Fuck, Nora," I groan, and she fucking smiles around my dick. "I'm close."

She smirks, pulling me out of her mouth just to kiss along my length, still looking up at me. My head rolls back, looking at the ceiling. I can't bear to look at her right now.

"Eyes on me, pretty boy," she demands, and I groan in response, my dick twitching. Where the fuck did this woman come from? A raspy laugh leaves her lips as she continues sucking me in and out of her mouth. "Do you like that, Wes? Do you like being told how fucking hot you look when you're deep inside my throat?"

Fuuuck.

The fewer words I say, the more she keeps talking. I should probably tell her to stop saying those things to me, but I can't bring myself to. I grip my cock as she leans back, and she opens her mouth so fucking willingly that I slide right back into where I belong, releasing.

"Can you swallow all of it for me, baby?" Nora nods when I pull out of her, swallowing before licking her lips. She has the audacity to smile at me while doing so. "Just like that."

"Like that?" she asks innocently, blinking up at me before she swipes some from her chin, sucking it into her mouth. I swear I'm going to pass out. "Or like that?"

"Fucking hell, woman," I mutter, still trying to make sure I can breathe normally. "Lay back on the bed. Keep your arms above your head."

NORA

Completely surrendering myself to Wes was not in today's plans, but I'll gladly do it. The way he's worked my body up just to bring me back down is irritatingly sexy and just pure irritating. I don't mind a little push and pull, but the way he's instructed me to keep my arms above my head as he trails his tongue down my body has me thinking otherwise.

"Keep your hands up there, or I'll stop," Wes instructs. His glorious face disappears between my legs after I part them. I nod in agreement, but no sound comes out. "Got it?"

"Yes," I breathe. He rewards me, pressing his lips to my heat, tasting me like he's starved. My entire body comes alive when he touches me. I drop my head back between the cushions, unable to keep looking at him.

He slows down his pace to the way I like it, sucking my clit into his mouth painfully slowly. His tongue works over me, and I'm left panting like my breath is running away from me. "Is this good, Nora?"

"Yes," I gasp.

Nothing leaves my mouth when he continues licking me, tasting me, increasing the speed just to slow down again. I'm completely drenched, covering his lips with my arousal, and he doesn't seem turned off by the way I immediately get worked up. He pushes two fingers inside me, stretching me until my back arches. He pumps his fingers inside me, working with his tongue, making sweats break out across my body.

"*Wes*," I moan, my hand reaching down to grip his hair as he toys with me, drawing me closer to the edge just to pull me back. "Don't stop. Please don't stop."

"I won't. Keep still," he murmurs, pressing his free hand on my stomach and pushing me back down. His words are so soft compared to the quick and harsh movement of his tongue and fingers.

"I'm trying," I whimper.

"Try harder," he presses, flicking his tongue over me again, looking at me. My eyes roll back in my head at the sight of him – his face flushed, his hair messy, his mouth glistening with my juices.

"Can you not argue with me right now?" I press. He pumps his fingers into me faster at my question.

"You sure you want me to stop? I thought it was turning you on," he challenges, licking his lips as he tilts his head to the side. I moan at the motion. "Or do you want me to call you a good girl instead, huh? Do you want me to tell you how well you're doing, baby?" Again, nothing leaves my mouth other than a desperate whimper as he leans back down to get back to work. "Then you've got to listen to me, okay?"

I don't have the energy in me to continue arguing with him. I let him do what he's way too fucking good at. He drags me right to the edge, licking and sucking me like he was paid to do it. He treats it the way it needs to be treated. My heels dig into his back, dragging them down as my hands tighten in his hair.

"That's it," he whispers. "You're perfect, Stargirl. You're being so good for me."

My whole body shakes when the words leave his mouth, moaning his name in response. My legs tingle, tightening around his face as I try to ride out the release. Wes continues licking all of me, cleaning me up before he works his way up my body, kissing across my stomach until he gets to my mouth. I'm still panting, my stomach clenching as he kisses my jaw.

"Are you getting tired, pretty girl?" he mutters.

"Not even a little bit," I say, letting out a laugh as I turn to meet his gaze. "I want you to fuck me."

"You want— You want me to–"

"I want you to fuck me, Wes," I whisper, dragging my lips across his jaw. He sucks in a breath. "I want you to fuck me until I forget my name. That orgasm was great and all, but I don't want my legs to work in the morning. I want to feel you everywhere. Do you think you can do that for me?"

He doesn't even need to answer because I see the arousal on his face the way I just spoke to him. He presses a rushed kiss to my temple, tearing away from me to find the jeans that he discarded at the end of my bed. When he climbs back over me, rolling on the condom, my breath hitches. He pulls me further down the bed, pinning my hands above my head again. He picks up a tie that he left here a while ago. He said he'd never wear it again after the interview, but we've found other ways to put it to use.

"You're going to keep your hands up here whilst I take my time with that sweet pussy of yours," he explains, tying the soft material to my wrists against the headboard. My lips part at this almost animalistic side of him. "You've got to keep your hands to yourself."

"Okay." I'm agreeing and nodding before my brain can even process it. He raises an eyebrow when he nudges his dick against my entrance, a cocky grin on his lips. Fuck. I want this so bad. "Okay, Wes," I reiterate.

That annoyingly sexy smirk spreads across his face as he holds one hand on my hands tied above my head and the other on his cock, slowly sliding through my folds. We both gasp when he pushes into me. He lets go of my hands, using both of them to grip my hips, pushing into me a little deeper. He gives me a second to adjust to his size before he starts sliding in and out of me at a slow pace.

"How's this?" he husks, leaning down to pepper kisses across my breasts.

"Good," I pant, writhing against the restrictions he's put on my hands.

"Just good?" he taunts. I nod aggressively. He knows my body like the back of his hand, knowing exactly the way to make me feel good. He swipes his thumb against my clit as if he's trying to prove to me how good it really is. "Don't get quiet with me now, Sunshine. Talk to me."

"It's good, Wes. *Really* good," I whisper. He pushes into me harder at my words, gripping so tight onto my waist that he might leave marks there.

"Do you like this, hm? Do you like letting me wreck your pussy whilst you can't touch yourself?" I only moan in response, my back arching off the bed. "I do, too, Nora. It's all I fucking think about. There's nothing I've imagined more than the sight of you beneath me, needy and begging for more."

His words turn my inside out, but I still have the strength to say, "I don't beg."

"Are you sure?" he teases, stretching me even more to rub his fingers against my clit. Both stimulations and the fabric pulling against my skin make my nerves sing. "Because I won't let you come unless you ask me nicely, Stargirl."

I close my eyes, wishing he could stop talking. He slows down his pace, and his thrusts become shallow just to torture me. "I hate you," I bite out, hating the way he's managed to edge me closer and closer and still not get me where I want to be. My head might explode at all this back and forth.

"What was that?" He smirks at me when I open my eyes.

"Wes. I don't think I can. I can't—"

"You can do anything you want, and you know that. This isn't any different. You've just got to ask nicely," Wes whispers. He's waiting for me to crack, and I'm trying to hold out as long as I can. As much as the teasing and edging is fun, it's single-handedly ruining me.

When he pushes himself into me again, I give in.

No orgasm is worth this torture.

"Wes, please let me come," I beg, doing exactly what I swore I wouldn't do. This must be paining him, too, because his face is twisted with pleasure, groaning with each stroke. *"Please."*

My plea finally gets him to break, and his thrusts become faster. He pushes into me with force, bending my legs until he gets to the angle that makes him hit the right spot. His thrusts are relentless, leaving me gasping and begging for more. We're both sweating, panting each other's name until he brings us both to climax.

He groans when he comes, his cock jerking inside me, still holding me as the orgasm passes through me in waves. He kisses his way up my body like he always does as he kisses between my breasts before untying the tie from my wrists. He kisses the marks that were left there, and I melt into his touch.

After we've both freshened up, I collapse back onto Wes's chest on my bed.

"I'm exhausted now," I whisper, tucking my head into his neck. He laughs, running his hand down my spine, soothing me. "That was… Almost life-changing."

He chuckles. "Almost?"

"Yeah, I can't give you too much credit," I mutter, looking up at him. He just shakes his head at me, grinning before pressing a kiss to the corner of my mouth. "I'm hungry, too. Do you want a snack?"

"As long as that snack is you," he teases. I push off his chest, hitting him in the arm playfully as I stand off my bed. My heart feels like it's glowing when I step out of my room, only to be disturbed by the loud noises coming from the TV.

Fuck. When did Elle get home? She's sitting on the couch, a bowl of cereal in front of her, as she watches a very loud cartoon episode. I cover my ears, feeling a headache about to fester.

"God, why is that so loud?" I groan. Elle turns to me, sizing me up and down. It's only then that I realize my shorts are on backward and I'm wearing Wes's shirt. I grimace. "You heard that?"

She wrinkles her nose. "Unfortunately."

"Sorry," I laugh, my face heating as I walk into our small kitchen area.

Elle laughs, too, blowing a raspberry. "You're not."

"You're right," I say, opening a cupboard to pull out a box of Pop-Tarts. "I'm so fucking happy, Elle-Belle."

I turn back to her, feeling completely alive for one of the first times in years. There's no one in this world who can make me feel the way Wes does, and I hope this feeling will last forever. I'd trade every single material thing I own if I could exist in a bubble with just him forever.

Elle's lips tug into a smile. "Finally."

THIRTY-NINE
WES
THE BAILEY'S

I'VE ALWAYS LOVED a good party.

Not always to get drunk, but mostly to spend time with the people I care about. Walking around a room full of smiling faces is better than any drink or drug. There's something so special about having a party, celebrating something, getting together, and everything just slotting into place.

The Bailey's are experts at that. Over the years, a range of parties has been held in their house across the street from mine. They get the whole block together, the front yard full of random kids, a baby passed out in a bedroom down the hallway, and an endless supply of food. I never pass up on a Bailey birthday party, especially since it's Emma's birthday.

After spending the morning refreshing my email to see if I got a place on the teaching course at Drayton that starts next semester, I dragged myself into the shower to forget about it. I've spent days feeling sick over it, and now that exam season is over and the semester has ended, there's nothing more for me to do than distract myself. The nausea wore off after my shower, only to resurface when I checked my email for what I promised would be the last time and saw the congratulatory email. That immediately put me on a high for the rest of the day.

Even now, as I stand in the study with Mark while he gives me tips. He's been a history teacher at the high school for almost eight years, so there was no way I would ignore the perks of being in the same house as him. Early 2000s pop songs play from outside the room, making the study bounce with the vibrations.

Mark turns to me, his kind blue eyes searching my face. "What are your intentions with my daughter?"

"What?" I gasp, practically choking. We've been talking about teaching and the school system for the last twenty minutes and Nora's name has not been brought up once. I can hear her somewhere in the house, screaming lyrics at the top of her lungs, though. *That's my girl.*

His hard expression falters as he sighs, taking a seat on one of the chairs. I follow him, sitting across from him. "God, I can't keep it up for more than two seconds," he mutters. I chuckle awkwardly, running my suddenly sweaty palms down my thighs. "But, are you and Nora actually serious? I've seen the way you've looked at her since you were kids, but Ryan really did a number on her. She's my only daughter, and I don't think I could bear to see her heart get broken again."

His words knock the wind right out of me. The thought of Nora getting hurt again is enough to make my stomach turn, especially if I'm the cause of it. "Yes, it's serious. You know that I'll do anything for her. You've watched me trail after her for years. I'm going to continue to make her happy and protect her as long as she lets me."

He lets out a laugh. "Yeah, as long as she lets you. You might think you've got her under control, but you don't. She's a loose cannon, that one."

"I know. I don't want her to be tamed or even controlled by me. I love her the way she is. All wild and free," I admit, my own words making my eyes sting. There's nothing quite like the feeling of spending years chasing after something to finally catch it.

"You love her, huh?" Mark wiggles his eyebrows at me.

"More than anything."

"Good," he says, sighing a little. There's clearly something he's holding back from saying, and I'm just waiting for the words to get out. "Look, I've uh... sensed something off with your parents. I know it's hard. My parents split up when I was pretty young, too. I know your relationship with Nolan has always been a bit strained, but you can always come to Emma and me. You know that, right?"

My throat burns. There's always been something unsaid with the way Emma and Mark looked after me, the times my dad would get annoyed at me or train me too hard, and I'd spend the weekend with the Bailey's. They never said anything or questioned me or my parents. They just let me stay.

"I know," I whisper. "And thank you for everything you guys have done for me. But we're in a better place now, all of us. They're working on their own relationship, and I'm working on mine with them."

Mark nods, standing to his feet. "Good. I'm glad. Now, let's get out there before the birthday girl calls a search party."

I laugh as we walk out of the room, making our way through the crowds of people to the backyard. I can't hear Nora's insane singing or even see her, which is weird. The backyard is full of people I haven't seen in a while, friends I would consider my cousins, and food that I want to shove down my throat, but my eyes snag on two people mingling around the barbecue. Catherine's dad is working on the barbecue as he talks to my dad. God, I can't remember the last time I saw those two in the same place.

I jog over to them, my heart feeling like it's two sizes too big for my chest. "You're both here."

My mom smiles, her bright eyes reminding me of every time that she'd tuck me into bed at night. "Of course we are. A new normal, remember?"

Dad scoffs, listening in to our conversation. "Even if that means hanging out with all these lot."

"Oh, they're not that bad," I say, turning to see a bunch of familiar faces. I turn back to my parents. "I'm glad you guys came."

My dad grins, a sight I've weirdly missed. "Us too."

I spend a few minutes catching up with the three of them before I start to desperately miss the other half of me. You'd think we were attached to the hip with the way I miss her. We came to the party together, but I haven't seen her since Mark dragged me off. I excuse myself from the conversation, making my way back into the house.

I scan the kitchen and the open living room, and she's nowhere to be seen. My heart begins to rattle in my chest, the uncertainty of her whereabouts freaking me the fuck out. She wouldn't run off from this party, right? I mean, it's her mom's birthday. She's known to disappear, but I thought I'd be in the loop this time, considering I'm boyfriend of the year and all. I take the stairs two at a time, coming to a halt when I hear a soft cry coming from one of the rooms.

I push open Nora's childhood bedroom door to find her on the floor, crying into her hands. Cat, Elle, and Connor are around her, not doing anything to console her when she's fucking crying. I rush over to her, almost knocking Cat over in the process as I kneel in front of her.

"What happened, baby? What did they do to you?" I pull at her hands, trying to see her face, and they all stay silent. I turn to Connor, my eyes squared. "Connor, I swear to God. What did you do?"

His eyes widen, holding his hands up as he stands. He's got an annoying kink in his mouth like he's finding this funny in some way. "Why would I *make* my sister cry? She does a lot of that without my help."

"I don't fucking know!" I probably shouldn't be shouting right now since Nora is currently sobbing in my arms. I turn and they're all standing now, a weird look on their faces as they slowly move towards the door.

"We'll give you two some privacy," Cat says, grinning as she shuts the door.

I tilt Nora's face up to me. "Hey, talk to me, Sunshine. What's going on?"

She sniffles, rubbing her hand across her face. "I got it."

"Got what?" I search her face and I slowly realize that these aren't sad tears. She gives me a watery laugh, a smile tugging at her lips. "Oh my god," I mutter.

Her face explodes like sunlight, and I don't think I've ever seen anything more beautiful. "Yeah, oh my god!"

I pull her into my arms, falling onto my back, and she collapses on my chest as I pepper her face with kisses. "I'm so fucking proud of you. I knew you'd be able to do it." She giggles, leaning up off me to rest her arms on my chest. She's giving me that real Nora Bailey smile, and I want her to look at me like this forever. "You're going to be in a movie, Stargirl."

She presses her lips together, trying to contain her smile. "It already feels like I'm in one."

I drop my forehead to hers. "If this is a movie, I don't ever want them to yell cut."

We stay locked in the moment for a few minutes. This has been the one thing she has strived for. I've watched her for years trying to get her name out there, and this is the perfect opportunity for that. Being in a movie is one thing, but being in a movie produced by A24 is another. This is her big break, and I'm so fucking lucky to be here with her for this.

"I'm going to have to go to the city a lot starting from next month. I might not be home a lot, and I'll have to change my classes," she whispers, thinking aloud.

"Okay."

"And they're shooting at a lot of different locations around the country," she explains.

"That's okay."

"And they don't have a set date for when filming will end," she says.

"That's okay," I say again, unable to stop smiling at her.

"But—But you might not see me as often. You might get bored of me because I'll be tired when I'm back, and then you might start to hate me and resent me for taking this opportunity when we've only just started *really* dating, and—"

"I could never hate you," I say, cutting her off.

"But what if—"

This time, I cut her off with a kiss so deep that she sighs into my mouth, her body relaxing. I wish this girl could give herself a break. She's constantly working herself too hard. Worried about how everyone else will feel instead of going after what she wants.

I pull back from her.

"Hey, Nora?" She bites her bottom lip, nodding. "Shut up for once in your life. I'm here for you. I'm never going to get bored of you. I'm never going to make you feel the way he did. I'm here to support you, okay? Through everything."

She sniffles. "I'm here to support you, too."

"Great. Then why are you worrying about it?" I ask, laughing softly.

She shrugs. "I dunno. It's kinda my thing." She leans down and kisses the corner of my mouth before pulling back. "We'll be okay, won't we?"

"Of course, we will. I didn't spend my whole life loving you just to let you go this easily," I admit, pushing back the hair that's fallen in front of her face. "I won't ever let you go, Nora. The world would have to split in two, remember?"

"Yeah," she whispers. "Even then."

"Even then."

I hold her closer to me then because as long as Nora Bailey is in my life, I won't have to worry about not feeling enough to be loved. I've always been hers, and she's always been mine. Even the measly thing we call our planet can't contain the amount of love that I have for her. The amount I'll continue to have forever.

EPILOGUE: THAT SUMMER
NORA

I'M CONVINCED no one loves their job as much as my boyfriend. Even when I was working at my favorite bookstore, I don't think I smiled nearly as much as Wes does whenever I pick him up from his summer job tutoring kids in our old neighborhood. He's been working with them all summer. Some sessions are online, but most are in person. Just watching him interact with children makes my heart ache. And also makes my stomach tingle with the need to have babies with this man. *Desperately.*

Not only is Wes having a good time, but the kids *love* him. I've never seen kids so happy after having a two-hour tutoring session. I used to hate tutoring when I was a kid. I would dread it every week because Connor was always the smarter twin. But Wes manages to make all the dull parts of my life scream with color, and I have no doubt that he does the same for them.

The car door barely closes behind me before one of the kids he's been working with all summer runs right up to me.

"Nora!" he screams, stopping in front of me.

"Hi, buddy!" I match his excitement and drop down to a crouch so we're eye level. "Did you have fun with Wes today?"

His cute mouth turns into a frown. "No. He made me learn fractions!"

"Fractions are fun. Aren't they, Wesley?" I ask, looking up at him as he bounces Leo's little sister on his hip. God, I'm never going to get over him with kids. He beams at me as Mia uses her tiny little grabby hands to mess up his hair. He's completely unaffected, like holding the baby is part of the job.

"Fractions are the *most* fun, Leo. And if you say that again, we'll do them for the rest of the month," he explains. Jesus. I love the bossy side of him even more. I want him to boss *me* around like that.

I give Wes a thumbs up as if to say, 'Good job,' and he rolls his eyes at my teasing. I turn back to Leo. "Don't worry. He doesn't mean it. He says that to me all the time. But tell you what?"

His little eyes light up. "What?"

"I always get my way. All you have to do is give him that adorable smile of yours, and he'll crack like a baby," I say, ruffling his hair.

"Awesome! Thanks, Nora," he says, flashing me a smile. His r's still sound like w's and I'll never get over how adorable he sounds when he says my name.

"No problem, little dude," I say, standing back up. Leo grips onto my hand as we start walking back up the front yard. "Are you ready to go, Wessy?"

"You let your girlfriend call you 'Wessy'" Leo manages to get out through his fit of hysterical kid-giggles.

"Your mom still calls you sugar-plum, so you're not one to talk," Wes says, full-on arguing with a kid. Leo makes an angry grumbling sound, and I have to hold in my laughter as his mom shakes her head. "Besides, that's my future wife we're talking about. She can call me whatever she wants."

"Your wife, huh? Does she know that?" Leo's mom asks, grabbing the baby from Wes as he picks up his bag.

"She does now." Wes's gaze clashes with mine, his cheeks the cutest shade of pink, and I have to keep all my composure not to melt right now. "We'll see you guys next week. It was a pleasure as always."

We exchange goodbyes, and I get a sloppy kiss on my cheek from baby Mia. All of the families Wes gets to work with are so nice and beautiful in their own way. They even treat me like I'm helping with the tutoring when I just come to pick Wes up most days. There's been the odd time where I help out if there's younger kids if the mom is alone. This is the perfect job for Wes, and I'm so lucky to be able to watch him flourish.

He leans over the console when we get in my car, curling his hands in my hair to kiss me. "Hi, baby."

"Hi," I whisper, his lips still against mine. My stomach does a weird dip thing like it does every time, and I pull back. "Good day?"

"Even better now that I've seen you." I laugh as I reverse out of the driveway and get onto the road. He slips his hand comfortably on my thigh like it belongs there.

"You saw me this morning when we woke up," I reply, quickly glancing at him to find him already looking at me.

"I'm a needy man, Nora. I'd spend every minute tethered to you if I could."

"You've got to suck it up because I've got to help Cat move the rest of her stuff in, remember?" He lets out the most dramatic groan at that. "Come on. We've just got the rest of the stuff today, and then we're done."

"You better be," he grumbles, rubbing his thumb against my thigh. "I want to take you out tonight. Just me and you."

"Just me and you," I repeat, my cheeks hurting from how big I'm smiling. "I like the sound of that."

"I'M GETTING OLD. I can't do this anymore," I groan, pulling what I hope to be the last box into the house. I don't know when she got all this shit, but it's just made this whole process a lot harder.

"Put your back into it, ladies," Elle calls, easily pulling a box full of books onto Connor and Cat's new bed. I guess all that dancing has given her superhuman strength.

"Can we have a break now? I'm exhausted," I ask, swiping the sweat that's been gathering on my forehead.

Wes must hear me from outside the room because he calls, "Let them have a break, Catherine. I don't want my girl to be tired. We have plans later."

I smirk at the sound of his voice and the frown on Catherine's face. She rolls her eyes, "Fine."

I swear most of the stuff she "always had" materialized a few days ago. As sad as I am to see Cat go, I know how much she's going to enjoy living with my brother. They're always together anyway, so it makes the most sense. Besides, Elle and I have hung out with June a few times since Elle came back from camp, and she's already seeming to fit in with our dynamic. Still, no one will ever replace the Catherine-sized hole in our hearts.

We trudge down the stairs, laughing about how much more we still have to do before we meet the boys out in the backyard. Wes is sitting on the grass, playing with Jarvis. Connor and Archer are at the table, enjoying the summer sun. Cat slips into Connor's lap, and Elle and I take seats across from them.

"Almost done?" Connor asks.

"Not really," Cat says, biting her bottom lip.

"I don't know why you didn't just do this when classes finished," Connor groans.

"Moving in together during summer would have been hell, and you know that. The heat would get to the both of us, and we'd end up killing each other," Cat explains. She turns to us. "Besides, I needed my girls here to help."

Elle has spent the entire summer at dance camp. She hasn't

been in a couple of years, but after fully completing rehab and getting back into dancing full-time, she took the opportunity to stay with Archer's parents in Aspen whilst his mom hosted the camp. I've been driving in and out of Denver and taking flights across the country, working on the film. Working on a real movie set has been an out-of-body experience, and making new friends has also opened up my range of opportunities. With school starting up again soon, I'm taking all the chances I can get to get my name out there.

"How was your summer, Elle? You've not said much about it," I say to her, bumping my shoulder into hers.

She shrugs. She's been insanely private about what happened at camp. Usually she talks our ears off about every single day down there, but she's hardly said a word. "Maybe it's a secret."

Archer coughs, and I turn to him, eyeing him suspiciously. He just twists his hat around, covering himself from the sun. I lean into Elle and whisper, "Oh my god. You totally hooked up with someone at camp."

"What? No, I didn't," she argues, her face turning red. I turn back to Archer, who must know something about what's happened.

He raises an eyebrow. "You sure about that, Harps?" They exchange a look that's too fucking weird to decipher right now. I let my gaze travel down to where Wes is trying to teach Jarvis to jump into circles, and he is not having it. I don't think he'll ever let go of the fact that Jarvis isn't like a dog or that he ever will be. He just wants to snuggle and eat, and there's nothing wrong with that.

He catches me staring at him and grins. "You ready to go, Stargirl?"

"That depends. Where are you taking me?" He's been oddly secretive about today's plans, and I'm dying to find out what he has in store.

"Just follow me, and you'll find out," he says, standing to his feet. He walks over to me, holding out his hand to me. "Are you ready to play?"

"Always," I say, slipping my hand into his.

Maybe I should have known that when he means play, he actually does mean play. He takes me to an arcade in town and I almost beat him at every game. Air hockey is way too much fun with Wes because he gets riled up too easily and then hits the puck too hard. Bowling was a lot harder, but I still won. Part of me is wondering if he's just letting me win for the sake of it.

"Okay," I breathe, trying to catch my breath after the arcade basketball game we just played. "What's going on? You brought me all the way out here to beat you in everything?"

He grins. "That was not exactly part of the plan. I just wanted to take you somewhere close by before the sun sets."

I tilt my head to the side. "Why?"

He doesn't answer me and instead tugs my hand, threading his fingers through mine. I follow him out of the arcade, and we go through the back alley. *This isn't sketchy or weird at all.* He leads me up the stairs at the side of the building until we reach the empty roof. I look down at the town, confused as to why we're up here before Wes turns me around.

My breath catches when I see the sunset. All the colors in the sky have faded into a beautiful pink and red color. The clouds swirl together, the sun hanging low beneath them as they rest behind the mountains, framing our beautiful town. I could stand here forever, taking into account every single part of the sky.

I turn to Wes, and he's already looking at me. "This is beautiful," I whisper. His smile softens. "Thank you."

He just shrugs as if it's no big deal, and he slowly falls to his knees in front of me. My breath hitches. We've had our fair share of public sex, but this is where I draw the line. There could be rats up here, for all I know. Instead, Wes ties up my shoelaces that I didn't notice were untied. I'm wearing the pink Converse he got me for my birthday. No matter what outfit I'm wearing, I find an excuse to put them on anyway.

"These are all the boyfriend perks I need," I laugh when he rises back up.

"What about the other perks?"

I frown. "What other perks?"

"You know, the ones where you're on the bed, screaming out a particular person's name," he muses. I furrow my eyebrows in fake confusion.

"Oh, you mean when I get off thinking about Ryan Gosling in *The Notebook*."

He rolls his eyes. "Shut up."

I step closer to him. "Why don't you make me?"

Wes's hand curls in my hair, pushing our chests against each other as he kisses me deeply. Kissing him feels like fireworks are exploding. Everything about it is so *him* and so damn perfect. I grip onto his jacket, needing him as close to me as possible. When he pulls apart, he's got one of the sweetest smiles on his lips.

"Hey, Nora?" His voice shakes, and my stomach dips.

I smile. "Hey, Wes."

"I've never been this happy in my life. Ever. There is not a single moment I can pinpoint that has made me feel as good as I do now. Maybe the day you agreed to fake date me counts as one," he says, his words rushing through me like water.

"Me too," I whisper. "I think my life restarted that day. Like you put me into a factory and put all the broken pieces back together."

He shakes his head. "You were never broken, Nora. There were just cracks, but tell you what?"

"What?"

"You still shined through them anyway," he whispers softly. Wes never fails to amaze me with the words he says to me. It's like there's a part of my brain that he can only activate with his words. He reaches into his pocket. "Speaking of…"

My pulse hammers against my neck as I look down at the black box in his hands. My lips part when he opens it to find a silver necklace with a star on the end, exactly like the one I lost. "So, I couldn't find the original one. I tried looking in your room again, and nothing. Do you remember that time you were in Denver for a whole week?" I nod, remembering how hard that week was without him. "I actually went back to New York to look for it. I know it is stupid because the city is massive, but I had to try." No thoughts are coming to my brain as he lifts the necklace from the box. He pushes my hair to the side, seamlessly clasping it around my neck. "I want this to be a reminder of how special you are."

My eyes are watering now, my lip quivering. "What if I lose it again?"

"That's why I got this." Wes slips off his jacket, pulling his shirt over his head. I'm about to question him before he draws my attention to a star that has been tattooed on his shoulder, the same design as the one I have behind my ear. "This is for you. You're all I need, all the time, forever. You're my Stargirl for a reason, Nor, and it's about time you start believing that."

"Wes," I stutter. "I can't be that for you all the time. My spark might die out."

He laughs, pulling his shirt back on. "You're not doing it for me. You're doing it for yourself, and I'm just a selfish motherfucker who wants to believe that there are parts of you that shine just for me."

I let the tears fall now, in complete disbelief of the man in front of me. "That is the most romantic shit you've ever said to me."

He chuckles. "Don't worry. I'll one-up myself on our wedding day."

I tilt my head to the side. "I think you're missing one vital step there, loverboy." His eyes flash with something I can only describe as mischief as he keeps his eyes locked with mine, slowly sinking down to one knee. No fucking way. "Wesley. No. Get up."

He laughs as if that's a funny joke to make. "Oh, come on. I wasn't going to propose to you on the roof of an arcade."

"Knowing you, you probably would," I say, pushing him on the shoulder. He pulls me towards him, slinging his arm over my shoulder as we turn back to the sunset.

"No, Sunshine. I've got it all planned out," he whispers, kissing me on the cheek.

"I guess we'll have to wait and see," I reply.

"Guess so."

THE END

ACKNOWLEDGMENTS

I'd like to start by thanking the three-am delusion that made me believe I could write this series without finishing the first one. I had always thought my love for romance and writing would die out after my debut, but it only got stronger and led me to write this book. Wes and Nora hold an insanely strong place in my heart and I am sure they will do forever. Friends to lovers has always been my trope and I couldn't think of more perfect characters to bring that to life with.

Thank you, reader, for picking up this book and allowing Wes and Nora into your hearts and your homes. As soon as I announced these characters in the Drayton Hills series, a lot of you staked claim on Wes and Nora's story and I hope I did them justice. Thank you for continuing to support me, my endeavors and my journey as a baby author. Thank you to my readers who have been here from my debut and a special thank you to any new readers who have trusted me enough to take you on this journey.

I can't even begin to describe how grateful I am for the friends that I have made whilst being in my author era. To Emma, you are my everything. This book was dedicated to you and your incredible support for my books and for my own personal growth. You've done more than you can imagine and Wes and Nora's story would be nothing without you. Thank you Maine for letting me read chapters of this to you and not getting bored of my voice. Thank you for all your incredible work with the promotion of this book and your talent continues to amaze me every day. I love you and your brain so much.

To Ella, for always believing in me when I didn't believe in myself and for being there when I told you I'd be postponing your favorite book to write this one. Thank you for making me laugh until my tummy hurts. I love you BIG TIME.

To Emily, my absolute world. Thank you for existing and doing everything you can to encourage my delusions and remind me that I'm still me without my books. Thank you for loving every part of me, even the parts I hate, and being there to talk me out of my mind. I fear I'll never be able to describe how much I love and appreciate you all. I love you bigger than the whole sky.

Thank you to my amazing support system and the team that I've built over the last couple of months. To my DHU girlies, Sophia, Alex, Megan, Mylla, Haya, Char, Kay, Keoni and Niamh for always having my back and being the best girlies forever hyping up my books and being my cheerleaders. I would have given up a long time ago if it wasn't for you, so thank you a million times.

A special separate thank you to my Soso for being so incredibly supportive and spamming me with all your thoughts. Thank you Zarin for being one of the most incredible and funniest people I've ever met. I owe you everything!

To my best friend, Pyro, thank you for putting up with me talking about these books and pretending to be interested. Thank you for letting me talk for hours and falling asleep whilst I read to you. I appreciate you more than you know. I love you, queen.

Thank you to my amazing editor, Cassidy, for your beyond helpful suggestions and making my writing more coherent for the common reader. Working with you has been a pleasure and I can't wait to keep sharing my work with you and your talent.

Thank you to Layla for producing the most beautiful cover I have ever laid my eyes on. I close the book every time I open it just to stare at the cover. Thank you for bringing my vision to life and gracing us with your talent.

Thank you to my assistant Morgan for carrying the load of my chaos and helping me out with everything. You're doing God's work and I am so incredibly grateful for you.

And to everyone I haven't mentioned because my brain is running on hot chocolates and bagels, thank YOU. This book would be absolutely nothing without your constant support. Here's to more unhinged characters and sickly sweet stories!!

ABOUT THE AUTHOR

Janisha Boswell is an nineteen-year-old romance author known for her heartfelt and steamy stories. Her popular 'North University' series delves into the lives of college students, exploring themes of love, career aspirations, and personal growth. Janisha's debut novel, 'Fake Dates & Ice Skates,' has garnered widespread acclaim on social media, earning praise for its engaging characters and relatable narratives. Her second college romance series, the 'Drayton Hills' connects all of her characters seamlessly and dives into a different, playful and spicy side of romance. Her work is celebrated for its warmth, diversity, and emotional depth, resonating with readers who seek romantic and inclusive tales.

Printed in Great Britain
by Amazon

42110806R00209